KOBANI

A Future War Novel

by FX Holden

© 2020 FX Holden.

Independently Published

137,000 words

Typeset in 12pt Garamond

All rights reserved. No part of this publication may be reproduced, distributed, or transmitted in any form or by any means, including photocopying, recording, or other electronic or mechanical methods, without the prior written permission of the author, except in the case of brief quotations embodied in critical reviews and certain other noncommercial uses permitted by copyright law. To contact the author, please write to the email address below.

bigfattfreddy@hotmail.com

Maps© OpenStreetMap

Each Future War novel is a self-contained story, with occasional recurring characters.

Other titles in the Future War series:
Bering Strait, 2018
Okinawa, 2019
Orbital, 2020

Science fiction in the Coruscant series
Deep Core, 2019

COMING 2021
Golan: This is the Future of War

With huge thanks to my fantastic beta reading team for their encouragement and critique:

Gabrielle 'Hell Bitch' Adams
Bror Appelsin
Mike 'Mad Dog' Ashworth
Johnny 'Gryphon' Bunch
Dave 'Throttle' Hedrick
Martin 'Spikey' Hirst
Greg 'Hawkeye' Hollingsworth
Graham McDonald
Mike 'Nuke' McGirk
Darren 'Wobbly' Warner

And to editor, Brigitte Lee Messenger, for putting the cheese around the holes.

Contents

Contents 5
Cast of Players 7
Ripples 9
The Turkey-Syria situation 11
Dog days 20
An Israeli GAL 46
Some things don't wash off 58
Linea Ignis 104
The wages of war 129
The Bloody First 132
Hunting Tita Ali 168
A surfeit of ships 197
Sisterly love 201
On the wings of BATS 235
Volcanic force 276
If a butterfly flaps in Syria 296
The ways of a dog 301
Belladonna poison 312
Corpsman for a day 320
Unconventional weapons 345
Persian playmates 370
Data deluge 372
No greater sacrifice 387
Going out clean 410

Glossary 429
Maps 442
Preview: GOLAN, This is the Future of War 445
Author notes 451

Cast of Players

By affiliation and order of appearance

THE WHITE HOUSE
Director of National Intelligence, Lt. General (Retired) Carmine Lewis
Secretary of Defense, Harold McDonald
Vice President Benjamin Sianni
US President Oliver Henderson

COALITION, COP MEYER
'Gunner' James Jensen, Marine Gunnery Sergeant, 'Lava Dogs'
Mary Jo 'MJ' Basim, Thomson Reuters News, journalist
Hospital Corpsman Third Class, Calvin Bell, 'Lava Dogs'

KURDISH MILITIA, KOBANI
Daryan 'Al-Kobani' Khalid, sniper, Kobani Women's Protection Unit (Yekineyen Parastina Ji, YPJ)
Lieutenant Colonel Jamal Adab, Intelligence Chief, Kobani People's Protection Unit (Yekineyen Parastina Gel, YPG)
Nasrin Khalid, merchant

SYRIA, KOBANI
Colonel Imad Ayyoub, commander, Syrian 138th Mechanized Infantry Brigade
Lieutenant Andrei Zakarin, sniper, 45th Spetsnaz Airborne Brigade (attached)

RUSSIA, INCIRLIK
Lieutenant Yevgeny Bondarev, pilot, 7th Air Group, 7000th Air Base
Captain Dmitry Bebenko, pilot and commander, 7th Air Group, 7000th Air Base

Second Lieutenant Sergei 'Rap' Tchakov, pilot, 7th Air Group, 7000th Air Base

COALITION, INCIRLIK

Flying Officer Karen 'Bunny' O'Hare, pilot, Royal Australian Air Force (RAAF), 3 Squadron

Flight Lieutenant 'Red' Burgundy, pilot, flight leader, RAAF 3 Squadron

Flying Officer Anaximenes 'Meany' Papastopoulos, pilot, Royal Air Force (RAF) 617 'Dambusters' Squadron

Flight Lieutenant Arthur 'Rex' King, flight leader, RAF 617 'Dambusters'

Lieutenant Ted Sun, Tactical Control Officer (TCO), US Army 5th Battalion 7th Air Defense Artillery Regiment

Sergeant Alessa Barruzzi, Tactical Control Assistant (TCA), US Army 5th Battalion 7th Air Defense Artillery Regiment

Corporal Ronald Allenby, Communications Systems Operator, US Army 5th Battalion 7th Air Defense Artillery Regiment

ISTANBUL CONSULATES

Shimi Kahane, Signals Intelligence Analyst Grade 4, Israeli SIGINT National Unit (ISNU), Unit 8200

Carl Williams, Signals Analyst, Signals Analysis Development Program (SADP), US National Security Agency (NSA)

Ripples

Russia's Middle East ambitions grow with Syria battlefield success

Moscow uses conflict to expand its role as regional powerbroker

When the Syrian government and rebels meet in Kazakhstan next week, the chances of the warring parties agreeing on a political solution to end their near six-year conflict will be slim. But for Moscow, the main sponsor of the peace talks, one crucial thing has already been accomplished: sending out the message that Russia is back as a player in the Middle East.

With a 15-month bombing campaign in Syria and shrewd political maneuvering, Moscow rescued President Bashar al-Assad from defeat, tilted the military balance in his favor and paved the way for a nationwide ceasefire.

In addition, there is an economic incentive – the Middle East has traditionally been a big market for Russian weapons sales, an important export, particularly to Egypt, Syria and Iran. Mr. Putin also eyes investment opportunities for Russian companies in the oil and gas-rich region.

In Syria, Moscow has achieved many of its goals for now. It is expanding its naval base in Tartus as well as a new air base near Latakia, giving it a large, permanent military foothold to project power. – **Financial Times, 2017**

How a 4-Hour Battle Between Russian Mercenaries and U.S. Commandos Unfolded in Syria

The artillery barrage was so intense that the American commandos dived into foxholes for protection, emerging covered in flying dirt and debris to fire back at a column of tanks advancing under the heavy shelling.

It was the opening salvo in a nearly four-hour assault in February by around 500 pro-Syrian government forces – including Russian mercenaries – that threatened to inflame already-simmering tensions between Washington and Moscow. – **NY Times, 2018**

Turkey evacuates largest military base in Syria

Turkish forces have evacuated their largest military base in Syria's northeastern province of Idlib, Germany's DPA reported on Monday.

"Convoys carrying military personnel and equipment were seen leaving the Morek base in the northern Hama countryside," explained the agency.

Morek was one of 12 Turkish posts established in the region to monitor a fragile ceasefire in the nine-year-old conflict. Last year, the base was encircled by Russian-backed forces loyal to Syrian President Bashar Al-Assad. – **Middle East Monitor, 2020**

The Turkey-Syria situation
White House Situation Room, 30 March 2030

THE 5,000 square foot room under the West Wing of the White House was ringed with LED monitors showing dynamically updated maps of various regions of the world. At the front of the room, a few feet from the end of a long mahogany table, a wall-to-wall monitor showed the images of the dozen participants who were joining the hastily called meeting by video link.

Only six members of the National Security Council and a couple of aides were physically present. Director of National Intelligence Carmine Lewis; White House Chief of Staff Karl Allen; Secretary of Homeland Security Allan Price; Secretary of Defense Harold McDonald; National Security Advisor Bill Lee; and Vice President Benjamin Sianni. They were waiting for the US President, Oliver Henderson, to join by video link from his motor vehicle. He had been in transit to a function in Pennsylvania when he'd agreed with Homeland Security Secretary Price to call the Council together.

The atmosphere in the large room was tense, as it always was when a meeting of the Council was called on short notice. There were those in the room and on-screen who knew exactly what was happening, those who knew vaguely, and those who had almost no idea at all and, at that moment, weren't even really sure they needed to care. After all, the topic was 'Update on Turkey-Syria border conflict' which was one of just several geopolitical crises they were managing right now, and not the most pressing. Not on the surface, anyway.

The President's screen blinked to life, and he could be seen sitting back in his seat, the shoulder of a Secret Service agent beside him just visible, a bottle of water in one hand and a sandwich in the other. He took a bite, then leaned forward, chewing. "We live now?"

The Homeland Security Secretary leaned forward. "Yes, Mr. President, sorry to pull you from your dinner appointment."

Henderson sat back, swallowed and smiled. "Did me a favor, Allan, I'll miss half the speeches. Alright, go ahead and tell these good folks what you told me."

Price nodded to the aide managing the briefing slides. In the situation room, and on the monitors of the participants wherever they were around the country, or the globe, a map window appeared on the screen showing the eastern Mediterranean, Israel, Lebanon, Syria and Turkey. Price cleared his throat. "Short and sweet, the Russian-backed Syrian offensive into Turkey to reclaim their northern territories and establish a so-called 'buffer zone' on the other side of the Turkish border has taken an unexpected turn. Literally." Price looked across the table at Director of National Intelligence Carmine Lewis. "Get us all on the same page please, Carmine."

Carmine Lewis had only been DNI for three months. She was the first former military Director to sit in the chair for nearly ten years, after the new US President, elected in 2028 and more confident in his skin after two years in the job, decided to break with a series of entirely political appointments. Until December the year before, she had been Lt. Gen. Carmine Lewis, deputy chief of staff for intelligence, surveillance, reconnaissance, and cyber effects operations in the US Air Force.

She'd inherited a National Intelligence Office riddled with executives who were party political hacks with no military or intelligence service records, and a core staff frustrated at seeing inconvenient reports buried, critical briefings edited beyond recognition and intelligence assessments 'contexted' with opinion, rather than facts. She was only at the beginning of the long journey of putting the organization back on a professional footing. But she'd earned a reputation for telling the Council what they needed to hear, rather than what they wanted to hear. It hadn't made her universally popular, for example, with the

President's Chief of Staff, but she had been handpicked for the job by Henderson and he was still in her corner.

She clicked the slide control in her hand. Now the border area between Syria and Turkey was shaded with red, showing Syrian army zones of control. Alert Council members would have noted they had expanded significantly since their last meeting. "Thank you, Mr. Secretary. Here, you can see the area along the Turkish border now under Syrian army control. They have extended their 'no drive, no fly zone' as far as the outskirts of the Turkish city Gaziantep, twenty-seven miles over the border. Turkish forces have held them there, and at our last meeting, I briefed that all our intelligence indicated Syria was satisfied that it had achieved its operational objectives and there would be no attempt to capture Gaziantep, or the Turkish port of Iskenderun on the coast."

"Because we finally made Turkey's fight our fight," Vice President Sianni said. Worried about Russia's growing influence in the Middle East, he'd been instrumental in pulling together a Coalition of Nations to back NATO ally Turkey, and persuading Henderson to support it, albeit in limited fashion. Led in principle by the UK, the Coalition included Turkey, Germany, Australia and the US. Henderson's support for the action had been conditional. After nearly two decades of antipathy between Turkey and the US, he didn't want the US to be seen to lead a multinational force supporting its regime. He also did not want to sow the ground for a head-to-head US confrontation with Russian ground or air forces, so the US contribution was to be limited to intelligence, logistics and finance. Sianni had expanded that beach-head a little, getting Henderson to agree to base a small force of Marines in Kurdish-held Kobani to support their resistance against Syrian government forces, and a US Army anti-air artillery regiment at the NATO base in southern Turkey at Incirlik. But Henderson, as most members of the Security Council, saw Russia's Middle East ambitions as a distraction from the main game, which was curbing Chinese political and military influence in East Asia.

"Send them an AWACS early warning aircraft, *Patriots*, unarmed drones, Ben. But I don't want to read about our troops or aircraft going toe to toe with Russian forces on the ground or in the skies, is that clear? You say the Brits and Germans are willing to step up and take the heat on this one? Let them, it's their eastern border."

Carmine flipped forward to a series of satellite surveillance images that showed a convoy of upwards of fifty vehicles: trucks, troop transports, light armor and heavy haulers carrying tanks. "In the last week we started picking up chatter that Syria was going to renew its offensive. Yesterday, we received these images, showing a large Syrian mechanized infantry force ... moving *west*." She zoomed in on an image showing a column of Russian-made T-90 battle tanks. "We have identified this new spearhead as Syria's elite 25th Special Missions & Counterterrorism Division. As I've mentioned before, this unit fields the latest in Russian-made tanks, mobile anti-air and armored vehicles and operates under the effective control of officers of the Russian 1st Tank Guards Army."

"West? Deeper into Turkey?" Sianni asked. "What's their objective?"

Having anticipated the question, Carmine flipped to the next image. Another satellite image, it showed a large air base, with a large number of fighter aircraft and large transport aircraft parked around the perimeter and outside hangars. Several of the larger aircraft had American markings.

"This is Turkey's Incirlik Air Base. It is also NATO's largest air base inside Turkey and is only a hundred miles west of Gaziantep. It is also the main base for Turkish, UK and Australian fighter aircraft and US AWACS, drones, transports and tankers operating in the theater."

"A *NATO* base?" the Secretary of Defense said incredulously. "They would never…"

"Mr. Secretary, we have credible intelligence from multiple sources indicating that Syria does indeed intend to take Incirlik. It is the greatest threat to their western flank, and they believe they can justify the action on the basis it is first and foremost a Turkish military target and aircraft there are used to conduct attacks on Syrian forces."

"Syrian forces *inside* Turkey," the President said. "Correct, Carmine?"

"Not exclusively, Mr. President," she said. "As you know, we have a force of Marines besieged at Kobani in Syria. Aircraft operating out of Incirlik have also conducted operations in support of Kurdish and American forces in Kobani."

Henderson frowned. "Which is exactly what I did not want to see happening, Ben."

The Vice President hesitated uncomfortably, but the Secretary of Defense came to his aid. "Mr. President, we had close to a battalion of Marines in Kobani. It was supposed to be a deterrent against Syrian attack, but Syria hadn't read that playbook. Our boys stood for three days against an assault by a division of Syrian troops and together with the Kurds they held that town. Syria backed off and put the town under siege and since then we've got all but 200 of them out. We want to leave the rest in place."

Sianni found his voice again. "Mr. President, we pull them out now, or let the Syrians run over them, we're giving Russia their biggest political coup of this conflict."

Henderson ran a hand over his face. "Carmine, tell me Turkey can stop this latest move like they stopped the Syrians at Gaziantep."

"A week ago I might have said yes, Mr. President," Carmine said. "The fighting outside Gaziantep has stabilized. Turkey could theoretically pull forces off the line there and send them west, even though that would leave them open to a renewed assault, which could also be the play here."

Chief of Staff Karl Allen had picked up on the first part of her sentence. "Until a week ago? What happened a week ago?"

Flipping a few images ahead, Carmine showed a series of images, more detailed this time, of aircraft on the ground at an airfield, or taking off. "Several months ago, Russia moved additional fighter aircraft into the theater. These photographs were taken by a human source, outside its Latakia airfield inside Syria. Russia has been operating *Okhotnik* unmanned attack aircraft out of Latakia since the start of the conflict, but these photographs also show Su-57 *Felon* stealth aircraft of its 7th Air Group, 7000th Air Base." She hesitated, weighing her words. "Until a week ago, these fifth-generation front-line aircraft were only involved in exercises inside Syria. A week ago, they started operating inside Turkish airspace alongside other Russian aircraft. This significantly increases Russia's ability to provide close air support deep inside Turkish territory."

"Our assessment is that the *Felon* is inferior in many ways to the F-35 *Panther* which our UK and Australian allies have brought to this fight," Secretary of Defense McDonald pointed out.

"That's our assessment, yes," Carmine agreed. "But it has never been tested in combat."

"And it won't be," Henderson said forcefully. "I want the rules of engagement reinforced with our allies over there, Ben. They are not to engage Russian fighters."

"And if the Russians attack *them*?" the Vice President asked. "Mr. President, we have shared this latest intelligence with our Coalition allies. They have repeated … no, they have strengthened … their request for additional US forces to be committed in Turkey."

"We already have a Marine battalion stuck on a hilltop in Kobani, Ben," Henderson said straight away. "And air defense troops at Incirlik, against my best judgment. I don't want the Syrians parading a captured American pilot in front of the cameras too."

Sianni was quiet, but Carmine knew why. He'd done his lobbying in advance of the meeting and was going to let someone else pitch the next ball. That someone was Secretary of Defense McDonald.

"Mr. President, we are talking about a measured but resolute response to the threat to Incirlik. I propose putting the B-21 *Raiders* of the 131st Bomb Wing at Ramstein in Germany on readiness, to support US forces at Incirlik if a ground attack develops. They can operate at standoff range, not going anywhere near Syrian-controlled airspace."

Henderson took a bite of his sandwich. "The German Chancellor would be alright with this? So far we've only been sending supply and AWACS flights in and out of Ramstein, right?"

"It's why we worked so hard to get Germany in on this Coalition," Sianni said. "In case it came to this."

The President pointed the crust of his sandwich at the camera. "No US aircraft are to enter Syrian airspace or engage with Russian fighters, is that understood? And if those Syrian tanks get within striking range of Incirlik, you will pull our troops there out."

"Yes, Mr. President."

"Then I'm OK with it. Anyone else with objections?"

McDonald interrupted before anyone else could speak. "Sir, we can't rely on Turkish ground forces alone to secure Incirlik. We may need to reinforce…"

Henderson looked angry and leaned toward the camera. "I know you are *not* going to ask me to commit ground forces to Turkey again, Harry. We just spent ten years drawing down our troop levels in the Middle East to be ready for the Chinese move on Taiwan you all keep telling me is imminent. We are not about to go back in."

"No, sir. But I assume it would be acceptable for my staff to plan for all contingencies."

"Plan, sure. Act on, no."

"Yes, Mr. President."

Carmine sat back as other members of the Council weighed in on the argument. She was trying to gauge the level of support around the virtual table for increasing US involvement in the theater. The level of enthusiasm was low; no doubt a function of decades of Turkey thumbing its nose at NATO and the US, climbing into and out of Russia's sphere, and only turning to the West for help when Russian drones started dropping ordnance on Turkish military targets in Istanbul. The meeting came to a quick conclusion, not least because the President's limo was approaching the venue for his dinner appointment.

The briefing finished, but as Carmine and the others in the room gathered their folders to leave, Secretary of Homeland Security Price turned to her and spoke. "Hang here a moment, Director. I need you for my next meeting."

After all but Vice President Sianni had left, Price asked his aide to open a new video channel. Defense Secretary McDonald came on screen again. "Well, that went as well as expected," Price said immediately.

"Or as badly, depending how you look at it," Sianni agreed. "I'll keep working on the President. At least you got on the record that we can start contingency planning."

Carmine was trying to follow. A former Lieutenant General, she was no stranger to backroom dealing, but whatever this was, she hadn't been let in on it, until now. Price pointed at a screen showing the area of operations, from the Syrian border to Incirlik Air Base. "How long before those Syrian tanks hit Incirlik, Director?"

She swallowed. "That depends on what Turkey can put in their way, Mr. Secretary. This move caught everyone by surprise. We thought Gaziantep was where they would stop."

"My people say a week," McDonald said. "Two at the outside."

Carmine had been living and breathing all available intel on this one for the last 24 hours, preparing for the Council meeting. She was less optimistic. "Five days," she said. "If you are looking to move US troops to Turkey to mount a defense, about your only option would be 1st Division's 18th Infantry Regiment, which is cycling up for combined arms live-fire exercises at Fort Riley right now."

"The Big Red One. 'No Mission Too Difficult.' Do we have the airlift capacity?" Sianni asked.

"That's one of a million questions I'll be asking my staff when I get off this call," McDonald said. "While you work on the President."

Dog days
Kobani, Northern Syria, 1 April 2030

MARINE Gunnery Sergeant James Jensen had not imagined he was being promoted to 'Gunner' in order to become a dog handler. But that's where he was after seven long years in the US Marines – a heavily armed dog walker.

As he crept through the rubble of a bombed-out grade school in Kobani with his two dogs by his side, he was telling himself this was definitely *not* what he'd thought he'd signed up for. The role that had been described to him was 'new weapons systems research and development'. He'd imagined spending a lot more time on a range at Quantico, drinking bad coffee while evaluating new rifles, grenade launchers or surveillance drones, and a lot less time getting his goddam ass shot at by Syrian army snipers.

On the floor above he heard a scraping sound. Like a foot, sliding on a dirt floor. He was holding a modified 9mm Sig Saur 18 out in front of him and spoke softly. "Easy, boys. *Listen*."

Called in by Kurdish militia taking fire two blocks away at the former Ayn al-Arab prison, he'd been hunting a Syrian sniper for the last two hours. The dogs had led him here and it looked like their instincts had been right.

Both dogs stopped, lifting and swiveling their heads. There it was again! The scrape of a boot on a floor above.

Jensen pointed his pistol toward a set of stairs at the end of the corridor that appeared still to be intact. He used the laser sight on the gun to paint a dot on the wall at the end of the corridor. "Brutus. Stealth. To the marker, go up the stairs, scout," he whispered. The dog, Brutus, dropped to a crouch and moved carefully around the fallen bricks and smashed furniture to the end of the corridor, then started slowly slinking up the stairs, head and shoulders low. "Spartacus, with me."

The second dog waited, and as Jensen began to follow Brutus toward the stairs, it paced along behind him.

Both dogs were streaming vision from their body-mounted cameras into the visor on Jensen's helmet. If the sniper was upstairs, Brutus would find him, and Jensen would see him. What happened next was up to the enemy soldier.

As he reached the bottom of the stairs and put his foot on the lowest step to start moving up, he saw Brutus's camera vision jerk crazily and heard the sound of heavy feet thudding across the floor above, then a muffled shout. Bounding up the stairs with Spartacus in his wake, he slammed into a door frame at the top of the stairs and bounced through, rolling onto his stomach with his pistol steadied on the ground in front of him.

He was just in time to see Brutus slam into the legs of a fleeing Syrian soldier, sending him down onto his knees. The man had landed on the rifle he was carrying, but he twisted, pulling a handgun from his waist and firing it into Brutus's head. The dog collapsed on top of him, but not because it was dead. Its legs splayed as it dropped its 220 lb. body on top of the man and pinned him to the floor with its actuator grapple around his throat. The man emptied his pistol into the dog's torso, but it stayed on him, adjusting its weight to keep him trapped as he scrambled to pull himself out from under it.

Jensen checked for other threats, saw none, and then jumped to his feet. He pointed with his pistol again, putting the targeting dot on the Syrian soldier. "Spartacus, attack. Gun!"

The second dog bolted ahead of him. In two seconds it was alongside the Syrian soldier and had clamped his weapon hand to the floor. As its jaws squeezed, Jensen heard bones in the man's wrist snap sickeningly and he screamed, his handgun falling to the ground. Jensen ran up to him, kicked the gun away, and pointed his pistol at the whimpering man's head as he reached down and pulled the sniper rifle out from under his body, jacked out the round that the sniper had loaded, and threw the gun against a wall.

The upstairs room was suddenly quiet, except for the panting of the man on the floor, trying to draw breath through crushed ribs and a clamped windpipe, whimpering at the pain in his broken wrist. He was looking at Jensen with a mixture of horror and hatred.

Jensen knelt down beside him, Sig Saur casually pointed at his head. "I'm going to pull that dog off your throat now. If you move, the other one will bite your hand off. Nod if you understand."

The man winced and nodded slowly, eyes fixed on Spartacus.

Jensen stood. "Brutus, with me."

The dog lifted itself off the Syrian soldier one leg at a time, then stepped away, backing up so that it fell in behind Jensen but kept a clear line of sight to the Syrian. The prisoner whimpered, feeling his throat fretfully.

"Now my other dog is going to let go of your hand. You are going to roll onto your stomach and put your hands out so I can tie them behind your back. If you do anything else, they will attack again. Nod if you understand."

The man looked at the dogs, looked at Jensen's pistol, maybe weighing his chances. He apparently decided they were zero, and nodded again.

"Spartacus, release and step back," Jensen ordered. The dog holding the man's wrist opened its jaws and took two steps back, head still low, legs crouched and ready to jump if ordered. Jensen motioned with his pistol for the man to roll onto his stomach, and when he had, bound the man's hands. He gave a cry as the carbon plastic ties bit into his broken wrist, but Jensen was a little short on sympathy.

Jensen sighed and stood, looking around him. No sign of a spotter, the man had been working alone. "At ease, boys," he told the dogs, and they both sat back on their haunches.

He reached for his field comms unit. "Crimson One to base, requesting prisoner transfer detail to my position. North side of the old Girls' School. One package. Include a medic in the detail, prisoner has light injuries."

"Good copy, Crimson One, detail to your position, base out."

Jensen took a step back, leaned up against the wall and took in the unreality of the scene. On the floor, a Syrian sniper, muttering something in Arabic, probably complaining about his broken hand. Beside him, two Legged Squad Support System LS3 *Hunter* units, one of which had just taken a full *Tokarev* 7.62mm clip to the head and body and wasn't even showing a dent. He pulled a command pad out of a leg pouch and ran a diagnostic on Brutus just to be sure, but apart from a slight heat warning on his rear hip actuator, the dog was reporting that all systems were nominal.

Jensen shook his head. It was a take-down that would have entailed far greater risk if he'd been working alone, or even in concert with a small squad. Being able to send in the dogs meant that he wasn't putting himself or any of his men in the line of fire when the sniper reacted to the assault.

But it hadn't gone perfectly. He'd have to flag some concerns in his after-action report.

He had ordered Brutus to *scout*, not to attack. It should have reached the top of the stairs, located the sniper either by sight, sound or infrared, and then sent the data and vision to Jensen's helmet-mounted display so that Jensen could plan the assault. For example, he would have sent Spartacus out and around to the building's other exit to block it or pursue in case the man managed to escape. Instead, the dog had seen the target, or the target had seen Brutus, and when he'd tried to flee, Brutus had charged him and pinned him. The LS3 had an 'always on' link to a cloud-based neural network system that was constantly learning and adapting as Jensen put it through its front-line field trials. It had a level of autonomy regarding non-lethal actions such as recon, pursuit, and apprehension. But in this case, it had chosen to exercise that autonomy in a way Jensen had not ordered.

Sure, the end result was one sniper, in the bag. He couldn't fault the system for that.

There was a sound outside and both dogs' heads snapped toward it, but it was just a pigeon taking off and they returned their attention to the Syrian prisoner on the ground in front of them. Jensen had to laugh. In that respect, they were like every dog throughout history. All it took was a pigeon to take them off task.

But they didn't look like dogs, not really. They had four articulated legs that ended in tennis ball-shaped pads, a narrow boxy body with rounded edges, their actuators and electronics built around a 125kw hydrogen fuel cell which made up the bulk of their weight.

At the front of the LS3 was a head that didn't look like a head at all. It was an interchangeable robotic arm that Jensen could swap out depending on the mission profile. There was a weapons arm that could be fitted with projectile weapons, tear gas or a grenade launcher, even a harpoon for pulling open wooden or light metal doors like car doors. Or it could be fitted with manipulator arms, like the ones Brutus and Spartacus were fitted with today, that enabled the LS3 to do everything from pin a man's hand to the ground, grab his throat, open a door or window by the handle, pick up and move an explosive device or stab a man in the heart. The head also carried the infrared sensors that weren't its only eyes.

In the center of its body it had a 360-degree pan-tilt-zoom camera that it used for environmental pathfinding, object manipulation and image capture. All vision was streamed to a cloud-based AI which managed target identification, macro navigation, systems and power distribution. In addition to the compact and quiet power source, it was the cloud-based AI that made the LS3 system possible. Brutus and Spartacus were linked to quantum computing platforms able to take in the inputs from their sensors, marry them to Jensen's commands, and issue orders to the dogs to carry them out at a speed even a real dog would have trouble matching.

Which was also their primary weakness, because if it lost its link to the AI in the sky, an LS3 would become nothing more than a handy packhorse, falling back on basic programming to follow its master around like a small mule. You could get it to carry your junk for you, but it couldn't do anything except follow you around until you managed to get an uplink again. Which was fine as long as you were working in bombed-out buildings with walls and roofs a radio signal could penetrate, but useless if you were deep inside a concrete reinforced bunker.

The dogs were programmed to move at random intervals, not to freak out anyone watching, but to keep their joints evenly lubricated, and both Brutus and Spartacus chose that moment to stand and then settle on their haunches again. Jensen saw the Syrian flinch as they moved, and breathe out in relief as they settled again.

Jensen holstered his Sig Saur and crossed his arms, leaning back against the wall and looking down at the sniper rifle that he'd thrown across the floor when the man was taken down. He didn't have to inspect it to see what it was. Orsis T-5000; five-round magazine, probably chambered for the long-range Chey Tac 9.5mm round. He sighed. Jensen was hunting one sniper in particular, and this man wasn't him.

Jensen and his dogs had been hunting the other guy for weeks. Jensen knew this soldier wasn't him, because that guy used a 10.36mm round. There were a few sniper rifles chambered for this rather unusual round, but only one that had been relatively common in Syria – the Russian SVLK Lobaev *Twilight*. Popular with Russian and Syrian snipers during the Syrian civil war, many had been 'souvenired' by veterans and used as hunting rifles in the short period of peace after that war. A single-shot rifle, it was deadly accurate even out to nearly two miles, in the right hands.

And his guy was no slouch at using it. In the last two days alone his target had shot two Marines at a range at which the shots couldn't even be heard. The besieged First Battalion, 3rd

Marines, had sent its own sniper teams out to hunt him, but so far they'd all come back empty handed. He never used the same position twice. The most shots he'd fired in any engagement was three. He never tried for headshots, preferring to play the percentages. Most of his casualties were caused by shots either to the torso, legs or groin. He appeared as happy to wound as to kill, which made sense because a serious wound would require a medevac rotor to be sent in, creating a juicy target for circling Russian aircraft and Syrian anti-air missiles.

The guy apparently moved around the city at will, evading Kurdish militia, finding nests in ruined buildings from which he could fire down on Marine patrols. The city was defended by thousands of Kurdish People's Protection Unit (YPG) militia, but he never attacked those. Only Marines. Like it was personal.

He had seventeen notches on his rifle butt so far.

He couldn't fire into Combat Outpost (COP) Meyer, which occupied the highest ground looking down over Kobani, though he had managed to get a hit from an abandoned radio tower along a ridge a mile to the south before US aircraft took it out. But any Marine in an observation post or tower who exposed themselves for more than a couple of seconds was fair game. His most recent hit had been one of those and when the medics recovered the bullet from the Marine's shattered shoulder blade, it had been a 10.36mm.

He was a ghost. A cipher. A bogeyman. They called him 'Tita Ali', the Hawaii equivalent of 'Bitch Ali'; and any boot in an observation post dumb enough to stick his head above the sandbags would get it shouted in his face, "Do you *want* Tita Ali to put a bullet in you, Marine?"

Jensen had made it a matter of personal pride that he would be the one who brought Tita Ali down. No one was better equipped than him to do it. His dogs couldn't sniff the guy out, but they had hearing and sight that was beyond anything in the human range and an ability to step quietly through rubble and wreckage a tap dancer would have trouble navigating. They had

High Definition 40x optical and 200x digital zoom lenses, infrared and movement sensors, and could move across firm open ground at 60 miles an hour – as fast as a cheetah. And they were butt ugly, which was enough to freeze grown men in their tracks sometimes.

Jensen looked down at his prisoner again and grimaced. *Patience, JJ, patience*, he told himself. Tita Ali might still be out there, but he's not a ghost, he's human. And like any human, he'll screw up.

PATIENCE was not something Lieutenant Yevgeny Bondarev of the 7th Air Group, 7000th Air Base, had an overabundance of. And what little he had, had been sorely tested since he'd joined Russia's Syrian Air Group from his squadron's base in Chkalovsk.

Bondarev had been a cadet pilot at Armavir when border skirmishes between Syria and Turkey had blossomed into a shooting war. Bondarev was one of what his trainers called the Su-57 '*Felon* babies', the first generation of pilots brought in specifically to fly Russia's new 5th-gen fighter, rather than transition across from older 4th-gen airframes. Russia had wanted to see what a new crop of pilots without any of the legacy habits of previous generations would be able to do with its most advanced fighter aircraft.

Not bloody much, had been Bondarev's own conclusion. Not that they weren't skilled at flying the Su-57 *Felon* by the time they graduated. But their instructors, like his new CO, Captain Dmitry Bebenko, were legacy thinkers, and had trained their pilots in exactly the same tactics as they had been trained in themselves. To Bondarev and his pilots, the *Felon* was made to roam the skies like a hawk on the prowl and pounce on its targets with unexpected speed and force. It was not made to fly like *this*, in strict finger-four formation. He looked out over his port wing at the three other aircraft in his flight as they bobbed up and down alongside and ahead of him, their formation-keeping radar locking them in place beside the next aircraft in line.

If Bondarev had been General of the Air Army, he would free his force of twin-engined *Felon* stealth fighters to roam far and wide, alone or in pairs. Because a *Felon* pilot was never really alone: the *Felon* was able to pull data from orbiting early warning aircraft, other fighters or ground radar, giving it a commanding view of the battlesphere around it. And its unique *IMA BK* integrated avionics AI simultaneously performed the role of weapons operator, navigator and electronic flight engineer, freeing the pilot to concentrate on his tactical environment. Fewer aircraft would be needed because every Su-57 was worth four or five 4th-generation fighters.

But the commanding officers of the Syrian Air Group were all 4th-generation themselves and were fighting this war the way they had fought over Georgia, the Ukraine and Syria before the *Felon* had entered service. And don't even get him started on their approach to the use of even newer aircraft like Russia's *Okhotnik* (Hunter) unmanned combat aircraft!

The smaller *Okhotnik* was virtually invisible to radar, could get up close and personal with its targets, carry 2,000kg. of air-to-air or air-to-ground ordnance internally and 4,000 on external hardpoints, and complete high-G maneuvers that would render human pilots unconscious. Most importantly, tests early in its development had shown it could be successfully slaved to the Su-57's AI system and perform as a 'virtual wingman' in combat.

Had his far-thinking generals pursued this opportunity? No. Instead they had decided that the *Okhotnik* should be used like the older two-crew Su-30 *Flankers*, flown by a remote operator and a weapons officer sitting in a trailer five hundred miles from the battlefield instead of a pilot in the sky above it! Now the system required two officers instead of none, and was relegated almost exclusively to ground attack missions like the drones of old.

Bebenko's voice broke his train of thought. "Siniy Flight, Siniy leader. I am showing a temperature anomaly on my port engine. I am returning to Khmeimim Air Base. Siniy two, you stay with me. Siniy three, you are flight leader. Keep a cool head and finish the patrol, Lieutenant Bondarev. Out." With that, Bebenko's aircraft peeled out of the formation, taking his wingman with him as he turned toward the Russian airfield a hundred miles to the south, on the Syrian coast near Latakia.

Bondarev acknowledged the order and changed his flight status to lead aircraft, giving himself command authority over the weapons of his wingman's aircraft if needed. *Keep a cool head?* He had done nothing but keep a cool head since arriving in theater. He had not fired a single shot in anger in the course of nearly ten sorties. And no wonder. One stealth fighter was almost impossible for Turkish ground or air-air radar to detect. Two in close formation were also highly unlikely to be picked up. But four, flying in a tight air-parade style formation? It was no wonder the timid Turkish F-16s had stayed well out of missile range on all of their patrols – any low-frequency ground radar or patrolling early warning aircraft could probably get a return off the formation. Not enough to plot an intercept perhaps, but enough to know they were there.

He keyed his mike, reaching out to his wingman, Second Lieutenant Sergei 'Rap' Tchakov. Rap was a '*Felon* baby' like himself and had gone through fighter school at Armavir at the same time, though in a different flight. He'd earned his nickname from the music he had thumping in his ears whenever he was lying on his bunk or working out at the Armavir gym. Checking that Captain Bebenko was truly disengaged and still moving away, Bondarev opened a channel to Tchakov.

"Welcome to the new century, Comrade Tchakov," he said, unable to keep the smile out of his voice. "What say we fly these *Felons* the way we tried to tell them they should be flown, back in Armavir?"

"Roger that, Siniy leader," Rap replied cautiously. "Your orders?"

Bondarev called up his navigation screen. He would send Rap to cover the easternmost point of patrol route, and he would cover the westernmost point. "You patrol grids Echo Four Seven and Foxtrot Four Seven. I will cover Delta Four Seven and Foxtrot Four Six. We overlap in the middle, over … Kobani. Understood?"

"Understood, Siniy leader," Rap replied. "You are perhaps hoping Turkey will think the sector is unprotected and will try to sneak a supply flight into Kobani?"

That was exactly what Bondarev was thinking. The Turkish and American quadrotors that delivered supplies to their besieged comrades at Kobani had an uncanny ability to sneak in through gaps in the Russian air patrols to resupply the forces there and evacuate the wounded. Or worse, to strike at Syrian ground forces with their ground attack aircraft. Bondarev's plan was to split his force and create the impression of a gap.

This particular patrol had an added edge to it. It was Bondarev's first patrol inside Turkish airspace since the *Felons* of the 7th Air Group had transitioned from training and exercises to combat operations a week earlier. And he was patrolling a sector that stretched from Kilis in Syrian-held Turkey to Kurdish-held Kobani inside Syria. It was a rich hunting ground, and the rumor was that Russian-backed Syrian forces were preparing for a big push on the big Turkish and NATO air base of Incirlik in the west. Bondarev's group had been given new rules of engagement, with orders to engage any and all hostile aircraft in their sector in an attempt to achieve air dominance in advance of the attack.

Including Coalition aircraft.

"Rap, I sincerely hope they will try," Bondarev said. "It's about time we showed our commanders what the *Felon* is really capable of."

ROYAL Australian Air Force Flying Officer Karen 'Bunny' O'Hare was also looking forward to finding out what the *Felon* was capable of. Because until now, although she had heard a *Felon* squadron had been moved to Syria, she had yet to see any evidence of it. All she'd seen in two months of patrolling the Turkish border with RAAF 3 Squadron had been skittish fourth-gen Sukhoi-34s and Mig-35s which tended to operate deeper inside Syrian airspace and bug out at the first sign of Coalition fighters.

A 'limited conflict', they called it. Not war. Coalition forces were only authorized to engage Syrian forces, not Russian. Russian troops and aircraft had focused their attacks on Turkish forces, not Coalition. On the ground, Russian regular army and Iranian Republican Guard special forces backed their Syrian allies, the US 3rd Marines shored up their besieged Kurdish allies, and all the while, Israeli fighters were busy harassing Syrian troops in the west of the country, nervous they were shaping to move on Lebanon, no doubt.

Bunny O'Hare wasn't running combat air patrols, she was 'reinforcing the NATO-mandated no-fly zone'. In a flight of F-35 *Panthers* loaded for bear. With rules of engagement which said she could only fire on hostile aircraft if fired upon or ordered to engage.

And no, it wasn't a war. Of course not.

Listening to the panicked call for help now coming over her radio, you could have fooled Bunny O'Hare.

"Coalition flight Virtue Able, this is Quarterback, vector to heading one two three degrees for sixty, twenty thousand feet. Turkish F-16 flight Delta Four Niner engaged with hostile aircraft. Buster. Commit," the Turkish Air Controller (Quarterback) circling behind Turkish lines in a Boeing 737 *Peace Eagle* said with urgency in his voice.

"Good copy, Quarterback, turning to heading One Two Three, sixty miles, twenty thousand," her flight leader, Flight

Lieutenant 'Red' Burgundy, had confirmed, wheeling their three F-35 *Panthers* onto an intercept heading and pushing their airspeed above Mach 1. "Can you patch through data on the enemy group, Quarterback?" The Turkish F-16s couldn't send data on the threat they were facing directly to the Australian F-35s, but the AWACS could, if it had picked them up on radar.

"Negative, Virtue leader, we have no fix on the hostile aircraft. Reports of two to four bogeys, fast movers. Turkish pilots report air-to-air missiles fired. One F-16 retiring, damaged, three still engaged," the AWACS replied.

Bunny pulled up her tactical situation display, seeing the *Peace Eagle* AWACS, two other Coalition flights, the position of the Turkish flight about forty miles away but sure enough, no enemy aircraft symbols. Stealth? How else could it be that the *Peace Eagle* couldn't pick them up less than a hundred miles away?

"Virtue flight, Virtue leader. Sending in the BATS. Roll out, pilots," Red drawled.

Bunny was flying about two hundred yards off his starboard wing and banked right immediately, increasing her separation to ten miles. Close enough to be able to assist if one of their flights needed help, but giving them a forty-mile-wide front over which the three aircraft could search for the hostile aircraft on infrared (IR) and electro-optical Distributed Aperture Sensors (DAS). If missiles were flying, the range at which the *Panther*'s DAS could pick them up would be even greater.

Her paired Boeing Airpower Teaming System *Loyal Wingman* drone, or 'BATS', had been in trail mode, following along dutifully behind her. But as she broke away, now under the control of her flight leader, it joined with the other two BATS and moved ahead of them, spearing directly toward the intercept as the F-35 formation moved to bracket the estimated location of the hostile aircraft.

If the question was 'how are 5th-gen stealth aircraft going to fight each other when they can't see each other?' BATS was the answer. By teaming an unmanned 4th-gen combat drone with a 5th-gen stealth fighter like the F-35, you could flush the enemy out, force him to engage, and when he did, he was no longer invisible ... he was dead.

It didn't matter that the BATS drone was easily seen, targeted and attacked – unlike its piloted master, it was expendable. And it couldn't be ignored. It had a high teen percentage chance of detecting a stealth fighter inside a twenty-mile range. At longer ranges it could be used as a firing platform, launching an attack based on data from other aircraft or radar sources. And if a hostile aircraft was forced to defend itself or chose to attack it, the minute it launched its missile, the F-35s behind the BATS had a vector on their enemy.

And BATS hunted in packs. You might shoot down one, but if you didn't kill them all, the chances were you would be on the receiving end of a volley of advanced short-range CUDA missiles either from the remaining BATS or from the F-35 pilots holding their leash.

Which was why in every instance where Coalition F-35s had moved into a sector and deployed BATS, the Russian Su-34 and Mig-35 fighters had bugged out.

"Turkish F-16 flight Delta Four Niner, this is Coalition Virtue flight of three F-35s with BATS support, closing on your position. Report status please," Red said on the Coalition comms channel, in a tone much calmer than Bunny could have mustered.

"Virtue flight, we are under air attack!" the Turkish commander replied. "One aircraft damaged. Active targeting radar identified and missiles fired. We are low and out of energy, circling over Kobani, please assist!"

"Delta leader, do you have an ID on the hostile aircraft?" Red asked.

"Negative, Virtue, we can't see the bastards!" the Turkish pilot exclaimed. "Dammit. Another aircraft down, aircraft down, withdrawing to Diyarbakir!"

What? They were only forty miles away. She could clearly see the three, now *two* Turkish aircraft circling above Kobani. But still no hostiles on IR or DAS! Not even a missile track?

"Unidentified aircraft over Turkish airspace near Kobani," Red said, opening a channel on the international Guard radio frequency. "This is the commander Coalition fighter force in your area. Please identify yourself or withdraw. You may be fired on if you do not comply. I repeat UI aircraft, you may be fired on if you do not comply."

They wouldn't respond, Bunny knew that from previous engagements. They never did.

"Eyes on DAS," Red warned. "Putting BATS in active search mode. Arm CUDAs and prepare to engage on my order."

Bunny tapped her weapons screen and her CUDA air-to-air missile loadout turned green, ready to fire. Her thumb hovered over the firing button on her stick. Thirty miles away, the three BATS lit up their phased-array radars. If there were hostile aircraft in the area, even stealth, they should be able to pick them up as they closed range. On the flip side, the wildly radiating BATS would be like a string of strobe lights in the sky, lighting up the enemy threat alert systems as they bored in on the hostile aircraft.

Would the hostiles flee or fight, that was the question. She bet they'd run, as usual. Two Turkish fighters down, job done for the day, why would they hang around?

A chime sounded in her helmet and Bunny's eyes flicked from the quarter of sky she had been checking to her tac screen as Red's suddenly terse voice broke in. "BATS 1, target lock! Stay cool, people."

Bunny saw a new aircraft icon flashing, twenty-five miles out of Kobani. The label underneath it was one she hadn't seen over Syria before.

Su-57! She bloody knew it. After two years of fielding fourth-gen Su-34 and Mig-35 fighters, Russia had finally brought its big guns to the fight.

And this guy showed no sign he was running away. Bunny watched the icon for the Russian aircraft spin, turning to face the threat from the BATS now all converging on it, their phased-array radars locked onto it. Did he know what he was facing? The BATS used the same phased array radar system as an F-35, so there was some debate about whether the Russian threat warning software could tell the difference between a manned or unmanned American aircraft.

But this guy had cajones. He was boring in on the BATS even though he must have had targeting radar warnings ringing in his ears and was looking at data that showed he was outnumbered three to one.

Unless he wasn't.

BONDAREV processed the information his screens were feeding him at the speed of thought, and even that was barely fast enough.

The Coalition fighters had a radar lock on Tchakov.

Bondarev had an electro-optical lock on three of the hostile aircraft, but his combat AI could not classify them. The radar was showing US-made AN/APG-81 radar signatures but the aircraft carrying them were not stealth optimized. Possibly upgraded Turkish F-16s, but his instincts told him he was looking at Coalition BATS. They had not launched missiles. They were no doubt just trying to spook Rap into running.

Which, for today at least, gave the Russian flight a massive advantage. Tchakov's aircraft had been identified, but Bondarev remained hidden, twenty miles away and ten thousand feet above the Coalition aircraft.

"Siniy two, Siniy leader, engage the three hostiles. I will stand off and support."

"Roger, Siniy leader, engaging," Tchakov said.

Rap should be able to deal with the drones. Bondarev was looking for the F-35 *Panthers* he knew would be hiding behind them.

BUNNY'S right hand tightened on her stick. Their three-plane formation had split about thirty miles out from Kobani, Red and his wingman moving south of the target, Bunny alone to the north, as the BATS drones closed on the hostile unit from the east. She was seeing no new electronic signatures on her sensors and could only hope the Russians had all their focus on the incoming BATS and hadn't picked up the Australian F-35s yet.

Later, she could replay what happened in slow motion in her head, but in the air north of Kobani it took just seconds.

"Missiles fired. BATS 2 *down!*" Red called. "Target still locked. BATS 1 *Fox 3*, BATS 3 *Fox 3* … hostile down. BATS evading…"

Bunny blinked, trying to make sense of her tac display. The Russian fighter had launched on the three BATS! She'd never seen that kind of aggression before. The other two BATS had reacted instantly, based on their programmed rules of engagement, and fired at the Russian as soon as they were fired on themselves. Two missiles had been directed at the Sukhoi from just ten miles distant and from radically different points of the compass. He may have been able to spoof one of them – apparently he couldn't spoof both. The Russian fighter had been hit.

BONDAREV cursed as he saw Tchakov's *Felon* signal it was going down.

"I've lost control, punching out!" Rap called. The next second his emergency beacon started flashing on Bondarev's screen. Bondarev checked his location. They were east of Kobani, over Syrian-held territory. If he lived through the ejection and landing, he'd probably make it back. That was tomorrow's problem.

Bondarev still had a position on the remaining two hostile aircraft, sure now they were drones by the fact they had evaded Tchakov's missiles. Few human-piloted aircraft could outmaneuver a K-77M missile fired at that range. Bondarev gave up any idea of trying to smoke out the lurking F-35s. He had already claimed one Turkish F-16 destroyed and one damaged, plus one BATS, for the loss of one Su-57. He needed some additional quick kills to justify the loss of Tchakov's aircraft, followed by an even quicker tactical withdrawal.

After engaging the Turkish fighters earlier, he still had five K-77Ms in his weapons bay and launched them all at the remaining two BATS.

"Missile launches!" Bunny called, seeing missile tracks detected by one of the remaining BATS flash on her screen. A second Sukhoi had engaged the BATS and given away his position. He was well north of Kobani at thirty thousand feet, inside Turkey and within range of her CUDA missiles. "I have an imputed target. Permission to fire?"

Before Red could respond, the BATS fired again. Each carried four CUDA missiles and they had already fired one each. Now they volleyed another CUDA each at the new target, before they disappeared from Bunny's screen with a frightening finality. Both were down!

Bunny watched as the BATS' missiles speared toward the origin of the missiles that had been launched against them, then cursed as they ran on without registering a hit.

But she still had a vector on the Sukhoi, and missiles armed and ready to fire.

"Virtue three requesting permission to fire!" she repeated.

"Negative, Virtue three," Red directed. "Virtue flight, turn to heading zero niner zero and reform in sector lima three two. Quarterback, Virtue flight is withdrawing to lima three two, requesting additional Coalition support at rally point in case of follow-up attack."

What? They were bugging out? Bunny's AI had calculated a firing solution for her CUDAs and even though she didn't have a lock on the new hostile aircraft, she could launch in sensor-seeking mode and the missiles would guide themselves to the intercept point and look for the target on radar, infrared and optical, much as the BATS had. She had a solid chance of a kill!

Grinding her teeth, she swung her *Panther* around and pointed it west again.

When she got to the ground after the patrol, she didn't wait for her ground crew to clamber up on her machine and help her out. She ripped off her helmet, unfastened her harness and jumped out of the cockpit before the small automatic ladder that dropped out of a side panel under the cockpit had even finished extending, and landed with a thump on the tarmac. She doubled over to Red's aircraft and was waiting for him when he climbed down himself.

She'd been too angry to confront him while they were still airborne and had bottled it up all the way back to base, but it came flooding out now. "What the hell kind of call was that? Turks lost one damaged, one destroyed. We lost three BATS, but we took one Russian down. I had a firing solution on a second but you pulled us out?!"

"Easy, Bunny," Red warned, holding both hands out to keep her away. He was taller than her, but his height wouldn't help him if she crash-tackled him, which she looked like she was about to do. "Cool the hell down."

"We were fired on!" Bunny continued, not 'cooling down' in the least. "We were entitled to engage under standing ROE, but you bloody bolted." She sounded as disgusted as she felt.

"You are out of order, Flight Officer O'Hare," Red warned again, more formally this time. "You can raise your concerns in the mission debrief. Now step aside."

Bunny had stood her ground, glaring at Red. Realizing she wasn't going anywhere, he moved to one side himself and walked past her, as a half dozen airmen approached the aircraft. She turned, hands on hips, watching him walk away.

As she'd walked into the mission debrief she'd been advised by Red she was being put on report and confined to quarters. So she'd kept her mouth shut all through the debrief, even when Red had delivered his BS mission summary to their CO.

"We got a target ID from BATS 2 on a Russian Su-57. The Russian engaged the BATS with missiles. BATS 2 was destroyed. BATS 1 and 3 responded with counterfire and destroyed the Su-57. BATS 1 and 3 were then attacked by a second Su-57 and destroyed. By that time the remaining Turkish F-16s had been able to withdraw under cover of our fighter screen, and I judged that we were at risk of an escalating engagement with Russian forces. I chose to de-escalate by withdrawing. Turkish and Coalition forces in the air incurred no further losses." He'd made it sound like a victory, not the rout it was.

De-escalate? You bloody ran away, mate, Bunny thought to herself. But she kept her mouth zipped and only answered questions when asked. She hadn't waited for their CO to wrap up, though. Without being dismissed, she had stomped out of the debrief and back to her quarters. She was already on report, what more could they do?

It wasn't the first time she'd been placed on report and it wouldn't be the last. She knew she'd be given a night confined to barracks to cool off and be flying again tomorrow. It wasn't like 3 Squadron had an oversupply of pilots, with three currently down with diarrhea. O'Hare's stomach was just fine.

She quite liked Turkish food. And Turkish beer. And the heat. She even enjoyed the 'call to prayer' that wafted out over the loudspeakers at the base five times a day.

But as she lay on her bunk, watching a six-inch spider in the corner of the room devour a bright orange cockroach, she was in a foul mood.

She felt like she was the only one who could see that the Turkish-Syrian conflict had just moved to a new and deadly phase. Russia had put its newest, most lethal fighter aircraft on the front line. It had just gone head to head against a Coalition BATS-supported F-35 combat air patrol, without hesitating. The attack on the Turkish F-16s may even have been intended to pull the RAAF *Panthers* into a fight and send the Coalition a message. Yes, the BATS had done exactly what they were intended to do and allowed the RAAF pilots to fix and fire on the Russian stealth fighters. They had knocked down one, and she might have knocked down a second if she'd been allowed to take the shot. Russia had claimed nothing but a brace of easily replaced unmanned drones. Call it a draw, if you were being generous to both sides.

But Bunny knew in her bones there would be worse to come. Ten dollars would get you one, they started seeing Russian attacks on Coalition forces all across the front line; on the ground, and in the air now. The 'limited conflict' in Syria was about to turn into a war.

As if on cue, her watch chimed with a news alert and she wearily reached over and turned on her TV. The tickertape across the screen under a breathless news anchor told her all she needed to know. *Syrian general warns 'multinational' troops to evacuate Turkey's Incirlik Air Base ... says base is being used for attacks inside Syria ... Leave or you will be 'collateral', says Syrian general.*

Still wearing her flight uniform, Bunny turned off the TV and her bedside light and rolled onto her side. She decided she'd be sleeping fully dressed from now on.

ROYAL Air Force Flying Officer Anaximenes 'Meany' Papastopoulos had never been to war.

But his great-grandfather on his Welsh mother's side had.

His great-grandad, Flight Lieutenant Dai Jones, had flown Bristol *Beaufighters* with RAF 255 Squadron in Algeria in 1942. His own grandfather had given Meany a 1:48 scale model of a *Beaufighter* when he turned ten and helped him build and paint it. Meany had been entranced by it. The midnight black fuselage, two massive 1600 horsepower Hercules engines, four nose-mounted 20mm cannons, plus wing and fuselage-mounted torpedoes and bombs for tearing apart tanks, ships and submarines.

'Whispering Death', the Axis forces had called it. As he had proudly set it on the bookshelf over his bed, Meany had resolved there and then that when he grew up he was going to be a fighter pilot like his great-grandad.

As he climbed up onto the wing of the bat-like RAF *Tempest* at Turkey's Incirlik Air Base, he thought back to that day, running his hand across the aircraft nickname painted in flowing letters under his cockpit: 'Whispering Death'. He wondered what his great-grandfather would have thought about – or whether he could ever possibly have imagined – the aircraft Meany was about to fly.

Dai Jones's nickname had been 'Sonny', after Sonny Stitt, the famous jazz saxophonist of the time. Meany also had a fantastic recolorized photo of his great-grandfather playing saxophone in a tasseled red fez in one of the bars and cafés of the Casbah in Algiers. Sonny might have recognized his *Tempest* for what it was – a multirole aircraft like the *Beaufighter*, suited to air-to-ground or air-to-air operations. He might have asked Meany where the hell the aircraft's weapons were, since no visible ordnance disturbed the lines of its sleek black 5th-gen stealth airframe. But the missiles inside the modular weapons bay would have looked vaguely familiar, similar in shape and form to the eight 130lb. RP-3 rockets his *Beaufighter* used to carry over Algeria. Except that Meany's weapons were two ASRAAM short-range 'lock-on after launch' air-air missiles which used phased-array multispectral seekers to home on their targets from twenty miles out and two *Meteor* radar-guided data-linked homing missiles which could be launched at a range of sixty miles, taking their guidance from their own radar or any Coalition unit with a target lock, whether on the ground, at sea or in the air.

What his great-grandfather would certainly not recognize, nor even begin to grasp the idea of, were the thirty US-made *Perdix* Autonomous Microdrones loaded into one of Meany's flare launchers. Fired out of his flare launcher in their canisters, the small drones had a wingspan of only one foot and weighed less than a pound – half of their weight being the 40mm grenade inside the body of the drone. Sure, his great-grandfather might be able to grasp the idea of a small autonomous aircraft – after all, he had seen V1 and V2 rockets raining down on London during his war. But the idea of a small autonomous aircraft that could be launched from a jet flying at greater than the speed of sound, right over the heads of enemy tanks and troops: an aircraft that would then form a swarm, syncing data and vision with the pilot of the jet and a fire support coordinator on the ground, allowing him or her to direct the drones to attack the enemy with unholy precision and devastating effect...

That, his great-grandfather could never have imagined.

But that was exactly the mission Meany was about to fly, together with his flight leader, Flight Lieutenant Arthur 'Rex' King.

AS Meany taxied his *Tempest* out behind Rex and surveyed the dead brown fields at the northeast end of Turkey's Incirlik Air Base runway, he still felt a slight bewilderment at finding himself at war in the Middle East, ninety years after his great-grandfather's war. Two weeks earlier, he'd been in the Premier

Enclosure at the Wolverhampton Racecourse outside his native Birmingham, watching his last £100 disappear into the bag of a bookmaker after the 'sure thing' his mate had put him onto had turned out to be a donkey.

There had been rumors, of course, that 617 Squadron (the Dambusters) might join the conflict in Turkey. Weekly rumors that had turned into daily rumors, that Meany had regarded as less and less likely as each day passed without any official confirmation. After all, the Dambusters had only just completed the transition from the US-made F-35 *Lightning* to the brand-new RAF *Tempest*, and were still ironing out some kinks. But everyone could see the conflict against Syria was going sideways for Turkey and unless someone stepped in on their side, there was a very real chance that Syria would roll over Turkish forces and then do as their new President, the thirty-year-old Hafaz al-Assad, had promised repeatedly they would do: drive the Coalition air forces from their nest in Incirlik.

The 'limited conflict' over Syria was the ideal opportunity to test the RAF's newest airframe in combat. Supposedly, RAF operations were limited to air-to-air and air-to-ground defense of Turkish forces inside Turkish-held territory, provision of training and logistical support, and ground-to-air missile defenses. On arriving at Incirlik in southern Turkey, Meany quickly learned the definition of 'Turkish-held territory' was a very fluid one.

As he waited for his turn to roll, Meany was busy setting up his multifunction displays for the ground attack mission ahead of him. There wouldn't be the luxury of time once he was airborne, as they were only forty minutes' flying time from their target today – a Syrian 25th Special Missions & Counterterrorism Division unit dug in southwest of Kobani.

Six miles *inside* Syria.

He would have liked to be carrying the *Tempest*'s directed energy weapon turret on this mission, but the added weight of the *Perdix* drones had made that impossible. The small 50-

kilowatt laser pod, powered by a kinetic generator, was very handy for blinding incoming enemy missiles and infrared sensors but he'd have to rely on his allies for this mission. The RAF attack was timed to follow an anti-air 'wild weasel' run by Turkish F-4s, so Meany and Rex just had to hope they would do their job properly.

Checking his kneepad for his mission briefing notes, Meany's eyes were drawn to the intel he had circled in red.

Turkish and Coalition ground forces at Kobani have been encircled as Syrian forces continue their successful push from the Turkish regional capital of Gaziantep to the west. Trapped within the city are Kurdish militia forces and the US 1st Battalion, 3rd Marines.

The threat of triggering a broader allied air offensive was probably the only thing keeping the Syrian 25th Division from rolling into the coalition combat outpost at Kobani and making everyone there dead. But Meany had to wonder how long their patience would hold.

Once his *Tempest* started dropping autonomously guided 40mm armor-piercing and anti-personnel grenades on their heads.

IT was 0500 on 1 April 2030.

In Kobani, Gunner James Jensen was picking his way through the rubble to COP Meyer, wondering who had died while he was gone. Every couple of days, the Syrians dropped a mortar round on their heads. Every day they faced the threat of sniper fire from the slopes below, or contact with a Syrian patrol. Listening to the whine and click of the dogs trailing behind him just served to remind him how alone they were out here. If that sniper's furious volley of pistol fire had struck something vital, he could easily have been down one dog and his supply of spare parts was running dangerously low as Russian patrols increased their attacks on US supply drones.

Twenty miles south of Incirlik, Flight Officer Meany Papastopoulos was settling in for the short run into Kobani with a bellyful of *Perdix* drones, hoping against all odds the bloody Turkish anti-air fighters would get through this time, so that every damn Syrian anti-air missile on the ground down there wasn't pointed at him as he blew through.

In the RAAF ready room at Incirlik, Flight Lieutenant Red Burgundy was telling Bunny O'Hare that she had just been given her last chance. One more act of insubordination would see her demoted to Pilot Officer, otherwise known as a 'bograt', and placed on non-flying duties for the rest of her rotation. They would be patrolling east of Kobani and all he wanted was for her to follow bloody orders up there, nothing more, nothing less.

And Lieutenant Yevgeny Bondarev was already airborne, his *Felon* headed for a target that until now had been forbidden by their rules of engagement due to the large US presence there.

But the rules had changed, and the Turkish Incirlik Air Base was about to learn what that meant.

An Israeli GAL
Israeli Consulate, Istanbul, Turkey, 1 April

SHIMI Kahane wasn't anybody at all. Not really. But he was a member of the largest unit in the Israeli defense and security apparatus.

Not the army, air force or even Mossad, but Unit 8200, the Israeli Signals Intelligence National Unit. Israel's cyber-warfare equivalent to the US National Security Agency (NSA).

Shimi had never been in the actual Israeli armed forces. Rather than do military service he'd applied to go to Magshimim, a state-sponsored hacker college in the middle of the Negev desert. He was not the shining light in his class. His roommate had come up with a final year project which had been a bat-sized drone that could autonomously fly from window to window outside target buildings, find vulnerable wifi access points and then attach itself to the building to provide an attack vector to the hacker controlling it. A girl in his class had found a way to infect the keyboards of an American-Swiss manufacturer during production, with a virus that would enable Unit 8200 to record the keystrokes of anyone using any of the infected keyboards.

That stuff was *fire*. Shimi? Shimi had studied the way COVID-19 virus had spread around the real world and wrote a little piece of code that enabled an exploit to mimic the spread of COVID-19 by using the telephones of millions of non-target users to hit a target system from multiple vectors. Shimi showed that if he infected the phone of a random person walking past him in a crowd, within three months, his test virus had a 50 percent chance of being found on any internet connected system, anywhere in the world.

"Who wants to wait *three months* for an attack with a 50 percent chance of working?" his tutor had asked, giving him a low C grade.

He was convinced he was going to fail, but instead he was offered a job in Unit 8200. The Captain who recruited him was a balding, chubby man with a salt and pepper beard called Nir Erfrati. Erfrati had studied Shimi's final year paper and had it on the desk in front of him when he'd interviewed Shimi, though 'interview' was a pretty formal word for it. They'd had coffee in Aroma café in Be'er Sheva. Shimi had a ticket in his pocket for a bus back to Katzrin, convinced the interview would lead nowhere.

Erfrati had spun the paper with a couple of fingers while they were talking and finally pinned it in place with his thumb. "This code of yours, it's like a real-world virus? The closer you release it physically to the target system, the faster it will get there?"

"Exactly; like a sneeze full of virus, except on cell phones, spreading from one phone to another," Shimi had told him. "But you don't have to be in the same neighborhood, even the same city. You want to infect a system in Tehran, you could release the virus in Houston, Texas and inside three months it would have a 50 percent chance of reaching your target system in Tehran. But if you released it from, say, Baghdad, your chances would be over 80 percent inside the same three months."

Erfrati had drained his little espresso and handed Shimi a different bus ticket. "In two weeks you will report to Urim for induction. After that, we'll see."

'We'll see' had turned out to be the Israeli Consulate in Istanbul. And the target had turned out to be the Syrian Navy Data Transfer Center at Tartus, Syria.

Shimi had released his virus at the Grand Bazaar in Istanbul, 800 miles from Tartus, on 14 March 2027. He could track its spread like virologists tracked the spread of a real-world virus, watching it jump from cell phone to cell phone. In days it had infected 258,000 telephones in Istanbul. Within a month, 2 million throughout Turkey. It started spreading west, through Bulgaria to western Europe first. Not what he'd wanted.

Then it hit the southern Turkish city of Gaziantep, bordering Syria. Gaziantep was the staging post for most of the troops and supplies going from Turkey into the Turkish-controlled 'buffer zone' inside northern Syria. His first significant hit inside Syria had been in the Turkish-controlled city of Afrin. Inside a month, Shimi's virus had reached Latakia on the Syrian coast, just forty miles from Tartus.

Then the Syrian government issued an ultimatum to Turkish troops to leave Syria. Ten years of training, support and equipment purchases from Russia had emboldened the Syrian regime to challenge Turkey's self-appointed status as a regional superpower. Turkey moved more troops into the border area, and inevitably, conflict broke out between Turkish and Syrian forces in September 2028.

Borders were shut down, traffic and commerce ground to a standstill inside Syria and so did Shimi's virus. In a series of lop-sided battles, Turkish ground and air forces had driven back assaults by the Syrian army, but in January 2029 Turkish hubris led it to attack a Russian air base outside the Kurdish-held city of Kobani. Despite a strong presence in Syria, Russia had largely stayed out of direct involvement in the conflict, supporting Syria mostly with arms, training, satellite and air reconnaissance. Even when Turkish fighters engaged and shot down two Russian Su-35 fighters patrolling the Syrian border, Russia held back.

But when troops of the Turkish 1st Army overran the Russian airfield, killing nearly fifty Russian personnel and destroying a large number of Russian aircraft including a $200 million A-100 airborne warning and control aircraft, Russian patience ran out. Together with Iran, it signed the Syrian Sovereign Defense Pact obliging it to come to the aid of Syria in the face of 'any foreign aggression'. And it responded to the Turkish attack on its forces inside Syria with a raid by stealth drones on the Turkish 1st Army's Selimiye Barracks in the heart of Istanbul.

By February 2029, despite regular air raids deep into each other's airspace and clashes on the border, neither side had declared war. A declaration of war by Turkey would compel its NATO allies to come to its aid, and after ten years of turning its back on the West, Turkey did not want to expose how weak it was. Syria wanted to preserve the legitimacy of its storyline about reclaiming its own territory, which a declaration of war would undermine.

But as Russia began landing more equipment at its naval base at Tartus and transporting it north to the conflict zone on the Turkish border, the north-south traffic intensified, and Shimi's virus took flight again. By 1 March 2029 it had reached Tartus and on 14 March Shimi was able to confirm that it had infected the servers at the Syrian Navy Data Transfer Center.

Shimi had bought himself a small tray of baklava at the Grand Bazaar to celebrate, and shared it with the other Unit 8200 personnel at the consulate, none of whom he could tell just exactly what he was celebrating. But Captain Erfrati had called him and congratulated him.

"Do you have a new target for me?" Shimi had asked, hopefully. He was tiring of Istanbul. Though there were 20,000 Jews in Istanbul, most were from Europe. The Israeli Jewish community was small and very claustrophobic.

"No, but I will send you a flight ticket," Erfrati told him. "You are to return to Urim for training. You are being promoted to signals intelligence analyst, grade four. Congratulations."

Shimi's promotion found him right back in Istanbul, in a flat in the same building he had just vacated. Now, instead of trying to penetrate the Syrian Navy Data Transfer Center at Tartus, he was sifting through the data his exploit was pulling off the Syrian servers, classifying it and forwarding it to Be'er Sheva for further analysis.

The one highlight so far had been a naval logistics command report indicating that the Syrian 25th Division 'Tiger Force' was being resupplied for a 'pivot' away from its stalled attack on the

Turkish city of Gaziantep to strike at Incirlik. A Turkish air base only a hundred miles west, so a logical target to relieve the pressure from air attacks by Turkish and Coalition aircraft, but it was also a NATO base. He'd called Israel a minute after he'd pulled the report off the Syrian servers and saw what he had. The Syrian intelligence desk back in Urim had told him to calm down. Syria attack a *NATO* base? There was no chatter corroborating that.

A week later, Syria pulled two thousand troops and sixty armored vehicles out of the fighting at Gaziantep and sent them west, straight at Incirlik. Of course the analysts at Urim called him and apologized for dismissing his analysis. Not.

But otherwise, it was mind numbingly boring work, and he could share his work with no one, so he applied for and was granted bandwidth on one of Unit 8200's natural language neural network AIs to do most of the work for him.

Still not long out of his teens, he named his AI assistant 'GAL' after the 2004 Miss Israel and Wonderwoman actress, and gave it a voice to match. In his spare time, of which he had plenty, he was given permission to contribute to GAL's programming.

Ironically, he *was* allowed to discuss his work on GAL with other Unit 8200 employees, and even with the US NSA, which was working on its own natural language AI prototype, which it called 'HOLMES'. Being able to discuss his work on GAL didn't really make sense to Shimi, since his work on the AI was a lot more interesting and potentially more advanced than any of the work he was doing sifting through the servers at the Syrian Navy Data Transfer Center.

The NSA programmer Shimi had been authorized to share his work on GAL with was a chubby young guy with thick round glasses and a mop of black hair that was already starting to go gray in patches, even though Carl Williams couldn't have been more than twenty-five.

"GAL made a joke? Not just one it found on the internet, but a real joke it made up itself?" Williams asked, talking around a mouthful of burger.

Shimi wasn't your only-eat-kosher kind of Israeli, and he was chowing down on fried chicken and coleslaw on a brioche bun because both he and Carl had agreed that they just wouldn't do *pide*, the Turkish pizza, ever again.

"Yeah, or, it was more like a comeback, you know," Shimi explained. "Like I said to it, 'GAL, we got new tasking'. Told it what the tasking was which, you know, even I was thinking it was tedious."

"My life," Carl muttered.

"Tell me about it," Shimi told him. "Anyway, it comes straight back with, 'Wow, Shimi, you really know how to make a girl hot'."

Carl nearly dropped his burger. "You programmed it to say that?"

"No, spontaneous. It's amazing, right? I mean it could have just come back with 'that is boring, Shimi, give me something that uses my full capabilities', but instead it's throwing *sarcasm* at me."

"But it must have learned it somewhere ... you said it had been monitoring text interactions between Unit personnel..."

"Yeah, but how much are you going to learn watching geeks talk to each other?" Shimi looked a little sheepish. "So I signed it up for Netflix and HBO."

"How does that even work?" Carl asked.

"I made it an account and wrote a little code that either chooses shows semi-randomly or it can choose whatever show it wants to watch itself. I started feeding it with documentaries about computers and AI..."

"Yeah, makes sense, I guess."

"Yeah, but then it started choosing its own."

Carl's eyes widened. "Like what?"

"It's watched all ten seasons of Friends. Game of Thrones. Vikings. Mad Men. But it seems to go for comedies. Family Guy is its favorite. It's watched all thirty-two seasons. Twice, so far."

"That's too weird. How does it even 'watch' a TV show?"

Shimi shrugged. "Downloads an episode, runs the show frame by frame through its image recognition software, listens to the soundtrack."

Williams shook his head. "HOLMES can't spontaneously start a conversation on anything. Let alone throw sarcasm in there."

"Yeah but the sarcasm wasn't the big deal." Shimi pointed with his fork at a group of women at a nearby table. "GAL self-identified as a *girl*."

"So, it just took its name literally; GAL equals girl. Or you could have triggered it. Like 'good morning, GAL, how's the girl today? You done with that data fetch, girl?' That kind of thing."

Shimi frowned. "Does that sound like me? I would anthropomorphize a cloud-based analytical AI?"

"Yeah, no, I guess not." Carl looked innocently over his burger. "So, this Netflix code you wrote. That's not classified, right? You could share that with me?"

"Maybe ... but you know the deal, nothing for nothing, Carl."

Carl looked around the bar like a cartoon villain checking to see if anyone nearby could hear them. "Alright, how about this. We're picking up chatter says the action in Turkey is just a curtain raiser for something bigger."

"Bigger, how? Like what?"

It was Carl's turn to shrug. "Unclear, so far. But the amount of hardware and 'advisors' Russia is moving in is way more than Syria needs to hold its little 'buffer zone' on the Turkish border. Then there's this whole Incirlik play, what's the idea there?"

Shimi thought about that. He was just a lowly Analyst 4, he didn't see geopolitical threat assessments, only intel that was relevant to his very specific target. But he followed open source sites that analyzed the politics of the region. "Lebanon?" he suggested.

"Why Lebanon?"

Shimi counted off the fingers on his right hand. "It's a failed state, economy is a basket case. Iranian-backed Hezbollah is already running the entire south of the country. Syrian troops have occupied the central and eastern provinces since that harbor explosion took out half of Beirut in 2020. Lebanese government forces are more or less only in control of Beirut these days and hanging on by a thread. Now Syria has got its northern border buffer zone, say it neutralizes Turkey's biggest southern air base. That frees them to move on Lebanon. Syria takes Beirut from the east, Hezbollah moves up from the south, and they divide the country up between them, just like in the 1980s."

"Yeah? And how would Israel react to that? Hezbollah, Iran, Syria and Russia running the show in Lebanon?"

"Not well," Shimi predicted. "We didn't sit back and watch in '82, I doubt we would this time."

"You didn't have Russian troops and aircraft on the ground in Syria in '82," Carl pointed out. "Andropov had just taken over from Brezhnev, Soviet economy was going backwards, Afghanistan was a bloody mess ... different Russia today."

"The question for you, Carl," Shimi responded drily, "is how would America react if Russia and Iran effectively take control of Lebanon? Russia might be different, but America is a different America today too. Obsessed with China, to the exclusion of just about all else. Does America care what happens in the Middle East anymore?"

Carl put his burger down, wiped his napkin across his face and placed it carefully beside his plate. He looked suddenly grave. "Tell you a story. There's a cemetery across the Potomac River from Washington called Arlington. There's a tree in that cemetery called the Cedar of Lebanon. It stands in the middle of the graves of nearly three hundred Americans who died in Beirut in the 1980s." His voice grew hoarse. "Every year on October 23, the anniversary of the day an Iranian suicide bomber drove his truck into a Marine barracks in Beirut and killed 241 Marines, I go to that cemetery with my dad to put flowers on the grave of my grandfather."

"I'm sorry."

"Yeah, well. You're right, the White House and Pentagon are obsessed with China. But the guy sitting opposite you here has a very personal interest in what happens in the Middle East and, yeah, he cares."

ANOTHER American with a personal interest in the Middle East was US Vice President Benjamin Sianni. Before he had become Vice President, he had been a Secretary of State, two Presidents previous. In that role, he had fought tooth and nail against the US pulling troops out of, first, Afghanistan, then Syria, and finally Iraq. When he left office two elections ago, the US had only ten thousand troops in Afghanistan, four thousand in Iraq, and fewer than a thousand in Syria. By contrast, it had 64,000 in Japan following Korean reunification, 35,000 still in Germany and 22,000 in the UK and Italy.

Sianni had spoken in the Security Council, in the United Nations and in Congressional Committees, pointing out that nature abhorred a vacuum, and if the US disengaged from the Middle East, Russia would move in. He highlighted, at every opportunity, acts of Russian aggression such as its annexation of Crimea, its role in the civil wars of Georgia and the Ukraine, its meddling in Nagorno-Karabakh and the increasingly provocative patrols of its strategic bombers over both the

Baltic Sea and Bering Strait off Alaska. He pointed, loudly and frequently, to continued US economic interests in the region's oil and gas.

His warnings as Secretary of State fell on deaf ears, and in the years between his time as Secretary of State and his later elevation to Vice President in the newly re-elected administration, the US drawdown in the Middle East only accelerated.

Despite achieving a position of power in one of the most influential roles in the most influential nation on the globe, Sianni had been forced to watch time and time again as Russia attacked its weak neighbors and persecuted or assassinated voices of democracy and dissent, both at home and abroad, almost with impunity. It seemed to him that his country had become immune to the outrages that Russia visited on the world around it, and it had certainly tired of him pointing them out.

He was sitting in his car on the way back from a personal briefing at the Pentagon, about new intelligence indicating Russian-backed Syrian forces and the Iranian-backed Hezbollah militia were now preparing to seize power in Lebanon. 'I told you so' did not even begin to sum it up. It was Russia's Cold War domino strategy all over again. First make alliances with North Korea and Iran. Then get a foothold in Syria. Try to win Turkey away from NATO: failing that, isolate it through proxy control of its neighbor Armenia and threaten it through Syria. March into Lebanon and topple the already crippled government there. Next? Support an Iranian-backed opposition takeover in Iraq probably.

And so what, his detractors would say. America is no longer dependent on Middle East oil. Let Russia play its games in the Middle East, just like China plays its games in Africa. America's position as a superpower is not strategically dependent on either the Middle East or Africa. Asia is where the real threats are.

Yes, but every action has an equal but opposite reaction. Let Russia and Iran increase their influence in the Middle East and you isolate the one ally you can't afford to ignore, Israel. Or, having allowed Russia to achieve its ambitions in the Middle East, NATO suddenly finds itself on the back foot in the Baltics or, closer to home, in the warming waters of the Arctic seas between Russia and Alaska. He'd shared the bitter fruit of these convictions with his peers, and their seeds had too often fallen on barren soil.

So he had tired of words. He was Vice President of the USA now, and he was going to force his country to face the realities of forty years of indifference to Russia, even if he had to drag it kicking and screaming into a conflict that its President very much opposed. There were at least a few powerful allies inside the administration who saw the world the same way he did.

He reached for his cell phone, closing the glass window between himself and his Secret Service complement, seated in the front of the armored limo. He dialed the Secretary of Defense.

"Harry. Yeah, I just left the briefing. You were right, this is what I need to get the President off the fence." He traced a finger across the window, drawing a map of Syria in the condensation from his breath without even realizing it. "No, I'm sure. You can start loading the cavalry onto C-5s and get it in the air, I'll make sure you have the President's signature on the order tonight." He listened to the other man for a few minutes. "I know what Carmine thinks. She said days ago the amount of hardware and manpower Russia was moving into Syria couldn't just be about Incirlik and I agreed. Now we know what their long game is, and it's time for everyone who can't see it to throw their damned rose-colored glasses in the trash."

He hung up and wiped the map on the window away with his hand. Sianni had more than once been accused of having an anti-Russian bias, motivated by his links to the US oil and gas industry which generously funded his re-election campaigns.

But in this, his adversaries were wrong. Benjamin Sianni was in fact motivated by a deep and abiding *personal* hatred of Russia.

Because his family name was not actually Sianni at all. It was Shishani. His emigrant father had changed the family's surname when they fled to the USA in the 1990s to escape Russian persecution of Chechen Muslims. Not long after they left Chechnya, Russian paramilitary troops attacked the family's hometown of Samashki, on the border with Russian Ingushetia. Between 7 and 8 April 1995, more than 200 civilians in the town were forced into their houses, shot or burned alive with flame throwers by Russian OMON police units.

In that single period of 24 hours, Sianni's father, mother and their only son had lost every single member of their families.

No US news outlet had picked up on that forty-year-old chapter in his personal story.

Some things don't wash off
Syrian 138th Mechanized Infantry Headquarters, 2 April

DARYAN 'Al-Kobani' Khalid had lain in the filthy sewer pipe for five stinking hours. Ten or fifteen times an hour, a flood of putrid excrement and urine washed past her, and though she had plugged her nose and held her breath each time she heard it coming, the stench made her stomach heave.

But she stayed. It was her twelfth visit to the sewer pipe and the first in which she had brought her Kalashnikov PL-15K 9mm silenced pistol into the sewer pipe with her. Barely able to squeeze her light frame into the pipe, on the first two trips she had brought only a drill and fiberscope. The sewer line inside the Syrian army's base outside Kobani had been laid hastily and buried only five inches under the ground. Boring through the top of the pipe with the drill, she'd then used an old teacher's telescopic pointer to push a hole through the dirt covering the pipe and poked the lens of the fiberscope through the hole so she could check her position.

Her first two surveys had been wasted. The first hole she drilled too close to a guard post, the second was under a structure of some sort and she hit solid concrete. But she judged the third right, and her camera emerged out the back of the Syrian command building in the middle of an old farming compound in the ruined village, between the rear entrance to the farmhouse and a latrine block built up against a wall twenty yards away.

The Intelligence Chief for the Kobani People's Protection Unit (YPG), Lieutenant Colonel Jamal Adab, had discussed sending her in with an IED, an improvised explosive device, but for that to have been effective would have required that they could successfully keep a drone overhead for surveillance (something that had proven impossible so far) or plant a transmitting video device in the sewer, whose signal would have been vulnerable to detection or jamming. Instead, Adab had sent Daryan in armed only with a PL-15K pistol.

Daryan had been given a very specific target. Lt. Col. Walid Ganem, the officer in command of the Syrian forces besieging Kobani. Despite their failed attempt to take the city, despite constant raids on their positions by Kurdish militia and Coalition aircraft, it seemed impossible to break the Syrians' morale. Colonel Adab's intelligence had led him to believe Walid Ganem was one of the reasons. The man was only in his command post from 0400 to 0600 daily. The rest of the time he toured the line of control around Kobani like a hunting tiger, dropping in on his men at seemingly random intervals to get updated, to provide encouragement or just give them recognition. Prisoners taken by the Kurds had defiantly bragged that more than once, he had been involved in firefights during Kurdish probing attacks which had only enhanced his reputation as a fighting leader.

A warm wave of putrid air washed over Daryan, presaging another flood of piss and feces. She drew a choking breath and held it. When it had passed, she put her eye to her camera again. On her sixth visit she had found a good position and begun carefully preparing her 'nest'. Her first priority was to open a hole to the surface for the camera, which was mounted at the end of a fiber optic tube. It could be flexed and rotated to give her 360-degree vision, but the pipe she was in ran against a wall on her right, so she only needed to cover her left flank. She had watched the headquarters personnel going to and from the latrines daily for three days before she was certain she had identified Ganem. The long-faced man had a distinctive, loping gait and ever-present twelve-o'clock shadow.

And like many senior officers, he was a creature of habit. Daryan had learned he visited the latrine at around 0555 each morning, just before leaving the headquarters building for the day. When not observing Ganem, Daryan was preparing her shot window. She had drilled a second hole around the level of her chin and used the telescopic pointer to gently widen it so it could accommodate a two-inch-wide plastic tube which she pushed down the hole to stop the dirt around it collapsing. She made the hole wider at the base so that she could put the silencer of the pistol in the tube and swivel it, giving herself about ten degrees of freedom for aiming. She didn't push the tube all the way through to the surface ... she would only do that at the moment she planned to fire.

As she worked to set up her nest, it was both satisfying and frustrating to see her target lope back and forth to the latrines each day. And more than a little irksome to know that after the man had made his visit, Daryan would be showering in his waste. But she allowed herself to be visited that indignity, knowing he would soon be dead or incapacitated. The PL-15K was based on a sports-shooting design, and its small magazine held only eight rounds. Daryan figured she would need one or two shots to align her fire, giving herself two or three shots on her target with three in reserve if the man was still moving and within her field of fire after that.

By day nine, her nest was ready. Daryan did not share her quarters with anyone else from the Women's Protection Unit, the YPJ. She had a small bolt hole in the basement of a shattered office building well outside Kobani, in Qawal, which she used as a base for this mission. It had a working shower hooked up to a water tank on the roof which she used at the end of each day to clean the sewage out of her hair and ears. She had found a soap which another soldier, a former abattoir worker, had recommended. It helped, but the scent of human waste still wafted around her like a cloud when she lay herself down to sleep. She sometimes wondered if she would ever get rid of it.

On day ten she was ready to commit, but Ganem did not show. He could have been sick, or had commitments elsewhere. After Daryan had made her way out again she checked in with Colonel Adab, but there had been no new intelligence indicating the Syrian had shipped out. Though Coalition fighters prowled overhead, the Syrian supply and communication lines back into the heart of the country were still open. It was possible Ganem had been wounded and evacuated, but Adab told Daryan he should have heard if that was the case. He sent Daryan back in. Day eleven was the same … no Ganem. The Syrian headquarters had been subject to a Coalition bombing raid while Daryan was lying in her pipe, and she had closed her eyes and prayed as the earth around her shook. The attack may have explained why Ganem didn't show that day either.

Now it was approaching dawn on day twelve. Zero five forty-five. The only upside of Ganem's biological routine was that the predictable time window meant Daryan only had to be inside the pipe for about four hours – thirty minutes wriggling headfirst into position, about double that to wriggle out again, with two hours on station in case Ganem made an unscheduled bio-break. The early hour also meant that traffic in and out of the latrines was limited compared to the 'peak hour' around lunchtime that she'd had to endure on her first few days. Daryan kept her eye on the video feed playing on the left eye of her goggles as she panned her camera around the compound, settling on an object and taking a practice shot in her mind as she did so. Anything to take her mind off the smell.

The heavy metal door at the rear entrance to the Syrian command building swung open and a young soldier, who Daryan guessed was the officer's aide, stepped out. Beside him … Ganem! Daryan took a deep breath, pushed the housing of her pistol against the tube so that it moved forward a quarter inch and broke gently through the smaller opening to the surface.

Five more steps. The PL-15K was self-cocking and had a short 7mm trigger pull. *Four steps.* She had the pistol against her chest, adjusting the tube in a gentle, continuous sweep to track Ganem as he walked. The aide was on Ganem's right side and wouldn't occlude the shot. *Three steps.* Daryan wouldn't know how close her aim was until she fired the first shot. And she was firing from a low position, upward, so if she missed, her shot would simply fly into the sky, not provide her with a visible splash she could use to correct her aim. *Two steps.* She took another deep breath and held it, laying her forefinger on the trigger.

One.

She fired. Amplified by the long tube, the muffled cough of the PL-15K sounded like a dog's bark to Daryan inside the pipe. *Miss!* Ganem kept walking, not even looking toward Daryan. Daryan adjusted her aim quickly, a quarter inch down, a little to the left. She fired again. *Hit!* Ganem staggered, clutching his thigh. Before he could move again, Daryan adjusted her aim up two millimeters and fired again. The next 9mm bullet caught Ganem in the ribs and he fell against the aide. The man looked at him in surprise, and then shock, trying to hold him up as Daryan fired a final time. Hit the Syrian colonel in his back as the aide started dragging him toward cover.

Daryan quickly withdrew her fiberscope and then the firing tube, wriggling it to destroy the hole she had made as she did so. Laying the tube down, she stuck her gun and fiberscope to Velcro pads on her chest, reached her arms over her head and, by a combination of pushing with her hands and pulling with her heels, began to drag herself down the pipe again, inch by painstaking inch. Outside she could hear muffled shouting. It would be another hour before she would emerge at the underground tank in which the sewage from several latrines was collected and another twenty minutes from there along a never-used feeder pipe to the ruined building outside the Syrian compound where she entered and exited.

She wasn't panicking. The Syrians would assume a sniper had fired from long distance and would be looking at surrounding buildings first. But that would just puzzle them, since all the buildings surrounding the walled Syrian compound had been leveled and provided no good sniping positions. The small caliber of the wound would also confuse them. They might think blue on blue, the presence of the aide clouding the situation. Even though she'd used a suppressor, if the shots had been as loud out in the open air as they were down in the pipe, then perhaps the Syrians would start searching their base for an enemy infiltrator. But they'd be looking above the ground, not beneath it. A bomb disposal dog might be able to find the hole she'd used to shoot through by the scent of the gunpowder, if there were any dogs still alive inside the base. She doubted they'd find it before she was outside.

As she pushed down the pipe, her mind was already moving ahead to the day that awaited her. There would be no time for celebrations, no congratulations, no medals. Daryan was not a regular fighter in the Kobani Women's Protection Unit. She had never been through formal training. She held no rank. As a child, Daryan had been one of those Colonel Adab called the Rats of Kobani. A network of civilian informers who provided Adab with intelligence on the movements of the occupying Turkish forces who had flanked Kobani to the east and west, before the Syrians had rolled in. His 'rats' knew every corner of every alley in every village surrounding the city, could slide through cracks in walls or crawl through tiny subterranean passages between buildings. They were invisible even in plain sight, the occupying Turks and Russians looking straight past them in their dirty jeans and shawls as they stood on street corners clutching footballs and dolls, or leaned out of windows. Drones were shot down as quickly as he put them up, but his rats were Adab's eyes and ears outside the Kurdish Kobani line of control.

A special few, the ones who had shown special aptitudes, Adab had given additional training. The fourteen-year-old Daryan had been brought to Adab after YPG fighters detained her in possession of a rifle. She'd refused to give it up, claiming it was the one thing of her father's she had left after he had been killed at a Turkish roadblock. An old rifle from just after the turn of the century that had belonged to her grandfather, she'd fought like a wildcat when the soldiers had tried to take it away from her.

They'd bound her hands behind her back and brought both Daryan and her rifle to Adab.

Colonel Jamal Adab had grown up in Aleppo, eighty miles and a world away from Kobani. Adab was a shopkeeper's son, not a hunter. But he knew a hunter when he saw one. He had regarded Daryan from under gray bushy eyebrows, stroking his mustache as he turned the old rifle over in his hands.

He had put it back down on his desk as the girl squirmed in front of him, trying to free her hands from the ties around her wrists even as she sat in front of the Colonel. Adab arched his eyebrows. "You told those men you used this thing to shoot rats?"

Daryan stopped squirming and glared defiantly at Adab. "Rats, and cats. Sometimes people pay me to hunt dogs with rabies. I shot a hawk once," she had boasted. "On the wing."

Adab stood up and walked over to the girl, who shrunk from him, expecting to be struck. But he gently lifted the collar of her shirt away from her shoulder and looked at it. A rifle like the girl was carrying had a powerful kick. Sure enough, the girl's shoulder showed new blue and older yellow bruises. He lowered the shirt and nodded. "Where do you get your ammunition?"

The girl did not meet his eyes.

"Well?"

"I find it," she said. "Or trade for it with the militia."

"Trade what?"

"Errands, and … favors," the girl said simply, looking at the floor.

"How old are you?"

Daryan looked up now. "Fourteen."

Adab turned back to his desk, picked up the rifle and walked past Daryan. "Follow me."

At the time, his 'office' had been a tent in a village called Halinjah, a crossroads town about five miles outside Kobani. He had lifted the flap at the entry and looked back at the girl. "Are you coming? I want to see you shoot." Adab's adjutant fell in behind them, his hand resting lightly on the holstered gun at his hip. He was accustomed to the Colonel's impromptu walks with the strays his fighters brought in. Their guests did not always join them for the return walk.

They walked to the edge of the village where dead brown fields stretched off to the horizon. Along the way, Adab had pointed at stray bottles and tin cans lying by the side of the road, and his adjutant had picked them up. As they reached the field, Adab had pulled a large hunting knife from his belt, razor sharp on one side, wickedly serrated on the other. Grabbing the girl roughly by the shoulder he spun her around and sliced off the plastic ties that bound her hands behind her back. Before letting go he leaned down and said into her ear, "You are thinking of running, I know. But if you do, you will never see your grandfather's rifle again." He looked in the girl's face for confirmation she understood, then stepped back. His adjutant paced out ten meters, put down a can, then another at fifty meters, and finally, a bottle at a hundred meters. Then he walked back.

Working the bolt on the rifle, Adab opened the breech and checked it was empty. From his pocket, he pulled four rounds one of his men had given him. He handed the gun to the girl, together with one bullet. "Now you are thinking you could load it and shoot me." Adab jerked his thumb at the adjutant, who was standing at ease but with his hands crossed in front of his belt and his handgun unholstered in his right hand. "Or him. But you only have one bullet, and there are two of us, so…"

Daryan took the gun and the cartridge. It was a heavy gun for a fourteen-year-old girl, and it was long. With its butt sitting on the ground, the muzzle came up to her shoulder. She held the butt in against the button of her dirty jeans and worked the bolt handle that opened the breech, feeding in the long round and closing it again. With a last look around her as though still weighing up her options, the girl put one knee down on the dirt and brought the gun up to her shoulder, resting her elbow on her other raised knee and peering down the gun's old optical sight.

Adab was impressed by how she'd created a solid firing position for herself, kept her sightline clear of the small rocks and bushes strewn across the field, and held herself steady as she aimed. Neither did she seem nervous or rushed, unobtrusively licking the small finger of her trigger hand to help herself judge the wind and lifting her eye off the gunsight to adjust the sight, before settling her eye behind it again. It seemed like a fair bit of drama for a shot at a can sitting ten meters away, but Adab let her be – no doubt she was trying to impress.

It looked to Adab like she was aiming high. She squeezed gently on the trigger and the gun bucked against her shoulder. Adab saw her wince, but she stayed anchored and didn't stumble.

And … she missed. *Ah well. It had been bravado after all.* But Adab could still use bravado. If the kid was this cool under pressure, even if she couldn't shoot…

Daryan wasn't aiming at the can ten meters away. Or the one at fifty meters. Or the bottle at one hundred. As she stood, she rested the rifle on the ground and gave Adab a disdainful look, pointing out into the field with her right arm. "Hedgehog," she said. "About two hundred meters that way."

Adab laughed disbelievingly, but nodded to his adjutant, who started trudging out into the field, pacing the distance. At about a hundred and fifty paces, Daryan called out. "To your right! Now, another fifty!"

At about two hundred paces, the man stopped, bent down and held something in the air. Adab could barely see it, but the soldier held the small lump out to one side and held a thumb up with the other.

Adab turned to Daryan. "Who taught you to shoot like that?"

"My father, before the Turks killed him. If I work for you, will you let me kill Turks?" the girl asked.

"If you work for me, you will do whatever I damn well tell you to do," Adab said. "And you will be glad I didn't just shoot you in the stomach and leave you in this field. Is that clear?"

The girl didn't answer. She lifted the rifle and put her arm through the strap, swinging it over her shoulder. "I lied about shooting cats. I have already killed three Turks. Your fighters give me a chicken or ammunition for every one I kill. I will do whatever you ask, as long as I can keep my Lobaev."

WORD of the assassination of the Syrian Commander was quick to reach the ears of Reuters Middle East correspondent Mary Jo 'MJ' Basim. But then, MJ had cultivated a host of well-informed friends inside and outside Kobani over three years reporting on the conflict between the Syrians, the Turks and the Kurds. She had reported from Syria during its civil war, from Iraq during US troop withdrawals there, covered the reunification in Korea. She had been embedded with a Turkish armored platoon as it crossed the border into Northern Syria to enforce its 'buffer zone' and she had been living side by side with the Kurdish militia in Kobani when the Syrian 138th Mechanized had rolled up from the south and laid siege to the city, preventing her from escaping.

But if there was a polar opposite of the chain-smoking, combat vest-wearing, hard-drinking, hard-bitten war correspondent, it was Mary Jo. She was, for a start, only five foot four tall. Before being sent to the Middle East she had been short, soft and round. After six months in Northern Syria she was short, wiry and lean, but not in a way her Lebanese American mother regarded as healthy. "Eat something, for the love of God," her mother said at the end of every call home. "Easier said than done, ma," she'd reply. She was Muslim, to an extent – didn't pray as often as she was supposed to, but didn't drink either. She had her father's ginger hair, which she kept tied in a bun at her neck because she couldn't wash it often enough. And a freckled complexion which despite her Middle Eastern DNA was not made for the harsh desert sun, so despite lathering her face in sun block, her nose was always peeling.

MJ was a regular at COP Meyer, because the cell and satellite phone reception there was relatively stable and the Marines didn't mind her calling on their dime, as long as she kept the world aware of what was happening in Kobani and filed reports that let their families know they were still here, still hanging on.

"This assassination could change the equation in your favor," MJ was telling a Lava Dogs corpsman, Calvin Bell. "Whoever the Syrians send to replace him might not be the hero that Ganem was."

They were standing outside what was nominally COP Meyer's battalion HQ but what was, in reality, a shell-pocked, two-story, roofless and windowless concrete shell. The combat medic Bell surveyed the inside of the combat outpost with a lot less optimism than MJ was projecting. The outpost on the summit of Mishte-nur Hill was a hexagonal patch of ground about the size of two football fields, ringed with head-high concrete walls built by Russia ten years earlier. To the north, an observation tower looked out over Kobani and the Turkish border. To the south, a second observation tower watched over the approach to the main gates, which were also guarded by a .50-cal gun emplacement and concrete blocks to prevent a direct approach by any vehicles. As combat outposts went, it was not the worst she had seen.

COP Meyer had several natural and man-made advantages. Armies had used the summit of Mishte-nur Hill as a stronghold since before the time of King Cyrus the Great in 600 BC, as it offered unobstructed views over the plains below in all directions. At the end of the Syrian civil war in 2019 Russia had fortified the summit, building a garrison on Mishte-nur Hill for a hundred personnel and repairing the walls that ringed the base. Conscious of the threat from Turkish long-range artillery over the border just ten miles away, the Russians also dug into the bedrock of the small hill, carving out two interlinked bunkers which in true Russian fashion were totally over-engineered. An exit at the base of the hill on the north side and the bunker entrance inside COP Meyer's eastern wall were sealed behind thermobaric blast-proof doors, while the bunkers themselves went forty feet down, under enough reinforced concrete to resist anything short of a tactical nuke.

MJ had visited combat outposts in Afghanistan and Iraq at the bottom of valleys or mountain ranges, with the enemy dug in on the slopes all around the US soldiers inside. In her opinion Bell had no cause to be as gloomy about his tactical situation as he was, but it seemed to be his default setting.

"The equation?" he scoffed. "Off the record ma'am; the equation, is that this unit is dug in on top of an exposed hilltop inside a rotting Russian fortification they abandoned ten years ago..." He pointed to a part of the hillside under the concrete western wall that had collapsed, leaving a hole in the wall the Marines had filled with sandbags. They called it 'The Suck', which described both the way it constantly ate sandbags, and also what the Marines thought about the never-ending job of filling and hauling the sandbags to feed it. "Which is about as secure as a New Orleans pole dancer's virtue."

"Sure, but..."

"And," he twirled a finger in the air, "we are surrounded by Russian-trained, Russian-armed Syrian regulars who outnumber us and the Kurds three to one, while Russian fighter aircraft run combat air patrols overhead shooting down two in three of our supply or medevac flights. How can the death of one Syrian officer change anything in that 'equation'?"

MJ looked up at the skies. "Well, the Russians don't have it all their own way up there. And one out of three of your supply drones is getting through. I'm just saying..."

"I guess you got to be upbeat to sell your stories, ma'am," Bell interrupted. "But I gotta deal with the messed up reality."

With that he turned and headed for the underground bunker where she knew he would spend a few hours sleeping before he was sent outside the walls again.

She sighed. The situation at COP Meyer was taking its toll on everyone, even MJ. At thirty-five, this was not MJ's first rodeo. She'd been a correspondent in Korea, during the brief reunification conflict. She had done two assignments embedded with the US Army in Iraq during the chaos known as the Drawdown. Yeah, COP Meyer could break anyone's spirits. If you weren't baking out on the hilltop in the desert sun, you were skulking down in the dank and musty concrete bunkers like a turd in a sewer pipe waiting to be flushed. MJ had learned how to spot a soldier about to crash, and Bell was on a bad glidepath.

He was an interesting character and she'd really wanted to do a portrait of him in the stories she was filing. A twenty-one-year-old from Greenfield, Indianapolis, he liked restoring cars from the 1950s with his old man. She'd also grown up with a car obsessed father who had played 'name the car' with her every time they went anywhere together, so she'd struck up a kind of friendship with Bell. It helped that he was also a fellow ginger - they were few and far between.

She'd tried writing about him as a heroic corpsman in an embattled company-sized remnant of besieged survivors, holding his bleeding buddies together with nothing but gauze tape and spit. But it hadn't sat right and she'd spiked that story. Bell was no picture-perfect hero. Every day another squad of Marines would saddle up, head out through the main gates, or the northern ground-level tunnel exit, and make their patrols. More often than not, Bell went along with them. If they were lucky, they'd all make it back in one piece. Too often lately, not all did. And with every one he had to patch up, or who died before he could get them on a medevac flight, Bell got angrier and angrier.

She knew the signs by now, and a sneak peek in his pack one day had confirmed it. *Modafamine* addiction.

A combination of modafinil and amphetamine, supplied by the US Department of Defense to frontline troops and pilots to keep them awake at times of extreme need, its addictive properties meant it was intended for use only one or two days at a time. It could keep you awake and alert for up to 48 hours; after that, you cracked. Unless you micro-dosed. In which case the result was mild euphoria, with side effects including sleeplessness, of course, but also anxiety, depression, obsessive-compulsive behaviors, paranoid delusion and, in extreme cases, auditory or visual hallucinations.

MJ had not been too worried about Bell early in the siege, when the Marines had just been concerned with shoring up their defensive position, clearing out the debris from the disused bunkers under the hill and setting up their workshops, barracks, chow hall, armory, heads and infirmary. And while the siege was still fluid, and Syrian troops still establishing their lines and patrols, casualties were light.

But of the two hundred Marines who had survived the first Syrian assault and held onto the summit of Mishte-nur Hill, three more had been killed and ten wounded. Two of the wounded had never made it out to Turkish Gaziantep, their medevac drones shot down én route. Bell had taken those deaths hard. Kept saying if they'd stayed inside the walls of COP Meyer, they might still be alive.

"What the hell point is it me putting them on a medevac rotor," Bell had told her after the last loss. "If the Russians or Syrians are going to shoot them down between here and Turkey? I might as well shoot them my damn self and save the plasma."

MJ watched Bell go; a fast, twitching walk, clicking his fingers like he was listening to some inner drum beat.

She hadn't reported his drug use to anyone. What right did she have to judge him? The COP was subject to almost daily mortar attack from Syrian artillery, Russian aircraft circled overhead, and lately, they had been taking more and more casualties from sniper fire. But Bell kept saddling up and going out on patrol and if a few pills were what he needed to get his job done, then good luck to him.

Almost on cue, she heard an explosion somewhere on the other side of the city, and a short time later a pair of jets blasted over Kobani from the south, with a crackle of small-caliber ground fire following them over. She couldn't see the aircraft, but she had heard their whining growl often enough to know what they were. Russian Sukhoi-35s.

Not for the first time, she asked herself, *Where are the damn Coalition air patrols that are supposed to keep them away?!*

She could hear the Russian aircraft recede into the distance, but the dull roar didn't disappear completely. Probably circling around, hunting. Her heart rate rising a little, she looked over at a group of Marines pulling a camouflage cape over a drone that had come in during the night. Her instincts would never be as good as those of a battle-worn Marine. She always looked to the soldiers and militia men around her for cues as to whether she should be worried.

As the roar of the incoming jets increased, they looked up, but kept working on securing the drone.

She didn't stand and watch them. She was already jogging past The Suck to the observation post, or OP, in the northwest corner of the walls that the Marines called 'Pearl'. With typical irony, the Lava Dogs had given every OP an exotic Hawaiian name – Pearl, Iolani, Mauna Loa, and Banyan. Only one OP had escaped the Hawaiian theme – OP 'Stink' – so named because the outflow from the COP latrines spilled out onto the hillside directly underneath it.

Scrambling up a ladder to the flimsy scaffolding they'd erected around the inside of the ten-foot-high, six-foot-thick concrete walls the Russians had built around the Mishte-nur outpost, she ducked down below the top of the walls and ran to OP Pearl, surprising the two Marines on lookout there, a private and a corporal whom she recognized.

"Ma'am." The corporal acknowledged her with a nod. The private had his eyes glued to his stand-mounted binos.

She strained her eyes, looking for the Russian fighters. She could see dirty brown contrails on the horizon, could hear them out there… "Where away, Denaro?" she asked. With only a couple of hundred personnel in the COP, she knew most of them by name by now.

"Three four niner degrees, low," the private with the binos replied. "We called in a wild weasel strike by Turkish F-4s on Syrian northern anti-air positions. Ivan just arrived to chase them away."

"Turkey still has F-4s flying?" MJ asked, surprised. The venerable F-4 *Phantom* had been in the Turkish inventory since the 1970s. MJ had heard most of them had been either mothballed or shot down in the first weeks of the conflict by far superior Russian fighters.

"I guess they're running low on everything, but they still got a few of the old F-4Es they got upgraded in the early 2020s," Denaro said. "We saw some secondaries northeast of the city at ground level, then the Russians arrived and the Kurds started banging away with that old 14.5mm peashooter of theirs."

"Mind if I get some footage?" she asked.

He stepped away from the wall and picked up a helmet, handing it to her. "Mi casa su casa, MJ."

She put on the helmet and pulled her Korean smart phone out of a utility pocket on her trousers. The days when war correspondents carried bulky SLR cameras around with them were long gone. The phone in her pocket had a 200 megapixel shake-stabilized lens and 20x optical, 100x digital zoom. As soon as she stopped recording or photographing – as long as she had a cell or wifi connection – it automatically compressed and squirted her images or video to the Reuters cloud servers so nothing would be lost. It was important she didn't have to worry about losing it. She'd smashed, dropped or drowned about twenty of the phones in the last two years, and had five more in the bag on her bunk down in the COP Meyer bunkers.

Standing on a sandbag, she saw the Russian aircraft now and started recording. They had gone up to about 15,000 feet where the Kurdish light anti-air gun couldn't reach them. They were low enough to just be within range of man-portable *Stinger* missiles, but the YPG had exhausted their supply of those some weeks ago, and what few *Stinger* B's the Marines had in their inventory they were holding for a rainy day. The Sukhoi-35s were circling over the city like watchful hawks, then suddenly the two silhouettes banked around, pointed southeast and lit their tails, screaming overhead again in pursuit of the Turkish *Phantoms*, which were no doubt beating a hasty retreat. She stopped recording, disappointed. Vision of a Russian-Turkish dogfight would have been a scoop. Even better if she managed to get video of Russian vs. RAF or RAAF fighters, but there was fat chance of that.

Theoretically, Coalition forces weren't at war with Russia. The Russians were happy to attack Turkish aircraft inside Syria or their 'no-fly' zone on the border. And Coalition aircraft were happy to attack Syrian ground targets inside Turkey or around Kobani. But until now, Coalition and Russian aircraft had avoided trading missiles with each other and the US had resisted sending any fighter aircraft at all to help the unreliable 'ally' that was Turkey. Tankers, drones, early warning aircraft, yes. In limited numbers. Pilots in cockpits and boots on the ground? No.

Except for the small Lava Dogs force. Theoretically, the 3rd Marines had only been in Kobani providing training and logistical support to the Kurdish militia facing off against Russian-armed and trained Syrian army regulars. When Turkish troops rolled into northern Syria in 2019 to create a buffer zone in the Kurdish territories, Kobani found itself isolated. Turkish forces eventually controlled an area twenty miles deep to the west and east of them, but Kobani remained under Kurdish control, isolated in the center of the Turkish buffer zone.

Following the general drawdown of US troops across the Middle East, the last remaining US force of three hundred Marines in Syria was moved to Kobani in 2028 to provide a slim measure of international support to the Kurdish cause.

It was a situation that could not last. When the Russian-funded, trained and equipped Syrian Arab Army began its operation to force Turkey out of northern Syria, it also moved on Kobani. The Kurds who had been fighting a guerrilla war to keep Kobani free of Turkish control from the north suddenly found themselves facing a heavily armed foe from the south.

The Lava Dogs had been ordered to defend their own positions throughout the city and help their Kurdish allies call in indirect fire and air support, and it had taken three bloody weeks before the Syrian assault abated. By the time they had pulled back, the Syrians had lost three hundred troops, seven armored vehicles, and eighteen unmanned aircraft. The Lava Dogs had lost fourteen Marines killed or seriously wounded, but they had held the critical high ground on Mishte-nur Hill and evacuated nearly 100 personnel, wounded civilians and militia fighters through COP Meyer before the Syrians realized what was happening and moved anti-air and regular troops into place to shut the evac down. After their failed assault, Syrian troops pulled back to the city outskirts, the bulk of their armor and infantry was redeployed west, and the troops of the Syrian *Panther Force* they left behind dug in for a long siege.

The remaining two hundred Marines were pulled out of billets in the city and found themselves in an outpost built to hold half that number.

The city of Kobani was no stranger to siege. In 2014 it had been the focus of an epic battle between forces of the self-declared Islamic State and local Kurdish YPG and Women's Protection Unit YPJ militia fighters. At the main crossroads leading into the city from the south stood the statue of a winged angel, a tribute to YPJ fighter Arin Mirkan, who had sacrificed herself defending Mishte-nur Hill. US airpower and the fierce determination of the Kurdish militia defending the city had proven too much for Islamic State and the attackers had been driven out in a defeat that marked the turning of the tide for the 'caliphate'. President Assad had apparently decided he wasn't going to make the same mistake, so he ringed Kobani with troops and left it to wither on the vine.

Syria might not have been officially at war with the USA, but it had no intention of letting the best part of two US Marine companies disturb its efforts to push Turkey out of Syria and take out Incirlik, the biggest threat to Russian control over its airspace. Russian aircraft roamed the skies overhead, trying to intercept anything that crossed the border from Turkey into Syria, including unmanned US supply flights into Kobani and medevac flights out. Syrian snipers harassed US troops manning the walls of COP Meyer and posed a deadly threat to the patrols that went out to gather intel. Not to mention the mortar rounds landing inside the COP walls at random times of day and night, which kept the bulk of the Marine complement hunkered down inside the bunkers for safety, and which made every trip above ground a roll of the dice.

MJ turned her eyes to the skies again, watching as the circling Russian fighters suddenly banked and headed west. Despite the futility of it, the single anti-air gun inside Kobani opened up again, flinging tracer impotently into the sky behind the departing Sukhois. She couldn't hear them now, they were just two silent black specks headed for the horizon. In seconds they were gone, and the gun inside Kobani fell silent. Somewhere, an ambulance or fire siren began wailing.

She patted the corporal on the shoulder, handing back the helmet. "False alarm."

"My favorite kind," the corporal replied, watching the contrails from the Russian fighters drift away in the breeze.

AS MJ climbed back down from the walls, she saw one of her other favorite Lava Dogs coming through the main gates.

Gunner Jensen made a strange sight, sloping in with his two robotic dogs in formation behind him. She'd been allowed to do a profile on the way the Marines were using their robotic dogs which got huge syndication, and ever since she'd been angling for a follow-on.

For a moment her hopes lifted as she saw he was carrying a long-barreled sniper rifle and the three-man patrol entering behind him were bringing in a prisoner. But he saw her look and shook his head. *Not Tita Ali, then.* That would have been a great story.

She walked over to Jensen and waited as he ordered the dogs down into the bunker engineering workshop to recharge. The prisoner would be taken for interrogation before being turned over to the YPG. Most Syrian prisoners were bled dry of any intel they might have carried by the YPG and then kept to exchange for militia prisoners at a later date, but as he trudged past them, the Syrian hung his head, knowing what his near future held for him.

"Clean takedown, Gunny?" she asked as Jensen turned to her. He was six feet of Viking DNA with a lopsided smile that rarely left his face, though he rarely cracked a joke. MJ had told him once to lighten up a little, but he'd just raised an eyebrow and shrugged. "I do know a joke, MJ," he'd said. "If we ever get out of here, I'll tell it."

"Clean enough," Jensen said, nodding. "Though one of the hounds went off reservation. Showed a bit too much initiative, if you get my meaning."

MJ looked over at the Syrian, who was being led underground. "That why the prisoner has a busted wing?"

"I couldn't speak to that."

She checked out the Syrian rifle Jensen was still holding. "That's, what? A T-5000?"

"You know your hardware. It's not a Lobaev, if that's where you're going," Jensen said. "I figure this guy for two recent hits. Ballistics will confirm it."

MJ nodded and handed the rifle back. A Marine private had been killed by a sniper two days earlier while on a recon patrol. And a corporal had been shot in the thigh delivering a prisoner to the YPG headquarters in the west of Kobani. She didn't report on individual casualties, it was Reuters policy families shouldn't find out their loved ones had been hurt by reading about it on social media. But the toll was starting to mount and word spread fast among Marine Corps families. She'd heard there were some pretty vocal people agitating with Congressmen to get their boys and girls out of Kobani.

Jensen sounded tired. MJ had just been briefed by her source on yesterday's Homeland Security sitrep and decided to share her thoughts with him. "Buck up, Gunny. I hear the Syrian 'Cheetah Force' has been stopped south of Gaziantep. They're licking their wounds, doubtful they have enough in them for a second push. Their 'Tiger Force' is making a hell for leather push on Incirlik and the Turks are crumbling in front of it, but..." She looked around herself, careful there were no others nearby. "... My sources tell me the Pentagon finally got off their asses and ordered a regiment from the Big Red One onto C-5s out of Kansas to Incirlik yesterday. 'Tiger Force' is going to find more than a few lightly armed MPs waiting for them if they move on that air base."

"Might be just what Ivan is hoping for, don't you think?" Jensen observed.

MJ frowned. She listened when Jensen talked, because he knew what the men around him were thinking. "What do you mean?"

"Well, apart from dropping bombs on Syrian heads, we've mostly kept out of Turkey's fight so far. The Syrians pick a fight with the US 1st Infantry Division, we're in it up to our necks. Then Syria and Russia move on Lebanon – I call that a when, not an if – and we're engaged on two fronts. Unless Israel nukes Damascus, we're going to be bogged down in this damned war for years, Ivan is laughing all the way back to

Moscow, and all of this…" He gestured to the bombed and patched walls around him. "Maybe it's for nothing."

First Bell and now Jensen? This sort of attitude was dangerously contagious and she could feel the mood inside COP Meyer turning. She didn't see it all as doom and gloom. "If you hold Kobani, if the Bloody First stops the Syrian push short of Incirlik, it puts a kink in their grand plans. They'll need every man, woman, truck and tank in their inventory if they move on Lebanon and you've got the best part of a mechanized regiment tied up here, right where you want them."

Jensen straightened up and squared his shoulders. "Hope you're right, MJ. Apologies for the misery shower. Been a long day's night."

As he finished speaking a siren started wailing. She recognized it immediately and felt the bottom drop out of her stomach. *Incoming fire!*

There was no time to run, so she followed Jensen's lead and dropped to the ground.

With a deafening *crack* off to their right a mortar round impacted atop an unoccupied section of wall about a hundred yards away. Concrete dust and smoke drifted up into the sky. Getting up from the ground, MJ flicked her eyes at Jensen to see if she should run for cover. But the siren cut out and he was standing looking up at the sky.

There was a shouted command from across the other side of the compound. "*GATOR lock, counterfire, three rounds, out!*" The shout had barely died out when there was a thud from an emplacement inside a ruined building inside the compound and an 81mm mortar round launched into the air in the direction the Syrian shell had just come from. It was followed six seconds later by a second, then a third.

COP Meyer's G/ATOR (Ground/Air Oriented Task Radar) had tracked the incoming shell and calculated the source of the attack. As soon as it had a GPS coordinate, it was relayed to an 81mm mortar crew which sent a spread of three GPS-guided rounds straight back at the Syrian *Podnos* mortar crew. After some early losses the Syrian crews had learned, and mounted their mortars on trucks now so that they could shoot and scoot to avoid the GATOR counter-attack. But one out of every three Syrian *Podnos* mortar crews didn't make it out of the Marine 81mm's 300-foot lethal blast range.

MJ would have thought that would make it hard for the Syrians to find volunteers for their mortar crews, but it seemed as quickly as they lost one, the Syrians got another *Podnos* crew up and firing again. On her regular forays into the besieged city, she often reflected it was almost safer down among the ruins of Kobani than it was up here on Mishte-nur Hill.

She turned to Jensen. "Miss is as good as a mile," she smiled, brushing dirt off her knees.

"I take every one of those as a compliment," Jensen told her, doing the same. "It shows they still see us as a threat. We just have to keep it that way."

AS she walked into her sister Nasrin's office inside the Cardamom Markets, Daryan Al-Kobani was given another lesson in the fact that Nasrin was not a woman given to dishing out compliments. Was she, for example, grateful that her sister Daryan put her life on the line every single day to keep her family safe?

"What the hell is that smell and what the hell do you need now?" she asked.

"Is that any way to greet your sister?" Daryan sighed.

"Everyone who comes in here calls me 'sister'," Nasrin told her with a thin smile. "Just because you're family doesn't get you special treatment."

Daryan pushed some hair out of her dirty face. She felt like saying something smart, but instead pulled a piece of paper from her pocket. "Ten sacks lentils, 10 rice, 20 chickpeas, wound dressings, saline…" She looked down the list. "… And ten thousand rounds of 7.62x39mm." She handed the paper to Nasrin.

Nasrin looked at it, running a long fake pink nail down the list. "Do you people think Kalashnikov ammunition grows on olive trees? Ten thousand rounds?!" She threw the list on the table. "Go ask your American friends."

"We did," Daryan said. "They said they are a little short on *Russian* ammunition at the moment. Sister." She hefted the rifle that never left her shoulder. "And I am running low on 10.36mm for father's rifle."

Nasrin gave her a sour look, reached down into a drawer and pulled out a makeup mirror, checking her lashes. Not satisfied with what she saw, she reached into the drawer again and pulled out a tube of mascara, giving her eyes a small touch-up.

"Well?" her sister asked, exasperated.

Nasrin slapped the mascara down on the desk. "Your 10.36mm is impossible, you know that. The rest ... I'll look into it. I promise nothing."

"You never do," Daryan said wearily. She looked around the neat and newly painted office. "And that smell is the smell of war, sister. I'm not surprised you don't recognize it." She turned and left.

Daryan reflected it would be hard to find siblings more unalike than the two Khalid sisters. She had been thirteen when the first Turkish soldiers appeared in Kobani, her sister Nasrin, ten. The town had only recently survived a full-scale assault from the forces of Islamic State, which had driven Daryan, Nasrin and their mother into hiding in the countryside. For a few brief months after the defeat of ISIS, they had been reunited with their father and returned to their gutted apartment in the ruined city with something like hope in their hearts, when Turkey started its campaign to create a 'buffer zone' around Kobani. Not long after that, their father had been killed at a Turkish roadblock outside Kobani for 'approaching at high speed'. Witnesses said he had been driving behind a Turkish army truck and had pulled out to overtake it, clearly not aware a new roadblock had been set up just hours before. He had jammed on his brakes as soon as he saw it, but died in a hail of gunfire from troops at the roadblock.

Daryan hadn't grieved. She'd reacted by pulling their father's rifle off the wall and telling her mother she was going to 'kill some Turks'. Their father had taught her to shoot. He'd been so convinced that his first-born child was going to be a boy that he even gave her a unisex name – Daryan. He hid his disappointment when his beautiful girl was born, but that didn't stop him bringing her up exactly as he would have brought up the son he didn't have. He taught her to fish, to shoot, to hunt. From the age of ten, he taught her to drive, to repair flat tires, plug punctured radiators. He'd fought in the YPG against ISIS and though he sent her to school, he told her when she turned sixteen he expected her to sign up for the YPJ and become a proud defender of Kobani and her family. She'd walked out the door the day after her father's death and done just that.

When she'd finally reappeared six months later in the doorway of the small apartment, with the same rifle still over her shoulder, she'd changed her name. She wasn't Daryan Khalid, she was Daryan Al-Kobani now. Her mother cried for days.

Nasrin had not been impressed.

"You sleep with that thing?" Nasrin had asked her, noting how the rifle was never more than a foot away from her sister's side, even when she was sitting at their dining table eating.

"Maybe," Daryan grunted.

"Between your thighs?"

"Nasrin!" her mother had exclaimed, boxing her ears.

At seventeen Nasrin got married to a Syrian businessman from Dubai she'd met at a night club when he was home visiting family. At eighteen Nasrin was married with an apartment near Dubai Healthcare City, a Filipina maid and her own car. By nineteen she was divorced. Her husband had been stupid enough to brag to her about the fact that he was siphoning money from a deal with a minor Emirates prince, and after compiling a nice thick dossier with evidence of his crimes, Nasrin placed it with a lawyer and then told her husband that if he didn't grant her a divorce and pay her a hundred thousand US dollars, she would give it to the prince's connections. A lowly Syrian commoner in Dubai, he knew what cheating royalty would mean if he was outed, so he agreed to a divorce and eighty thousand US dollars.

Nasrin had returned to Kobani a rich nineteen-year-old. She bought her mother and herself an apartment near the Cardamom Markets. With the remaining money she rented an office in the market from which she imported generic Indian drugs. She traded shamelessly on her ex-husband's connections to set herself up and soon proved a much better businessperson than he had ever been. She quickly became the number one trader in over-the-counter drugs in Kobani. And *under*-the-counter drugs. As the resistance against the Turkish presence heated up, new opportunities presented themselves. Logistics were logistics. She had contraband suppliers from Jordan and Turkey to Iraq, all looking to make a dollar and not too worried about how. She knew people; they knew people. And the Kurdish militias had CIA dollars. She started importing weapons and ammunition from Kurdish forces in Iraq to equip the local YPG and YPJ.

Then when Nasrin was twenty-one years old and Daryan twenty-four, the Syrian army rolled across the plains from the south and east and started firing artillery into Kobani.

Daryan had stopped killing Turks and started killing Syrians. As for Nasrin, business *really* started looking up.

Not for the first time, as she trudged out of the market and toward the YPG headquarters, Daryan asked herself why she did what she did. If she wasn't fighting the Turks to avenge the death of her father anymore, then why? For the safety of her mother? Yes. So that her vain and graceless sister could continue to make money selling supplies to the militia? Maybe. As long as that money was used to keep their mother housed, fed and healthy and those weapons were being used to keep the enemy outside their gates. But still, there were days like today, watching her sister fuss with her lashes, when Daryan wished a mortar or bomb would take out the southwest corner office of the Cardamom Markets.

After all, there was a Syrian *Buk* anti-air battery a couple of miles away, behind the government lines. She'd seen and heard it firing at Coalition and Turkish aircraft. Surely it wasn't unrealistic to think an errant bomb or missile could…

As though Allah was reading her mind, Daryan heard the *whoosh* of an incoming missile just before the crump of an explosion, some distance away. She spun around, looking back over the markets, and saw a cloud of smoke rising from behind the Syrian lines. She turned and kept walking.

Oh well, not today. She hoped it had at least caused Nasrin to ruin her eyeliner.

"Goblin two, Goblin leader. Turks are reporting four *Buk* units down, three still radiating," 'Rex' King called with unnatural calm as he and Meany closed on their target outside Kobani. Turkish F-4s had attacked minutes before with HARM Homing Anti-Radar Missiles, intended to take down the medium-range *Buk* anti-air missile radars that ringed the village of Mamayd, where the Syrian 138th Mechanized Division had its HQ. "I'm showing two fast movers over Kobani. AI is calling them Su-35s. No lock on us, they're chasing the *Phantoms*. We're still clean."

Meany scanned his threat warning display. It was showing a long-range radar in central Syria well to their south, and the same *Buk* radars and Russian fighters around Kobani that Rex had tagged, but none that had locked onto the small, delta-winged *Tempests*. "Two is also clean," he replied tersely.

The Turkish anti-radar strike had only knocked out four of seven known *Buk* launch vehicles. Every launch vehicle had a crew of four and had six missiles ready to fire as soon as they had a target. After losing four of their comrades, Meany was in no doubt the remaining three would be on high alert, expecting the worst.

And the worst was what Rex and Meany hoped to give them. Each of their *Tempests* carried thirty *Perdix* drones armed with 40mm grenades. It was a payload the Coalition hadn't deployed against Syrian forces at Kobani yet, but photo recon had shown that as quickly as Coalition aircraft flattened the tents, stores and vehicles around the village of Mamayd, the Syrians crawled out of their trenches, cleared away the debris and set up camp again. Short of a weapon of mass destruction, such as a fuel air explosive or tactical nuke, there was little in the Coalition armory that was effective against deeply entrenched troops, and Syria knew it.

Or thought it did. Meany had been training with the *Perdix* drones for the past week, and today both the Coalition and Syrian forces were about to see if they lived up to their hype.

Unlike a lot of air-launched systems, *Perdix* drones didn't require weapons pods attached to the fuselage or wings of the launching aircraft, which would have compromised the *Tempest*'s stealth. They were designed to be fired like bullets from a gun, out of one of the two flare launchers that lined the belly of the *Tempest*. Once free of the aircraft they fell a hundred feet and their launch casings split open, the *Perdix*'s wings folded out, their electric engines deployed and they started looking for each other, synchronizing positions. Then they started hunting their targets.

Meany felt his stomach churn as his machine crested a ridgeline below, automatically rising and falling again as it followed the terrain below at five hundred feet altitude and six hundred miles an hour. He'd prefer to be cruising at an airspeed of eight hundred, the better to evade those damn Russian fighters if they were spotted, but the *Perdix* couldn't be launched at anything over five hundred miles an hour, so for the next few minutes they were going to be hamstrung.

"On terminal, clear to arm," Rex announced. "Arming *Perdix*." Meany glanced over his wing at the lead aircraft, barely visible two miles off.

Meany hit an icon on his weapons screen and watched it turn solid. "Two armed," he confirmed. They were well inside the kill zone for the *Buk* launchers at Mamayd, approaching from the southeast so that they were less exposed to any surviving units on the other side of the besieged city. Boring straight in on the Russian-made radar trucks, he knew he was virtually invisible, but that would change the minute he banked to make his escape. He felt himself grinding his teeth and forced himself to breathe deep. He ran through the launch checklist in his head ... *arm, airspeed 500, fire, fifteen seconds to deploy, report launch, safe, break and bug the effing hell out.*

Rex broke into his thoughts at exactly the same time as a threat warning began warbling in his ears. "*Buk lock*. No missile. Ready for launch in five ... four ... three..."

"Come on, come on, come on," Meany muttered out loud.

"*Missile!*" Rex called. "Hold for launch. Launch, launch, launch!"

"Launching *Perdix*," Meany confirmed. He triggered the flare launcher that would spit the drones out of his belly, but his eye was on his threat screen which showed four Russian-made *Pensne* ground-to-air missiles flying straight at them at *three times the speed of sound*.

Ten more seconds until the last *Perdix* was away. Literally a lifetime.

THE new commander of the Syrian 138th Mechanized Infantry, and therefore of the new Siege of Kobani, had already spent a lifetime at war. That was how he felt.

Colonel Imad Ayyoub was fifty-eight years old. He'd fought in the Syrian civil war and led a company of T-90 tanks in the 25th Special Missions & Counterterrorism Division as it had rolled across Syria from south to north, driving the Syrian rebels and ISIS militants in front of it. With the civil war crushed, he supervised the training of his tankers with upgraded tanks and training from Russia. For the big push on Gaziantep he'd been made commander of an armored battalion and had fought his way to the outer ring road of the city before being ordered to halt.

Syria wanted to tie Turkish troops up in the defense of the city, but it was not their goal to capture it. It simply wanted to rid Syria of the Turkish military presence that it had tolerated since 2019 and establish its own buffer zone, holding Turkish forces twenty miles north of the Syrian border. Part of that plan had involved capturing the Turkish and NATO air base at Incirlik so that it could not be used to land western air mobile armor or infantry close to Syria's new northern front.

Because the scuttlebutt said Syria had its eyes on a bigger prize, for which securing its northern border was only Phase One. Ayyoub had not been briefed on it yet, but the rumors were too strong to be wrong. The Syrian 4th Army based at Damascus was being built up, supplemented with Russian irregular troops training alongside their Syrian army compatriots in Syrian uniforms. Beirut – it had to be. Lebanon was on the verge of collapse, with Hezbollah poised to take the Lebanese capital for itself. Syria wanted a piece of the spoils, so it made sense to move as soon as its northern border was secured from Turkish or NATO interference. As the rumors had intensified, Ayyoub had expected any day to be called up to join the spearhead of Syrian armor rolling over the border into Beirut.

But as a reward for my success at Gaziantep, they sent me to Kobani, he observed wryly. Where he had been 'promoted' from commanding a battalion of T-90 main battle tanks to commanding an entrenched Mechanized Brigade barely worthy of either name. A brigade it wasn't. After its failed attack on Kobani, the 138th was barely two thousand infantry, more than a battalion but less than the regiment it was supposed to be on paper. And armored it wasn't. Not in the true sense of the word. It could muster just sixteen Russian-made *Terminator* infantry fighting vehicles, or IFVs. Despite being built on the same chassis as the T-90, they weren't tanks but tank support vehicles, armed only with missiles and light 30mm autocannons. They were designed to fight in the close-quarters urban environment of Kobani, if the Syrian army had managed to penetrate the Kurdish defenses and get into the city proper. They never had, so the *Terminators* of the 138th were still unblooded.

Ayyoub also had nominal command of two companies of troops and equipment of the 154th Artillery Regiment, which comprised a handful of truck-mounted *Podnos* mortars and a battery of *Uragan* 220mm rocket launchers – for which he had no ammunition – protected by an air defense company fielding SA-19 *Tunguska* anti-air artillery and seven SA-11 *Buk* surface-to-air missile batteries. Against this, he was facing four thousand seasoned Kurdish militia fighters inside Kobani, plus an unknown number roaming the countryside, striking at weapons and fuel depots, transport routes, bridges and electricity infrastructure. And if that wasn't enough, he also had a US Marine force of unknown strength holed up on the highest ground in Kobani, calling down airstrikes on his troops any time one of his units moved into the open.

His orders were to contain the Kurdish militia within the city limits of Kobani and prevent them from disrupting the vital east-west highway inside Turkey about twenty miles to the north. And to keep the US force bottled up inside its Combat Outpost until they were either evacuated or strangled into submission, giving Syria a valuable political and PR victory.

For a war fighter like Ayyoub, his promotion was a no win, no glory command.

At least his predecessor, the late Colonel Ganem, had managed to restore and maintain the morale of the men under his command, despite their earlier defeat and despite the soul-crushing nature of their duty. They were inflicting more losses than they were taking. Russian air support was keeping the Kurds' heads down and stopping them from moving more troops or heavier weapons into the city. Whenever the Americans ventured outside the walls of their outpost, they were sent scurrying back again, carrying their wounded with them.

Ayyoub had stepped outside the rather gloriously named 'command compound' in which Ganem had been shot, sucked in his slight paunch, tightened his belt and surveyed the sea of empty tents around him. It was a deceit created by Ganem of which he'd approved. A canvas decoy that had absorbed tons of Coalition high explosive and to which they apparently never tired of returning.

He snapped his fingers, beckoning to his adjutant. "Damage report, where is it?"

They'd just driven off another Turkish air attack, but his anti-air commander had reported losses. *How many, where?* His anti-air units were spread in a ring around the city, and communications were poor. Precious minutes were ticking past in which…

Sure enough, as though the thought itself was enough to tempt fate, Ayyoub heard the unmistakable sound of a *Buk* battery launching missiles at another wave of unseen attackers and he walked quickly back inside the compound to the comms station in time to hear the voice of his air defense commander announce a Beriev A-100 early warning aircraft over Raqqa had picked up a weak track … *unidentified fast-moving aircraft inbound your position, from the southeast.*

Weak track? Stealth fighters.

British or Australian, it didn't matter to Ayyoub. His *Buk* units hadn't claimed a single stealth fighter kill yet, not a credible one anyway. And the Russians might try to scare them off, but they were not supposed to engage. So whatever the Coalition fighters were carrying, it was sure to be coming his way any damn second. More of those damned *Stormbreaker* glide bombs they had been peppering Mamayd with since the first day of the siege? An F-35 could carry eight of the high-explosive 100lb.-warhead bombs in its weapons bay, and the Coalition fighters usually struck in pairs, delivering more than a dozen bombs in a matter of seconds.

Ayyoub sighed. Luckily, all his *Terminator* IFVs were protected in earth-walled, sandbagged berms, their fuel and ammunition were buried deep, his men were huddled six feet down in steel rebar reinforced trenches and he had plenty of tent canvas. But a few more casualties were inevitable.

"*Perdix* out, jamming and evading!" Rex called. Flicking his eyes to his wing, Meany saw his flight leader change his angle to the incoming missiles and fire off a volley of tinfoil chaff and flares to confuse the missile radar and infrared seekers aimed at his aircraft.

Give me a green, you bastard ... Meany thought, the muscles in his arm tensed to twitch his stick and copy Rex's maneuver as soon as his last *Perdix* was away.

"Pilot override, missile proximity alert," a female voice said in his ears. And with that, the *Tempest*'s AI wrenched control of the aircraft away from Meany, aborted the launch of the last *Perdix* drones and hauled his machine into a screaming, skidding, face-melting turn as it desperately tried to avoid the two incoming Syrian missiles. He'd waited too long.

Meany's flight suit inflated explosively, trying to protect him from the force of the radical high-G turn and keep the blood flowing to his head, but his vision turned gray, then black. He felt the aircraft shake as a missile exploded somewhere behind him, but how close? He had no idea. Hell, he couldn't even have told you his name right there and then. He felt the aircraft lurch and roll, then reverse its turn. Blood came flooding momentarily back into his head and he heard warning tones screaming in his ears before his head snapped sideways and the world went gray again.

At the altitude they'd approached their target, the AI had no downward angle to play with. All it could hope to do was jam, out-turn or decoy the Syrian missiles and it didn't pay much mind to the useless meatware lump strapped inside its cockpit. The *Tempest* had been designed to fly as either a crewed or unmanned aircraft, and right now it was behaving like its pilot didn't exist.

Meany felt a final rolling lurch, or imagined one, and then he passed out.

KURDISH militia Colonel Jamal Adab looked up at the sound of jets in the distance, rubbed sand out of his eyes and motioned to his adjutant to close the door that the young woman had left open. In front of him was the intelligence report on the assassination of the Syrian commander at Mamayd. It lay on top of the casualty list from a mortar attack of just a few hours before, which he couldn't help but think of as retribution.

Daryan sat quietly, chewing on something she'd scrounged from the YPG base mess, rifle butt on the ground, the body of her Lobaev rifle between her clamped knees.

'Base' was a pretty grand name for the Kurdish HQ inside Kobani. Bombed-out ruin, that was another. The YPG fighters stationed there huddled behind broken walls or in the few still remaining basement rooms to keep themselves safe from Syrian artillery and drone strikes. Luckily, the Syrian commander seemed satisfied the headquarters had been pretty much leveled and wasn't still in use, so the hourly mortar and rocket strikes had become merely daily now.

Occasionally the Syrians got lucky. Two days ago he'd lost a valuable commander and four men to a drone strike which had landed a fragmentation grenade right in the middle of their cooking fire. It was another unit he couldn't afford to lose. He cocked an ear, hearing the sound of explosions in the distance and jets overhead. That sounded like a Coalition attack. He hadn't been notified, but that wasn't unusual. He snapped his fingers at his adjutant, and the man disappeared to find out what was happening.

Adab scanned the intel report one last time and laid the paper in front of him, fixing the girl with a neutral gaze.

"The Syrian commander is dead," he told Daryan.

The girl stopped chewing, then started again with a shrug. "I told you."

"*You* didn't kill him," Adab told her. "He died in hospital after being evacuated."

The girl wasn't fazed. "Because I put three bullets in him from inside a stinking sewer pipe full of turds." She stopped chewing. "I want what you promised me."

Adab looked up at the ceiling, playing dumb. "Ah yes, what was that? A chicken, I believe?"

"*Not* a chicken. A Zenit X42 Picatinny-rail digital scope with laser range finding," the young woman said slowly. "And low light vision."

"Ah yes, a Zenit something something, with laser," Adab said, waving a hand disinterestedly.

"*And* low light vision," the girl added.

"Where did you hear about such a thing?" Adab asked her, nodding at the girl's rifle. "How do you know it can even be fitted on that old blunderbuss?"

"The internet," the girl said, deadpan. "You heard of it?"

"Funny. Well, how about this instead?" Adab said, reaching down and pulling open a drawer. Inside it was a small box. He pulled it out and set it on his desk in front of her. "Just the thing to help an amateur like you who refuses to work with my best spotters."

The girl leaned forward, pulled the box toward her and regarded it dubiously. It was small and square, too small to be a scope. She lifted it, feeling the weight. "What is it?"

Adab reached into his drawer again and pulled out a piece of paper, squinting at it. "Kestrel Nomad Elite 2030," he read off the page. "Ballistic calculator."

Daryan looked at him skeptically, opening the box to pull out a small device that looked like a short, fat telescope. "What does it do?"

Adab looked down the page. "It has a laser on it that is good out to three kilometers. You point it at your target, it tells you the wind speed, temperature, humidity and air pressure…"

"That's…."

Adab held up a finger to stop her interrupting. "… Air pressure. Plus spin drift, aerodynamic jump, and, uh, Coriolis effect, and it has ten different drag models." He raised an eyebrow. "Ten, Daryan."

The girl looked pained and patted the scope on her rifle. "The problem, Colonel, is this scope. I can't see two kilometers with this stupid scope." She pulled it off the mount and handed it to Adab. "You look."

Adab put the page down and took the scope. It was filthy. Giving Daryan a disapproving look, he reached for a water glass, dipped his shirt tail in it and cleaned the lenses on the scope. Putting his eye to the viewing lens and pointing it out a window, he saw his efforts hadn't helped much. It was like looking through a window smeared in butter. Where the crosshairs met was a large chip that obscured a tenth of the field of view.

He handed it back to the girl. "I find it interesting you can hit *anything* with this."

"You know it," the girl said. "But only out to a kilometer. Maybe 1500 meters. I want to be able to shoot from Mishtenur into Mamayd," the girl said.

Adab had a map on his desk and located the Syrian HQ. With his thumb he measured out the distance to the American outpost. "That's 2,100 meters," he said.

"Two thousand two hundred," Daryan said. "I got one of your men to measure it. He said it was an impossible shot for a 'kid like me' and I should go back to shooting cats and rats."

"I'm sure he was just being kind," Adab said. "To save you disappointment."

"He was an asshole," Daryan said. "I put him on my list."

"Your list?"

"People I wish were Syrian," Daryan told him.

"Am I on that list?" Adab asked.

"Not yet."

"Good," Adab said, reaching down. "Or else I might think twice about giving you this." He pulled a second package from the drawer and slid it across to Daryan.

It was the right size and shape to be a scope, but the girl didn't bite this time. "And that is?"

"Zenit Z42, with laser range finding," Adab told her. "Newer than the X42. With low light vision. Oh, and it has the ballistics computer built in."

The girl couldn't contain herself. She dropped the hand-held ballistics computer he had given her and almost leapt across the desk, tearing the box open. The heavy scope looked huge in her small hands. She turned it over, peering into and at it as though it was a magical artifact.

The torn box lay on Adab's desk and he swept it into a wastepaper basket. "You're welcome," he said. The girl wasn't listening, she was still lost in her inspection of the scope. Adab slapped his palm on the desk, snapping her head up. "It took me more effort than I like to get you that scope, girl. I have a special mission for you."

Daryan lowered the scope. "All your missions are special," she said drily.

"You'll like this one," Adab told her, handing her a written order. "A Syrian prisoner told us that a month ago the Russians brought in a new instructor to train their sniper teams. Supposedly, he is the best sharpshooter in the 45th Spetsnaz Airborne Brigade." Daryan looked unimpressed. "His name is Zakarin. Apparently he specializes in shooting Americans. The Marines call him Tita Ali."

"What has this to do with me?" she asked, holding the order up to the light. It was written in English, which she could speak, but had trouble reading.

Adab pointed at it. "You will take those orders and present them at the American outpost. Ask for a Gunnery Sergeant James Jensen."

"Why?"

"Because the two of you are going to hunt down this Tita Ali and kill him."

THE all-clear siren blasted out across Mamayd and Ayyoub unfolded himself from his crouch, motioning to his adjutant against the other wall to open the metal blast door he'd had bolted into the sandbagged walls of the command building.

Stepping outside he surveyed the skies. All he could see were the contrails of the *Buk* missiles drifting away. Strange. There had been no strike, no canvas casualties. Not a single missile, rocket or bomb. A feint? Testing their defenses, trying to wear them down? Or had the Russian fighters actually driven them off for once?

He put a finger to the earpiece in his ear. "Salem, report," he said, calling his air defense commander.

A burst of static and some loud voices in the background. There wasn't a lot of space inside the *Buk* command vehicle and any voice was loud. He heard his Captain order his men to shut up. "Yes, Colonel. Two enemy fast movers detected and fired on at a range of … twenty miles. They appear to have either been destroyed or driven off."

"Stealth?"

"Undoubtedly, Colonel," the man confirmed. "We have lost the track."

"Get a patrol out looking for pilots or debris," Ayyoub said. "I'll believe you hit them when you show me wreckage."

"Yes, Colonel!" the man said. "Sir, I have one *Buk* launcher destroyed, three damaged, but we are confident we destroyed a Turkish F-4 in the earlier…"

"Yes, well done," Ayyoub said. "But you have four launchers destroyed or damaged, do you not? And there are no commendations to be won bringing down an aircraft designed in the 1960s, Captain."

"No sir." Ayyoub heard the man swear under his breath. "If those damn Russian fighters would do their job…"

It was a land warrior's lament a hundred years old. *Where was the Air Force?*

"You do your job, Salem," Ayyoub told him. "Let the Russians worry about theirs."

He saw a squad of men jogging toward him, while others climbed from their trenches, no doubt either looking for orders or looking to avoid them. He turned to his adjutant. "See that Salem gets that patrol on the way immediately. If there is a British or Australian pilot out there, I want us to be the ones who find him. And get medics and engineers out to those damaged *Buk* units if they aren't already on the way."

The man saluted. "Yes Colonel." He turned, then halted, looking up at the sky, then tilted his head to one side. He turned back to Ayyoub. "Colonel, do you hear…"

Ayyoub waved him away with an annoyed flap of his hand. "Hear what? Just get on your…"

Wait. There *was* something. He spun around, straining his ears. A lieutenant came running up behind him.

"Colonel, requesting your…"

"SHUT UP!" Ayyoub yelled at him.

DARYAN had left Adab's YPG HQ with her rifle over her shoulder, the scope in her hand. What she felt like doing was sliding the new scope into place on her Lobaev and going out into the countryside to start shooting with it, not humping across town to the American base. She'd stood looking at the militia fighters moving lazily from one place to another, or squatting on their haunches on street corners, as they always did between gun battles.

Sergeant James Jensen? He could wait. Squatting quickly in the sand as she pulled off her old scope and mounted the new one, she slid her old scope into a trouser pocket and stood.

COP Meyer was an hour's walk through Kobani, over rubble and roads strewn with burned-out cars and vans. Not to mention a half dozen checkpoints she'd have to argue her way through, even with Adab's orders in her hand. Or, she could take a shortcut, outside the city and through Syrian lines – half the distance. It was still daylight. She preferred sneaking through at night, but she knew the blind spots in the Syrian positions by heart. She would go right through the Martyr's Graveyard – the superstitious Syrian soldiers never patrolled there – then the ruins of Tarmik Bijan, behind the Syrian trenches, and as the sun started to drop in the sky, scramble up the slopes of Mishte-nur to the US outpost.

And on the way … a little practice session.

She found a deep depression south of Tarmik Bijan where the echo in the ruins would confuse anyone trying to locate the sound of her shots. Kneeling on the slope above the defile, she looked carefully for Syrian patrols through her new scope. The countryside around her seemed clear, though she could hear jets somewhere overhead. Not close. Descending into the depression, she pulled her rifle off her shoulder and lay down on the sand, on her belly, feet spread. There was a bush about five hundred yards further along the depression with spiky branches that would do nicely.

She reached into her tunic pocket and took out five 10.36mm rounds, laying them in a line beside her trigger hand. Sighting through the scope, she felt like she'd felt the day her father had given her her first rifle. A .22 rabbiter. Looking down the barrel over the little notch at the end of it, and seeing it bob around as it settled on an unsuspecting rabbit for the first time, she'd never forget that. She felt like that right now. Adjusting the focus on the Zenit scope, the bush downrange sprang suddenly into clarity. It was like something on a high-definition TV! She'd never seen such a crisp image!

Without looking, she reached beside herself, picked up a round and chambered it, settling down behind the scope again. Her father had taught her a few things before the Syrians killed him. He'd taught her that breathing was important, but it wasn't as important as the pull. It didn't matter how calm and centered your breathing was if you rushed the trigger pull. If you pulled even slightly right, a fraction of a millimeter on the trigger could mean shooting a yard wide at the target. Tip of the finger, straight back, firm and smooth. That was the way.

She felt a breeze on her cheek. Centered the topmost branch of the bush in the scope, dialed in the range and then lifted it a few millimeters up and right, allowing for the drop of her shot and the effect of the breeze at the crest of the depression. Touching the range dial on the side of the scope had woken its electronics to life and it was showing her what looked like a compass reading, maybe windage and ... a projected strike point? She ignored all of the information, focused on what she could see through the lens, and ... fired.

Miss. But not a total miss. The branch had shivered from the passage of her bullet, so she'd gotten close.

She wasn't concerned. It was normal for a new scope. Without taking her eye from the lens, she ejected the spent round, chambered another and settled the stock against her cheek. She rolled the range dial on the scope a fraction forward. A fraction back. Tip of her forefinger on the trigger. Firm and smooth.

The branch rose slightly as the breeze on the crest of the depression lifted it, then fell again.

She fired.

The branch spun away in the wind, chopped clean across at the base.

Not perfect. She'd aimed further right than that, but good enough.

With her remaining three bullets she chopped off another branch, registered another miss, adjusted the fit of the scope and then chopped the bush in half with an easy shot through the trunk. It was a shot she could have made with her old scope … but she'd made it so *easily* with this one.

She rolled onto her back, holding the rifle above her face, regarding the Zenit with wonder.

Daryan looked up at the sun. She didn't own a watch. Had never needed one. Her eyes were enough to tell her there were a few good hours of daylight left. Plenty of time to get through the Syrian lines and make contact with the American.

She pulled a water flask off her hip and took a sip. As she fastened the cap again she hesitated.

What the…

She almost ducked as a swarm of what sounded like angry bees darkened the sky overhead, headed west. There were dozens of the things, moving at a hundred miles an hour, and in a few seconds she lost sight of them over the lip of the depression, only a lingering buzz from that direction telling her she hadn't imagined it.

She rolled onto her stomach and raised herself onto her feet, putting the Lobaev over her shoulder as the buzzing sound receded.

She gave a mental shrug. Whatever that had been, she wouldn't want to be wherever it was headed.

"There!" the adjutant said, one hand cupped to his ear, the other pointing east. "Can you hear that?"

Ayyoub could. In Deir ez-Zor, where Ayyoub had grown up, there was a wind they called *Dhiib* – the Wolf Wind. It was so called because in winter it came out of the western desert with a bite like a wolf and if you were caught out in the open, it could drain the warmth from you like a predator feasting on your blood. It announced itself with an evil humming sound as it tumbled stones and clouds of sand in front of it.

That was what Ayyoub heard now. But this ... the *Dhiib*, here? Blowing in from the east, in Kobani? Impossible! Looking where the man was pointing, Ayyoub saw the slightest discoloration in the sky. Not a cloud ... more like a shadow.

The soldier inside Ayyoub reacted before he even had time to process the fear he suddenly felt.

"COVER!" he yelled. "GET IN COVER!"

THE two clouds of *Perdix* drones had formed two swarms. They had only been slightly affected by technical failure and the aborted launch of the last of Meany's drones. One swarm comprised twenty-six drones, the other twenty-one. Half of them carried 40mm anti-personnel grenades, the other half were armor-piercing, designed to cut through both flesh and up to 2 inches of steel plate.

They were self-guided and didn't need a human to identify their targets. As they approached Mamayd, one swarm swung left toward the known positions of the 138th Syrian Mechanized, the other swung right toward the camouflaged mortar and rocket artillery park of the Syrian 154th Artillery. As they closed within a hundred feet of their assigned kill zone, they rose a hundred feet into the air as one and fixed their micro-electro-mechanical system (MEMS) sensors on the ground below.

The anti-personnel drones targeting the troops of the 138th used infrared sensors and were optimized to detect human bodies. Each drone had only limited processing capacity, but as a swarm, they comprised a single powerful AI. In seconds, each drone had identified a human target, prioritizing those positioned close to other humans. They swooped toward their targets, sitting in trenches, standing in groups out in the open, running for cover or climbing into vehicles. Each anti-personnel drone was packed with 115 razor-sharp, two-inch-long flechettes and had a kill radius of twenty feet.

Colonel Ayyoub heard the terrifying scream of a buzzing rotor right behind him as he reached his command post and dived inside. With a sickening *crump* a grenade exploded right outside, flensing the open metal door. He heard dozens of other explosions ring out across the base.

Over the artillery park, the anti-material drones hunted for their targets – trucks, jeeps, towed artillery, heavy machine guns or mortars. To protect them from standard bomb blasts, the Syrian vehicles had been parked in defilades or inside depressions in the ground surrounded by low-walled sandbagged berms designed to deflect a ground-level bomb burst up and over the vehicles inside. With the soft sand absorbing most of the blast, it meant that, so far, the Syrians had lost very few parked vehicles to Coalition air attacks.

The *Perdix* drones used optical image recognition to pick out weapons and vehicles and skimming just above the ground they closed to within feet of their targets. They ignored the reactive armor-plated T-90 hulls of the *Terminators* but went for the soft-skinned support vehicles and towed weapons, whether they were stationary or frantically being driven away by troops trying to escape. Hovering inches above each target, they detonated.

MEANY woke with a start and grabbed for his flight stick. His neck felt like someone had tried to wrench his head off by brute force. Turning it gingerly, he tried to focus on the dancing numbers and icons in his helmet-mounted display.

"Welcome back, Flight Lieutenant," a voice said. "Easy does it."

Looking over his starboard engine nacelle Meany saw the *Tempest* of Lieutenant King holding formation about a hundred feet away.

Pilot, do you wish to resume manual control? the combat AI asked him.

Did he? He still felt groggy and checked he was flying straight and level. "What's..." He licked dry lips. "What's the situation, sir?"

"Your systems are all green, Goblin one," King told him. "I'm not seeing anything but a low fuel state as a result of you gyrating all over the damn sky..."

"Not me, sir," Meany told him. "AI."

"I figured. You nearly got a *Buk* missile up your tailpipe, Flight Lieutenant. You ask me, you should buy shares in British Aerospace, because their AI saved your skin."

"Just wanted to get the shot away, sir," Meany said. He could already see more clearly. Clear enough to see the frown on King's face through his helmet visor a hundred feet away.

"One drone more or less isn't going to make the difference, Meany. You dying delivering it gives Syria a political and material victory they don't deserve. Next time you have a missile approaching lethal range, you will evade in good time. Am I clear?"

"Yes, sir," Meany said. "Loud and clear."

There was a pause, which Meany used to run his eyes across his multiple screens. King was right; miraculously, he was seeing no system warnings. He looked outside and down, seeing the Syrian coast sliding past at about two thousand feet as they headed out over the Eastern Mediterranean.

"When you're up to it, follow me around to 352 degrees and five thousand," King said. "And keep an eye on that fuel burn rate. If you've got an undetected leak I don't want to have to call sea-rescue to fish you out of the Med, Flight Lieutenant."

"No, sir."

"Goblin leader out," King said, and put his machine into a slow starboard banking turn.

Meany leaned gingerly forward and hit an icon on his flight control screen. "Pilot resuming manual control," he told the AI. He matched his flight leader's turn and saw Cyprus, a sliver on the far horizon, slide away behind his port wing. The effort of coordinating both throttle and stick just about made him throw up, so he hit another button on his screen, changing his mind. "Autopilot, hold formation with Goblin one until we enter Incirlik airspace, confirm?"

Holding formation with Goblin one. Will alert you five minutes prior to entering Incirlik air traffic control airspace.

Meany released the stick and throttle and let his head slump onto his chest. His head was pounding and his back and neck ached like he'd been given a good kicking by a gang of football hooligans.

If this was what surviving a *Buk* missile near-miss felt like, he almost wished he hadn't.

Linea Ignis
Incirlik Air Base, Turkey, 2 April

A hundred miles due north of Meany, US Army Lieutenant Ted Sun had an aching back too, for an entirely different reason. He was lying on the hot ground glaring at the mass of cables and wires under his truck-mounted Engagement Control Station (ECS) and trying to work out just which one Private Angelo Demori had managed to pull free when he'd snagged it with a damn forklift.

Like Sun didn't have enough problems keeping his damn *HELLADS* (High Energy Liquid Laser Area Defense System) battery operational, without random grunts cutting his umbilicals. There. An auxiliary power cable running from the nearby diesel generator to the underside of his ECS had been pulled clean out of its mount and socket. That idiot Demori must have been booking in that forklift.

Sun heaved on the cable to give himself some slack to work with and reached for the tool belt lying in the dirt beside him. He'd have to reseat the socket so that the cable would lock into it again, and then see what could be done with the mount to make it harder to pull the cable out next time. He got to work with his Gerber multi-plier. Yeah, he could have called in a hot-crew, but Sun preferred to do the simple stuff himself first and listen to their bitching later if he had to call it in. It also saved him from getting questions from their CO, Major Carlson. Sun had grown up working in his old man's electrical shop, repairing and reselling the defective fridges, washers and tumble driers that people traded in, so a lot of what went wrong with his truck he could fix himself.

He'd have to get that aux power cable buried deeper. They still had a mains supply but if that was cut, then the generator was the only way to keep his ECS up and feeding targets to the battery's five truck-mounted High Energy Laser units. *No ECS, no HELLADS*, it was as simple as that. His team could independently track up to 100 incoming missiles or aircraft and fire on five at a time, with a 10-second recycle time between engagements. That 10 seconds could be an eternity if you had supersonic missiles or aircraft inbound, but against subsonic cruise missiles or aircraft it was enough for five or six rounds of precision fire out to a range of twelve miles, meaning that whatever the *Patriot* Missile batteries missed, his HELLADS team should be able to mop up.

They'd done well enough in exercises, for sure. The standard setup was against multiple strike aircraft, usually Turkish F-16s but sometimes F-35s, boring in on Incirlik, trying to get within anti-radar missile range. The *Patriot*s would engage first, their anti-air missiles able to hit a target anywhere from twenty to forty miles range. But only 40 percent of the time. They overcame the low hit rate by firing multiple missiles at every aircraft, but all too often Sun had seen one or two attacking aircraft break through the *Patriots*' defenses – usually stealth fighters that were hard to pick up at that range, even when you knew they were coming. It meant there was always a brace of simulated air-ground missiles for them to engage, but that was the kind of challenge his men and women lived for.

Linea Ignis – 'Line of Fire'. That was the motto of E Battery, 7th Air Defense Artillery Regiment. He had it tattooed on his back over a line of dancing flames. If an enemy missile or fighter got through the outer air defenses at Incirlik, it was the job of E Battery to burn it out of the sky. And if the lasers couldn't get a lock or weren't burning through, then Sun's crews had a 'weapon of last resort' … the HPM or High Power Microwave secondary weapon mounted on every laser transmitter truck. Otherwise known as 'the toaster'. If a missile, drone or aircraft got within two miles of one of his HELLADS trucks, the nearest HPM would lock it and fry it with a targeted burst of microwave energy that would scramble its infrared and electronic systems and drop it from the sky.

That was the theory anyway. It had never been tested in actual combat.

"Lieutenant! You better get up here, we have possible incoming!"

Ted started, banging his head on the chassis of the ECS. What? "Projectiles or aircraft?!" he yelled, dropping his multitool and crabbing out from under the truck. The voice was his comms sysop, Corporal Allenby. As he rolled onto his feet, Sun saw the man hanging by one arm out the door of the ECS and holding out a hand to help him up. Allenby hauled him inside and Sun immediately sensed the charged atmosphere inside the command vehicle.

Sun dropped into his chair beside his Tac Control Assistant, Sergeant Alessa Barruzzi. She had her face against the view guard on her monochrome screen and had barely reacted as he barreled into the truck.

"Talk, Barruzzi."

"Info Coordination Center reported unidentified air contacts fifty miles west. A large group of fast movers, under 1,000 feet, headed our way," Barruzzi said evenly. She had been assigned to him six months ago and he liked her no BS style.

"We been given a target?" Sun asked. He looked at an instrument panel. "Why aren't we cycling up?"

The *HELLADS* had some inherent flaws. The first was that each laser array pulled 200kw of power and a firing battery had to be assigned fire authority by the battalion Fire Control Officer because if every battery in the battalion tried to suck that much juice at the same time, they'd probably black out the whole of southern Turkey.

"No target yet, sir," Allenby told him. The boy had gotten back into his comms station and had his eyes glued to multiple monitors. "Turkish AWACS aircraft over Mersin picked up the track. SPACECOM confirmed a hit on motion-sensing satellite. *Here*. But they don't have a real-time plot."

Sun looked at where Allenby had his finger on a map screen. "That's Kilis. Inside *Turkey*," Sun said, thinking out loud.

"Hit like that has to be stealth. Ain't no such thing as a Turkish stealth fighter, sir," Barruzzi said. "I think the shit is about to get real, TCO."

Sun swallowed. Barruzzi only called him TCO or 'Tac Control Officer' when she thought Lieutenant would take too much time.

They'd talked about it for weeks now. Syrian troops encircling Kobani, cutting off Gaziantep. Syrian armor bypassing Gaziantep, headed *west*. Incirlik had to be the target, there was nothing else that made sense; especially after the ultimatum for multinational forces to leave Incirlik. But stealth fighters? Turkey had none, and Syria certainly didn't. Was Russia about to open full frontal hostilities with the Coalition? With NATO?

Sun reached over and hit three switches on his control panel. In case of loss of comms, he had a manual command override that could start pulling power into the capacitors of his laser and microwave arrays so that they could be ready at a moment's notice.

Barruzzi looked over at him. "Oh, you are bad, TCO. Gonna get your wrist slapped for that."

"If we live through whatever this is," Sun told her. "I'll wear it."

THIRTY thousand feet above and five miles north of Incirlik, Bunny O'Hare was also thinking about going seriously off-reservation. 'Red' Burgundy had just acknowledged an order from Coalition Sector Air Defense to hold over Incirlik, and holding over Incirlik he was. In picture-perfect air-show diamond formation, with Bunny and two other RAAF 3 Squadron F-35 *Panther* pilots.

While unidentified Russian fast movers made a beeline for the air base somewhere ahead of them!

All Burgundy had done was dispatch a flight of two BATS into the projected path of the unidentified aircraft.

"Cabot three to Cabot leader," Bunny called, trying to keep the frustration out of her voice. "Requesting permission to break south with Cabot four to patrol grid alpha four zero, so we can at least flank the threat?"

"Negative, Cabot three," Red replied. "Hold formation. If they're there, the BATS will see them."

Bunny fumed. *And by then they'll be what? Twenty miles out? Inside Russian standoff missile range. So even if they are picked up by the BATS, they'll be able to launch on Incirlik!*

"Sir," she continued. "With respect ... we have about two minutes before..."

"Shut it, Cabot three," Red barked. "If they're Russian it's just a probe. We don't want to give our hand away."

Now she exploded. "Was it just a *probe* yesterday, sir?" she said tersely. "We lost three BATS! We have to lose a *Panther* too, before you..."

If there was a God, she intervened at that point to save Bunny from a court martial. With a simultaneous ping that was heard in every *Panther* cockpit, a new icon appeared on their threat warning and helmet visor displays simultaneously.

Red rolled his aircraft onto a new heading and Bunny followed him around. "Quarterback, Cabot leader, BATS 2 is tracking. Target identified, Sukhoi-57, bearing zero niner three, altitude 1,000, range thirty miles, Cabot flight requesting permission to intercept."

There was no hesitation from the tactical director aboard the airborne warning AWACS aircraft. They were looking at exactly the same contact and it was already twenty miles *inside* Turkish airspace.

"Cabot flight, Quarterback, you are cleared to engage. Repeat, you are cleared to engage the bandits while they are within Turkish airspace."

Bunny grunted. Good. At least there was to be no BS about hailing the approaching aircraft and politely asking them to turn around. The events of the day before had at least woken up someone in the command chain.

"Cabot flight turning zero nine zero, angels one for thirty," Red confirmed. "Cabot two, with me. Cabot three and four, hold here."

Bunny hammered the cockpit glass above her head. Red was ordering her and her flight leader to cover him while he engaged the bandit. But it was standard RAAF doctrine, so she just bit down the disappointment and eased her stick back and left, pushing her throttle forward to keep her airspeed up as she followed the other *Panther* into a banking climb. "Roger, Cabot leader. On me, Cabot three," the other pilot called. She glued herself to his wing.

Bunny flicked her eyes over her displays, the skies, her control surfaces, her displays again. The Russian contact was still boring in, but her AI was predicting a track that would take it slightly *north* of Incirlik now. That didn't look to Bunny like an attack heading, it looked to Bunny more like the Russian was trying to drag their air cover north. Which meant...

She searched the skies to the south, knowing her Distributed Aperture Sensor system should pick up any target long before she registered it on her Mk 1 eyeballs, but looking anyway.

Wait. Was that the glint of sun off a canopy? She dropped her wing and squinted. It was there against the clouds and then gone again. Nothing registered on DAS.

"Cabot four, I have an unidentified object on visual," she said. "One zero eight degrees, estimated altitude ten thousand, range, uh, ten miles. Just checking it out."

There was a pause. "I don't have anything on DAS, Cabot three," the other pilot said. "Are you sure?"

"Five seconds, Cabot four," she said. She put her *Panther* into a powered dive, airspeed rising over eight hundred miles an hour. *No mate, I'm sure of nothing. But I'd rather be wrong than leave Incirlik a sitting bloody duck*, Bunny thought.

YEVGENY Bondarev could see the nearby BATS remotely piloted combat aircraft, and he was absolutely sure it could now see him.

That had, after all, been his intention.

When his CO Bebenko had outlined the mission objective and invited his pilots to discuss how they would achieve it, Bondarev had seen a chance to redeem himself after the dubious results of his actions the day before.

"The problem as I see it is those damn BATS," Bondarev said. He pointed at a map, indicating the skies east of Incirlik. "We know they have them patrolling the skies like pearls on a string, two deep, with overlapping radar, optical electric and infrared coverage from Kozan a hundred miles north to the eastern Mediterranean in the south. We will have to pass under or through them at a range that even our stealth systems will not be able to defeat. One or two of us might sneak through, but not more. They'll pick us up while we're still out of range, and every one of them is armed with four medium-range anti-air CUDA missiles. They'll swarm on us like hyenas. And behind them are the Coalition *Panthers*. It could be a slaughter…"

Bebenko regarded him with a sideways glare. "Thank you for a wonderful summary of the bloody obvious, Bondarev. Do you have a proposal for how to deal with this situation, or is that the sum total of your contribution?"

"Yes, I have a proposal," Bondarev said cheerfully. "Sub-launched hypersonic cruise missiles fired from north of Cyprus."

His fellow pilots looked at Bondarev, then waited for Bebenko to react.

They were not disappointed. The man barely let the words land in his ears before he laughed bitterly. "Which the USA has said they will regard as equivalent to a *nuclear* attack and provoke a proportionate response. Plus, of course, you have your own attack submarine moored on the seabed off Cyprus, presumably, since we have about four hours to execute this strike? No? Brilliant idea, Bondarev." He turned to the rest of the squadron. "Anyone else?"

Bondarev coughed. "That was only my first suggestion, Comrade Captain," he said. He pointed to the airspace northeast of Incirlik. "My second suggestion ... I go in ahead of the main strike force. I should be able to pick up the nearest BATS before it detects me. When I get within sensor range, I derogate my stealth profile..."

Bebenko frowned. "Derogate your..."

"Blow my cover," Bondarev explained. "Open my weapons bay, drop flaps and deploy air brakes, present my broadside to the BATS."

Another of the pilots caught on before Bebenko did. "Decoy. You pull them away."

"More than that. I pop up like a star shell in the sky, radiating like a second sun, get their attention, and then engage. I pull them toward me, the rest of you sneak through the gap and launch."

Bebenko wasn't laughing any more. "I like it," he said. "But one fighter is not going to be a big enough decoy."

He splayed the fingers of both hands, flying one hand through the air on his right, and the other on his left.

"We go in two waves. The first wave, five aircraft, the decoy. You engage the BATS and hopefully draw any circling *Panther*s to you as well. The other wave of five goes in a minute behind you and twenty miles south. Launches standoff missiles at the first sign of detection and bugs out."

It wasn't perfect, but they fine-tuned it until everyone was satisfied the proposal had a chance.

Bebenko looked around the room. "Alright. Decoy flight. Any volunteers other than Bondarev?"

WELL north of Bunny, things were heating up. "Missile alert! BATS 2 evading. BATS 1 engaging," Red announced as a Russian aircraft fired at the drone and the BATS wingman returned fire automatically. But it was much further out and a kill against a *Felon* at that range unlikely. "Cabot flight light up the sky. Let's find them," he said, ordering his pilots to engage their radars and start actively searching for targets.

Bunny leveled her aircraft, still looking for the source of that flash of light on glass, but she didn't engage her radar. Doing so increased her chances of finding a target, but it also painted a great big 'shoot me' target in the sky for any *Felons* within range. She scanned her DAS display, radar and threat warning screens. On her radar warning screen a dozen bright spheres lit up as her *Panther* flight and every BATS drone patrolling east of Incirlik put their radars in active search mode and drowned the sky in radiation.

Immediately four more red icons flashed onto the threat screen as more Russian *Felons* were identified, flying in loose line astern formation behind the leader who had been identified. Automatically, all BATS within range were assigned targets by the AWACS aircraft and a volley of CUDA medium-range missiles arrowed toward the Russian fighters.

The Russians also responded instantaneously, missiles lancing out from their formation toward the threatening BATS.

"Cabot flight, hold at twenty miles, lock your targets but do not fire," Red ordered. "We'll mop up any who are left."

Five fighters? You don't attack the biggest western air base in the Middle East and declare open season on the Coalition with just five fighters, Bunny thought, eyes searching the space around her.

A chime sounded in Bunny's ears and her eye fixed on a new icon in her helmet-mounted display. Her passive optical target identification system had picked up movement below her and drawn a box around a swarm of dots. Aircraft! *She bloody knew it.* The boxes the system had drawn around the targets were dashed, meaning her combat AI had not been able to identify them yet.

"Cabot leader, Cabot three, I have five fast movers right below me, bearing zero four three, speed eight hundred, altitude under one thousand…" As she reeled off the contact data, one of the target boxes went solid and the ID for a Sukhoi-57 *Felon* appeared above it. "Confirm Russian Su-57s, permission to engage?"

Red didn't hesitate. "Confirmed, Cabot three, commit. Quarterback, Cabot leader, request you vector BATS and reserves to assist. Cabot three, assigning you BATS proximity control."

Bunny had already pulled up her weapons screen and started validating the targets her combat AI had suggested. She had five targets and only four CUDA missiles in her internal weapons bay. The AI had allocated a single missile to each of four targets and she cancelled that, putting two missiles on each of two targets. She could see two BATS drones within range of the Russian flight, and each of those carried four missiles. As she tapped her screen allocating her own missiles, the control of the ordnance on the two nearby BATS was handed to her too and she quickly added them to the mix. Now she had twelve missiles and five targets! She liked that math much better.

For another second, she had the element of surprise. She stayed high as the Russians passed twenty thousand feet below her and brought her machine slowly around to shadow them. She knew that as soon as she fired, she'd be giving herself away. "Cabot three, Fox 3."

With a single press of the trigger on her joystick, twelve CUDA air-to-air missiles flamed to life, aimed at the Russian formation. And in the same motion, Bunny dropped her nose and set her DAS to 'target following' mode, locked on the rearmost Russian fighter.

She might be out of missiles now, but if any of the aircraft below survived the onslaught of CUDAs, she still had 180 rounds of 25mm to continue the fight with.

THIRTY miles north of her, Yevgeny Bondarev had survived the first volley of missiles from the Coalition BATS drones and returned fire with a single missile of his own. His anechoic skin and physical decoys had broken the lock the BATS missiles had on him and he was now climbing through ten thousand feet having knocked one of the BATS out of the sky.

Unlike the inferior *Panther*, his *Felon* carried six air-air missiles, not four, and unlike the other *Felons* on the mission, he wasn't carrying air-to-ground missiles, so his internal hardpoints were fully dedicated to air-to-air ordnance. He had four *Vympel* medium-range radar and optically guided missiles and two short-range off-boresight infrared missiles. And Bondarev did not intend to waste them on the unmanned BATS. With their radars blasting out energy like small suns, he could now see the Coalition stealth fighters lurking behind the drones which were his real target. Theoretically they were already in range, but the closer he got before firing, the less time his enemy would have to react.

But he would not have the luxury of an unimpeded ingress, that much was obvious as another missile warning flashed on his visor, another BATS firing on him. He turned his machine toward the missile, pushing his throttle forward, following the cue in his visor that gave him the ideal vector, angle of attack and airspeed for a successful evasion. His flare and chaff countermeasures were set to automatically fire when the missile was close and as he heard them fire he rolled his machine onto a wing and pulled it into a radical high-speed turn that slammed his head against the side of his headrest and nearly ripped it off his shoulders.

He didn't hear the explosion behind him, but his *Felon* felt like a giant had given it an almighty shove as the shockwave of the blast overtook him briefly. No new warnings flashed in his eyes, and he leveled out, hunting the nearest *Panther* again. His *Vympel* targeting system was blinking insistently at him. *Fire, fire, fire* … It had a target locked, and in range. The equation was simple to the AI. But Bondarev also knew the *Vympel* had only a 60 percent hit rate in combat, and that was against older fourth-generation fighters. It had never scored a kill on a *Panther* because … no *Felon* had ever fired on one. But he had to assume its kill rate would be dramatically lower.

The enemy pilot reacted now, no doubt seeing Bondarev's machine on an intercept course directly for him. The *Panther* changed heading, turning to meet him fifty miles away.

That's it. Closer, my friend.

AS she broke through the sound barrier, trying to close the gap to the Russian formation which was now in disarray as its pilots flung their aircraft around the sky, trying to avoid the onslaught of the Coalition missiles, Bunny quickly clocked the tactical situation. North of her it looked like two of the *Felon* group had been hit by BATS. But at least two had escaped the first and probably second volley of missiles from the drones and had penetrated past the Coalition outer air defenses to the Cabot Flight F-35s behind. As she watched, the three F-35 *Panthers* entered the fight, their first volley of missiles spearing out toward the two remaining *Felons*.

Get some, 3 Squadron! Bunny yelled inside her head. But secretly she was dismayed. Only two of five *Felons* downed in the merge. That meant she had to expect there to still be two or three *Felons* out of the group in front of her still alive in …. five seconds from now. Three against one? She didn't like those odds.

With uncharacteristic caution, Bunny pushed her throttle through the gate and started turning her energy into altitude, climbing over and ahead of the scattered Russian fighters. Three against one was not a fight she could win with guns. In seconds she put ten more miles between her and the five *Felons* and she watched with bated breath as her brace of twelve missiles reached the violently maneuvering Russians.

Because the *Panther*'s electro-optical cameras were still tracking the Russians visually, even though she was running away from them, she saw the bright flashes of missiles exploding, and the even brighter balls of flame that were aircraft and their pilots being torn apart. One ... no, *only two* down! The map screen also showed the *Felons* and *Panthers* to the north furiously engaged.

"Quarterback, Cabot three is Winchester, will hold ahead of remaining Russian force and continue tracking. Confirm?"

Bunny could only imagine the stressed atmosphere inside the airborne warning aircraft as the controllers tracked the swirl of combatants and missiles and vectored reserve forces to the fray. But a second later they returned to her. "Cabot three, Quarterback, hold at grid Charlie four niner, thirty thousand feet. Vectoring Dart Flight, six F-35s and six BATS to that position, you are Tac Lead, copy?"

"Good copy, Quarterback, moving to grid Charlie four niner, thirty thousand, Cabot three is Tac Lead, out."

Tac Lead. *Crikey*. Bunny had just been made a mini-quarterback. Without weapons, it would be her job to vector the fast-approaching reserves to intercept the remaining Russian force, and she would theoretically have command over every missile the six incoming BATS were carrying. She'd done it before *in silico* and in exercises, but never in the real.

Grid Charlie four niner? She checked her nav screen. The remaining Russian air group was now only twenty miles out from Incirlik. What the hell was the range of a Russian standoff missile?

TED Sun knew the answer to Bunny's question. As Tactical Control Officer for his battery, or TCO, he took the targets that were passed to him by his Tactical Director and made the call about how and when to engage them. And there was no shortage of targets already. Though they had been detected fifty miles out, he was looking at a variation on the same tactical situation map that Bunny had access to and he didn't like what he saw. The Russian air group to the north was fighting air-air at beyond visual range with the Coalition screen of BATS and *Panthers*, but the group to the south, or the remainder of them, were reforming and boring in on Incirlik again with Coalition fighters scrambling from Incirlik but not yet in a position to intercept them.

The range of the Russian *Krypton* homing anti-radar or HARM missile, which Sun bet would be the first to launch, was sixty miles maximum, thirty miles optimal – and if the Russians hadn't been engaged by Coalition fighters, Sun was sure they would already have launched.

"Bring the toaster online, Barruzzi," Sun said quietly. The second of the first-generation *HELLADS* battery's flaws was that while it could bring either its High Power Microwave (HPM) or its laser array into play, it couldn't power both at the same time. So unlike a *Patriot* missile battery that just had to lock and fire on its target, Sun had to lock and choose *what* to fire.

"You figure *Kryptons*, sir?" Barruzzi asked, tapping her screen and arming the HPM system.

"I do, Barruzzi, I do," Sun said. "I've talked to so many Turks the last few months I almost feel I can understand them without a translator, but the message is the same every time.

First Ivan hits your air defense units with *Kryptons*, then he follows up with Mark 2 *OVOD* cruise missiles."

"Sir, those *Kryptons* have stealth coatings, anti-reflective housings, ceramic laser-hardened nose shields…"

"I know, Barruzzi, but the *OVODs* don't, so we drop the *Kryptons* by toasting their brains with microwaves and save the laser array for the second wave, because if there is one thing Ivan isn't, it's creative. He did it that way a hundred times against the Turks, he's going to try it the same way against us."

"Bringing toaster online, sir," his TCA confirmed. "Awaiting targets."

Sun had the hot seat today. His battery was positioned east of the airfield, facing the most likely direction of attack, Syria. Each laser could engage at twelve miles, while the HPM 'toaster' was limited to two. His five laser arrays were spread ten miles apart – to allow for beam scatter in poor atmospheric conditions – giving him coverage of a forty-mile front in ideal conditions.

But conditions around Incirlik were never, ever, ideal.

"Atmospherics?"

His comms sysop, Corporal Allenby, read off the screen in front of him. "Light cloud, 89 degrees, humidity 59 percent, chance of precipitation 2 percent, wind ten feet per second, beam tight out to, uh, … eight miles."

Damn moisture in the air. Eight miles. Outside that, his laser would scatter so much it wouldn't even give a human sunburn. That meant there were gaps between the arrays through which *OVODs* could leak. He'd been right to go with HPM. Hadn't he?

Sun shifted in his seat. This was the part he hated. The wait. You knew the other guy was going to try to kill you. In 'Stan he'd been TCA on a *Patriot* missile battery, where he'd been defending against insurgents and drones or rockets. If you were lucky, you'd get intel about a planned attack and then all you could do was wait. You were double lucky, the attack never came. If it did, you had minutes, sometimes seconds, to knock it down or hand it off. This was his first time facing off against a superpower foe, but the wait was the same. And whether the attack came or not, if you were still alive, you were a wreck later, awash with adrenaline burnout, muscles cramping and eyes dry.

"Question is, how many he's got left," Sun said. He knew it was nerves that made him talk, but it helped him cope. "We're seeing three bandits on an attack vector. One *Krypton* apiece? Or a mix of *Kryptons* and *OVODs*? Barruzzi."

"Fifty bucks says a mix, Lieutenant," she replied.

"Oh, playing safe," Sun smiled. "Allenby."

"Not a betting man, sir," the boy said. He wasn't a drinking or cussing man either. Sun didn't mind that. He'd rather have a sober man in Allenby's chair than a hungover party animal.

"I'll stake you," Sun told him. "Give me your guess."

"Not a guess," Allenby said evenly, pointing at the tactical map. "They brought ten *Felons* to the air-ground fight. Three are left. If this is their air defense suppression play, then there is a second wave out there. These are *Kryptons*."

"I'm with Einstein," Sun said. "*Kryptons*."

Barruzzi rolled her shoulders. "Three? With, what, two missiles apiece? We can do six missiles in our sleep. We can do six just with HPM. They aren't taking us seriously, Lieutenant. I'm offended."

He laughed. She was right though. For a declaration of war, it did seem a little ... understated.

"Missiles inbound!" Allenby said suddenly. "Vector zero niner three. AI is calling *Kryptons*. I have a good lock. Designating targets alpha one through six."

Simultaneously a voice broke in over their internal comms. "*HELLADS* Echo, this is Fire Control, missiles incoming, confirm state."

Sun checked his status panel. "Fire Control, Echo, we have five arrays on standby, five HPM generators primed, targets locked, *HELLADS* Echo requesting permission to engage when in range?"

"You are good to commit Echo, good luck, Control out."

"Luck, who needs luck?" Barruzzi said as the call was cut, blowing a raspberry. "We got *fire*."

Sun ignored her, watching five red lines lance toward his position from the three Russian aircraft, which were now turning south to make their egress, their payload successfully delivered. If Allenby's AI was right, then at least one of those missiles coming at them at just under the speed of sound was aimed directly at his battery. Lieutenant Ted Sun wouldn't mind a little luck in about ... thirty seconds from now.

"Lock broken, I've lost track on target alpha three!" Allenby called.

So much for luck.

IN planning the Russian air attack on Incirlik, Dmitry Bebenko wasn't relying on luck. He also wasn't relying solely on Yevgeny Bondarev's decoy strategy to carry the day. He had in fact decided to turn the entire anti-radar attack by his *Felon* squadron into a decoy. He knew that if they were detected, the price he paid in machines and pilots could be high, but he'd been ordered to take it. So he had also taken out insurance.

In addition to the *Felons* of 7th Air Group, Bebenko commanded a squadron of fourteen unmanned *Okhotnik* drones, each of which could carry two of the *OVOD* air-to-ground cruise missiles in its internal weapons bay. Three of his *Okhotniks* were down for repair or service, but he'd been able to put eleven into the air for this mission.

He'd sent the small deltoid drones out over the eastern Mediterranean at wavetop height and ordered their land-based crews to loiter them off the west coast of Syria, eighty miles southwest of Incirlik.

As Bebenko and his surviving *Felons* wheeled east after delivering their anti-radar missiles, the *Okhotnik* crews spread their machines out like the spokes of a wheel with Incirlik at the hub and slid in over the eastern Mediterranean at treetop height, showing a radar cross-section no larger than a steel marble. Just off the Turkish coast near the national park at Karatas, forty miles from Incirlik, they quickly opened their weapon bay doors and launched their twenty-two supersonic *OVOD* missiles.

Each missile contained five 20lb. double-charge cratering bomblets and twenty 5lb. area-denial mines; the first intended to buckle slabs of runway concrete and the second to kill the personnel or destroy the equipment sent to clear or repair the runway.

At 2.2 times the speed of sound, they would take just over a minute to reach the Turkish air base.

BUNNY had been working her targeting screen, allocating the fleeing *Felons* she was still tracking to the six *Panthers* and BATS that were now joining her flight. She never got to execute the pursuit order.

"Cabot three, Quarterback. Priority retasking, pushing data to you. Missiles bearing one eight five, angels one, range forty, engage immediately!"

"Good copy, Quarterback, I have handshake, Cabot three out," Bunny said tightly, wiping her screen clear and waiting impatiently for the data on the new wave of enemy missiles to download. It took a precious second, but then she saw them. A host of them. She had no hope of manually assigning the targets; instead she handed targeting control to her combat AI. It spread all the air-to-air missiles of the six BATS across the incoming missiles and her helmet visor signaled it had them locked. The six *Panthers* headed for her position were already firing at the *OVOD* missiles. Bunny thumbed her missile release and sent twenty-four CUDA missiles from the BATS downrange.

Even as she did so, she knew the chances of a CUDA scoring a hit on the supersonic *OVOD* was infinitesimally small.

INSIDE the *HELLADS* control trailer, any overconfidence was quickly extinguished. Allenby spoke tight and fast. "Missiles, second wave! Bearing 180 to 165 degrees, angels one, range forty, velocity Mach 2, time to impact ... one zero one seconds. Fire Control authority received. Designating group Beta One through Beta ... twenty-two!"

Sun started and spun his chair toward Allenby. "Did you say twenty-two missiles inbound?"

"Yes, sir!" the sysop said, his voice pitching higher. "Coalition fighters engaging."

Sun didn't waste time confirming Allenby's call. "Priming laser arrays one through five. I'll manage the laser engagement. Barruzzi, you have the HPM." He gave his TCA a quick look. "You take down the first wave, Barruzzi, or we won't even get a shot at the second, is that clear?"

The High Power Microwave defenses of the five *HELLADS* units were set to automatically trigger if a threat entered their two-mile perimeter, but Barruzzi's task was more complicated than just lighting the fuse and waiting for the HPM to fire. If two missiles were flying one behind the other and she let the HPM fire at the first, it would not have time to recycle before the second hit. She would have to take manual control, let the first get dangerously close, and then fire when the second crossed the perimeter, to have a hope of taking both down.

She zoomed the missile plots on her targeting screen and made a quick mental calculation, leaving three of the HPM triggers at the default two-mile setting and bringing the other two, including the one mounted on her own truck, to just ... five hundred yards. It was the only way to account for the one missile they had lost track of. It was going to be hella close, but also their only chance.

Sun had a different challenge. The track for the missiles fired by the unseen *Okhotnik*s showed they were headed for Incirlik's runways and infrastructure, not the air defenses. He only had three laser arrays in position to engage the missiles fired from the south. But he wasn't working alone. Even as he made his target assignments, he heard longer-ranged *Patriot* missiles streaking from their launchers across the base toward the incoming near-hypersonic missiles.

Twenty-two targets between three arrays. Each array could knock a missile down with a one-second on-target burn and they would have about five seconds in which to do it. That meant even with a 100 percent success rate, he could only hit fifteen missiles and with the atmospherics they were dealing with today, 100 percent accuracy was not going to happen. As he locked his arrays on the incoming missiles, he spoke softly and calmly to Barruzzi. "As soon as you trigger the toaster, realign on the second wave and reset arrays 2, 3 and 5 for autofire. Understood?" It was a long shot, but if the missiles passed close enough to the three laser arrays, a second HPM burst might also take down a couple.

"Arrays 2, 3 and 5, set for autofire on second wave, yes sir," she repeated. She saw the blizzard of Coalition air-to-air missiles merge with the Russian second wave.

Come on, Air Force...

They were all seeing the same data on their tactical monitors, but Allenby called it out anyway. "Ten seconds to first wave ... eight, seven, six..."

"HPM firing!" Barruzzi called. A tone sounded inside the truck to signal the HPM toaster arrays were firing, because otherwise they were soundless. Almost immediately, they heard an explosion about four hundred yards away as a Russian missile lost flight control and buried itself in a field outside the air base. Then another. But that was all.

"Incoming!" Allenby called and Sun could see a missile still tracking, headed directly for their position. There was no point diving for the floor, it would shred their truck and anyone outside like paper. All he could do was turn his eyes to the ceiling.

He heard a screaming whine, then his eardrums nearly caved in as the missile passed overhead, rocking the truck with its subsonic wake.

"High miss," Allenby announced. "It's flying wild."

"Yeah baby!" Barruzzi shouted, hammering a fist on her console.

"Round two," Sun reminded her.

"Bring it," she muttered grimly. "Recycling, retargeting."

"*Patriot* interception, group Beta..." Allenby intoned, continuing his running commentary. "Fighters knocked four down! *Patriots* three. Fifteen missiles remaining. Still a good lock on all incoming."

It wasn't enough. Not nearly. Sun felt helpless, a passenger now. His AI would handle the final interception. With missiles closing on Incirlik at double the speed of sound, he couldn't target and fire manually with anywhere near the speed needed.

"Fourteen," Allenby said after a second volley of *Patriots* lanced out at the incoming Russian missiles. The OVOD missiles were now inside the *Patriot*'s minimum strike range.

With a sound like tearing paper, the 20mm autocannons of multiple *Centurion* close-in weapons systems around the base opened up. Sun knew they had a snowball's chance in hell of hitting an OVOD.

A new tone sounded in the truck and it hummed with an ominous sound of heavily loaded capacitors as the lasers mounted outside fired for the first time. Then the HPM tone sounded as Barruzzi's secondary microwave weapon discharged.

There was no more they could do, the enemy missiles were upon them.

'RED' Burgundy had waited to see the result of the BATS attack on the Russian aircraft below him before he wasted his own missiles on them, but when the nearest *Felon* easily evaded the BATS attack and then turned as though looking for a firing solution on him, Red let fly.

"Fox 3," he called, releasing two of his active-homing CUDA missiles at the *Felon*, still forty miles distant. Almost simultaneously the Russian fired too, and the four missiles passed each other in the sky at twenty miles as they tracked their respective targets. The two pilots reacted to the threats each in complete accord with their personalities. Red put his *Panther* into a tight turn, pushed his throttle forward and extended laterally away from the approaching Russian missiles, forcing them into a tight turn. As they drew closer he fired his decoy chaff and flares and then radically tightened his turn until he was almost facing toward Bondarev's *Felon* again. Bondarev's missiles completed a tight arc in the sky, but couldn't follow Red's last jink, settling on the decoys and detonating harmlessly behind him.

BONDAREV continued to close with the Coalition *Panther*, changing his intercept vector to keep himself pointed right at the enemy aircraft, almost ignoring the CUDA missiles boring toward him. At ten miles separation, his *Felon* began actively jamming the enemy missiles, trying to scramble their radar lock. It burned through one of Red's missiles, sending it wide, while the other had picked up Bondarev on its infrared seeker and kept straight at him. Rolling onto his back when the missile was two miles out, Bondarev hauled his stick back into his stomach, fired off a stream of decoys and pointed his machine straight at the ground. The CUDA was blinded by the sun-bright decoy flares and detonated in the midst of them, as Bondarev twisted like a corkscrew and pulled back on his stick again, turning his Mach 1.2 airspeed into altitude as he pointed himself back at the Coalition *Panther*, now just twenty miles distant.

And fired again.

RED saw the incoming *Vympel* K-77M missiles but held his fire. He had altitude, he had a good lock on the Russian, but he had only two missiles left. At the last practical moment he fired one CUDA at the approaching Russian and then turned oblique to the incoming Russian missiles, forcing them to turn hard. Then he rolled and reversed, forcing them to change direction again. Ten miles. *Eight*. He kept his eye on the boxes around the incoming missiles on his helmet display and waited for the AI cue that would tell him when to radically tighten his turn and evade. As the two Russian missiles closed, their icons flashed red and he reversed his turn once more, pulling his nose down toward the ground and firing decoys as he watched his own missile close the distance to the Russian.

BONDAREV again ignored the single incoming CUDA. His automatic jamming system was pouring energy at the enemy missile to try to blind its radar. He had to hope it would be enough to save him. He had a long-distance visual lock on the enemy *Panther* now and waited for the Coalition pilot to begin maneuvering radically to evade his missiles. As he pulled a high-G inverted turn trying to get under the Russian missiles, Bondarev fired one of his last two missiles. The enemy CUDA flashed over Bondarev's cockpit, less than 100 meters distant, but didn't detonate. At a distance of just eight miles, his own missile locked onto the Coalition *Panther* immediately. The enemy pilot was fully fixated on dodging the missiles already coming at him, which he did, and spun his machine away from Bondarev for a fatal second, presenting his engine baffles at the missile Bondarev had just fired.

It detonated just feet behind the *Panther*, sending superheated shrapnel directly into the Coalition fighter's Pratt & Whitney turbofan engine.

Kill!

Breaking away and scanning the battlesphere around him automatically for undetected threats, Bondarev grunted with satisfaction as he glanced at his targeting display and saw the Coalition pilot blast out of his cockpit and into the sky behind him.

The airspace around him was clear. He checked his tactical screen. His flight had lost two aircraft, but both pilots' emergency beacons were flashing, indicating they had reached the ground below. Dead or alive, he would find out soon enough. No longer actively engaged, the remaining enemy *Panthers* had disappeared from Russian radar but he could still see several Coalition BATS drones searching the sky with active radar. He saw the icons for the surviving members of Bebenko's ground attack flight already back inside Russian-controlled airspace, and further out, the *Okhotnik* strike squadron moving southeast toward the Syrian coast. He couldn't take the chance all of the Coalition fighters had withdrawn – they might still be hunting him – so he turned his machine toward home.

Whether the mission was deemed a success or not would depend on the bomb damage assessment. Had they hurt Incirlik enough to force the Coalition fighters to pull back? Now that his elation over his personal kill was fading, he damn well hoped so. The 7th Air Group had opened a new front in the conflict with a direct attack on a NATO base, but lost several aircraft and who knows how many men trying to put a hurt on the Turkish airfield.

He looked down over his wing at the brown and white landscape scarred with barely visible roads and the pinprick dots of villages. Somewhere down there, the troops and tanks of the Syrian 25th Special Missions & Counterterrorism Division were either rolling toward an airfield that was a burning ruin, or celebrating having survived a blizzard of Russian *OVOD* missiles.

The wages of war
Office of the Dir. of National Intelligence, Virginia, 2 April

THE constant murmur of traffic from the expressways bounding the 51-acre Liberty Crossing intelligence complex in McLean, Virginia, was completely inaudible in Carmine Lewis's windowless, airless office. It didn't bother her, not really. She was very rarely there, but tonight was an exception. She'd dropped in for a briefing and had been about to leave again for the Pentagon when she'd received a message to stand by for a call from President Henderson.

She knew what he would want to talk about and realized the conversation could put her in a difficult position. But she also knew who had appointed her, and to whom her loyalties lay.

The telephone on her desk – a throwback to a different century, but still more secure than even an encrypted cell phone – began ringing, making her jump.

"Carmine."

"Mr. President."

"Hell of a thing."

He'd gotten her flash alert. She had sent a brief to all members of the Homeland Security Council as soon as her people had confirmed the reports. Russian aircraft had directly attacked the Incirlik Air Base, and more than a dozen US and Coalition personnel were dead, many more wounded.

"Yes, sir."

"Called Harry straight away to ask him how we should respond; he said he had an armored cavalry regiment waiting in Kansas to load aboard air transports. *Raiders* on the runway at Ramstein, engines running. I just had to say the word."

"Yes, sir. There is another option."

"That's why I called you, Carmine. I already know what the Vice President will say. I want to hear your objective view before I bring the National Security Council together on this."

Objective view? Did such a thing really exist? She'd been shocked, horrified … then *outraged*. Not since the Syrian civil war had US and Russian forces exchanged fire. And that incident in 2018, in which private Russian 'security contractors' had attacked US soldiers guarding an oil installation, had resulted in Russian deaths from US air strikes, but no US casualties. This attack was a bald-faced threat, delivered by cruise missile in hundred-foot-tall high-explosive letters. *You have no business interfering in this conflict, and if you don't accept that, you will pay in blood.*

Russia could claim it had not specifically targeted US troops. It had attacked a 'legitimate' Turkish military target, after warning multinational troops to evacuate. Carmine was no diplomat, but she could see how Russia could so easily go hat in hand to the UN Security Council and say it was all an unfortunate misunderstanding, and in future it would work more closely with the US to ensure such things could not occur in the confusion of the fast-moving Turkey-Syria conflict.

In the darkest corner of her heart, she wanted Henderson to rain hellfire on the Syrians and their Russian protectors. But she also knew that ruin lay in that emotion.

She ran a hand through her hair. She was fifty-eight years old, with a thick glossy mane that had turned silver when she was about thirty. Strangely, it had caused people always to assume she was older than she was and take her more seriously as a result. She hadn't fretted about it once she realized that.

"Sir, you can withdraw all US forces from Incirlik. You don't have to take them out of Turkey, just move them off the line." She had been looking at a map of Turkey on a tablet PC before the President had called, and spun it to face her now. "Coalition air force commanders are already talking withdrawal. Turkey is planning to move its aircraft to Konya in central Turkey, the Brits and Australians to RAF Akrotiri on Cyprus.

Without air cover and US air defenses, Incirlik will almost certainly fall, but there will be no more US casualties."

"But Russia wins, and we look as weak as … water." Henderson rarely swore. Carmine wondered what it would take for him to do it, if now wasn't one of those moments.

"We have bigger concerns than a border dispute in Turkey, Mr. President," she said. "The Chinese blue-water fleet is currently exercising in the East China Sea between Taiwan and Japan and there have already been two close calls…"

"And the Vice President would say that if we cave in to Russia, it will only embolden China."

Carmine nodded to herself. The Vice President was right. "There is a middle ground," she said, thinking on her feet. "A strategy of proportionate response. Russia attacks Incirlik, we send in the Bloody First to defend our troops and assets and launch the *Raiders* as the Defense Secretary proposes. Stop the Syrians in their tracks, send them back east with their tails between their legs. Turkey is not Iraq or Afghanistan, it can look after itself once it gets the breathing room. As soon as the situation stabilizes, we put the infantry back on their transports and bring them home."

"In body bags?" Henderson asked. "Because it is inevitable some of those men and women will pay the ultimate price."

That hit home. What could she say? "Yes, Mr. President. It is. But they will be giving their lives to protect their fellow Americans. Isn't that why they put on the uniform?"

Henderson was quiet. "Thanks for the perspective, Carmine. I'll ask you to represent it at a National Security Council meeting in about thirty minutes. In the meantime, I need to think about whether I agree with it."

The Bloody First
Incirlik Air Base, Turkey, 2-3 April

Lieutenant Ted Sun was also thinking hard. On the one hand he was still alive, and so was his squad. But it was a bit hard to feel good about that when so many other good men and women weren't.

Sun and his *HELLADS* battery had taken down three of the first wave of subsonic *Krypton* anti-radar missiles, and five of the second wave of *OVODs*. *Centurions* had knocked down the rest of the *Kryptons*. Of the second wave, a second *HELLADS* battery, poorly positioned relative to the attack, had claimed another four *OVODs*. *Patriots* and *Centurions* had claimed nine.

Four *OVOD* missiles had breached the airbase perimeter. Two released their payloads over the single runway, cratering it in dozens of places and scattering hundreds of mines. One hit the aircraft park at the southwest end of the runway, destroying four Turkish F-16s, two British *Tempests* and killing dozens of Turkish and British personnel. The last hit the apron outside the main military hangars, cratering the apron, damaging a US E-3 early warning aircraft, and destroying a Turkish C-130 and two quadrotor supply drones. For better or worse, all Coalition *Panthers* had been airborne at the time of the attack, though one had been destroyed in air combat east of the base.

Though it had only one runway proper, Incirlik had two broad taxiways each side of its main runway that could be used to launch and land any but the heaviest aircraft, and they were quickly cleared to allow the returning Coalition aircraft to land, rearm and refuel, in case Russia had planned a follow-up attack.

Sun, Barruzzi and Allenby had handed control of their battery to a relief squad, debriefed and spent the night helping to ferry the shocked and wounded to the base hospital medevac transports.

Later, Sun found himself sitting on the wheel of a three-wheeled electric tool transport and looking out across the ruined, smoking airfield. He flinched as a robot mine detection vehicle tripped a mine about five hundred yards away, the flash and sharp report coming a second apart. The small metal-detecting ground vehicles were like oversized floor-vacuum robots and within an hour of the Russian attack they were at work detecting and exploding the Russian mines. But the heavy cratering of the runway and apron meant the bots couldn't be used everywhere and until all of the anti-personnel munitions had been cleared, work on repairing the runway couldn't begin. Army mine-clearing crews would have to do the dangerous work of climbing in and around broken concrete and cratered dirt to finish the job.

As he watched, a pair of RAAF F-35s spooled up their engines about a hundred yards away on the taxiway and then leapt forward, lifting their noses and climbing into the night sky. Incirlik could still launch and land the nimble stealth fighters, but anything bigger would have to fly out of Konya, 160 miles northwest.

"Penny for 'em, Lieutenant."

Sun turned and saw Barruzzi standing behind him, thumbs tucked into her nylon web belt. She was only wearing her t-shirt, having taken off her blood-stained jacket sometime during the night after helping Allenby carry a wounded airman to an aid station. She had curly black hair courtesy her Italian ancestry, and even at twenty-four looked to Sun like she could be the matriarch of a Sicilian mafia family, the way her steely gaze could drill into you if you said something she didn't approve of.

"You first, Sergeant," he replied.

Barruzzi sat herself on a wheel guard beside him. "Well, sir, to be honest I was just thinking, this must be what Pearl Harbor felt like, the day after," she said.

Sun reflected on that. "Except they caught us with our pants down at Pearl. We stopped 90 percent of what Ivan threw at us yesterday," he said. He nodded at the F-35s climbing into the sky. "And we're still mission capable."

"True that," Barruzzi nodded. "I guess we did pretty good, considering."

He'd just come out of a briefing by their battalion CO and decided to share a little of it with Barruzzi.

"We did *damn* good," he said. "Our anti-air took out the entire first wave of missiles and most of the second." Another mine detonated and he pointed. "We clean those up, pull up the broken concrete, lay down steel mesh patches, Air Force will be landing heavies on that runway again inside three days."

"Quicker than I figured," Barruzzi said. "I was thinking maybe a week."

"Yeah. But I'm not going to sugarcoat it, Sergeant, it isn't all good news."

She squared her shoulders. "I can take it, sir," she told him.

"You heard the Bloody First is on the way here to fortify the base perimeter?" Sun asked.

"The whole base heard about it before it even hit the radio waves. Two battalions. Yes, sir. About time Washington got off the fence and decided to put boots on the ground here. Incirlik isn't just Turkish, it's a damn NATO base!"

"Yeah, well, they're in the air right now. But C-5s can't land here with no runway. Can't land east at Gaziantep either – Syrian anti-air and Russian patrols make it too risky."

"Where they putting down then?"

"Konya, central Turkey," he said. "Two hours away. They land in a few hours, by the time they saddle up, say another four hours."

"Still. That's what? A couple thousand troops, M1A1 tanks, remotely guided *Bradley* and *Hyperion* fighting vehicles, JLTV armed recon vehicles, right?" She smiled. "Everything mamma ordered."

"Hmm," Sun said, not looking at her.

"Come on, Lieutenant," she said. "Spill it."

"Alright. Earliest they'll be here is 1500 hours tomorrow afternoon. The Syrian 25th Armored Division just broke through Turkish lines at Erzin. They could be here first." Sun slapped his thighs and straightened up, pushing away from the electric trike. "I'm going to check out a carbine from the armory. You round up Allenby and do the same."

DARYAN had never been inside the American outpost. Yes, she'd seen it from just about every angle, because it sat up over Kobani like a concrete crown on the highest hill for miles. A hill hundreds of Kurdish fighters had died defending, losing and then retaking from ISIS during the Syrian civil war. It rankled that foreign fighters now sat up there looking down on Kobani over their guns, even if they were on the same side. But just as they had under the siege fifteen years earlier, they needed the Americans to coordinate air strikes and counter-battery fire, so the heights were the only logical place for them to base themselves.

Entry to the outpost from the Kobani side was via a tunnel dug deep into the base of the hill by Russian engineers, just wide enough for two people to pass without having to turn sideways. It went five hundred yards under the crest of the hill and connected to a repurposed office lift and emergency stairwell that rose up into the bunker complex.

The entrance to the tunnel was guarded by two US Marines and two YPG fighters. The YPG fighters leaned on concrete anti-vehicle barriers, smoking, and barely looked at her orders before waving Daryan past. The US Marines by the tunnel entrance – a corporal and a private – looked carefully at her, at her rifle, and then at her orders. The sergeant handed her orders back, then held his hand out for her rifle.

She stared at him uncomprehendingly.

"You aren't going in there armed," he told her.

"Then I'm not going in there," she said. "I give this rifle to no one."

The Marine corporal looked at the private, raised an eyebrow and crossed his arms. Daryan sized them up and then took two steps back and sat down in the dirt.

"You can't just sit there," the corporal said, frowning at her.

"Then let me in, or go and get Gunnery Sergeant James Jensen," she said. "You are the ones who sent for *me*, I didn't ask to come here."

The sergeant stared at her for a good minute, then he sighed. "Show me the breech is empty," he demanded.

Daryan stood, ejecting the shell that was in there and showing it to him.

"Pat her down," the sergeant ordered the private. He did so, but not very thoroughly. If she'd had a folding knife between her butt cheeks, he wouldn't have found it. "Take her up, Johnson," he said, reaching for a field telephone. "I'll call it up."

The private had a hand on his sidearm and nodded toward the tunnel. "After you, ma'am," he said.

As she walked ahead of him, she reflected that this was a strange way to treat an ally. But then, the history of Kurd and American had been a troubled one the last ten years. Close allies in the fight against ISIS, the Americans had left them to the mercies of their NATO friends the Turks when Turkey came across the border to create its 'buffer zone'. The Kurds had been forced to accept Russian and Syrian regulars in Kobani as a bulwark against the Turks, and then found themselves once more alone when Syria pulled out of Kobani to push Turkish troops back over the border. With the Turks pummeled all the way back to Gaziantep, when the Syrians and Russians had tried to re-enter Kobani, the YPG and YPJ fighters had held them out. The token force of US Marines had arrived just in time to help fight off a concerted attack by the Syrian 138th Mechanized Division and this time, with Kobani under siege, the Americans had stayed. Not that they had much choice.

Daryan was no student of international politics, but even she shook her head at the 'in today, out tomorrow' commitment of the Americans in her region. *Whatever.* They were here today, and both Americans and Kurds wanted the Syrians and Russians gone tomorrow, so for now, that was all that mattered. At the lift she paused and the Marine private pushed a button to call it. "Someone will meet you at the top," he said, and waited in awkward silence. She enjoyed his discomfort.

"You have nice eyes," she told him. It was the truth. Kurdish men only had brown or green eyes. His were bright blue.

He flushed red at the throat and stared at the wall above her head, not replying.

"I'm sorry, I did not mean to embarrass you," she said, smiling. "We have a saying: *what the heart feels, the mouth speaks.*"

"You didn't … uh, here you are," he said, obviously relieved as the lift arrived and even more obviously relieved as the lift doors closed and took her up.

Another private pulled open a security gate to let her out of the lift and she stepped out into a brightly lit, bare, white-painted room. It contained only the private guarding the lift entrance and – standing with feet slightly apart, hands behind the small of his back, with a slight smile on his face – one of the biggest men Daryan had ever seen.

"You're the sniper," he said. He held out a hand to shake. "They didn't tell me you were…"

"A woman?" she asked, taking his hand. It was so smooth.

"So young, I was going to say," he said. "I'm Jensen, Gunnery Sergeant," he said. "And you are?"

"My name is Daryan," she said, then saw he was looking at something behind her. "What?" she asked, turning around.

"Your rifle…" he said. "Is that a Lobaev?"

"Yes."

"Chambered for ten thirty-six millimeter?"

"Yes, why?"

"That's … it's just the sniper we're hunting uses a Lobaev."

She shrugged. "Then when we kill him, allow me a minute to relieve him of his ammunition. It is not easy to come by."

The Marine laughed. "You are pretty confident."

She looked him up and down. "How many Syrians have you killed?" she asked.

"We don't keep track of that kind of thing."

"If you are human, you do," she said.

He was not smiling now. "Three," he told her. "That I know of."

"I have killed twelve," Daryan said. "And seven Turks. And one Russian."

"Then you win."

"I am not boasting," she said, frowning. "And I am not confident or unconfident, I am just good at getting into places where I am not expected, and staying still, and shooting."

The Marine stared at her a moment. "You are the one who killed that Syrian commander a few days ago."

She lifted her shirt to her nose and smelled it. "Do I still stink?"

"What? No…" He looked confused. "Look, if you'd like, we can get a cup of coffee or tea, talk this through, then you can meet my commander." He started for the corridor.

She nodded. "Tea is good. Do you have sugar?" she asked hopefully.

O'HARE also preferred tea over coffee. With two heaped teaspoons of sugar. And she'd already had four cups since waking up in the ongoing chaos that was Incirlik. Arriving back from their sortie, she and the others from 3 Squadron had been forced to enter the pattern over the air base and hold for nearly twenty minutes while the air controllers worked out where the heck they could put the returning fighters. It would have made sense to O'Hare for them to rebase at Konya in central Turkey, which was only an extra thirty minutes' flying from the area of operations, or the RAF base at Akrotiri in Cyprus, but someone somewhere wanted to show the Russians their strike hadn't knocked Incirlik out.

So she put her *Panther* down on the southern taxiway, fully expecting to have her landing gear blown off by a mine any second. She almost wished it had. A trip to the sick bay would have been more enjoyable than the conversation she had just had with the very irate Lieutenant Red Burgundy, who had been choppered back to Incirlik after bailing out west of Gaziantep. Why he felt he had to take out his filthy mood on Bunny, she still couldn't fathom.

"You broke formation, why?" Red asked. He'd called her into the transportable truck that was serving as 3 Squadron briefing room, and sat himself at the CO's desk, which she regarded as typically presumptuous. He'd put a chair in front of it which he indicated she should park herself on. She felt like a schoolkid about to get detention.

"I saw an unidentified aircraft and decided to check it out, which…"

He crossed his arms. "I reviewed your DAS feed. There was no 'unidentified' aircraft visible."

"It was there," she insisted. "As events proved."

"You saw an aircraft at a range of over ten miles, which a high-definition 40x optical zoom lens and infrared sensors could not pick up…" he said.

"Obviously," she said. "Where are you going with this? I shot down two bloody *Krypton*-armed *Felons*!"

"Where are you going with this, *with respect, Lieutenant*," Red said in a dangerously low and even tone.

Bunny gritted her teeth. "With respect, Lieutenant, two kills. I'm nearly halfway to a damn ace, but you are treating me like a deserter."

Red let out a bitter laugh. "You? An ace? You were assisted by two BATS units that put eight missiles on target O'Hare. I'll see you get credit for a third of two kills, which is less than *one* kill. Some ace."

Bunny glared at him. Don't say it, O'Hare. Don't say it.

She said it. "Could the Lieutenant, respectfully, be a little upset that he got his arse shot out of the sky yesterday?"

To his credit, Red didn't rise to her bait. He picked a pencil off the CO's desk and tapped it thoughtfully, looking at her. "Do you know your military history, O'Hare?"

"No sir, too busy making it," Bunny shot back.

"Very droll. Since you are so keen on making ace … who was the leading Australian ace of World War Two?"

She knew that one. "Clive Caldwell."

"Correct. Twenty-seven kills between 1940 and 1943, awarded the Distinguished Service Order, Distinguished Flying Cross and bar, promoted to Wing Commander in 1943…" Red pointed a pencil at her. "I just read his biography. You remind me of him."

"I'm flattered, sir," Bunny said, knowing there would be a catch.

"Don't be. After being promoted to Wing Commander, he was charged with mutiny, cleared, but then found guilty of bootlegging booze, court-martialed and busted back down to Flight Lieutenant."

"I feel a moral coming, Lieutenant."

"No moral. Call it more of a … premonition. You are a good pilot, O'Hare. And you got lucky up there yesterday." He took the pencil and held it in both hands. "But one day you are going to push your luck too far and, like Caldwell, you will come crashing to earth."

"Well, you are the expert in that area, sir," O'Hare said.

He narrowed his eyes, snapping the pencil. "You have a combat patrol in three hours, report back here at 1100. Now get out."

Sitting on a chair outside the trailer, she watched a pair of RAF *Tempests* roar into the sky from the northern taxiway as a bulldozer pushed slabs of uprooted concrete into a pile. Most of 3 Squadron was airborne, fencing with Russian fighters east and south of Incirlik as Syrian mechanized troops began their big push. She should be up there too, but Red had been grounded by the Squadron medico and he'd kept her on the ground with him, as a landing accident yesterday meant they now had more pilots than they had machines.

She hammered the arm of her chair. You could put all the propaganda spin on it you wanted, Ivan had suckered the Coalition combat air patrol into an air-to-air engagement in the east, and then hammered Incirlik from the unprotected south. They'd had too few aircraft airborne, and those that were, were in the wrong place. Now they were burying bodies and pouring concrete, with a Syrian tank brigade about to roll right through the front door.

Her attention was caught by a woman in US Army uniform who was making a beeline across the apron toward the 3 Squadron briefing hut. She had a carbine slung over her shoulder, dark curly black hair tucked up under her field cap, and a way of walking that said, "Get in my way and die." She was wearing Sergeant stripes. O'Hare hoped she was looking for Lieutenant Burgundy.

The woman stopped in front of her. "This RAAF 3 Squadron headquarters, ma'am?"

Bunny looked back at the container on a wheeled trailer that was their briefing room. "Closest thing we've got, Sergeant. How can I help you?"

"I'm looking for a Flying Officer O'Hare."

Damn. "And what did that idiot O'Hare do now?"

"Pretty sure she saved my life from what I heard, ma'am; just wanted to say thank you."

O'Hare stood and held out her hand. "In that case, I'm O'Hare."

"Barruzzi," the woman said. "Pleased to meet you."

O'Hare looked back at the chairs against the trailer. "Have a seat?"

"Thank you, ma'am," the Sergeant said, pulling the carbine off her shoulder and resting it against the trailer wheel. "I was asking around in flight control, and I was told you intercepted the main *Felon* strike yesterday?"

Bunny sighed. "No, as my Lieutenant just pointed out, my BATS intercepted the strike, I just helped."

"BATS?"

"Drone wingmen," Bunny explained. "I spotted the Russian group, but the BATS killed it."

"I'm TCA on a HELLADS battery, ma'am. At least one of those *Krypton* missiles was aimed at my radar truck. We only had to deal with five all up. If we'd had to take down ten, at the same time as we were preparing to engage that strike from the south … well, I don't think I'd be here to talk about it."

Bunny frowned. She wasn't used to people thanking her. "You're welcome, I guess." She looked over at the carbine. "HELLADS crews usually carry assault rifles?"

Barruzzi shrugged. "My Lieutenant says it's better to have a rifle and not need it, than need it and not have it."

"I like him," Bunny said. "You want to swap Lieutenants?"

MEANY also got back from the attack on Mamayd to find Incirlik in chaos. Unlike O'Hare, he and Rex King *had* been diverted to Konya. But he'd barely had time to land, debrief and get a medical check before they were ordered back to Incirlik. And given their next mission.

At 0800 the next morning, he found himself lifting off on King's wing again. And a hairy takeoff it had been. The taxiway they were reduced to using was five hundred feet shorter than the main runway. He'd had to apply full power while keeping his wheel brakes locked, the *Tempest* rattling like it was about to shake itself apart, before releasing the brakes and rocketing along the narrow taxiway and into the sky. They were the third RAF combat air support mission launched that morning, and another two were planned.

They weren't going back to Kobani today. Their target was much closer. Too close, if you asked Meany Papastopoulos. Which was why they actually turned *away* from the target as they climbed out of Incirlik, to give themselves the altitude they'd need to set up their attack on the tanks of the 25th Syrian Armored Division currently headed west along Highway 52 out of Erzin.

With nothing but Turkish light infantry and a couple of tanks between them and Incirlik.

Meany pulled up his wheels and settled his machine onto King's wing, running his eyes over the tactical display. It was pulling data down from satellite, long-range ground radar, an airborne warning aircraft thirty thousand feet above and twenty miles behind the ops area, and from the picket of RAAF *Panther*s and BATS to the east and south. As he watched, one of the drones picked up a radar return and fired a missile at it, but the return vanished as quickly as it had appeared.

"Russians are playing with us," King observed, looking at the same data as Meany.

"Seeing if they can sneak a few more *Felons* in under our guard you think, sir?"

"No. They think they have us on the defensive now," King said. "They won't waste missiles on the air-to-air pickets. They're running cover on the Syrian advance. They'll be looking for blaggards like you and me, Meany, who are trying to ruin their party."

Turkish F-16s had spent the morning on strikes around Gaziantep, trying to relieve the pressure on their southern front. The city was understandably seen by Turkey as a more important strategic asset than Incirlik, and they could not afford to let it fall hostage to Syria.

In defending Incirlik, the RAF had had some success already that morning. One tank and two armored fighting vehicles had been confirmed destroyed outside Erzin. Unfortunately, the enemy armored column was well protected against air attack and a large number of the *Tempest*'s missiles had been intercepted. But their aircraft had gathered invaluable data on the Syrian anti-air units embedded in the advance, which Rex and Meany were about to put to good use.

Inside their weapon bays, each *Tempest* carried a *SPEAR-EW* swarm-capable electronic warfare missile. The stealth optimized *SPEAR* missile was designed with a 'launch, loiter and cooperate' capability which allowed it to detect enemy radar and communications units, and then join with another nearby *SPEAR* missile if needed, to circle overhead and jam the enemy radar and radio signals. If one *SPEAR* missile was not enough to overwhelm the enemy unit's electronic systems, then it could call on a second to join it. If authorized, and before entering a zero-fuel state, the missiles would go supersonic and strike the units they were jamming, usually thin-skinned radar and comms trucks.

With the enemy air defenses and comms jammed, the remaining three missiles in each of the *Tempests*' weapons bays could be deployed. The *SPEAR-HEAT* missiles had a High-Explosive Anti-Tank warhead and were also designed to work together to destroy their targets. When enemy armored vehicles were located, the *SPEAR-HEAT* missiles within range would divide the targets between them, prioritizing main battle tanks and missile-armed infantry fighting vehicles.

With Syrian armor in the east now just thirty miles from Incirlik, Meany and Rex would be launching their attack from west of the air base.

As they climbed to twenty thousand feet, Meany armed his weapons.

"Assuming weapons authority," Rex told him.

An icon appeared on the *Tempest*'s weapons display and Meany tapped it. "Authority granted."

They banked through the sky, a mile apart, and oriented themselves east. "Launching *SPEAR-EW* in five ... four ..."

Meany held his breath. The moment when their weapon bay doors flipped open and closed again would double their radar cross-section. If a Russian *Felon* had managed to slip through the picket of BATS and F-35s and was invisibly circling Incirlik looking for a target, they were about to paint a big crosshair on themselves.

If you're up there, Grandpa ... Meany said to himself ... *now would be a good time to keep an eye out for your man Anaximenes. There's a lot of people down there who could be dead tonight if I stuff this up.*

YEVGENY Bondarev had not been congratulated for coming up with the strategy of the day before. It had resulted in the largest loss of aircraft in air combat by the Russian Aerospace Forces since two Russian aircraft had been destroyed by Turkey at the start of the conflict two years earlier. Five *Felons* had been lost and their vulnerability to the *Panther*-BATS 'teaming' strategy exposed. The damn Coalition pilots could hide behind their curtain of expendable drones and force their opposition to fight their way through them before they were engaged themselves.

Which Bondarev had done. And achieved the first air-air kill of a Coalition *Panther* in the Russian Aerospace Forces. For which he had received exactly zero recognition.

Bondarev was furious. In their debriefing, Bebenko had claimed full credit for the successful destruction at Incirlik, laying the success of the attack entirely at the feet of his

Okhotnik crews and downplaying the role of the *Felons* that had given them a free run at the target. Bondarev had tried to argue that the main reason for the failure of the *Felon* anti-air strike run had been the close formation strategy adopted by Bebenko for that attack, which allowed the entire formation to be identified as soon as one of the aircraft within it was exposed.

One of the virtues of long experience in war was that the Russian air forces had developed a principle known as 'besstrashnaya obratnaya svyaz' or *fearless feedback*. Junior officers were encouraged to speak their minds. It allowed them to vent. It did not guarantee they would be heard.

"The Comrade Captain is treating fifth-generation stealth aircraft as though they are fourth-generation aircraft, which need to maintain visual and radio contact to coordinate in combat. A single *Felon* can see every other *Felon* in the sky, no matter how distant. Its AI coordinates its attacks with the AI of every other *Felon* dynamically, without their pilots needing to communicate verbally. There is no need for a flight of *Felons* to fly in formation and no excuse whatsoever for an enemy being able to identify and engage an entire flight in a single sweep."

The reaction around the room was mixed. Those he knew well smiled or winked surreptitiously. Those he did not looked at the floor, or leaned away from him, not wanting to get 'splash damage' from Bebenko's expected response.

Bebenko waited, letting Bondarev's words die in a long silence.

"The *Felon* as Lone Wolf," Bebenko said at last. "That was the name of it. Your final treatise at the Academy?"

Bondarev did not respond. Bebenko already knew it was.

"After it was graded poorly by your instructors, I believe you sent a copy to your grandfather, did you not?"

Again, Bondarev remained quiet, but the other pilots leaned forward. To many, this was news.

"Your grandfather, former Colonel General of the Russian Aerospace Forces and Hero of the Russian Federation, Viktor Bondarev. Yes?"

"Yes," Bondarev admitted. "I did."

"You did. And he returned it to you, did he not, with a single comment?"

"Yes."

"Please," Bebenko said, indicating the assembled pilots with a wide sweep of his arm. "Tell us, what did your grandfather, former leader of an Air Attack Regiment and Hero of the Russian Federation, write on the cover of your treatise?" He looked hard at Bondarev as though daring him to look away.

Bondarev glared at him, refusing to break his gaze. "He wrote: *Wolves hunt in packs.*"

"Thank you for your feedback, Lieutenant Bondarev," Bebenko said, looking at the other pilots now. "Are there any *other* observations on yesterday's mission?"

Bondarev was about to speak up again, but Tchakov kicked his foot and shook his head. Bondarev had swallowed his words, but not his thoughts.

Which was why now, a day later, he was hopping his *Felon* over ridges and down valleys, north of Seyhan Beraji lake, just northwest of Incirlik, looking for a chance to prove himself right. He had flown the mission he and Tchakov had been assigned by Bebenko that morning, providing cover for the advancing Syrian armor. They had been vectored to intercept possible RAF *Tempests* which had just attacked a mechanized platoon, but had not managed to pick them up. They had been returning to their sector east of Incirlik when Bondarev had been locked and fired on at long range by what he assumed was one of the damned Coalition BATS.

He'd evaded the missile easily enough, but found himself down among the weeds over farmland east-northeast of Incirlik, all alone. Before he thought about what he was doing, he had killed his aircraft Identify Friend or Foe ID transponder and comms link and pointed his aircraft at the low hills ahead of him.

Tchakov would be panicking, he knew that. His flight leader plummeting to earth firing chaff and flares, and now disappearing off the comms grid? He'd hold station looking desperately for any sign of Bondarev, and then report him MIA. But done was done. Now Bondarev had to make it worth his own while.

He hit the low hills and engaged terrain prediction and following mode in his *Felon*, aiming for the rugged landscape northwest of Incirlik where a single *Felon* in 'dark mode', as he was, would be almost impossible to detect. He had been so focused on evading the BATS aircraft he could see on his tactical screen, and the *Panthers* he couldn't, that he hadn't given much thought to what he would do when he got there, but a plan had formed as his machine rose and fell over the low hills and then speared across a lake, so low it left a feather of water in its wake.

He was through the Coalition picket!

The hills north of the lake should be right under the takeoff and landing pattern for Incirlik's northwest-southeast aligned runway. Despite their successful attack the day before, Coalition air forces were still launching fighter aircraft from the air base. He'd hide in the radar shadow of the hills until one or more of the Coalition fighters appeared above him on his passive optical-electric sensors and he'd engage it. Then scram east.

For at least twenty tense minutes, he flew a racetrack-like pattern up an uninhabited valley, over a ridge to the west, down the valley on the other side, over the ridge to the east, and back up again. Over and over, his eyes on his targeting screen, looking for the telltale radiation or infrared signatures of Coalition aircraft. An ancient Turkish C-130 turboprop transport had crossed about ten thousand feet above him, but he'd ignored it. He was after tastier game.

He'd almost given up when, with a deeply satisfying chime, two Coalition fighters announced themselves on his sensors. His AI identified them immediately by their infrared signatures. RAF *Tempests*, climbing out from Incirlik on a westerly heading, no doubt preparing for another ground attack mission.

Careful not to bury himself in a Turkish hillside, Bondarev followed them out, like a shark in deep water stalking surfers above. His tactical position was not ideal. His targets were already fifteen thousand feet above him, moving to twenty. If he launched from as low as this, his missiles would have to make a radical climb to their targets, giving the nimble *Tempests* ample time and altitude with which to detect and defeat his attack.

He would let them increase separation, then he would move into their rear quarter, directly behind them, and try to close the altitude gap before he was detected. Incirlik passed his port wing only five miles away, its air defense radars oblivious to him.

The Felon as Lone Wolf. He was right – he knew it – and with the destruction of these two *Tempests*, he would prove it.

The aircraft above him leveled out and settled into a cruise as he swung around behind them. He eased his stick back and began a gentle climb. *No sudden moves, Yevgeny. Don't want ground radar or AWACs picking you up before you can fire.* Five thousand feet, five two … targets locked. Twenty miles separation. He armed all four of his *Vympel* missiles and a calm female voice began chanting insistently in his ears … *targets in range, shoot, targets in range, shoot* … his finger slid toward the missile trigger on his control stick.

Then from the bellies of each of the aircraft ahead of him, two air-to-ground missiles dropped and streaked east!

Damn. He couldn't get any higher, he had to engage *now*.

"*SPEAR-EWs* away and tracking," King announced. "If those tanks are still at the Highway 52 crossroads, we'll find them."

"Shut down the *Tunguska* anti-air vehicles and then go to work, yes sir," Meany affirmed.

Then a warning screamed in his ears. He froze. *Missile alert on their six?! What? No!*

"Break low!" King called, and Meany watched as the other pilot rolled his machine to port and dived, streaming chaff and flares.

Without further hesitation, Meany rolled to starboard and did the same. His *Tempest*'s optical targeting system had identified the missiles and was showing him their position in his visor, along with a steering cue to give himself the best chance of avoiding them. They were already right on him, arrowing up from low on his rear quarter, back behind Incirlik. Ground missiles? Not possible!

He grunted, breathing hard as he rolled his *Tempest*, chopped his throttle and held the control stick hard back, pointing his nose at the ground as he spiraled earthwards. The two missiles passed a hundred yards away on his port side, still screaming into the sky, and he looked down to where their contrails led, his targeting system following his eyes as he scanned the ground.

There, you bastarding bastard! Felon! His targeting system zoomed the view so he could see the target on his screen, though it was still beyond visual range. If he'd been carrying American CUDA all-aspect missiles he could have fired at the Russian there and then, but he was loaded for air-to-ground and *SPEAR* missiles were useless in air combat.

The Russian was back behind his starboard wing and now only ten miles distant as Meany began pulling the *Tempest* around, and the *Felon* fired again! As the missile alert sounded, Meany's AI painted a new steering cue on his visor and Meany pulled his turn tighter. It was no use, the Russian had fired at point-blank range. There would be no avoiding the Mach 2.2 missiles this time.

As Bondarev's last two *Vympels* closed to within two hundred yards of Meany's frantically skidding *Tempest*, his rear-aspect 30kw laser automatically locked onto them. Pulling its power from a breakthrough embedded-generator fitted inside the *Tempest*'s twin Rolls-Royce gas turbine engines, the missile defense laser that Meany hadn't been able to load on his last mission due to the added weight of the *Perdix* drones fired at the closest of the Russian missiles behind him.

Its seeker head exploded in a ball of high explosive, taking the other missile out with it.

"My turn, Ivan," Meany said out loud, pulling his nose further around so that he was head to head with the Russian. He reached for his gun trigger and laid the predictor sight on the dot that was the approaching *Felon*.

He tightened his grip as the dot grew larger in his visor. Out of missiles, it looked like the Russian was going to take him on, guns on guns, in a supersonic head-on merge.

Then the Russian aircraft exploded in a gaseous white cloud of flame which Meany blasted straight *through...*

He snapped his head over his shoulder in time to see the Russian's ejection seat spiraling through the ball of fire behind him as King's voice came over the radio. Meany pushed his nose down and leveled out, panting.

"Splash one," Rex announced, his machine appearing on Meany's port wing. "Well done, Flying Officer Papastopoulos."

Meany couldn't hide his chagrin. "With respect, sir, I had the bugger dead to rights..."

"Or he had you. Luckily we'll never know," King told him. "Now, back to work. As soon as those electronic warfare *SPEARs* start singing, we need to shoot and scoot before Ivan sticks another one up our backsides."

YEVGENY Bondarev had stayed conscious through his own ejection and was already focused on trying to steer his chute so that he didn't land on the four-lane motorway that he was looking at between his feet. His AI had saved his life, anticipating that the *Mauser* 27mm cannon shells about to strike his aircraft would have catastrophic consequences, and launching him into space just before they hit.

He pulled on the lines above his head, spilling air out, which increased the speed of his descent but slipped him over the motorway toward empty fields on the other side of some trees. He looked around himself. No tractors, no cars. No angry Turkish farmers with pitchforks.

The ground rushed up toward him and he hit soft-plowed earth, rolled an ankle as he fell, and had the wind knocked out of him. His chute collapsed around him as he gasped for air in a cloud of dust. He pulled it off his face.

Find cover.

He rolled out from under the chute and pulled it toward him, balling it up. Trying to stand he nearly screamed, and as he pulled up the leg of his flight suit he looked down at his ankle. It was already swelling, but there was no bone sticking out.

Suck it up, Bondarev.

Parachute clutched to his chest, he started hobbling toward the nearest trees. He looked at his watch as he scrabbled across the field. Mid-afternoon. Someone would have seen him come down. A Turkish civilian or soldier. They'd be searching for him. He had to find a vehicle, get moving east toward the Syrian advance.

He stumbled and nearly screamed in pain again, turning the sound into a bitter choking laugh instead.

Lone Wolf? Be careful what you wish for, Yevgeny.

IN the galley under the hilltop at Mishte-nur, Jensen poured a cup of tea from an urn for Daryan and pulled a big mug of coffee for himself, while she looked through the thin file he'd compiled on 'Tita Ali'.

There were only two pages, and she turned the last one over a couple of times, frowning as though reading them was a struggle. "This is all you have? A list of who he has shot, when, and a description of the Lobaev rifle?" she asked.

Jensen pointed at a page. "These numbers are our best guess at the direction he shot from, the distance, if anyone heard the shot." He leaned back in his chair. "We figure he's shooting from considerable distance, or he's not much of a shot, because so far he hasn't made a killshot. Only torsos, legs, groins."

"No one who can get into position so often and not be found is that bad a shot. He is not shooting to kill." Daryan pushed the folder back across the table to Jensen then spun it around again and looked at the name written across the top. "I understand why you call him Ali. A common Syrian name. What is Tita?"

"Bitch. In Hawaiian."

She laughed. "Good name. *This* is your Tita Ali." She reached into a pocket on her combat pants and pulled out a piece of paper of her own, unfolding it and handing it to him. "Andrei Zakarin. Lieutenant in the Russian 45th Spetsnaz Airborne Brigade. Georgian. Five foot eight – small, like me. Bald."

He looked at the page. There was no photo, but it was a lot more than he'd managed to put together.

"How can you be sure?"

"Russian prisoners talk. Also, he is a sniper instructor. Usually, Russians use the SV-98 or Dragunov rifle, but the prisoners said he chose the Lobaev because it is common here and he wants you to think he is Syrian."

"Well, that worked."

"Yes." She tapped Jensen's folder. "These kills are all in different places."

"He never shoots from the same hide twice," Jensen said. "The guys we've taken down, usually they have their favorite spots. Not this guy."

"That is not a problem," she told him. "Do you have a map?"

Jensen pulled a map from his own trouser pocket and spread it out on the desk between them. Daryan pointed at a slight rise outside the northwest shoulder of the Kurdish line of control. "Kunyan Kurdan. It is a hill, not as high as Mishte-nur, but still, good vision. The Russians are all camped there."

He frowned. "Our intel says they are at Mamayd, embedded with the Syrian command."

"Then your intel is wrong." She tapped the map. "The Russians are here. Zakarin is here. You drop a mother big bomb on Kunyan Kurdan, boom, no more 'Tita Ali'."

Jensen thought about it. A night strike perhaps, when most of the Russians in the camp were asleep? But Tita Ali had made three kills at night. What if they took out the Russian camp, but missed him anyway? And then there were the optics of it … if they laid a big hit on the Russian camp, there was nothing to stop Russia doing the same on COP Meyer. So far both superpowers had avoided going purely after each other in Kobani.

"No. A bomb can miss. I was told that you don't."

"Then either we go into their camp and find him and kill him, or we wait outside for him to leave and we kill him either going out, or coming back," she said. "There are only three tracks down from the top of Kunyan Kurdan."

"I like those odds," Jensen said. "We have a one in three chance."

"He does not sound stupid," she warned him. "He probably would not use the same track every time."

"That's OK," Jensen said. "I can watch one track, my dogs watch the others."

"Your dogs?"

He stood up. "Come on then. Let me introduce you."

The dogs' recharge stations were one 'deck' up at the end of a small, poorly lit corridor. The Russians had installed a big diesel generator four decks down, with air and exhaust ports to the surface, but they had long ago run out of fuel for it and there was no chance of getting any through the Syrian blockade. There was backup wind and solar that gave them enough juice to light the bunkers during the day, with surplus going to batteries which powered essential systems and low-energy lighting through the night.

And power to recharge his dogs, of course. Opening a door across which someone had scrawled 'KENNEL', Jensen led Daryan to two pods against the back wall among shelves of parts. At the end of a patrol the dogs backed themselves into the pods and engaged with the charging points. Jensen shut them in and then hit a button for what he called 'the rinse and lube cycle'. The dogs were shut in, sprayed with a water-based cleanser that washed the dirt and dust from their frames and joints, and then by a mister that covered their moving parts in fine droplets of lubricant.

The front panel of the pods showed they were at full charge.

Daryan was looking around. "There are no dogs here."

Jensen put two fingers in his mouth and whistled, the sound piercing in the closed underground space. Daryan held her ears.

The two pod doors slid open and Brutus and Spartacus woke. They didn't have glowing red LEDs, though Jensen had often thought that would be a cool addition. But they always started with a self-test routine. They sat in the pods on their rear haunches, just like real dogs. First, they rotated their 'head' joints, the multifunction sockets that could be fitted with sensors or weapons. Then they nodded up and down, left and right. As they started up, Daryan cursed in Kurdish and took a step back. After testing their multifunction arms, they rose from a sitting position and took two steps into the room, their 360 optical-electric sensor making a quick rotation around their girth. They then tested each of their four legs by straightening and bending them one by one. Finally, they lowered themselves to the floor and stood again, four times in rapid succession, like they were doing pushups. Daryan watched, wide-eyed. Only when they were finished did she turn to Jensen. "What are these?"

"Brutus and Spartacus, otherwise known as Legged Squad Support System or LS3, *Hunter* prototypes," he said. "Twenty-hour patrol endurance, teaming capability, carry up to 100 lbs. in cargo, or ordnance…"

"Ordnance? They are weapons?"

"They can *use* tools and weapons," Jensen said, pointing at the multifunction head socket. He walked over to his work bench and picked up various items. "Grips for picking up objects or opening doors. Explosive detector heads. Bayonets, long and short, smooth or serrated. Small-caliber automatic pistols or shotguns." He held up the shotgun attachment. "I prefer the shotgun if I'm taking them out armed. Their aim is pretty sketchy."

As he finished showing her, the dogs completed their self-test routine and sat back down on their haunches again.

"They are *loud*," Daryan said, disapprovingly. "Like an electric drill."

"In here, sure," he said. "And that was a problem with the early models. But these guys only put out 30 decibels when they're moving, which is about the same as a loud whisper."

She crossed her arms. "I am not traveling with these. I do not make 30 decibels of noise. These will get us killed."

"I'm not suggesting they travel with us," Jensen said. "They can go ahead of us, or trail behind. I'm thinking we get within a mile or so of that Russian camp, then I give them the coordinates of those tracks you were talking about. They'll go off and find cover somewhere they can watch the tracks with infrared and send the vision back to me. I'll watch the third track. Meanwhile you get into position wherever and however you damn like, as long as you and I can talk. We spot Tita Ali for you, and you hit him."

"This is not my way," Daryan said. "My way is to work alone."

"This is the Marine way," he told her. "We always use a team – one to spot, the other to shoot." She didn't look convinced. "You'd still be on your own," he told her. "We'd be nowhere near you. We can't give you away." Jensen reached over and patted Brutus on his back. "This ugly guy's sensor suite has saved my butt more than once, trust me."

She looked at the dogs again, then at Jensen. "I want to go up to the surface."

"Now?"

"Now."

"I thought we could meet the CO," he said. "Then I can give you the above-ground tour if you like…"

"I don't want a 'tour'," she said. "Just take me to the surface."

"All-righty," Jensen said with a shrug. Maybe it was claustrophobia. "After you," he said indicating the door back out to the corridor. The two dogs automatically stood to follow and Daryan shot them a suspicious glance. Jensen made a hand signal. "Stay," he said.

They sat down again and powered down.

It was only a short walk to the metal stairs that took them up two levels to the bunker entrance. They came out just as there was a change of guard on the walls, and so had to press themselves against a wall to let a platoon of Marines push past them, then emerged into the mid-morning sun. Jensen looked at his watch.

"About thirty minutes before our dinnertime mortar is due," he told Daryan. He gestured around himself. "So, welcome to COP Meyer. Drone landing pad and medical station in the center. That ruin is battalion HQ." He pointed at the observation posts around the wall. "OPs – we have five – plus one over that mess of sandbags filling the hole under the western wall. We've had a couple of infiltrations through there." He indicated left and then right. "South tower, North tower," he said, indicating the fifty-foot-high squat concrete guard towers. "Otherwise known as Heaven's Gate and Hell's Gate, because you stick your head up above the sandbags up there, it's a shortcut to the afterlife."

Daryan started walking toward the North tower, rifle butt bouncing on her thigh. Jensen hurried to follow. When she got to the base of the tower, she looked up. "I want to go up there."

Jensen wasn't sure he was exactly comfortable showing the woman what the setup atop the guard tower was, and hesitated. Then he mentally slapped himself. *She's your ally, soon to be your squad-mate, JJ. Lighten the F up.*

"OK, follow me," he said, putting a foot on the steel ladder that went up the eastern side of the concrete wall. Hand over hand he climbed, and then stopped just below the entrance to the guard post. "Gunnery Sergeant Jensen, coming up!" he called out.

"Aye, Gunnery Sergeant," a shout came back.

He looked down at Daryan. "Not a good idea to surprise them."

He climbed up into the guard post and nodded to the two Marines there, a corporal and private. The corporal was sitting at the surveillance station, while the private had a hand resting casually on the joystick for the Common Remotely Operated Weapon Station, or CROWS, a .50-cal gun mounted on the top of the guard post.

Both soldiers looked a little more alert as Daryan climbed up behind Jensen.

"Gentlemen, this is an ally from the Kurdish Women's Protection Unit. Daryan, can I introduce…"

She ignored both of the Marines and stepped up onto a small pile of spare sandbags against the northern wall of the guard post, trying to see over the top. "This is no good," she said, jumping up. "How can you see anything?" She turned and saw Jensen pointing at the bank of screens in front of the other Marines.

"Camera on top has motion detection, infrared and high-definition 100x zoom," he said.

She looked at the screens dubiously. "And if the enemy shoots it?"

"Well, we're high on top of the highest hill, so any shot from below is occluded by the tower. And glass is armored, ma'am," the corporal explained. "So is the gun mount. Took a direct hit from a mortar two weeks ago. Barely dented the CROWS casing."

Unimpressed, she hopped up on the sandbags again.

"I don't recommend that, ma'am," the corporal said, looking at Jensen. "Syrians camp out down there with their scopes on this tower, just waiting for one of us to do exactly what you're doing."

With a grunt, she pulled the top sandbag down, caught it and threw it to the floor at Jensen's feet. As he jumped back, she grabbed another and pulled that down too, creating a hole she could use to see out of the tower. Without any discussion, she took the two sandbags she'd pulled down, lifted one and put it on top of the other in the middle of the guard post, and then pulled her rifle from her shoulder and stepped up onto the sandbags on the floor. She put the Lobaev to her shoulder, aimed it at the hole and looked down her scope, as Jensen and the two Marines looked on, dumbfounded.

She was no fool, Jensen could see that. Only someone level with or above them could have shot through the hole she'd made and hit her, standing two feet back from the lip of the tower.

After about a minute, she stepped off the sandbags and handed her rifle to Jensen. "Your turn. Look north."

He stepped onto the sandbags and, with some difficulty, squinted through the scope of the rifle. It was starting to get darker outside and it took a moment for his eyes to adjust, but he saw the easternmost edge of the city and, beyond that, a small mound.

"You see the hill there?" she asked.

"Yeah." He could just make out some low buildings, a few tents. Soldiers and civilians moving around, but he'd have to play with the scope to get their faces in focus and he didn't want to mess with the woman's settings. "They're in Syrian uniforms."

"Yes. But they speak Russian," she said. "Get down now."

When he jumped down, she took the rifle and climbed up again, looking through the scope at the Russian camp again. "This position is good. I can kill him from here."

Jensen laughed.

She took her eye off the scope and glared at him. "Do you think I couldn't?"

He thought back to the image in the scope. "That has to be two miles away."

She lifted the rifle again and pressed a stud on the side of her scope, her lips moving as she did a calculation in her head. "No. Two thousand one hundred yards. One ... point two miles." She lowered the rifle and turned to the corporal. "Has anyone ever shot from here, at Syrian troops on the other side of the city?"

"Uh, no, ma'am."

"Not a rifle, not even a mortar?"

"No."

She climbed down. "Good. Then they will be careless. Also Tita Ali."

The corporal held out a hand to help her down and she looked at it like he'd just used it to wipe his ass. She slung her rifle on her shoulder. "I will meet your superior officer now and then I want to come back here and set up my hide. I will need an ordinary chair, an adjustable four-foot standing tripod and a box or pallets the same height as these sandbags. A low-light or infrared viewer or binoculars, with zoom. A piece of black cloth, six feet by six feet. Duct tape. Some bread and cheese. Two liters of water and an empty bottle to piss in. And a flask of tea." At last she gave Jensen a small smile. "With sugar."

Jensen looked over her shoulder. "You get all that, Corporal?"

The corporal was typing into a hand-held comms unit. "Yes, Gunnery Sergeant. I'm not sure about the tripod, though, we don't..." Daryan gave him a withering look and he bit off his sentence.

Jensen took her arm and led her back to the ladder down from the tower. "Don't worry, if you're going after Tita Ali, hell, we'll *print* you a tripod."

BONDAREV crouched in the shadow of a line of trees, scoping out the landscape around him, a plan forming. He was a hundred yards from the motorway. He could take off his uniform patches, make his flight suit as anonymous as possible. Hop the barrier and flag down a car. He had his *Grach* pistol ... he could commandeer the vehicle and head east until he hit the inevitable Turkish roadblock. Ditch the car, get around the roadblock, wait for the Syrian armor to roll through and try to talk someone into getting him a ride to the Syrian air base at Aleppo.

Most of the traffic was crawling west though, of course. Civilians, fleeing the Syrian advance. The only traffic going east was military; trucks and light infantry vehicles.

OK, plan B. Judging by the volume of traffic fleeing west, Syrian armor couldn't be far off. Hours? Maybe later tonight, at the latest. He could head south for Incirlik, hide out near the Coalition base and wait for the fighting to come to him.

One thing was clear, though. He couldn't stay here. As he watched, two cars pulled up to a nearby farmhouse and several men jumped out. They went into a huddle, and then he saw one of them point across the field in his general direction.

South it was.

MEANY had watched the Russian's parachute drift through the sky below him, unable to stop the thought that King might have been right. Yes, he had his sights on the Russian. But the opposite would also have been true. If King hadn't intervened, would it be him floating to earth? Or worse? He'd shaken the thought off.

While he and King had tangled with the Russian fighter, his *SPEAR-EW* electronic warfare missile had paired with King's and they had just reached the target crossroads and gone active. As they completed a fast circuit twenty thousand feet above the crossroads, the missiles mapped Syrian radio and radar signals, matched frequencies and started jamming at the same time as they sent targeting data back to King.

They each had three *SPEAR-HEAT* missiles in their weapons bays and as Syrian targets were plotted on Meany's tactical display, he picked out three that appeared to be in the company of several other vehicles. Their orders were to focus on armor, so he picked out two T-90s and a *Terminator* infantry fighting vehicle, all in the middle of separate convoys. He and King couldn't stop the Syrian advance, but they could sow chaos.

"Incirlik control, Cribbage flight. We have ground targets locked, shooting into grid Echo-three-niner. Confirm," King announced.

"Cribbage, you are clear to engage enemy in grid Echo-three-niner. Play the piano."

"Cribbage two, commit," King ordered.

With a press of his thumb, Meany's three remaining *SPEAR* missiles dropped out of his weapons bay and he banked to put himself on a heading for Incirlik, just minutes away. The missiles would guide themselves to their targets using the data from the electronic warfare missiles already over their targets, or if they were somehow lost, they would navigate to the target area and choose targets themselves using their image-matching AI.

Meany didn't need to babysit them. He and King had to get down, rearm, refuel and get the hell up again.

BUNNY O'Hare was itching to get airborne, but two aircraft short and out of favor with her Flight Lieutenant, she'd needed to wait for the machines on patrol to get back and get turned around. She paced the hangar like a caged animal, watching carefully as the RAAF fitters and armorers loaded her *Panther* with ordnance. With Syrian armor closing on them, stealth was no longer a priority. Her machine was being loaded in 'beast mode' – with all internal and external hard points being brought into play.

She and Red would be going up carrying four CUDA air-air missiles (two in her internal bay and two on her wingtip hard points) and six *Gray Wolf* swarming cruise missiles (four external, two internal), each with an 800lb. high-explosive warhead able to penetrate up to 15 inches of metal or cause lethal fragmentation out to a radius of 400 yards.

Bunny and Red had been tasked with causing the highest possible attrition among the Syrian troops, currently in trucks and troop carriers following their armor into the new front line east of Incirlik.

Red jogged up beside her, fresh from a situation update.

"How far out is the Bloody First?" she asked.

"They landed two hours ago. They'll be here in three, maybe four," he said.

"And the Syrians?"

"Brits just laid a hurt on them outside Yakapinar. Took out a brace of T-90 tanks and IFVs, but they're still advancing."

She frowned. "Yakapinar? That's…"

"Ten miles away," he said grimly. "Syrian 25th Armored could be here inside the hour unless the Turks can hold them up. We're pulling back to RAF Akrotiri on Cyprus once you and I have unloaded. The rest of the squadron will meet us there."

Bunny felt her blood rising. "We've already given up? We aren't going to put up a fight?!"

"I said *we're* pulling out," Red said. "Turkish ground forces are digging in about a mile east of the base. US Air Force is scrambling a couple of B-21 *Raiders* from Ramstein in Germany, should be overhead soon, and the US Army has five hundred personnel here."

"I met one this morning," Bunny said. "She looked tough, but she's no Ranger."

"Well, I hope she doesn't owe you money. She might not be alive to pay you back," Red said. "You done with your walkaround?"

Bunny felt like arguing, but even more than that, she felt like getting up and getting to work. "Yes, sir. Good to go."

"Mount up, Flying Officer," Red said. "We've got a combat air patrol of Turkish F-16s and a picket of BATS covering our takeoff, but we can't expect that to last. Russia is going to try to push on us in support of those tanks, and I don't want to be around when they do."

No, you want to be on Cyprus, eating souvlaki, Bunny thought. *While everyone else here does the dying.*

ABOUT half a mile away, Sun, Allenby and Barruzzi were piling sandbags about six feet out from the door of their Engagement Control Station. They had to stay at their stations until the last possible moment, in case the Syrians or Russians tried a missile attack under cover of the now inevitable firefight, but if they did abandon their truck, they wanted some cover to jump behind.

As they dropped the last sandbag onto the ground, Sun surveyed their handiwork. Their small pyramid-shaped berm was about ten bags wide, two deep, and six high. Propped up against it were three M-27 squad weapons and a case of 5.56mm magazine reloads. Sun had wanted some M203 grenade launchers for the M-27s but there had been none available.

"Back in the trailer," he told Allenby. "Run another systems check."

"I ran one thirty minutes ago," the sysop complained, wiping his brow. "Tac Director has us in data link mode anyway. He has fire authority, so what's the point?"

Sun could see why he asked. After they debriefed on the last engagement, battalion command had decided that they needed to cut the battery commanders like Sun out of the decision cascade, to save some precious seconds. All engagements would be run by the Battalion Tactical Director, with crews like Sun's being left in place only in case of a technical issue.

"The point is, we still have a job to do," Sun said, without rancor. "Run it again." As Allenby stepped up into the ECS trailer, Sun turned to Barruzzi.

"What do you think, Sergeant?" he asked. "Is it worth the effort?"

She looked at the small pyramid of sandbags as she walked around it, testing its stability by putting her weight on it. "More of a psychological barrier than a physical one," she said. She looked toward the airfield perimeter. "HE tank round, we're dead. Mortar round, we're dead. Rocket propelled grenade, we're dead." She looked off to the side and pointed. "They flank us, we're dead." They both turned their heads to the east as a dull boom rolled across the countryside. Barruzzi smiled. "But it's too late to build a concrete-lined bunker, so it's better than nothing, Lieutenant."

As Sun turned to join Allenby up in the trailer, the big auxiliary diesel generator about fifty yards away, to which it was coupled by thick umbilical cables, suddenly started up. Across the airfield, he heard critical incident alarms blaring and then the alarm on their own trailer started up.

"Saddle up!" Sun called to Barruzzi and jumped into the control center. As he climbed inside, his eyes adjusting to the low background light and glare of multiple screens, he thumped Allenby on the back. "Talk to me. We got incoming?"

"No sir," Allenby said. He was listening to something in his headset and relayed what he heard. "Base-wide power failure. Main grid is down. Auxiliary power kicked in automatically."

"Damn," Barruzzi said, standing in the door. "Cyberattack?"

"Unclear ... wait." Allenby cupped a hand to his earphones, then paled. "Power is down across the whole city. I'm ... comms is under attack too. Electronic jamming, worst I ever seen. We've got no link to Joint Tactical Information, no link to AWACS ... going to fiber optic backup..."

With power down and enemy mobile electronic warfare units jamming their satellite and radio comms, Incirlik had just been cut off from the outside world. Their ECS had a backup fiber optic link to their Tactical Director but with power down and comms jammed, the TD's information blackout would be similar to theirs.

"Cyberattack took down the grid, has to be," Barruzzi cursed, diving into her chair. "Or an EMP strike on a transformer station…" She frowned at her screens. "*Massive* jamming. If they had this kind of electronic warfare ordnance traveling with them, why didn't they use it for the missile attack yesterday?"

"Because they didn't want our aircraft to find it and blow it to hell before today is why," Sun guessed. "OK, people, you know the protocol." He tried to push the lump in his chest back down into his gut. "We're back on manual control. Detection *and* engagement. Ivan didn't do this for fun. There is some serious harm on the way. Definitely armor and infantry, probably indirect fire. Get those capacitors powered up. I want 360-degree coverage on the phased array. You see *anything* looks like an unidentified airborne target, missile or shell, you engage immediately. Is that understood?"

With their own radar up and radiating, Sun had at least some idea of what was going on around him. Perhaps a better idea than almost anyone else. The truck vibrated as a nearby aircraft roared past and lifted into the sky. On his monitor, he saw two RAAF *Panthers* taking off. Further out, a string of BATS drones patrolled to the east and south – one engaged with a Russian stealth fighter that was out of range of their *HELLADS* and *Patriot* batteries. As he watched, the BATS icon winked out. It had been destroyed. Another moved up to fill the gap, but they were a finite resource and every available BATS was currently airborne. Overhead, a Turkish combat air patrol of six F-16s was holding at thirty thousand feet, about five miles from the air base, but if Sun could see them, so could just about any other Russian aircraft. Neither the F-16s nor the base defenses had much chance of detecting a Russian *Felon* stealth fighter on their own, but the Russians would be able to target the ground and air defenses of the base with ease.

Things were about to get intense.

Hunting Tita Ali
COP Meyer, Kobani, Northern Syria, 3 April

MARY Jo Basim had met some intense individuals in her life, but the Kurdish sniper was in a class of her own. Jensen had approached MJ as she had been dozing over a cup of instant coffee in the COP galley after a long night out working her contacts inside the various Kobani militias. The news had been mixed. Reports of a Coalition strike on the Syrian HQ at Mamayd, but no casualty information yet. And the Syrians had responded with a rolling mortar bombardment across the depth and breadth of the Kurdish city, indiscriminately smashing houses, hospitals, schools and shops. Most of the remaining inhabitants were living in their cellars, so casualties had been light, but it reinforced how vulnerable the city was. "If they would just attack us," a YPG commander had complained to MJ bitterly. "Fighting house to house, we could beat them. But they just sit outside the city behind their artillery and kill and maim. There is no honor in this."

Jensen had pointed over to a young Kurdish militia fighter trying to work out how to get hot water out of the galley urn. "Kurdish sniper. Thought you might like to do a profile on her."

MJ looked her over. "Hard-ass Kurdish girl with a gun, it's been done a million times, Gunny."

"Hard-ass Kurdish girl with a gun who took out a Syrian general a few days ago? That been done?" he asked innocently.

MJ did a double take. "No way. *That's* Daryan Al-Kobani?" The young woman was already a legend among the militia of Kobani. The Syrian military had reportedly put a bounty of ten thousand dollars on her head and sent some of its best snipers to hunt her. She'd tagged at least two of them. MJ had seriously had her doubts if the woman even existed. Now she was standing right here! Short, wiry, black hair tied up in a plain green scarf, a big rifle slung across her back from shoulder to thigh. "She's here? Why?"

"We're hunting Tita Ali."

Now he had her full attention. She'd been putting together a piece about the Syrian 'ghost' who seemed to make a sport out of shooting Americans. If Jensen and the Al-Kobani girl were hunting him, they must have some hard intel.

"No shit. And you're letting me in?" she asked.

"Halfway. You can shadow *her*," he said. "So it's about the YPJ, not the Corp, you get my meaning."

"Yeah, sure." MJ stood.

Jensen took her arm. "Suggest you go slow with her. She's a prickly one."

Daryan hadn't appeared at all fazed when Jensen had introduced MJ as 'Reuters journalist MJ Basim'."

The girl had simply looked her over and spoke in Kurdish-accented Persian. "I have heard of you. You know what we call you?"

MJ understood Persian well enough. She grimaced and shot a look at Jensen, hoping he didn't. "The *Red Jaban*," she replied.

Daryan nodded. "Yes. The Red Coward." She jerked her head at Jensen. "Tell him why."

"No."

"Tell him, or I will."

MJ swallowed. Jensen was looking at her with eyebrows raised, waiting. "She wants me to tell you how I got my Kurdish nickname – Red Jaban. It means Red Coward." She looked at the floor then up again. "It was the early days of the siege. Syrian troops inside the city perimeter, the fighting was house to house ... I got trapped..."

Daryan snorted in disgust and looked away.

MJ ignored her, continuing. "I got separated from my minder, trapped in a side street. Syrians at one end, Kurdish

YPG at the other. There was a boy, in the street, he'd been shot…"

"By the Syrians. He was alive," Daryan said. "You were five meters away. You did nothing."

"He was badly wounded. There was no way to reach him without getting myself killed in the crossfire."

"You didn't try," Daryan said. "You made a *video*."

"To show the world," MJ protested. "To document what was happening."

"Get out your camera," Daryan told her.

MJ thought she was going to ask her to delete the video. "There's no point," she said. "Every video I take goes automatically into the cloud…"

"Get it out."

MJ reluctantly pulled her cell phone from her pocket and opened the camera app.

Daryan held up her middle finger in front of her face. "Document this."

"OK, girls," Jensen said. "Play nice, can we?"

AS they sat down in the galley under the hilltop, Daryan decided to ignore MJ and dive straight into a rapid-fire question and answer session with Jensen.

"When did most of the attacks take place?" Daryan asked.

"Middle of the afternoon, sometimes at night," Jensen replied.

"Every day?"

"Every damn day. Either a hit, or a close call. If he isn't lucky enough to ambush a patrol, he puts a couple of rounds into one of our OPs. He never uses the same position twice, and he never takes a damn day off."

"Has there been an attack today?"

"No."

"Then he will try to strike tonight. Show me the folder."

Jensen handed her a folder which MJ could see contained data on the US casualties attributed to the sniper. She would have died for a copy of it.

"They are mostly in the eastern part of the city," she observed. "He comes from the Russian camp, gets into the city or south, through the lines to Mishte-nur, waiting to ambush you as you come down from your outpost here. He knows your patrol routes, he sets up and waits. Doesn't like going too far. He wants a quick exit back to his base. Either careful, or just lazy."

MJ interrupted. "Did you say Tita Ali is working out of a Russian camp, or Tita Ali actually is Russian?"

"He is Russian," Daryan told her.

Whoa. This story was getting better by the minute. The occasional dogfight between fighter planes over a disputed border, that was one thing. But Russia sending out a sniper with specific orders to kill American troops?!

"It's a theory," Jensen said quickly. "He's in Syrian uniform."

Daryan ignored him, continuing with her questions. "Always he uses the Lobaev?" she asked.

"Yes. Or at least, always a weapon firing 10.36mm. I'm the one identified it as a Lobaev, but I'm pretty sure…"

She cut him off. "Why have you not already called an airstrike on that Russian camp?"

"We … it's a delicate situation," Jensen told her. "First, we hadn't confirmed it was a Russian camp. The Syrian uniforms, it looked just like another small outpost, not a real attractive target. There are civilians there. A field hospital…"

"Fake," she said. "And the civilians are human shields. If they are collaborating with the Russians, they know the risk."

"You say," Jensen said carefully. "We would need to confirm it. Plus it isn't certain we'd be given the all-clear to call a strike on a Russian military camp. So far, we've avoided targeting Russian-only positions in this conflict, and they've avoided targeting ours – like this outpost, for example."

Daryan gave him a withering gaze. "What kind of war is this, where America and Russia leave each other alone in Kobani, but in the skies you are shooting at each other with missiles?"

"There's a line," Jensen said. "It's dynamic. At Gaziantep and Incirlik, the war is between Turkey and Syria, not Russia and America. We are not directly engaged in fighting each other…"

A sonic boom sounded overhead as an aircraft flew over them. Dust or paint fell from the ceiling. Daryan looked up. "I make a bet that aircraft was Russian. I also make a bet that if it ran into an American fighter up there, it would be 'directly engaged'."

"Yes, but there's … conflict in the air is not the same as conflict on the ground," Jensen told her.

"Because on the ground, more people die, soldiers and civilians die," Daryan said. "Syrians die, Turks die, Kurds die. But Americans and Russians are not supposed to die?"

"That's not what I am saying."

"This Russian sniper, your Tita Ali, he is killing Americans. Only Americans," Daryan pointed out. "There have been no Kurds killed by a sniper using 10.36mm ammunition."

"Hiding behind the Lobaev, trying to appear Syrian," Jensen said. "We didn't know he was Spetsnaz, that changes the dynamic."

"Moves your invisible line," Daryan said. "But not enough for you to bomb the Russian camp."

"No," Jensen said. MJ agreed with his judgment on that. US forces call an airstrike on a camp full of Russians and Kurdish civilians? Never happen. Or, not yet.

"Do you have paper?" Daryan asked.

MJ did, of course. She pulled a notepad and pen from a trouser pocket. "Use this."

Daryan drew a rough map. "This is Kunyan Kurdan hill, the Russian camp, our lines here, the Russian lines. We are here, south. The three tracks leading down from Kunyan Kurdan are here, here, and ... here." She drew three lines down from the hill, two to the northeast and northwest, and one to the south. "They are cut into the hill, which is why I need height. From your tower, I can cover the track facing us on the southern slope. The other two would be more dangerous for him, since they are more exposed and our militia has riflemen on the roofs overlooking those tracks, shooting at anything that moves."

Jensen looked at the map. "So he's been coming in and out of that camp, right where we can see him, the whole time?"

"You thought he was Syrian, not Russian," Daryan said. "And you had no idea what he looked like. Finally, you have never shot into that camp from here. He thinks he is safe there."

Jensen put two fingers down, one on each of the northern tracks. "Knowing where this guy operates out of is half the fight. I'll pull some satellite imagery, but I'm pretty sure I can get the dogs into position to watch these two tracks at the back of the hill. Maybe even get in ambush range if there's any ground cover, bushes, that kind of thing. So you just have to cover the southern route facing us."

MJ drew a line on the notepad page with her finger, between COP Meyer and the Russian outpost. She knew Kunyan Kurdan hill. It had to be a couple of thousand yards out. "You plan to shoot at this guy from inside this outpost, that bullet is going to be in flight, what ... five seconds or more?"

"Three," Daryan told her. "If he is moving, I shoot where he is going to be, not where he is."

"That *sounds* clever," MJ told her. "But if you miss, he knows you're onto him. He'll just move base, change his routines and you're back to zero."

"I will not miss," Daryan told her.

MJ looked at her skeptically.

"Way I see it," Jensen told her, standing up, "this doesn't work, we're no worse off than we are today. I tell the CO we're getting intel on a Russian camp, he'll sign off on it for sure."

Daryan stayed sitting, looking at Jensen.

He motioned to her to stand too. "Well, come on, we need to print you a tailor-made shooting tripod."

YEVGENY Bondarev had made it to a ditch that ran alongside the motorway and limped at a crouch in the direction of the Syrian advance. His ankle wasn't broken, but it was swelling. He needed a ride. The ditch led him to a dirt service road that ran parallel to the motorway and he lay in long grass, watching for traffic, and was rewarded a few minutes later when a small 50cc motorbike came puttering up the road toward him. Just before it drew level, he stood up and stepped out onto the road, right in its path.

The surprised rider tried to swerve around him, lost control of the bike and hit the grass verge, going over the handlebars. He hadn't been wearing a helmet, and as Bondarev jogged over to him, *Grach* pistol at the ready in case he wanted to start an argument, he saw that the man was lying still in the grass, either unconscious or dead.

The bike, however, was still running. Bondarev searched the man's pocket for keys, found them and a telephone, and righted the bike. The front wheel was a little bent, but it was still rideable.

He considered the telephone. Calls to his unit at Latakia from Turkish numbers would be blocked, but if the phone had international dialing enabled, he might be able to get through to a number in Russia and let his unit know he was safe. He turned it on, but it was locked with a code. He shook his head. In action movies, no one locked their telephones, but of course here in rural Turkey everyone did. He threw it away in frustration.

His only option was to find friendly troops and get to a Syrian airfield where he could be picked up.

He got onto the bike and, feeling a little foolish, gunned the motor and took off toward the east at a blistering twenty-four miles an hour.

MEANY and King's *Perdix* drone attack on the Mamayd command center of 138th Mechanized Division had several consequences. It had resulted in a large number of casualties which the Syrian commander, Colonel Imad Ayyoub, had either to bury or evacuate to Aleppo. It provoked the use of a large amount of ordnance for no military gain, shelling the city of Kobani to satisfy the desire of his officers for some measure of revenge. It had also resulted in a long and uncomfortable lecture that night from the commander of the northern front, General Saheli Omran, about the inadequacy of his air defense preparations.

And the commander of the northern front was apparently not finished with him.

"General Omran on comms for you again, Colonel," Ayyoub's adjutant said, breaking into Ayyoub's daily logistics briefing. Ayyoub stood and excused himself. This was not going to be a call he wanted to take in front of his officers. He had a feeling Omran had slept on their conversation of the night before and decided on a new fate for Ayyoub more suited to his talents. Commander of some backwater military prison perhaps.

"Greetings, General," Ayyoub said, sitting at the desk in his office and taking up the handset there.

"Greetings, Colonel," the General replied. "How is the situation there today, Ayyoub?"

"We have evacuated all the wounded to Aleppo. Total casualties were thirty-two dead and about double that number wounded. We have recovered one of the enemy drones intact and have sent it to Damascus for analysis. There is a full report on its way to you, General."

"Good. I am bringing in someone else to take over the 138th and the siege of Kobani, Ayyoub," the General said.

His heart sank. *Here it comes.* "Yes, General."

"The action to neutralize Incirlik is ahead of schedule. *Tiger Force* is less than ten miles from the air base and meeting only light Turkish resistance. I anticipate achieving control of the airfield within the next twenty-four hours."

"That is excellent news, General," Ayyoub said carefully.

"Yes. With Incirlik out of play, the northern front will be secure. Our western adversaries will not be able to use the base to land ground forces and launch a major offensive against us from the north without significant forewarning." The General cleared his throat. "So with our Turkish objectives all but achieved, it is time to prepare for the second phase of the operation."

Ayyoub frowned. He still had not been officially briefed on this 'second phase'. "General, may I ask, what is the objective of the 'second phase'?"

"You will be indoctrinated into the details in good time, but not now. For now, you will fly to Damascus and take command of the 4th Armored Republic Guards battalion, effective next week. I don't mind telling you it is a shambles, but we will need it for the coming operation."

Not a prison command then. But a poisoned chalice nonetheless. Though it had modern equipment, the 4th had not had the benefit of Russian training. It was a 'showpiece' unit that had spent most of the recent civil war inside its base outside Damascus or parading through the streets for the benefit of television cameras. It was known to be riven with inefficiency, nepotism and outright incompetence. If thrown into combat tomorrow, it would be decimated. And unless he could turn it around, it was a command sure to get him killed.

"I am deeply honored, General," Ayyoub lied. "How long do I have to get the 4th into shape for the coming operation?"

"We have not decided on our final timetable for phase 2. But I will be flying into Damascus in one month to inspect the 4th Guards, and you will be expected to demonstrate to me that it is combat ready."

Ayyoub put the handset against his chest to muffle his curse, then lifted it again. That sounded like a definite timetable to him. "It will be ready, General Omran."

"One more thing," the General said. "At the request of our Russian allies we have tolerated the continued presence of the American outpost inside Kobani in order to avoid an escalation of the US engagement in our conflict with Turkey. That gesture has been ignored by the western Coalition. As yesterday's attack at Mamayd demonstrated, they have no compulsion about deploying weapons intended to cause mass casualties among our troops. Their aircraft are now aggressively targeting Russian defensive patrols inside the Syrian no-fly zone. And we have received intelligence that the Americans have landed several battalions of ground troops and armor at Konya, intended to prevent us from taking or holding Incirlik."

"American ground troops? In Turkey?"

"They are calling themselves a NATO force, but yes, troops from their 1st Armored Division. They have moved too late. Incirlik will be ours by the time they are able to deploy them. But that leads me to the US force at Kobani. Restraint is no longer needed. Before you depart for Damascus, you will eliminate the US outpost at Kobani."

Ayyoub swallowed. He had barely enough troops to maintain the siege of the Kurdish militia inside Kobani. His predecessor had failed to take the heights of Mishte-nur despite a three-day assault backed by armor and artillery. Yes, the US Marine and Kurdish force on the heights had been stronger then, but they were well entrenched now and still able to call on air support. Which *he* would desperately need if he was to have a hope of carrying out the order.

"Yes, General. Will Russian close air support be available?"

"No. There are no air-attack assets currently available for such a low-priority task. But I have diverted a battery of mobile artillery to Mamayd. *Sunburn* multiple rocket launchers – they should be with you by tonight. They will be attached to the 154th Artillery Regiment and placed under your command." Ayyoub heard someone in the background call on Omran. "That's all, get it done and get to Damascus, Ayyoub. Long live the Arab Ba'ath."

"Long live the Arab Ba'ath," Ayyoub replied automatically, cutting the call. *Damn.*

There was a knock on his door and his adjutant put his head into the room, but Ayyoub waved him away. He sat in his ruined office with his boots up on the old desk, staring at the peeling and cracked ceiling that was all that stood between him and a Coalition bomb. A quick death that might be preferable to what was to come. But he furrowed his brows, steepled his fingers under his chin and soon had the outlines of a passable strategy ready to present to his junior officers.

Despite the recent Coalition attack, he still had a platoon of *Terminator* infantry fighting vehicles, several thousand men and the *Podnos* 82mm mortars of the 154th Artillery, soon to be reinforced by a battery of two *Sunburn* 220mm rocket launchers. The *Sunburn* was a multiple-barreled beast built on a T-72 tank chassis that could fire twenty-four thermobaric rockets at a target up to six miles away inside ten seconds. It was specifically designed to kill troops inside buildings and above ground by flooding the air around them with a mist of fuel and then setting it on fire, either burning them alive or sucking the oxygen from the air around them.

His strategy for taking the American outpost atop Mishte-nur Hill would be very simple. He would initiate a decoy attack on the main gates of the outpost with scout infantry. The Americans would flood out of their bunker to defend the outpost, and he would roast them alive with his *Sunburn* rockets or suffocate them in their tunnels. He'd send another force to the bunker exit at the base of the hill to be sure no Americans got out to flank him that way. Finally, a company of his best troops would storm the summit of Mishte-nur under covering fire from the 30mm autocannons on his platoon of *Terminator* tanks and make short work of any Americans left overground at COP Meyer. By the time any of the surviving Americans underground tried to emerge, the summit would be his. Thankfully, he had not been asked to take prisoners. With control of the bunker entrances, he could flood them with poison gas if needed.

CLIMBING west out of Incirlik in her F-35 *Panther*, Bunny O'Hare was in a take-no-prisoners mood. As they'd set themselves for a fast ascent to twenty thousand feet, she'd seen smoke from the clash between Turkish and Syrian troops to the east and been shocked at how close it was. Ten miles? It looked closer to five.

She thought of the 3 Squadron techs, engineers and ground support staff she'd left on the ground at Incirlik, desperately turning recently returned fighters around so that they could flee for Cyprus, not sure whether they'd be able to get on a transport and get out of Incirlik themselves before the Syrians arrived. She thought of the US Army *HELLADS* Sergeant she'd spoken with the day before. They had momentarily lost contact with Incirlik Air Traffic Control as they'd made their egress, and when they came back they were reporting a base-wide power and comms outage. Their *Panthers* too were registering heavy jamming, probably from Russian *Belladonna* mobile electronic warfare units traveling with the advancing Syrian armor. They could cause headaches for airborne warning aircraft from two hundred miles away; at a range of ten miles from Incirlik they were probably putting out enough radiation to cause cancer. It didn't affect her and Red's own systems, but it made her worry for the drones and anti-air units down below that were protecting her rear.

Electronic warfare attacks alone shouldn't be able to bring down BATS drones. They were designed to go autonomous if their comms were knocked out, though their radar would have trouble picking up targets as they flicked from frequency to frequency trying to shake off the effect of the Russian jamming. But the US anti-air shield – its *HELLADs*, *Centurion* and *Patriot* batteries – would be blinded. She found herself mentally crossing her fingers the dour US Army Sergeant she had met would be alright.

"Sunset two, Sunset leader. Threat board is clear. Leveling out, coming around to zero four zero. Initializing *Gray Wolf*. Boot 'em up, O'Hare."

"Yes, sir. Booting." She reached forward to her ordnance management screen and tapped a sequence of commands to arm the small cruise missiles hanging on hardpoints both outside and inside her aircraft. On by one the icons for the missiles went green. Except one.

"Showing boot failure on one of my inboard *Wolves*. Repeating boot sequence," she reported. She went through the boot sequence again, but the icon stayed stubbornly red. It could be a comms failure on an otherwise good missile, or the missile itself could be dead, she had no way of knowing. "No good, sir, only five good boots."

"I've got six green. We'll go with what we've got," Red ordered. "Initiating Horde mode."

The *Gray Wolf* missiles were designed to work as a swarm, or in *Gray Wolf* parlance, a 'golden horde'. They were programmed with dozens of attack algorithms in an onboard playbook so that as the horde of missiles approached their targets, much like human pilots would do, they identified targets and threats, allocated them among themselves and chose their attack vector based on the dynamics of the environment they found themselves in. Launching into an environment in which enemy electronic warfare was jamming their communications? They had line-of-sight laser communications to allow them to work around that. Dealing with electronic warfare was just another play in the horde playbook.

O'Hare flicked her eyes between the ordnance screen, the skies, her instruments, Red's aircraft and back to the ordnance screen, satisfied as the screen showed solid links between her cruise missiles and Red's. "Horde handshake confirmed," she reported.

"Quarterback, this is Sunset leader, we are ready to launch greyhounds, please confirm," Red said tightly. All he got back was static. He had to repeat the request twice before he got a reply.

"… leader from Quarterback … are cleared to commit. Happy hunting," the controller said. Bunny had never experienced such heavy interference before.

"Launching in three … two …" Red began to intone. Bunny closed her finger on the weapons release trigger. They didn't have to pick targets. The missiles had been programmed with their targets before takeoff and the coordinates updated in real time as they climbed out. They would fly themselves to the Turkish-Syrian front line and then pick out their own targets – Syrian trucks, troop concentrations and light armor. Turkish troops and vehicles were equipped with Identify Friend or Foe signaling beacons, IFF, so the *Gray Wolf* missiles would know who was who in the inevitable chaos of the battle below. But Bunny knew from training with the system that it was far from infallible.

A rain of fire was about to break over the heads of the Syrian troops, and anyone nearby could find themselves without an umbrella.

"Launch, launch, launch…" Red ordered. "*Wolves* away."

O'Hare's finger twitched on the trigger and the first pair of cruise missiles dropped from their hardpoints, fell twenty feet through the air unpowered, and then ignited their jet turbine engines. As they speared away ahead of her, O'Hare felt the next two drop off her wings and follow after them. *OK then*, she thought to herself, waiting for the last missiles to drop out of her internal payload bay. *Do I have a dud in the hold, or was it just comms error?*

Only one more missile dropped and fired its engine, trailing along behind the others like a forgotten duckling.

"Five away, one missile failure," she confirmed. In front of her the contrails of eleven missiles streaked east.

"You can dump it over the Med on the way to Cyprus," Red told her. "Come around to one eight zero and follow me over." With that he banked to starboard.

Bunny checked her tactical display. Despite the Russian jamming, the Turkish Air Force *Peace Eagle* airborne warning aircraft 160 miles away over Konya air base, together with Turkey's own S-band and L-band radar network, might still be able to pick up returns from Russian stealth aircraft, if not provide a definite position. She was seeing multiple returns in the sector five to twenty miles out from Incirlik, which made sense if the Russian stealth fighters were providing close air support for Syrian troops.

Despite turning to follow him, O'Hare couldn't help herself. "Sir, we still have four air-to-air missiles and a full belt of 25mm cannon shells," she protested. "If we close on the Syrian advance, we might be able to get a solid return on the Russian air support…"

"You have four missiles and you'll still have four missiles when you land, O'Hare," Red told her. "This mission was not air-to-air, it was air-to-ground and you have successfully executed it. Those cruise missiles do not need us riding shotgun. Our orders now are to retire to RAF Akrotiri and regroup, and that, Flying Officer O'Hare, is what we shall do."

"We still have people on the ground at Incirlik!" she protested.

"Who will be on the next transport west bound for Konya, as soon as our remaining aircraft are refueled and airborne. So cut the damn chatter and do your bloody job, O'Hare. Out."

Do my bloody job? I thought my bloody job was to stop the bloody enemy from overrunning my bloody airfield, Bunny thought, fuming. *Which they certainly bloody will do if we do not do something about their Russian air cover.*

Think, O'Hare. She looked around the skies for inspiration, and then down at her multifunction displays. The malfunctioning missile was still blinking red on her ordnance screen, but she had amber lights across the board for all of her air-to-air missiles, which she could arm with the touch of an icon.

Don't do it, O'Hare, she told herself. She took her hands off her throttle and stick, as though they were about to act of their own free will. *Do. Not. Do. It.*

"The hell with it," she decided. Pulling her control stick left she slid to port and pointed her fighter back toward the north and Incirlik. It took Red a few seconds to react, but when he did, he didn't hide his temper.

"What in bloody hell do you think you are doing, O'Hare?" he asked. "Rejoin formation immediately!"

She ignored him, shut down her comms link to the other *Panther* and instead opened a channel to the Turkish Air Force *Peace Eagle* AWACS. "Turkish Quarterback, this is RAAF 3 Squadron F-35 Sunset two, currently on bearing zero zero nine, twenty thousand feet for sector ... Golf four. Available for air-to-air tasking."

She didn't have to ask twice. Coalition air operations planning officers may have decided caution was the best response to the approaching Syrian armor, but their Turkish counterparts were fighting a foreign enemy on home soil and it was their soldiers who were doing the dying.

"F-35 Sunset two, confirm you are available for tasking. Please proceed on bearing zero two two, angels twenty to grid sector gamma zero six and engage hostile attack aircraft in the area of Goztepe township. Commit."

She shot a quick look at her nav screen. Gamma zero six ... Goztepe? That must have been the smoke she saw taking off. Her stomach dropped as she calculated the distance from Incirlik.

"Good copy, Quarterback, Sunset two proceeding zero two two, angels twenty, grid sector gamma zero six, out."

As she looked up and around her again, she saw Red's aircraft slide onto her starboard wing, just fifty feet away. He was gesticulating wildly. She felt like gesticulating back at him, but instead focused on setting herself up for the possible engagement ahead.

Despite the Russian jamming, her threat warning system was pulling data from a battle net comprising multiple ground and air radars, and satellites with optical, infrared and motion detecting sensors. It was showing possible returns on two Russian fast movers, and another two more solid returns on rotary aircraft, probably Syrian helicopter gunships. The rotary aircraft were already in range of her missiles, but less of a threat as they were probably also being tracked by the Incirlik *Patriot* defenses. She couldn't see missiles flying, but with the amount of radiation Russia was pouring into the airspace, it was a miracle she could see anything at all, and didn't even bother engaging her own phased-array radar, deciding instead to rely on electro-optical sensors to find and lock any Russian last-gen or stealth aircraft in the area.

Glancing over at Red's *Panther*, she saw he was still trying to get her attention, rocking his wings in the universal gesture for 'back to where you were'. She tapped her helmet over the ear area, indicating comms difficulties, then continued steadfastly to ignore him. If he followed her into combat, all the better. If he broke off and left her alone, that was fine by her too.

She pulled up her DAS sensor screen and started working the Russian fighter contacts over Goztepe. If they were supporting the lead elements of the Syrian advance, then she was already late to the party. Goztepe was less than three miles from Incirlik.

THE front lines of a war were like a fire front in a forest fire, Bondarev reflected. As it bore down, you could try to hide from the flames, or drive like hell to get on the other side of it. Either choice could get you killed. As he crouched behind a low farm wall and watched the battle unfolding in front of him, he glanced across at the moped he had stolen and had to acknowledge that breaking through the Turkish defensive line at speed was not going to be an option.

The service road he had been following had led him to an olive grove outside a small town called Goztepe. Turkish combat engineers had recently blown the overpass that took the service road over the motorway, dropping hundreds of tons of concrete onto the motorway to block the path of the advancing Syrian force. He had heard it before he saw it; there was still a plume of brown smoke and concrete dust rising into the air. Their intent was clear – to force the Syrian vehicles off the motorway and onto dirt roads that offered a less direct route to Incirlik.

To the north of the motorway, Bondarev could see a company-sized formation of Turkish troops dug in around a small farmhouse, backed by a solitary wheeled 6x6 *PARS* armored combat vehicle, armed with anti-tank guided missiles and a 7.62mm coaxial machine gun. The troops were almost certainly also armed with American TOW anti-tank missiles.

To the south, the service road entered the main intersection going in to Goztepe where another company of Turkish troops was dug in, spread between farm buildings on one side of the intersection and an olive grove on the other. The main value of this position was that it looked down on the motorway, offering an unobstructed field of fire. Which explained why Turkey had chosen to position two ancient *Leopard* 1T tanks, hulls down, behind the rise.

But still, it was a paltry force that could do no more than delay the Syrian advance.

Invisible from the motorway, the tanks were not invisible from the air, and as Bondarev watched, a Syrian Mil-25 helicopter gunship inched down the motorway toward the Turkish positions. He admired the pilot's use of the terrain – any higher and he might get swatted by *Patriot* missiles fired from batteries around Incirlik, any lower and he'd be plowing the farmers' fields for them. He could probably see the Turkish tanks on infrared – both had their engines idling – but to get a shot at them with rockets or anti-tank missiles he would have to pop up at some point and gain altitude to fire.

He was apparently ahead of the main force of Syrian scouts and armor, though, because the pilot flared his machine five hundred yards back from the Turkish positions and hovered behind a line of trees. He was no doubt warning the troops behind him about the reception waiting ahead. Bondarev looked at the situation with a tactician's eye. The Syrian commander had several options. He had made dramatic gains during the last 24 hours, cleverly flanking Turkish defenses across the Ceyhan River by leaving the motorway and detouring south, crossing the river at the small, lightly defended town of Yakapinar before rejoining the motorway and moving west again.

That much Bondarev had been aware of before he'd jettisoned from his aircraft east of Incirlik. The Turkish force at the bridge over the Ceyhan River had apparently withdrawn and now Bondarev knew where they had chosen to make their stand.

The Syrian supply lines between here and Gaziantep were no doubt stretched tightly now, its armor having moved faster than expected. A concerted counter-attack south from Gaziantep by Turkish forces could cut that supply line, but Bondarev doubted the pressed Turkish army had the resources for a counter-attack. Nonetheless, the Syrian commander could decide to consolidate his gains and shore up his flank, holding outside Goztepe before a final push on Incirlik.

He could also choose to detour around the Turkish defenses again, going north or south around Goztepe ... but to the north was rough, hilly terrain, and to the south a large conurbation that would see him having to fight house to house before breaking out.

The more attractive choice was to call in air or artillery support, then fight through the Turkish positions and back onto the motorway, driving straight at the heart of Incirlik on four-lane asphalt. With American troops reportedly on the way, that was what Bondarev would do. Every second wasted at Goztepe was a second more that Turkey and the US could use to strengthen their defenses around the air base.

To the east he heard the rumble of vehicles and saw several staggered columns of Syrian tanks, armored combat vehicles and trucks inch into view. Overhead he could hear, but not see, jet aircraft circling. Russian or Coalition, he could not tell. It was a strangely surreal feeling, sitting at the base of an olive tree overlooking the battlefield. He felt like a spectator at a deadly game of football. The feeling only intensified as the sound of the overhead aircraft coalesced into a single, ominous roar. But from where? Called in by whom? He swiveled his head, straining his ears.

Then he saw it, a dart-shaped drone, boring in from the south. *Okhotnik*! But judging by its ingress height and speed it was not attacking the Turkish positions. A combat air patrol? Or just a reconnaissance overflight? It stayed high and did not engage the Turkish troops below.

Recon flight. And compounding the impotence of the display, the fool sitting safely in his trailer at the controls of the *Okhotnik* drone in Latakia decided he would engage in a little display of aerial showmanship once he had made his pass. At the end of his run he pulled his machine into a corkscrewing vertical climb, sending it thousands of feet straight up into the clouds above.

Idiot.

Bondarev turned his eyes back to the farmhouse north of the motorway, where the Turkish troops were building barricades of machinery and stone taken from a nearby fence. He also saw the Turkish PARS armored car backing into a position in a defile from where it could provide cover fire without exposing itself. He was reflecting on the fact these were not novice troops when from the east he heard the whine of jet engines and a swarm of low-flying subsonic cruise missiles flew along the motorway toward the Syrian troop columns to the west.

He tried to count them. *Eight ... ten ...* maybe more?

They were shorter than the ubiquitous ship-launched American *Tomahawk* missiles, and the direction of travel, though of course it could have been programmed to deceive, seemed to indicate an air launch, not a sea launch.

Swarm? Could they be *Gray Wolves*?

He held his breath.

BUNNY heard a low-pitched tone in her ears and an icon flashed on her threat warning screen. Target! *Okhotnik. Confirmed.* It had broken out of the clouds about ten miles ahead and been immediately locked by her Distributed Aperture camera system.

Freaking *way*.

She looked over her starboard wing to check the other *Panther* was still with her and flipped her comms channel to 'Red' Burgundy open again.

"Sunset leader, Sunset two, I have a target on DAS, bearing three five five, altitude ten thousand, engaging with CUDAs," she said, locking the Russian drone up and allocating two missiles to it.

She had expected Burgundy to explode into a string of expletives, but the voice that came back was cold and calm. "I have it too, Sunset two. Hold your fire…"

"Sir! I am going to engage, and you can…"

"Shut the hell up for *once* in your life, O'Hare," Red said in an almost pleading voice. "*Okhotniks* hunt in packs. Where there is one, there will be more, we just can't see them yet."

"So … what are you saying, sir?"

"We fall well back on this drone's six. He's going to lead us to the others, and then we take them all on. That alright with you, Flying Officer?"

"Yes sir!" O'Hare said, settling behind her controls.

Side by side, a mile apart and in total silence, the two *Panthers* sliced through the air twenty miles behind the Russian drone, just inside DAS range. It led them south into Syrian airspace, where a second and then a third *Okhotnik* joined it. They had a problem now, as the possibility of detection by the drones and anti-air radar inside Syria increased exponentially.

O'Hare was about to explode. "That could be all, sir," she said as the Russian formation turned south at about five thousand feet, toward Syrian airspace. "Three's a crowd, right?"

Red came back straight away. "Ivan flies these guys in flights of four. Always four. There's still one out there … oh *hell no*."

Bunny's threat warning chimed at exactly the moment Red cursed. Her DAS had picked up the last *Okhotnik*. Two miles below, and four miles *behind* them. Before she could react, her radar warning receiver began warbling as the Russian unmanned fighter engaged active radar and tried to lock up the Coalition *Panthers*. The aircraft it locked was Bunny's. She immediately rolled her machine onto its back and pulled into a vertical dive.

"Fox 3, Fox 3!" Red called, unloading his full complement of missiles at the three drones in front of him.

It was inconsequential to O'Hare now. She had a bat-winged hell hound on her tail that could pull maneuvers no human could possibly match. But she had help … her combat AI kept a fix on the position of the enemy aircraft, calculated the best maneuver and flight path for her to avoid a missile or guns lock, and projected cues on her visor. Reacting with a speed only possible because her life depended on it, she responded to the cues instantly, flinging her aircraft around the sky with seemingly random abandon. At the same time, she was thinking at the speed of light. *No missile warning. It should have had a missile solution by now. So it was guns only? A recon bird.* She grunted as the cue on her visor went from hard port high to hard starboard low and rolled her machine into a spinning inverted dive. *Guns only. Only guns. There's a solution here, O'Hare, think!*

She vaguely registered a target lock tone in her ears. Her finger twitched on her missile trigger before she even consciously registered it, and a CUDA missile leapt from her *Panther*'s belly as one of the *Okhotniks* Red had fired on flashed across her nose. It had dodged Red's attack, but she hit it point blank. Her missile detonated almost immediately and she saw the *Okhotnik* disappear in a blinding flash even as she reversed her current maneuver and pointed her nose at the ground, the Russian machine behind her following her effortlessly down.

"I've got your six, O'Hare," she heard Red say. "When I call it, you break high on fire. Alright?"

"Good copy."

"Get ready… *break*!"

Her AI cue was telling her to do the opposite. But she drew a big breath, braced both her legs, shoved her throttle forward and pulled her stick hard back.

The g-force slammed her head back and her flight suit inflated as she went from diving vertically at the earth to screaming vertically into the sky in the space of a second. Blood fled from her brain and she grayed out. She barely heard through the fog of near unconsciousness as Red called out. "Splash! Bandit down. Level out, level out!" She was still riding into the upper atmosphere on a tail of flame. Burning precious fuel, she took long seconds to shake off the fugue in her brain. With the barest twitch of her hand she managed to roll the *Panther* onto its side and take off some of the g-force. Gradually, feeling returning to her extremities, she regained situational awareness and rolled level.

Fifty thousand feet. She shook her head and dialed up her oxygen to clear her mind. She could actually see the curvature of the earth. Well, that was a personal record.

"You having fun up there in space, O'Hare?" Red asked. She checked her tactical display and saw he was still 'down' at twenty thousand feet.

She tried speaking and nearly threw up. Gathering herself, she managed a single word. "Rejoining."

She gently spiraled down to where Red was maintaining a leisurely racetrack path through the sky and joined on his port wing. She checked her threat display and saw it was clear. No system warnings either. She was alive, and so was her kite. Freaking miracle.

"Alright there, Flying Officer?" Red asked, looking over at her as she flew up alongside him.

"Not even close, sir," she replied. "But thanks for the assist."

"Day's work," he said. "Congratulations. Your second individual kill, I believe."

"It was? I did?"

O'Hare checked her ordnance screen. Three missiles? She'd fired a missile? The last few minutes flashed back through her mind. She honestly could not remember. She frowned. "Sorry, what?"

"And three to me. Drones, but still, my first combat victories."

"Well done, Red. Sir."

"Not how I wanted to do it, O'Hare," he told her. "Disobeying orders."

"No sir."

"When you are fully rested and refreshed, O'Hare, if it is entirely acceptable to you, we will bugger off for Cyprus."

O'Hare ran a quick check of her own heartbeat, breathing, and general mental state. Yeah, she was on her way back. Then she flipped through her instrument readout screens, double checking she'd really come through the dogfight without damage. She had. But not without issues. She punched some numbers into her navigation computer.

"Uh, sorry sir, that's negative," she told Red. "My fuel is at 11 percent after that SpaceX maneuver I pulled back there. I can't make Akrotiri." She wasn't lying this time, it was a simple fact. The *Panther* was a formidable fighter, but it had relatively short legs.

"Dammit, O'Hare!"

"Have to put down at Incirlik, sir," she told him. "Might be able to make it to Konya, but I'd be on fumes."

There was a moment of silence, the two of them flying side by side twenty thousand feet above the war below. "Alright, Sunset two, you are to proceed directly to Incirlik to refuel. And only to refuel. You will turn your machine around in record time and be back in the air again, bound for RAF Akrotiri *post haste*, is that clear?"

"Yes, sir."

"Farksake, O'Hare."

"Yes, sir."

He gave a visual signal to break and rolled away, pointing his *Panther* south, reporting their status to the AWACS as he did so.

Bunny set a nav point for Incirlik and saw it was now twenty miles northwest. She also couldn't help noticing she still had three CUDA missiles in her weapons bay.

Yes, she would proceed directly to the Turkish air base to refuel.

But if she should spot a suitable target on the way…

O'HARE and Burgundy's *Gray Wolf* cruise missiles were also on the lookout for suitable targets. Having overflown Yevgeny Bondarev, they followed the curve of the motorway southeast past Goztepe to where the satellite data they had pulled down fifteen minutes earlier indicated the spearhead of the Syrian 25th Special Missions Division should be.

The closer they got to the Syrian columns, though, the stronger the jamming they faced from the Syrian truck-mounted *Belladonna* electronic warfare units trailing the convoys. Two miles out from their targets, they lost contact with each other and went from being a horde of eleven missiles to eleven 'lone wolves'.

Each of them analyzed the target data they'd received, matched it with the images flowing into the lenses of the electro-optical and infrared sensors in their nose cones, and chose the play from their internal playbook that matched the rapidly evolving scenario ahead of them. Which was the reason they flew in train, in a single two-mile-long snaking line, and not clustered together.

Each missile carried twelve armor-piercing submunitions. The first *Gray Wolf* reached the Syrian vehicles a hundred feet over the top of the *Terminator* infantry fighting vehicles at the front of the column and over the heavily armored T-90s, scattering its small infrared and acoustic-guided bomblets as it passed. Each bomblet picked a truck or armored car and steered for it. The missile itself dropped its nose toward a fuel truck at the rear of the convoy. A ripple of detonations from its submunitions preceded its plunge into the cabin of the fuel truck, triggering a massive fireball that consumed the two trucks beside it too.

Reacting instantly to the destruction in front of it, the second *Gray Wolf* veered right, choosing a different group of vehicles, with much the same effect. And so it went, each of the cruise missiles behind watching what the one in front of it did, adjusting its flight path and terminal target accordingly so that none of the missiles struck the same target twice, and they spread their strike across the depth and breadth of the Syrian force.

MILES away and standing up so that he could see, Bondarev drew a sharp breath. The series of booming reports that rolled back across the landscape from the missile strikes sounded like someone beating a heavy drum. As bad as the dozens of smaller explosions had been, worse was the sound of secondary explosions, as fuel and ammunition cooked off, sending gouts of flame and sparks into the air, frighteningly bright even in the afternoon sun. The secondary explosions indicated the missiles had found their targets.

From down in the Turkish positions, he heard cheering and saw men jumping in the air, fists waving at the skies, some even firing their guns into the air.

Fools, he thought. *We men are such fools.*

From the small hillside on which he stood, he probably had a better view of the Syrian force that was still approaching, so he could forgive them that. Because yes, the Coalition cruise missile strike had certainly wreaked havoc among the advancing

Syrian columns, the boiling pyres of black and red smoke now rising into the sky attested to that.

But emerging from the smoke and destruction, the remaining T-90 tanks and armored fighting vehicles of Syria's most disciplined and experienced shock troops still rolled forward. He watched carefully over the course of the next twenty minutes, counting at least twenty main battle tanks behind a similar number of missile and cannon-armed wheeled or tracked vehicles.

In a very short time, they would reach the shattered overpass outside Goztepe, a terrible violence would ensue, and the cheering of the Turkish troops would be replaced with silence.

IT was approaching 1500 on 3 April 2030.

Marine Gunner James Jensen was in the engineering shop under the summit of COP Meyer, explaining to a bemused Kurdish sniper that although they did not happen to have a Lobaev standing rifle tripod in their inventory, they could download the plans for one and print it for her on their 3D manufacturing unit.

Colonel Imad Ayyoub had just briefed the commander of the newly arrived *Sunburn* battery that there would barely be enough time for his men to rest and eat, as the attack on Mishte-nur Hill was scheduled to begin with an intensive 82mm mortar barrage closely followed by a volley of 220mm thermobaric missiles from his launchers, in exactly ten hours' time.

Flying Officer Bunny O'Hare was flying a very non-direct course for Incirlik, scanning the skies and praying for a stray Russian aircraft to cross her path during her ingress. At the same time, Meany Papastopoulos was also turning back for Incirlik. The RAF ground crews still there were specialists at rearming and refueling their aircraft so that they could be turned around and sent up again within thirty minutes of landing, and their skills were about to be put to the test as they tried to get their aircraft headed for Akrotiri before the Syrian armored storm hit.

Lieutenant Ted Sun and his crew had their eyes glued to the screens in front of them, but their ears were attuned to the faint sounds of explosions outside their *HELLADS* command truck that told them war could soon be upon them. All the while wondering how it could take so damn long to unload a few thousand troops from the US 1st Infantry Division and a handful of *Hyperion* unmanned ground combat vehicles and drive them the 170 miles from Konya to Incirlik, *for Chrissakes.*

And in his tent on Kunyan Kurdan hill, sniper instructor Lieutenant Andrei Zakarin of the 45th Spetsnaz Airborne Brigade carefully cleaned the aircraft-aluminum upper receiver of his Lobaev *Twilight* rifle. At nearly fifteen years old, it was the same age as his oldest daughter, but a great deal better behaved. He lifted the anti-flash cover from his Breitling watch and looked at the time. Another two hours. He would have something to eat and then, as dusk approached, head out to hunt. He'd decided that his blind for tonight's ambush would be the roof of the Cardamom Markets, southwest corner. It was nicely located at the northern boundary of the Kurdish line of control, with easy exits to Syrian-held territory. And it gave him a clear line of sight down the city's main crosstown boulevard, across the central square all the way to the 'Angel of Kobani' monument that nearly every American patrol which passed through Kobani paused in front of to take a selfie. They were more careful in daylight since he had started hunting them, but had the ubiquitous carelessness of all youths at night.

A surfeit of ships
Israeli Consulate, Istanbul, 3 April

SHIMI Kahane put his feet up on his desk, took a sip of cold coffee and wiped white dust off his black sneakers. The powder had fallen from the sky as smoke settled from a Russian airstrike on the Fatih Sultan Mehmet bridge over the Bosporus that morning. Not for the first time, he was thankful he lived and worked on the Asian side of the city and didn't need to cross the bridge every day for work – a life or death trip since Russian drone and cruise missile attacks had intensified.

"GAL, run a report on all Russian warship movements in and out of Tartus and Latakia in the last six months, classify by ship class and trend against the same time last year, please," Shimi asked. "Send it to my desktop."

Yes, Shimi. Compiling, the AI replied.

He was looking at his personal messages on his cell phone at the same time and cursed out loud.

Sorry, Shimi, I did not copy that. Were you talking to me? GAL asked.

"No, it's nothing, just that girl I broke up with. She just messaged me, and I'm actually thinking about replying." He put his cell phone down. "I can't believe myself. It's never taken me a week to get over a girl before."

True. You've never taken more than a shower to get over a relationship, Shimi, GAL responded.

Shimi sighed. "Don't tell me, that was from 'Mad Men', right?"

Friends, GAL replied. *You get it?*

"I get it, GAL. Just run the report." It was his own fault, he knew that. Bored, isolated, and to be honest, quite lonely, he shared his life with the AI as though it was his own personal chatbot. He knew somewhere in Unit 8200 there was probably a psychologist looking at the reports of his conversations with GAL and shaking his or her head, but that was fine by him. Get me out of Istanbul and put me in a hospital back home for observation. Please!

Compiling. Shimi, you asked me to alert you to any coordinated multinational fleet movements?

"You got something?" It had been a long shot. He wasn't a cryptanalyst, and neither was GAL. His exploit had given him access to data on the Syrian navy servers at their base, but unless the data was stored using cyphers Unit 8200 had already broken, Shimi couldn't read it, he could only forward it to other units so they could try to crack it open. So far, he was able to read the traffic logs for shipping in and out of the port, comms between civilian ships and the Tartus coast guard, but not military ships, shipping manifests from civilian freighters, or other naval traffic which might refer to military operations.

Yes, Shimi. The message was sent using the coast guard cypher instead of a Syrian navy cypher. Translating. Putting onscreen.

He recognized the original language straight away. It was Iranian Farsi. The short message appeared to be a copy of a communication sent by the Iranian navy to the Syrian navy command at Tartus. Shimi speed-read it.

Jackpot! The title of the assessment was 'Naval Order of Battle for Operation Butterfly'.

Butterfly? He'd never come across that one before. The current Syrian operation inside Turkey appeared most often to be described as Operation Lynx. So what was 'Butterfly'?

An 'order of battle' was usually a summary of the major units allocated to an operation. As his eye ran down the list, his unease grew exponentially.

Cruisers: Slava class, Moskva
Frigates: Grigorovich class, Admiral Makov, Admiral Essen
Corvettes: Karakurt class, Mytischi, Sovetsk

Landing ships: Ropucha class, Korolev
Submarines Russia: Improved Kilo class, Krasnodar, Kolpino
Submarine, Iran: Besat class, Qaaem
Destroyers, Iran: Safineh class, Amol, Sirjan

That was all the message contained. No dates, no other information. Shimi whistled. A good part of Russia's Black Sea fleet seemed to have been allocated to this coming operation, whatever it was. Including a missile cruiser and a landing ship, the Ropucha-class *Korolev*, which Shimi had logged on a previous visit. The *Korolev* was more battleship than landing ship. It was armed with 122mm rocket launchers for ship-to-shore attacks, anti-air missiles to provide air cover, and could carry ten main battle tanks and three hundred plus troops.

What interested him just as much, though, was the inclusion of Iran's newest blue-water destroyers in the order of battle. The two Safineh-class, high-speed trimaran-hull destroyers had only entered service two years earlier, and had not ventured outside the Persian Gulf as far as Shimi was aware. Each had a helicopter landing deck and twenty-four *Khaliber* vertically launched cruise missile cells.

His blood went cold. It was Lebanon, for sure. 'Operation Butterfly' had to be the naval force Russia and Iran was sending to support the Syrian and Hezbollah takeover of Lebanon.

You are very quiet, Shimi, GAL said. *Is there a mistake in my translation or decryption? Or would you like more information on the units listed?*

"Thinking, GAL. In the meantime, prepare this to forward to Urim as a flash priority. Include a background summary of the profile of every ship listed in the order of battle."

Yes, Shimi. Compiling.

Cruisers, frigates, submarines, missile destroyers ... they had put together a task force of no fewer than eleven vessels able to fend off any significant naval threat. It was way out of proportion if Russia, Syria and Iran were expecting to be confronted only by the small corvettes, diesel subs or missile boats of the Israeli navy.

But it was exactly the kind of task force you'd put together if you expected you could be going up against a US Carrier Battle Group.

Report onscreen, Shimi.

Shimi reviewed the report quickly. He wasn't going to context it, it spoke for itself.

"Good. Send it. This is going to blow minds back at Urim, GAL."

Yes, Shimi. Freaking sweet, am I right?

He felt like smacking his head, but it was his own fault. "Was that Bart Simpson?"

'Family Guy'. What is the word?

He was afraid to ask. "I don't know, GAL, what word?"

The Bird is the Word, Shimi. The Bird is the Word.

Sisterly love
COP Meyer, Kobani, Northern Syria, 3 April

"If you weren't going after Tita Ali, I'd have had to ask you to get the CO to sign this off," Chief Warrant Officer Ellis told Jensen as they stood and watched the outpost's 3D printer do its thing. "I'm down to my last 50lbs. of alloy powder."

"I thought you could use all kinds of feedstock," Jensen said. "Polymers, composites, ceramics…"

"And we ran out of all that in the first couple weeks just replacing what you guys keep breaking and wearing out," Ellis complained. "AF-96 powder is good for most of what we need, and I literally had a ton of it, but now even that is running low." He looked around the near-empty storeroom in dismay. "What you see here is what we've got left. We're low on fuel for the generators, we've got about ten days of rations, small-caliber ammunition is alright but we're down to a few dozen rounds for the 82mm and we are desperately short of medical supplies, especially wound care."

Jensen had never met a logistics NCO who didn't moan about the state of the world, but the desperation in Ellis's voice was real.

They'd pulled the plans for Daryan's standing rifle tripod from a website and measured her for it. She'd chosen a Swedish hunting model that featured an eagle head motif on the upper grip, and it was just starting to appear.

MJ was standing off to one side, watching with bemusement. "Any chance you can print me a chopper to fly me out of here?"

"How does it work?" Daryan asked, walking around the printer in wonder. It was a hollow tubular rectangle not unlike an old phone box, nearly head high, with an input screen attached to one support and the robot printing head working away laying down layer after layer of metal and polymer on an adjustable base at the bottom of the box.

Ellis pointed. "Feedstock goes into the ... you know ... feeder," he said. "The printer's lasers melt the powders, spray them onto the build plate into a pattern and repeat over again until your object is complete. Like an ordinary ink printer does in ink for photos, except this one does it with liquid metal and plastics, for objects."

"Any object?" she asked. She pointed to a rifle on a bench. "Like that?"

"Sure, one part at a time," Ellis told her. "Give me the plans or the parts to copy, I can build you a rifle, a drone, or even a rocket engine. Could build you a howitzer if you gave me enough time. And feedstock."

"How about ammunition?" she asked. "Could you make Russian 10.36mm?"

He looked dubious and held out his hand. "Show me." She reached into a pocket on her trouser legs and pulled out a bag, tipping cartridges into her palm and handing him one. He held it up and inspected it. Then whistled. "That's a Russian .408 Chey Tac. Pretty rare. Looks like a 400, maybe 420 grain bullet?"

Daryan nodded.

"I could do the casing and bullets in alloy. The primer looks the same as a standard Russian 7.62mm primer. Might be able to use the gunpowder from a Winchester .300 magnum, maybe the primer too. But more effort than it's worth," he said, handing the cartridge back to her. As he finished speaking, the printer chimed and he opened the safety screen to pull out her tripod. He handed it to her. "No moving parts, but it's the exact height and configuration you ordered, ma'am."

She sat the tripod on the concrete floor in front of her, pulling her Lobaev off her shoulder as she did so. She laid the rifle into the U-shaped receiver at the top of the eagle head and pulled it quickly off again, frowning at the receiver. "I need a file and some duct tape."

Ellis turned to the workbench behind him and found both for her. She quickly filed some edges on the metal receiver head and then wrapped a layer of duct tape around it. She also taped the feet of the tripod to give them better grip. Laying her rifle into the receiver again she nodded in satisfaction. "This will do."

Jensen was looking at her stance with a critical eye. She was using the tripod to hold the forestock of the rifle, but was still gripping the rifle in both hands as she sighted down it. "Uh, can I come with a suggestion?"

"What?"

He stepped up to the tripod, taking her rifle from her. Laying the forestock in the receiver, he kept his right hand around the stock, finger next to the trigger guard, but used his left hand to steady the tripod, gripping it just below the receiver head, his legs spread wide. "Like this? You do it your way, the tripod will jump as you fire and you'll waste time resetting between shots."

She tried his suggestion, nodding. "Yes, alright. But you assume I will need more than one shot."

"*Jazooz*," Jensen said. "Don't take everything so personal."

Daryan grabbed her rifle back from him and threw it over her back again, picking up the tripod. "Thank you for this," she said to Ellis. "You said you are short of medical supplies?"

"Yes."

"Give me a list."

Ellis didn't need to be asked twice. He turned to a computer terminal, hit a few keys and printed out a page, handing it to her.

She simply nodded, folded the paper and put it in her pocket. Whatever she was thinking, she kept to herself. To Jensen she said, "I will go up the tower and set up my blind. You will need to leave now with your metal animals to get into position for tonight."

Jensen saluted her. "Aye aye, ma'am. And if it's alright, MJ will go with you, she knows her way around the outpost as good as anyone."

AS Daryan made her way out of the American bunker and back to the surface, she was boiling with anger.

She had provided them with the identity of the Russian sniper. She had given them his location. She had devised the plan for eliminating him. And they were treating her like she was somehow less than them, with their patronizing 'aye aye, ma'am' and their salutes and their raised eyebrows.

To cap the insult, they had given her the Red Jaban as a chaperone. A *civilian*.

"Up here, right and then left," the journalist said, leading the way to the surface.

As they emerged into the fading light of the small compound inside the walls of the fortification, Daryan put the tripod down and reached for the ammunition pouch in her leg pocket. Pouring the bullets out into her hand, she counted them. Twenty-one. Damn. One of the reasons the ubiquitous Lobaev rifles were hanging on walls in farmers' houses and not standing near their doors, ready to use, was the shortage of ammunition. Daryan had to scrounge every single round she had in her hand.

She made a quick calculation. Once she had her blind set up, she would need to take some practice shots at the same range as the Russian camp, to get comfortable with her new scope. She would also try the ballistics computer in it, see if it really did make any difference to her shooting. Ten practice shots. Despite her bravado, it was true she would probably need to take more than one shot at the Russian. Say three. That left eight rounds.

Every now and then Adab's men would deliver some 10.36mm to their ordnance depot and she'd get a call to pick it up. But the last such call had been two weeks ago.

She needed ammunition. There was only one person in Kobani who could find her the ammunition she needed, and it was a call she hated making, but she reached for her telephone. The only reason she could dial her sister at all was because the Americans had set up cell transmitters inside their observation towers, but she didn't pause to reflect on that. She was in no mood to be grateful.

She pulled out her cell phone and handed the tripod to the ginger-haired woman. "Hold this."

"What do you want now?" Nasrin said, picking up the call. She was probably in her office in the markets near the Ain Arab Museum. She always was, unless she was at their apartment, eating. She would be there placing orders, haggling with merchants in Hasakah, Mumbai and Mosul. Or dispatching smugglers from Kobani, who she paid a pittance to risk their lives slipping in and out of the besieged city to bring in her goods. The only reason her enterprise was tolerated was because she provided the militia with desperately needed food, ammunition and medicines.

"Hello, sister, how is mother?" Daryan asked.

"Like you care," Nasrin replied. Daryan could imagine her sitting at her desk, feet up, filing her nails with the telephone held in the crook of her neck, or looking in a mirror as she spoke. "When did you last see her, or even talk to her?"

"A week ago, maybe two," Daryan admitted.

"*Every single day* she asks me, how is Daryan? Have you seen Daryan?" Nasrin said. "Does she ever ask how I am? Hell she does. She's asking are you even still alive, you know that, right?"

Daryan pulled Ellis's list from her pocket. "I know. Look, I need that ammunition for my rifle, 10.36mm, and the Americans need medical supplies. Do you have a pen?" She read from the list, stumbling over the unfamiliar words. "Impregnated biguanide gauze dressings, antimicrobial silver dressings, moisture indicators, recombinant factor 7a..."

"Are you at the American base now?"

"Yes, they need..."

"They need, you need, everyone needs..." Nasrin sighed. But Daryan could hear her writing down the list. "You call mother, right now, I'll see what I can do."

"This isn't a game of barter, Nasrin!" Daryan exclaimed. "Without the Americans and their aircraft, how long do you think it will be before the Syrians overrun us, kill mother, rape you and string you up from a lamp post!?"

"Syrians take Kobani, it's just a new mayor and a different customer as far as I'm concerned," Nasrin said. "Now call your damn mother."

Daryan felt like throwing her cell phone at the nearest wall.

The journalist was watching her closely. How much had she understood? She could speak Persian, probably Arabic, but Kurdish had its own vocabulary and grammar, and Kurds of the Kobani region their own distinct dialect.

"Family," the American woman said, handing back the tripod. "Don't you sometimes wish you could just shoot them and be done?"

BUNNY found no new targets for her missiles as she made a rapid return to Incirlik. With the main runway out of action, the traffic controllers were using both taxiways to get aircraft out, and given the situation, they hadn't been planning for any new arrivals. But Bunny had declared a low fuel state, so they had to clear the northern taxiway for her and she stopped her machine and shut it down as close as she could to the NATO refueling facility, worried the ground crew there would have already departed for Cyprus.

But she found an NCO and some aircraftmen who hadn't got out yet and they quickly approached the unexpected arrival.

"Flight Sergeant!" she called out, dropping off the wing. "Fuel it up and kick the tires, I need to get airborne again stat." She looked beyond him. "Any cracker stackers still here?" While she was down, a missile reload wouldn't hurt. *Also be good to offload that dud Gray Wolf in my weapons bay.*

"Gunnies just lit out for Akrotiri, ma'am, in the last Turkish *CASA*," the Flight Sergeant told her. "Sorry." As he spoke, they heard a massive explosion from the east. He looked sheepish. "We were just about to turn out the lights and find ourselves a truck headed for Konya."

"Damn." She took off her helmet and started unzipping her flight suit to the waist. She also needed a toilet. "Alright, just refuel and point me back at the enemy, I guess," she said.

In the officer's bathrooms, she realized that in the rush to get airborne for the last mission, she'd left her personals in her locker. Not that she carried much around with her. Walking out to the locker she pulled it open. Inside was a small backpack. She knew what was inside it already, so she didn't need to check it. Passport. Hygiene pad. Credit cards. A small flask of vodka, because you never knew when you'd have the right time or place to celebrate or commiserate. And her non-regulation body jewelry: nose stud, lip stud, earrings, navel stud. The navel stud in particular she wouldn't want to lose – it was a tiny little blue sapphire on a silver drop chain and it had been given to her by her mother when she shipped out.

Some mothers gave their kids a rabbit's foot, a photo or a locket when they went to war, but Bunny's mother knew her daughter.

Pulling out her backpack, Bunny paused and ran her hand over the stubble on her scalp.

No. Taking her stuff with her, that felt like defeat. Like she wasn't planning on coming back. *Screw that.* Very carefully and deliberately, Bunny put the bag back in her locker and closed it.

Outside she jogged up to the aircraftmen busy around her airport and prowled around her machine, inspecting tires and control surfaces. It had got hairy up there, but her machine seemed to have come through alright. As far as she could see. There could be a million internal components that had got shaken loose, but there was no time even to run a system diagnostic. As if to emphasize the thought, they all looked up as a series of booms from rapid explosions rolled over the base.

The Flight Sergeant – she was good with faces but terrible with names – came around to her side of the aircraft as she was pulling her helmet on again. His people were backing the refueling dolly away from the machine.

"Good to go, ma'am," he told her. "Say g'day to everyone back at Akrotiri for us."

"Forget that, Flight Sergeant," Bunny said. "I've still got missiles on my kite. I'm going up there to kick some Russian arse and I'll be back here inside thirty looking for more fuel, is that clear?"

The NCO grinned. "Hell yeah, ma'am."

She held her fist out for a fist bump, and he obliged. "And if you could scare up some Turkish Air Force armorers who know how to put bombs and missiles on a *Panther*, that would be a bloody bonus."

Inside ten minutes she was airborne again. She headed west from the air base into clear air away from the Turkish jamming and checked in. "Turkish Quarterback, this is RAAF Sunset two, available for air-to-air tasking."

There was a pause before the Turkish forward air controller came back to her. He no doubt had to deal with a little surprise. But he obviously had no shortage of targets. "RAAF Sunset two, Quarterback, please proceed to grid Golf zero four, vicinity Goztepe town, Syrian rotary-winged aircraft reported, our troops are engaged."

She checked her threat screen but saw nothing. Her radar warning receiver was still showing massive jamming energy on all frequencies. So she'd have to pick the enemy up on infrared or optical. So be it. "Quarterback, Sunset two, proceeding grid Golf zero four. Out."

She banked her machine and pointed it east again. She didn't need to plug any waypoints into her nav system. She knew exactly where Goztepe was. What she didn't know was what she would find there this time.

BONDAREV was crouched under his tree again, trying to make a decision. A pitched battle was unfolding about a mile away. The spearhead of the Syrian armored columns had been engaged by the dug-in Turkish *Leopard* tanks, which had managed to stop one T-90 with a disabled track, and forced another to retire blowing smoke, probably from an engine strike. A Syrian Mil-25 helicopter gunship had fired several anti-tank missiles at them, but without apparent effect. It was now circling the battlefield, occasionally engaging Turkish troops with its cannon, but more probably providing tactical intelligence to the Syrian armor commander to allow him to direct his forces. He was probing the route off the motorway to the north.

The Turkish force in the farmhouse there put up stiff resistance. Turkish anti-tank TOW missiles took out two Syrian scout vehicles in quick order and they were pouring small arms fire on any Syrian troops or vehicles which tried to approach. Bondarev knew the Syrian commander would be desperately calling for Russian air support to flatten the Turkish position. In the meantime, he was maneuvering his tanks into cover onto a side road, hoping he could bypass the Turkish roadblock.

Bondarev could see this was not the fight the Syrian commander wanted to fight. That lay a few miles ahead, at Incirlik. And he wanted to get there before the US 1st Infantry Division rolled in.

The Turkish *Leopard* tank platoon had other ideas. Bondarev saw them pulling back from the verge of the motorway, out of sight of the Syrian force, probably moving to hit it in the rear as it pushed north. If only he had a damn radio! He could alert the Syrian commander to what he was seeing. The two *Leopards* didn't have the muscle to be able to stop the Syrian advance on their own, but they could certainly disrupt it.

Relax, Yevgeny, he told himself. *The Syrian chopper must see them. He'll call it in.*

O'HARE decided not to go screaming in over Goztepe without knowing what was waiting for her there. There were still three BATS circling nearby, their autonomous defensive routines engaged as they monitored the airspace for targets, authorized to engage Russian or Syrian aircraft if identified.

She called up her BATS control screen, identified the two nearest units and took control of them, then did a quick check of their systems and ordnance status. Both appeared in good shape, though one of them only had two air-to-air missiles remaining, and the other only one, so they had already been engaged. That might explain why there were no Russian fighters above Incirlik at that moment, for which she was very glad.

She called them to her so that she could communicate with them outside the Syrian jamming range. It took a few frustrating minutes before they responded, but they eventually started moving west.

Bunny O'Hare had struggled through life with a severe case of attention deficit disorder and that inability to focus on just one thing came to her aid right there and then. As she monitored the sky around her, the threat environment, her aircraft systems and instruments, she also called up the BATS nav screens and gave them waypoints over Goztepe – one at ten thousand feet, the other at twenty thousand, flying cover. She changed their rules of engagement to prioritize low-level ground attack and rotary-winged aircraft, which would affect the way they used their phased-array and synthetic aperture radars. Keeping an eye out for any Russian fighters which might be providing air cover, she sent the BATS in and followed them closely enough that she could keep contact with them.

She got a bite almost immediately. As her low-altitude BATS closed on Goztepe, it picked up a new target and classified it. Mil-25 gunship! *Bingo, baby.* She didn't have to tell it to engage. As soon as the BATS had the target locked and confirmed, it fired.

BONDAREV saw the missile before he heard it, or even saw the aircraft firing it. The white contrail caught the corner of his eye and his heart sank as he watched the missile scream down from about ten thousand feet, correct itself at the last minute, and then slam into the hovering Syrian helicopter. It was knocked sideways and fell to the earth like a burning sack of rocks.

His decision was made for him. There were one or more Coalition aircraft overhead. The Turkish armor by the motorway was repositioning. Without disciplined forward air control, the Syrian advance could be halted right here, outside Goztepe. Leaving the cover of his tree, he limped downhill and headed toward the nearest Syrian vehicle, still a mile away.

ITS target destroyed, the low-altitude BATS unit sent a message to O'Hare which was the AI equivalent of 'what now, boss?' She checked the fuel and weapons states of the two BATS. They both had about twenty minutes' fuel remaining. Each had only one air-to-air missile left, and no air-to-ground missiles. The jamming from the Syrian forces below meant she had only intermittent comms links to the drones and couldn't get too far from them. She called them both back up to twenty thousand feet and sent one north of Goztepe, the other south, to scan for incoming fighters. She would have to cover the air over the town herself. Using her DAS optical-electric targeting system, she looked down through light clouds and saw a large number of Syrian trucks and tanks maneuvering to get off the motorway and around the small town to the north.

With no air-ground weapons she was no more useful than a recon drone. In frustration, she called up her ordnance screen again and hammered on the 'arm weapon' icon for the remaining *Gray Wolf* in her weapon's bay. It stayed stubbornly red; not reporting a malfunction, but not arming either.

Focus, O'Hare, she told herself. *The task here is air to air. Keep the sky clear for the Turkish troops below.* The DAS system was designed to automatically lock onto possible targets and cue missiles to engage them, and it could pick up stealth aircraft out to fifty miles in clear air. But O'Hare wasn't the kind to leave an AI to do her job, and as she circled over Goztepe her eyes scanned the sky around her, her threat and radar warning screens, the data intermittently getting through from the two BATS she had slaved to her, occasionally paging the Turkish AWACS for any intel on Russian aircraft movements. But the AWACS was unreachable due to signal jamming.

She and Red had taken care of a flight of *Okhotniks*, but there *had* to be other Russian aircraft in play. They may even have seen the RAAF aircraft at Incirlik bugging out and expected to have the sandpit to themselves. If they weren't here already, they would be soon.

A voice came over her radio, breaking up badly.

"Sunset two, Incirlik … vectoring Gargoyle flight … your position. Patching … sync SAR data … lead. Incirlik out."

What? She pulled up her tactical screen. On it two new icons appeared about ten miles west of her. Friendlies. As quickly as they'd appeared, the icons disappeared again. Damn Syrian jammers! But the friendlies were RAF *Tempests* out of Incirlik. She'd seen that much. Synching data with them was going to be out of the question given the storm of interference around her. But the request to synch synthetic aperture radar data indicated they were on a ground attack mission, which left her as their guardian angel, whether they knew it or not.

She decided to get some data on the situation on the ground below for them and then get back to altitude to squirt through the data and resume her patrol. Bunny didn't want to risk using her own radar and alerting Syrian anti-air units below before she had to. So that gave her no choice but to get down below the clouds and get an optical lock on the Syrian targets.

YEVGENY Bondarev had approached the Syrian *Terminator* infantry fighting vehicle with his arms raised, hoping desperately the crew inside would recognize his Russian flight suit and the large flag prominently displayed on his left upper arm.

The 30mm autocannon turret of the IFV had swung ominously toward him, but he kept walking steadily forward. After a nervous minute or so, the hatch forward of the turret had popped open and an officer stuck his head out, holding an assault rifle which was also pointed at Bondarev. When he got to within fifty feet, the man yelled out to him. First in Arabic, and then in English.

"Stop there!"

Bondarev halted and turned his body so the man could see the Russian flag on his uniform.

"Russian?"

"Russian pilot," Bondarev yelled back. "I need a radio!"

"Come." The man waved the barrel of his rifle.

From the back of the IFV two other men emerged, both with rifles also pointed at him, one on each side of the vehicle. Bondarev kept his hands high and walked toward them. He stopped again ten feet in front of the officer.

"You need air support," Bondarev said, nodding toward the sound of fighting down by the Turkish farmhouse. "I can call it in for you. But I need a radio."

At that moment a dark shape dropped out of the clouds above. The Syrians looked up, moving closer to the illusory protection of their IFV. Bondarev made a quick assessment. *Panther*. Bombing run? No. The attitude and velocity were wrong. Recon run. Probably the bastard who just shot down that Mil-25 chopper.

The Syrians flinched as the Coalition fighter boomed overhead at about ten thousand feet, screaming across the Turkish force from north to south, firing chaff and flares as it did so. From the other side of the motorway a single *Verba* anti-air missile lanced into the air but it had no hope of intercepting the *Panther*, which was already screaming back up into the clouds out of reach of the Syrian missile.

As the sound of the sonic boom died down, Bondarev turned to the Syrian officer again. "That was a reconnaissance run. That aircraft just mapped every single tank, truck and jeep in your battalion. There will be cruise missiles or bombs on the way any second." He raised his voice. "I. Need. A. *Radio*."

The Syrian officer squinted at him, then pointed with his rifle to the back of the vehicle. "Get in."

Bondarev stepped around the IFV and the two armed Syrian soldiers standing by its rear doors. Ducking down and climbing inside he saw the officer pull himself back inside the vehicle, and three more crew members at their stations. Eyes adjusting to the low green light inside, and nose adjusting to the smell of sweating men who had been in close quarters, he identified the radio operator and moved to his shoulder. The radio set was Russian made, with the ability to switch from Arabic to Russian text on the multifunctional display.

"May I?" Bondarev asked the radio operator and indicated the chair he was sitting in.

The man looked at his officer, who nodded curtly. He climbed out of his seat and into the back of the vehicle.

Bondarev dropped into his chair and tapped the Russian-made screen in front of him, switching it to Cyrillic text. He quickly located the frequency for the Russian air controller, locked it in and grabbed the handset.

"Sector Control, this is Lieutenant Yevgeny Bondarev of the 7th Air Group, 7000th Air Base, currently embedded with Syrian ground forces at Goztepe. Come back please."

There was a long pause, and he was about to repeat himself when the radio crackled to life. "Lieutenant Bondarev, please authenticate with your service number and code for the day."

Bondarev reeled off his alphanumeric service number, read the code off a note on his digital watch and waited. "Service number confirmed. Your message please."

"Control, the Syrian ground force has been engaged by Turkish main battle tanks and at least two companies of Turkish troops. It is being held at the overpass by Goztepe town and is in need of close air support."

"Lieutenant, we are in contact with the forward air controller for the Syrian 25th. Your involvement is not..."

"Was he aboard a Syrian Mil-25 gunship?" Bondarev asked.

"I will check..." the controller said. "... Yes, a Mil-25, that is correct."

"Then he is dead," Bondarev interrupted. "That aircraft was just shot down by a Coalition fighter." Bondarev looked around the crew compartment and covered the handset. "Map? Someone have a *map*?" The Syrian officer reached down to the console by his command position and pulled a paper map out of a side pocket, handing it to him. Bondarev spread it on his lap, locating Goztepe. "Control, I am going to read you the coordinates for two Turkish MBTs and the two main groups of Turkish ground troops, do you read?"

"Go ahead, pilot."

Bondarev read off a series of latitudes and longitudes. When he was finished, he gripped the handset. "Control, do we have any assets overhead?"

"Affirmative," the controller reported. "We have a flight of Su-57s on CAP."

"*Ground attack* assets."

"We have a squadron of Su-30s on standby."

Bondarev thought fast. "Control, there are Coalition fighters or combat drones over Goztepe, why is that air patrol not engaged?"

"We have no Coalition aircraft on our plot over Goztepe," the man said.

"I just bloody saw one!" Bondarev exclaimed. "It did a low-level recon pass. Do you want to trust your radar or my damn eyes?" Forget this, he was talking to the wrong person. "Control, can you patch me through to the commander of that flight of Su-57s?"

"Patching you through."

Bondarev grunted, tapping the handset impatiently on his thigh. Something didn't add up. The biggest Syrian armored push of the war and there were no ground attack assets circling overhead, ready to unload?

After two agonizing minutes, a new voice came over the radio. A familiar voice. "Lieutenant Bondarev, this is Captain Bebenko," it said. "So the Turks haven't captured you after all."

"No, sir," Bondarev grimaced. "Not yet. Sir, I am with the Syrian 25th Armor. They are being held up by a small Turkish blocking force but I have provided coordinates, if an air strike was authorized on the Turkish armor south of…"

"We just lost four *Okhotniks* over that target, Lieutenant," Bebenko said, his voice cold and flat.

"Sorry, sir, what did you say?"

"You heard me. We just lost four *Okhotniks* returning from reconnaissance duties over the western area of operations. We thought the Coalition had pulled all its fighters out, but apparently not. I can't send in those Su-30s until we can see what they have in the air over Goztepe – we are probing, but with the exception of a few BATS drones, we have nothing."

"They have multiple fighter aircraft in the sector," Bondarev reported. "I just saw a Mil-25 shot down by an air-to-air missile fired beyond visual range. I am pretty sure I also observed an air-launched *Gray Wolf* strike a couple of hours ago and I saw a low-level pass by a *Panther*. I can confirm you are *not* alone up there, sir."

"Your report is duly noted. I look forward to hearing how you got yourself shot down so far behind enemy lines, Bondarev. In the meantime try and get yourself to … uh, Karsi. Turkish town about twenty miles south of you, now in Syrian hands. We can fetch you from the helipad at the hospital there," Bebenko said. "Understood?"

Another explosion outside, a large one this time. A Turkish or Syrian tank, it had to be. "The Syrian troops here are engaged in a firefight, Comrade Captain," Bondarev said. "I doubt they are minded to give a stranded Russian pilot a lift, unless we can do them a solid favor and get them through this blocking force."

"We are working on it. Keep your head down and get back in contact when you are safe. Bebenko out," the Captain said.

Sentimental swine, Bondarev thought, looking down at the handset. And cautious. Too cautious. His losses had made him timid.

The Syrian lieutenant gave Bondarev a hopeful thumbs up. "Air support, yes?"

Bondarev couldn't lie to him. "Not yet, no." He pointed to the air above. "Coalition fighters overhead. I need to speak with your commander. Which vehicle is he in?"

As Bondarev climbed out and looked downhill toward another IFV with a large antenna which a soldier was pointing out to him, a Syrian tank took another Turkish TOW missile hit. Its armor appeared to shrug it off this time, but the Syrians were well and truly stalled. He looked at the skies above. *Come on, Bebenko, show some guts and push those Coalition fighters.*

ITS rear-firing defensive laser system was not the only advantage the sixth-generation RAF *Tempest* had over its fifth-generation *Panther* brethren. Among them was an advanced electronic warfare suite that included defenses against jamming, and improved radio and radar direction sensors. As his machine closed on O'Hare's position just west of Goztepe, Meany's flight of two *Tempests* used the GE Avionics anti-jamming capabilities that allowed their synthetic aperture radar, or SAR, to frequency hop around the Syrian jamming and successfully scan the ground up to twenty miles ahead.

But using it was like an invitation to nearby Russian fighters to kill him. In a hot environment like this, every second the ground-mapping radar was active increased the risk of detection exponentially.

Meany wasn't flying with Rex King on this mission, he'd taken off under a different flight leader. Meany's flight leader had stayed behind to organize his other 617 pilots to relocate to RAF Akrotiri on Cyprus, from where they would continue operations. Meany's was to be the last strike out of Incirlik until the 'current threat environment' had been resolved, and after the last two missions in which he'd been shot at by anti-air missiles and ambushed by a Russian stealth fighter, he looked forward to getting this particular mission over with.

The mission planners had reviewed satellite imagery of the bomb damage assessment from the Coalition *Gray Wolf* strike and decide to go with a different ordnance package. Unlike the *Perdix* drones and *SPEAR* missiles he'd deployed in the last two missions, Meany was carrying self-guided iron bombs on this one. Their disadvantage was that they had no 'horde' capabilities, no advanced AI to help them dynamically adjust their attack profile. However, they had the advantage that they were effective at killing heavily armored tanks. Very, very effective.

In the belly of his aircraft were eight *Stormbreaker* glide bombs, each of which carried a 100lb. shaped charge specifically designed to penetrate the reactive armor of the Russian-made T-90 tanks fielded by the Syrian army. Dropped from twenty thousand feet and driven only by gravity, they would fly themselves to the coordinates provided by Meany's SAR system and then, using their own onboard millimeter radar and infrared sensors, lock onto any Syrian tank or truck in range. As they didn't have AI capabilities, two or more bombs might lock onto the same target. But against a heavily armored main battle tank like the Syrian T-90, that wasn't necessarily a bad thing.

"Confirm target data sync with payload," his flight leader called.

"Confirmed."

"Kill your SAR, arm bombs."

"SAR down, bombs up."

His *Tempest* hit an air pocket and he instinctively steadied it. The two RAF fighters were flying side by side, a mile apart, ten miles west of Incirlik and less than twenty miles from their targets.

"Send them."

His thumb closed on the bomb release, his payload bay doors dropped open and 2,000lbs. of ordnance fell away in a single salvo. As he followed his flight leader in a slow banking turn to Cyprus in the south, Meany kept himself busy with his nav screen, instruments, threat displays and system readouts, and tried not to think of the fact that if even half of the bombs he'd just dropped struck their targets and killed four tanks, he'd just sent twelve men to their deaths.

Poor bloody sods like him, just doing what their country ordered them to do.

WITHOUT the ability to pick up their IFF tracking beacons due to the Syrian jamming, the RAF *Tempests* were as invisible to O'Hare as they were to any patrolling Russian fighters. She just had to assume they were going about their job, so she went about hers.

Bunny *knew* there had to be Russian fighters nearby. But how many, what type and where? It was, however, the exact scenario the BATS system was made for – to enter potentially hostile enemy airspace, find and engage an enemy – and with no pilot's life on the line, she had no compunction about putting the two BATS units under her command in harm's way.

Unlike in previous engagements though, where she had full authority over the BATS – through line of sight laser optical links or satellite long-distance comms – thanks to the Syrian jamming, the moment her BATS broke out of laser range, she would lose the ability to control them.

Luckily, the BATS system had been designed by an Australian team, which had foreseen that the ability to 'boomerang' a BATS drone might be a very useful thing. So they had programmed the drones with a protocol that allowed a pilot to assign them a patrol waypoint, send them out in autonomous mode to search for and engage any hostile aircraft, and then if they survived, or didn't find a target, 'boomerang' back to the pilot controlling them for new orders.

Circling thirty thousand feet above Incirlik, Bunny was busy boomeranging her BATS into the skies over and beyond Goztepe, trying to flush out any Russian air cover, but it was a nerve-wracking business. As soon as they were out of line of sight, she lost laser-optical comms with them and had to wait what felt like eons for them to get back into range, reconnect with her and synch their data. She had checked her weapons again and armed them. Three live CUDA air-to-air missiles, one busted *Gray Wolf*, two BATS with a single missile each. Five lousy shots. And an untold number of Russian fighters nearby.

The question of the hour ... *if* she found them, would the Russians flee or fight? Unaffected by the Syrian jamming, the Russians would be able to see her BATS. They could already have engaged them, but so far had not. Probably cautious of the *Panthers* and *Tempests* that were usually ranged behind them. But now they had the advantage of a wall of electronic noise to hide behind as they launched their missiles. So would they try for a shootdown, knock the Coalition drones out of the sky? Or would they just slide away, trying to stay unseen, waiting for a bigger prize?

As she was checking the sky around her through her DAS system, she got the answer to her question. Only one of her BATS had returned from its latest scouting loop. She waited another two minutes, but soon concluded the other drone was gone, and stayed gone. *That could mean only one thing.* It had been engaged and destroyed. BATS didn't have a habit of dropping out of the sky for no reason and if this one had been running low on fuel it would have returned to momma, reported its low fuel state and then requested permission to return to base. She checked the grid reference the missing BATS had been sent to explore. The Russian fighters could, probably had, engaged the drone and then moved away, but there was a chance their patrol pattern would bring them back. She had a possible attack vector now. A weak one, but better than none.

And a plan.

She brought her BATS command screen up and programmed the remaining drone to get into formation slightly above and slightly behind her own aircraft, then adjusted their separation. *Closer, my darling baby, closer.* When it got to within a hundred feet, she locked its position.

She ordered it to keep sweeping the sky around it with its phased-array radar in a 360-degree search pattern so that it would shine on enemy radar warning receivers like a lighthouse above a shoal of rocks. She wanted it screaming to any Russian fighter out there, *BATS here, coming to get you. Better shoot me down before I do.* And she wanted to be hiding in plain sight right in front of it when they did.

If she was lucky, tucked under the nose of the drone, they would mistake her radar return for that of the BATS and underestimate the threat. If she wasn't, well, they might run, or they might fight, but at least she'd be taking the initiative instead of just circling impotently around the sky.

JAMES Jensen could have used an eye in the sky at that exact moment. Lighting out from COP Meyer with Brutus and Spartacus in 'trail mode', he had gone west from Mishte-nur Hill into the Kurdish-held hamlet of Halinjah north, which was only five hundred yards from the nearest Syrian position across a ring road and wasteland of mortar-cratered fields. But the Syrians were spread thin here, more concerned about protecting their own skins than stopping exfiltrators from leaving Kobani, so he was able to take the dogs west about a mile, circle around a Syrian dugout and then back toward the Russian camp at Kunyan Kurdan hill.

The detour had taken him nearly an hour, and it was dark by the time he'd gotten within visual range of the Russian camp. His helmet-mounted infrared camera and heads-up display should show him the body heat from any Russian sentries or patrols, though he would have liked a drone overhead also keeping watch around him. But the Marines' supply of small surveillance drones had been exhausted and even though they could print spare parts like rotors and bodies for their damaged units, they couldn't print electronics and batteries.

Still, he had his dogs. Crouching behind a low wall just east of the hill, Jensen pulled a small tablet off his belt and called up a map of his location. He laid down two pins near the tracks off the summit of the hill to the north that Daryan had marked as likely egress routes, and set the dogs to 'conceal and observe' at those locations.

He didn't have to give a verbal command. They reacted immediately, both slinking off into the night toward the north. They would travel in stealth mode, scanning the ground around themselves to be sure every time they put a foot down, it would create the least possible noise. If they heard or saw a human nearby, they would plot a course around them, or freeze and slowly lower themselves to the ground, and if needed, they would shut down all but essential power so that they reduced their infrared heat signature to almost nothing. If they were attacked at close range, they would automatically respond with their swivel-mounted semi-automatic 12 gauge shotgun and withdraw. If engaged at longer range they would seek cover and attempt to retreat.

As they crept from building to building, they sent back vision of what they were seeing, hearing and sensing directly to small windows on Jensen's helmet-mounted heads-up display. On his forearm was a small command pad for use when he was outside voice range. If Spartacus or Brutus spotted a squat, bald Russian hiking down one of those tracks carrying a sniper rifle, he could order them to attack.

In the meantime, he was creeping around to the southern track coming down from the hill, the one they judged Tita Ali was most likely to use because it couldn't be seen or fired at from the city itself, and offered the easiest access to the south of the destroyed city where a single well-trained individual could sneak past Kurdish guards.

As he made his way between two small abandoned farm buildings he reached for his throat mike. "Daryan, I'm at the farm, southeast corner of the hill, how is..."

"I can see you," the sniper replied. "There is a Syrian position a hundred yards north of you. They should not be able to see you. No traffic coming down the track. You are clear."

He was glad she was on overwatch, though at a distance of two thousand yards, if he came face to face unexpectedly with a

Syrian or Russian soldier, he could be dead in less than the time it took for a bullet to leave her barrel and reach his position. The next thirty seconds would be the most dangerous of his mission so far. He had to leave the cover of the farmhouse and get across open ground to a stand of olive trees, nestled at the foot of the hill. The track leading down from the Russian camp skirted the small plantation, and if the Kurdish sniper fired at a target on the track and missed, they would only have two choices; run back up hill to the protection of the Russian camp, which would be slow and exposed, or run for the bottom of the track and the cover of the trees, which would be the natural, human instinct.

He watched in his helmet display as Brutus and Spartacus picked their way around the hill, heading for its northern slopes. He could see exactly what they were seeing; an out-of-body experience that had taken some getting used to but was now second nature.

He looked across the open ground at the olive grove and tensed his leg muscles. *Okay, JJ, fast and low. Let's go.*

MARY Jo Basim had watched the Kurdish woman set up her hide with deep fascination.

First, she had hung black shade cloth from the ceiling, slice it down the middle and pegged the bottom corners back to create a hole she could shoot through. Beside her, she put a small table, her food and drink, and a chair. Then she set about getting her shooting position organized. As she started moving sandbags around, sighing audibly if one of the two Marines in the lookout got in her way, MJ had pulled out her phone and tried taking a photo. As soon as the Kurdish woman had noticed, she turned to MJ.

"No photo."

"It's going to be a great story," MJ tried painting it for her. "Kurdish YPJ sniper takes down the Spetsnaz Murderer from two miles away at COP Meyer. You'll be as famous as Arin Mirkan, maybe get your own statue."

Daryan threw the sandbag she was holding down in front of her. "You know the story of Arin Mirkan?"

"Sure."

"The real story?"

"Surrounded by ISIS tanks, stayed behind on the hilltop here, killed ten ISIS soldiers in a suicide attack so that her comrades could escape..." MJ told her. It was inscribed on the base of the fifty-foot-high statue at the entrance to the city.

Daryan shook her head. "You do not even know her real name." She picked up the sandbag again and put it beside another, building a step for herself to stand on. "She was Dilara Milak. Twenty-two years old." She lifted another sandbag, grunting with the effort. "Two children. She had been away fighting the Caliphate mercenaries so long, her mother, Wahida, asked to see her and she sent back a message. 'I will see you when Kobani is free.'" Daryan dropped the bag, pointed outside the tower. "She never saw her mother after that and she never saw Kobani free. She died, right down there." Shouldering another sandbag, she turned to MJ. "Do not ever compare me to her. I am not worthy."

"I'm sorry."

Taking the tripod, Daryan placed it in front of her sandbag steps and pulled the rifle from her shoulder. She put a round into the breech, rested the stock on the tripod and sighted down the barrel like Jensen had shown her, then turned to the Marine standing closest to her. "You, do you know how to use this scope?"

MJ had recognized the man when she climbed into the tower. His name was O'Halloran, a private from Boston, not far from where she had grown up herself. He bent over and looked at it. "It's got inbuilt ballistics," he said, straightening. "Yeah, I guess."

"Show me."

O'Halloran looked at his corporal, who nodded, and then climbed up on the sandbags. "Is your scope switched on?"

"Yes."

"Can I check it's set up?"

Daryan stepped back, and he pushed a button on her scope, peered into it and started paging through menus.

"Rifle type?"

"Lobaev SVLK-14S."

"Barrel length?"

"900mm."

"Muzzle break?"

"T-tuner."

"You ever use a suppressor?"

"No."

"Chambered for?"

"Chey Tac, 10.36mm."

"OK, got it." He straightened up. "Yeah, good to go." He pointed to a large red button on the side of the scope. "You find your target in the scope, laser it with this button, you can manually input things like wind speed and direction at the target if it's a long shot, then it does the calculation and sends it to your scope."

She bent to her scope and sighted down it. "The green cross?"

"Yeah, that's the calculation of where the bullet will strike. You put that on your target, not the crosshairs."

"I need to see if this is reliable," Daryan decided. She oriented the tripod so the rifle was pointing out into empty desert and pulled a handful of rounds from her trouser pocket. She held them out to MJ. "Hold these, hand them to me when I say 'bullet'."

MJ took a step back. "Me?"

Daryan frowned. "Yes, you. These soldiers have a job, you are sitting doing nothing."

"I can't … under the Geneva Convention I lose my protection as a journalist if I engage in combat, if I even *carry* a weapon." She looked at the rifle rounds like they were poisoned. "Or ammunition."

The Kurdish woman's frown deepened. "Will the Geneva Convention protect you if the Syrians attack us here?" Daryan asked. "Or do you expect these men to do it?"

"They are trained soldiers, I'm not," MJ replied.

"If they dropped their weapon during a battle, would you hand it to them?"

"Yes."

"Would you use it to shoot at an enemy who is shooting at you?"

"Of course. If the choice is life or death."

"Your life."

"Yes."

"Not theirs?" Daryan asked with a nod to the Marines. "Not mine?"

MJ saw the two Marines listening to the conversation with interest.

"Look, it's an ethical question, I can't…"

Daryan turned from her, lasered a target out in the desert and then sighted down her rifle, still holding the handful of 10.36mm rounds out to MJ. "It is not an ethical question. If you want to stay up here with me, you will hand me the bullets. If you want your photograph, you will hand me the bullets. If you care about the lives of your American Marines, you will hand me the bullets."

MJ stood, paralyzed by indecision. It could be the story of her career. But it could be the end of her career if it ever came out. With a snort of disgust, Daryan pushed the bullets into MJ's closed fist like she was loading a magazine. MJ didn't resist, but she didn't open her hand to receive the bullets either. Daryan turned back to her rifle. She fired, the report loud inside the confines of the sandbagged observation post, causing MJ to flinch. As it died away, Daryan worked the breech bolt on the Lobaev and held out her hand without taking her eye from the scope. "Bullet."

The two Marines watched MJ and she keenly felt the judgment in their eyes.

From the minute she had laid eyes on Daryan Al-Kobani, Mary Jo had been writing the opening paragraphs of her feature in her head. *The Kurdish sniper had been staring down her scope for hours. Just after midnight, a solitary shot rang out, the culmination of days of planning...*

Biting back her doubts, she rolled the cartridges in her palm, then handed one to the sniper.

IF Andrei Zakarin heard Daryan's practice rounds in the distance, he did not register them against the sporadic background of small arms fire, day and night, from different parts of the city perimeter. Syrian snipers firing in, Kurdish patrols testing for weaknesses in the blockade and being turned around. Inbound and outbound mortar fire, not least from the US outpost on top of Mishte-nur, with its 120mm mortar, which the Syrians seemed unable to silence.

Thankfully, though, it had never been turned on the Russian camp, or at least, not yet. Politics probably played a part in that, though he suspected the Americans were conserving their ordnance too.

Politics had sent him here. At the liaison post for the 45th Spetsnaz Airborne Brigade in Damascus, he'd received a very short briefing from a very tall GRU intelligence officer. He'd shown Zakarin a map of Kobani, putting a pointer on the location of the US combat outpost. "There were 500 US Marines stationed in Kobani. Many were evacuated after the initial failed assault. We believe anywhere between 200 and 300 remain. They skulk in their bunkers – bunkers *we* built – and despite the fact we are shooting down two out of three of their supply drones, the Syrian containment lines are full of holes, so we estimate the chances of starving them into surrender to be nil." He tapped his pointer on the map. "We can't drop a bunker-busting bomb on them, we don't want the Americans to escalate…"

Zakarin had laughed. "The rumors say we are soon to support a Syrian invasion of Lebanon," he said. "I'm pretty sure things will *escalate* the minute those tanks start rolling."

"Yes, the move on Lebanon has been sadly well telegraphed, but we don't want them to escalate *yet*…" the man emphasized. "We want all of our units in place, both in the air, under the seas and on land for the next phase of operations, before the Americans start sailing Carrier Battle Groups into the Mediterranean. So that is where you come in."

"I'm good," Zakarin said. "But even I cannot shoot a Marine hiding inside a bunker through the top of a hill. Let alone two hundred of them."

"No, but you can shoot them when they leave their outpost to patrol the city, which they do daily. Or as they transfer prisoners to the Kurdish militia. Or when they try to recover damaged drones and supplies."

"To what end?"

"To destroy their morale," the GRU officer said. "We have deliberately not jammed their satellite telephone link. They are still calling home to wives, husbands and children. Their democracy is their weakness. A steady flow of casualties will cause alarm, dismay, and weaken their resolve. They have abandoned the Kurds before, you will help persuade them to do it again."

"They can't get out anyway. As you said, they are surrounded by Syrian mechanized infantry and our aircraft fly overhead."

"Enough casualties and they will want to parlay," the man predicted. "Don't shoot too many at once. Just one or two per day, every day. They will open a channel and we can negotiate their passage out of the city through Syrian lines to Turkey. And film their surrender."

"It would be better to wound than to kill, then," Zakarin said thoughtfully. "If you are looking to demoralize them. Let them fear the world outside their walls, let them see what happens when they leave them. Let them try to evacuate the fallen rather than bury them."

"I leave that to you," the GRU officer nodded. "But one more thing. It should look like the work of a Syrian sniper. Work alone, and don't give yourself away."

"Wear a Syrian uniform?" Zakarin asked.

"And use a common Syrian rifle, ammunition – nothing can be directly tied to us. Understood?"

"No. You don't want a Russian sniper, you want a Syrian. Why send for me?"

"Syria has put two of its best sniper teams on this task already. One was killed and one wounded, both by the same shooter."

Zakarin leaned forward in his chair. "Now you have my attention."

The GRU officer reached into a folder and threw a grainy photograph across the table at Zakarin. "This is the only known photograph of Daryan Al-Kobani."

In his tent outside Kobani, as he did before every mission, Zakarin pulled the photo of the woman from his shirt pocket. It was a poor photograph, taken from a distance with a drone or zoom lens. The scarf-clad woman stood among a ragtag group of militia and could have been any one of hundreds of Kurdish female fighters, except for the long rifle strapped diagonally across her back from shoulder to thigh. Her age could have been anything from seventeen to twenty-seven.

"So I will have to deal with her before I can deal with the Americans?" he'd asked the GRU officer.

"She is not your mission," the officer had said. "But be careful; expect her to be hunting you, sooner or later."

Kobani was not a big city and he'd now seen a large part of its population through his sights, but never the girl with the rifle nearly half her size. And he'd been very, very careful. He spent the first period in any new hide meticulously scanning the environment around him for other shooters. The best chance of spotting an adversary was before he or she knew you had taken up residence. The minute you moved – or worse, if you fired – you were announcing open season on yourself. He'd fired thirty times in twenty-three days and, by his best estimate, scored seventeen clean hits. Each time he'd moved within minutes, not giving her a chance to locate him.

After consideration, he'd decided to shoot to wound, not to kill, aiming into the vulnerable area around arms and groins not covered by body armor. If the angle was wrong, he'd take a leg, aiming to shatter the thigh bone or pelvis. His misses had all occurred in the last week, as the Marines had responded to his growing number of attacks by staying closer to cover, moving quicker across open intersections and streets, rarely lingering out in the open. He didn't mind that at all. It increased the challenge if the target was moving.

He lifted the photo of the Kurdish woman to his lips and kissed it, then put it back in his shirt pocket.

Soon, Al-Kobani, he whispered in his mind. *From my gun to your heart.*

Lifting his weapon, he checked his uniform. Boots, laces, trousers tapered and secured. Desert camouflage cape folded tight in the left pocket of his trousers, concrete and steel camouflage cape in the right. Belt and ammunition pouch. Twenty rounds. Knife. Water bottle, full. Shirt buttoned to the throat. He worked the bolt on the Lobaev, checked the breech and loaded a single bullet, then lowered the rifle. Not swinging it onto his shoulder because a swinging rifle could catch on an obstruction. He wielded his rifle like a swordsman wielded an unsheathed sword, with care and deliberation.

Andrei Zakarin had a more than mild case of obsessive compulsive disorder or OCD. And he thanked his Tatar father for passing the defective gene along to him, because he credited his OCD with having kept him alive through four combat tours; in Syria, Afghanistan, Korea and now Syria again. He stood, arranged his belongings on his bed in the order he wanted them to be found if he did not return, and then bent down to leave his tent.

Something was wrong.

A smell? A sound? Or just a feeling? He looked around the tent. *Ah, of course, how could I have forgotten!* He reached into the wallet he had left on his bed and pulled out the photograph of his daughter, Viktoria. Patting his right pocket to make sure the photo of the Kurdish sniper was there, he put the photo of his daughter in his left pocket, over his heart.

Love was stronger than the strongest Kevlar, he truly believed that.

With a final look around the tent, he went out.

The northwest track tonight, Turkish border side of the hill. It was exposed, but the risk at night was acceptable. Few of the Kurdish riflemen posted on the roofs of the nearby buildings had infrared vision equipment and the Americans rarely patrolled at night. He would strike north to the dry creek bed that ran east-west outside the city, then take the southerly branch of the creek that led almost directly to the Cardamom Markets. It ended at a rusted and padlocked iron stormwater grate that led under the city, and he'd used it many times to sneak under the militia guard post north of the market. The padlocks were no problem because, well, they were his.

The stormwater drain leading from the creek ended in the back yard of a house destroyed in the civil war, which was no doubt why it had been forgotten. From there he only had to cover twenty yards of open ground to the rear of the market, from where the climb to the roof of the market building would take a mere thirty seconds. He had already climbed it twice, in planning this attack. Reducing the risk of being seen during his reconnaissance was a part of his method. If he wasn't discovered while researching his next attack, then the chances were pretty high he wouldn't be discovered executing it, and vice versa.

He nodded to the sentries on the main gate out of the Russian camp as he left. What they made of the lone sniper he didn't know, nor did he care. Although they were dressed in Syrian uniforms, they were mere regulars of the 15th Detached Reconnaissance Regiment. Not even Spetsnaz. Barely worthy of his regard. He was not here to make new friends, he was here to kill Americans and soon he would be going home.

Not because his attacks had persuaded the Americans to depart. His mission had been overtaken by the tide of war. As he'd been preparing for his next mission, an officer of the 15th Recon had interrupted him, telling him it was very unlikely he'd bag himself any Americans tonight, since word had just been received that the Americans' lease on Mishte-nur had expired. The Syrian 38th Mechanized was about to begin an artillery bombardment and infantry assault on the hilltop fortification.

"Infantry attack on the main south gates, then thermobaric artillery barrage at 1 a.m., followed immediately by an assault in battalion strength supported by IFVs," the officer explained. "So you might as well find somewhere to watch the fireworks with the rest of us. If there are any Americans left alive after the *Sunburn* launchers have done their work, they won't be in shape for sightseeing in Kobani tonight."

Zakarin had thanked the officer for the information. The attack would probably mean he would be recalled. The conflict was clearly entering a new phase if the Syrians were engaging in direct attacks on American troops. But he didn't change his plans for tonight. He had done his research very thoroughly before leaving for Kobani. Kurdish troops on Mishte-nur, supported by the Americans, had held off the Syrians once before, over three days of heavy fighting in which the Syrians used both artillery and close-support rocket fire from helicopter gunships. True, they had not used thermobaric shells, but Zakarin had also reviewed the engineering plans for the Russian-built bunkers atop Mishte-nur. Which clearly the new Syrian commander had not done.

If he had, he would have learned that the hilltop and ground-level entrances to the bunker complex were sealed behind airtight, thermobaric-blast-proof doors. Which would leave the American troops safe inside their bunkers and any Syrian troops or vehicles that made it inside the compound sitting on the summit of Mishte-nur alone and completely exposed to American air or cruise missile strikes.

No. He would still head into the city and settle in his hide. By his reckoning, the Syrian assault would probably blow itself out or be decimated by American airpower by dawn. At which time, he fully expected that the American commander and/or several of his senior officers would probably make the journey out of the base of the mountain, through the city to the YPG militia headquarters on Minaz Road, to coordinate a response.

It was neither luck, nor coincidence, but a matter of good site selection that the side entrance to the YPG headquarters which the Americans favored was clearly visible from the rooftop of the Cardamom Markets.

On the wings of BATS
Over Goztepe village, Turkey

THE Boeing Airpower Teaming System drone looked more like a grey nurse shark than a bat. Especially from where Bunny was sitting, parked fifty feet ahead and fifty feet under its squat, flattened cylindrical form. It had a nose sensor section that could be swapped out to allow it to perform air or ground recon, combat or electronic warfare roles.

It was thirty-eight feet long, only a little more than ten feet shorter than her own *Panther*. But it had a radar cross-section a hundred times larger because it was built fast and cheap and expendable. It didn't carry its weapons in stealthy bays but on wing and belly-mounted hardpoints, and she could clearly see its one remaining air-to-air missile at the end of its stubby starboard wing.

The BATS was riding in the baffles of her jet turbofan engine, which meant keeping on top of her stick and throttle so as not to make any sudden maneuvers, but it was not greatly different to the formation flying she'd had to train in back home and she made the small adjustments to her controls without thinking too hard about them as she focused on her DAS display, waiting for any sign that the Russian fighters she *knew* were out there had taken the bait and were coming for her drone.

For the first time in history, western stealth aircraft were fighting against Russian stealth aircraft, and *everyone* was on a steep learning curve.

Her other drone had been ambushed, the Syrian jamming preventing it from communicating with her to tell her it was under attack, and from where. Riding nose to tail with this drone, there was no danger another attack would go unnoticed. She'd taken command of its defensive measures so that it didn't immediately evade if it detected an enemy missile launch, but had armed its missile, as well as her own. She needed it to hold fire for just a few seconds if it was attacked. She was more than prepared to sacrifice the drone in the cause of flushing out the aircraft attacking it.

And she didn't have to wait long.

As soon as they entered the patrol area in which the last drone had disappeared, her neck started itching. Which was weird. She was neither psychic nor superstitious, but she got the definite feeling she was being *watched*. No warnings on her helmet heads-up display. Nothing on the DAS screen. She scratched her neck and followed the BATS into a slow starboard turn. Off the tip of her wing, through a gap in the thick clouds, she saw the village of Goztepe below her.

Missile launch!

Her threat warning system started screaming, though she hoped – no, prayed – the missile was aimed at the BATS. The drone automatically made a radical turn to face the source of the threat – *behind them* – and she mirrored it as best she could without blacking out, given her human limitations. The Russian missile was spearing in toward them at over Mach 2, from about twenty miles away. As it covered more than twenty-five miles a minute, she had only seconds to react to the shot.

Almost as fast as she thought it, her fingers tapped the BATS screen to put the drone on autonomous control and it reacted like a greyhound released from a starting gate. It fired blind, its remaining missile leaping off its wing on the reverse trajectory to the incoming missile, and it lit its tail, powering into a climb and forcing the Russian missile to follow it up.

She had no target lock herself. Watching the BATS' missile disappear into the distance, its seeker head looking for any indication – visual or electronic – of the enemy aircraft that had attacked it, she aligned her own much more powerful search radar on the patch of stubbornly empty sky behind the incoming Russian missile and sent a blast of X-band radar energy down the bearing of the enemy missile. At the same time, she pushed her throttle forward, breaking out of the shadow of the drone and moving toward the unknown enemy.

As her BATS cut power and turned its screaming climb into a supersonic dive with a speed that would have blacked out a human pilot, it fired off flares and chaff to spook the Russian missile now radically maneuvering to try to intercept it. Bunny ignored it. Whether it lived or died in the next minute was not relevant anymore, but she hoped her adversary had his full focus on it.

The *Panther*'s phased-array radar was designed to pick out non-stealth airborne targets up to a hundred miles away, or stealth targets within fifty miles. At that range it had the disadvantage of alerting its prey it was being tracked, but there was a time for hiding and a time for fighting, and the time had come for her *Panther* to show its teeth.

You beauty, she muttered to herself as not one, but three icons appeared on her helmet display. *Felons*, hidden from her DAS optical sensor by atmospherics and distance, not even showing on infrared. They hadn't been able to hide from her radar at such close range, though. One was maneuvering to avoid the BATS' missile, which had gone active and was pursuing. Her combat AI automatically assigned a missile to each of the other *Felons* and she quickly cancelled the decision, reallocating two missiles to the *Felon* that was already maneuvering, knowing the pilot would be compromised. Her thumb twitched on the missile release. "Fox 3, bitches," she called and as her missiles blasted away from her aircraft she rolled her *Panther* onto its back and pulled toward the earth below, knowing she had just stirred a hornet's nest.

DMITRY Bebenko was also cussing. "Pizdets!" he exclaimed as his calm and ordered world went to hell in a matter of seconds. What was looking like another easy kill on a Coalition BATS had turned into a fight for his life as first the BATS-launched missile began homing on him, and then his radar warning receiver started warbling in his ears, followed immediately by a missile launch warning, and he saw he now had not one, not two, but *three* CUDA missiles coming for him as the F-35 *Panther* that fired on him last made its retreat!

He didn't have time to issue orders to his flight; his combat AI was having a meltdown trying to decide how to minimize the probability of a hit from the three missiles. It had been giving him a steering cue to avoid the first missile, and he had been steering to that, waiting for the indication to break hard and dodge the missile. Now it showed him a new cue in a different quarter, and he rolled his *Felon* quickly left and pulled its nose up, trying to put it on the bearing the AI suggested, before the steering cue blinked and changed back to where it had been before. And back. And back again.

He knew what that meant. Take your pick, you will probably die either way.

Forget that. He hit the *Felon*'s 'panic button', which was the only option apart from the ejection handle left to a pilot in the face of certain doom. It simultaneously initiated every countermeasure the *Felon* possessed, firing infrared-blinding flares, radar-blinding chaff and a metal foil-lined electronic noise emitter on a parachute into the sky behind him. At the same time, his *Felon*'s own phased-array radar system locked onto the fleeing *Panther*, fired two K-77M missiles at it and then switched in a heartbeat to jamming the missiles now just seconds from obliterating him.

And it nearly worked.

The BATS' missile was spooked by the rain of flares and chaff and detonated harmlessly in a cloud of tinfoil. Bunny's first CUDA missile fell in digital love with the electronic noise emitter floating gently to earth on a parachute in Bebenko's wake and embraced it with a blast-fragmentation hug so close it generated a shockwave Bebenko could feel.

Bunny's second CUDA missile was not so disloyal. It only had eyes for Bebenko's *Felon* and, guiding itself to a position just in front of his twin Saturn turbofan engines, it slammed into his fighter and detonated inside one of the *Felon*'s fuel tanks.

Shaken into action by the violence of the explosion, Bebenko's combat AI automatically fired his ejection seat, launching him through the fireball of fuel and shrapnel and into the freezing sky above Goztepe.

The third-degree burns from the flaming fuel alone would have probably killed him, if he hadn't already had the back of his head removed by a piece of flying metal from the disintegrating aircraft. So it didn't really matter anymore to the late and fatally timid Captain Dmitry Bebenko that his parachute was going to land him just five hundred yards away from his former wingman, Yevgeny Bondarev, who was trying to warn the non-Russian, non-English-speaking commander of the Syrian 25th Special Missions & Counterterrorism Division that he had two bloody Turkish *Leopard* tanks about to attack his rear, *dammit*.

And Dmitry was even more unimpressed by the first detonation, between his gently swinging dead feet, of the first of the *Stormbreaker* glide bombs from Meany's *Tempest*.

"Tell the Colonel that he is not facing a platoon of bloody *Leopards*, he is only facing two, but that at this very moment they are relocating from that hamlet..." Bondarev pointed over the top of the armored fighting vehicle he'd been directed to, at the village across the motorway, "... down a utility road behind that embankment and they are about to smack him right in the ass if he doesn't do something about it!"

Bondarev had been halted by a Syrian army warrant officer at the rear of the vehicle and had been shouting over his shoulder at the nonplussed Arab colonel inside for nearly five minutes, with no sign anything he said was getting through.

"You go there," the warrant officer was telling him, pointing to a truck full of troops. "You wait, there."

Bondarev looked at the truck, then back at the warrant officer. "I am not going to sit in that bloody truck, I am going to..."

As he spoke, the truck disappeared in a cloud of dirt and flame. The ground around the command vehicle heaved, and Bondarev and the Syrian warrant officer were thrown into the back of the IFV and buried under about four hundred pounds of prime Turkish farmland.

BUNNY didn't register the RAF *Stormbreaker* strike, though if she'd had her cockpit open, she might just have been able to hear it. She was, literally, down at rooftop level south of Incirlik, with Bebenko's missile two hundred yards behind her. One of the visual navigation landmarks outside Incirlik was the old cement factory outside its southeast boundary, and she steered straight for its two huge mixing tanks. The gap between them was about a hundred yards, and she rolled her *Panther* onto a wingtip as she slid between them, before pulling her flight stick hard back against its gimbals, gritting her teeth and panting as her vision began to gray out.

Bebenko's missile slammed into one of the towers and she quickly righted her machine. "Incirlik control, this is Sunset two. Requesting clearance for immediate landing on taxiway two south." She had to repeat the message twice, the static on the air traffic frequency nearly drowning out the controller's reply.

As the controller came back to her with an approach vector, she quickly scanned her tactical screen. She had shut down her radar the moment her missiles had launched, and with it she'd lost track of the enemy aircraft. If she'd hit any of them, she would probably never know. But there *was* one aircraft showing on her DAS...

"Well hello, pupper," she said in surprise. About a mile behind her, faithfully following her back to the air base, was her remaining BATS. It had apparently evaded the Russian attack and, having exhausted its weapons, had set itself to autonomous trail mode.

"Incirlik control, Sunset two. Make that clearance for two aircraft," she said, smiling. As she set herself for a quick touchdown at the airfield just two miles away, she tried and failed to park her apprehensions. Would there be a ground crew waiting to refuel and rearm her own machine, let alone the drone? Or would every sensible noncombatant at Incirlik have loaded themselves onto a truck and high tailed it west?

THE problem with precision-guided munitions was their misleading name. They could be precisely targeted, but they were *dumb*. Launched in semi-autonomous targeting seeking mode, the *Stormbreaker*'s tri-mode seeker heads were able to identify targets and classify them – car, truck, building, tank, human – and prioritize them according to the protocols set when they were launched. The RAF pilots had been given Syrian armor as their primary targets and so had chosen a vehicle attack profile that prioritized tanks and other tracked vehicles. Only if they failed to identify those did they home in on transport trucks.

As they were glide bombs and not more maneuverable missiles, not all were in a position to strike the Syrian tanks, so they chose transports, like the one a short way from Yevgeny Bondarev, which had been vaporized, along with the twenty-two soldiers inside it, as two *Stormbreakers* slammed into it. But there were plenty of tanks within strike range of the remaining *Stormbreakers*, including the two Turkish *Leopard* tanks maneuvering to strike the rear of the Syrian column.

The dumb bombs were smart enough to recognize a tank. They were smart enough to guide themselves toward it. To reduce the risk of friendly fire, they were also fitted with Identify Friend or Foe transponders so that they would detect an IFF response from any Turkish tanks and veer away from them.

But thanks to the effectiveness of the Syrian jamming around its armored column, when the *Stormbreakers* interrogated the IFF transponders of the Turkish *Leopard* tanks, they got no response. They were not smart enough to tell the difference between the outline of a Turkish *Leopard* tank and a Russian-made T-90. Satisfied the Turkish tanks were legitimate targets, they locked onto the two Turkish tanks and their lone infantry fighting vehicle, and dropped on them.

With tragic effect.

SPITTING dirt from his mouth, his ears ringing from the shockwave of multiple bomb blasts, Bondarev crawled from the Syrian command vehicle to survey the carnage around him.

He could see ten vehicles burning. Most appeared to be tanks. It was Bondarev's first lesson in the lottery that was war. In a column of ten T-90s, the first, third and seventh had been struck. Those near them were pulling away, trying to get separation in case fuel or ammunition exploded. One had lost a track and was futilely turning in a circle.

One column over, both the first and last tanks had been struck, but all of those in between them were unscathed.

On the other side of the motorway, the Turkish side, he also saw two columns of smoke rising. No, could it be? The Coalition strike had taken out their own tanks?

He pivoted, looking over at the farm hamlet, where a Turkish infantry fighting vehicle had engaged the Syrian column with TOW missiles. It was gone, and so was most of the farm building it had been sheltering behind. He saw a burning Turkish soldier tumble from a doorway in the building and fall to the ground.

Now was their chance! The northern route around the Turkish obstruction was clear!

The Syrian warrant officer was hauling himself off the floor of the command vehicle and Bondarev pulled him roughly out.

"Thank you," the man said. "I am…"

"Shut up and look," Bondarev told him, pointing at the Turkish position by the farmhouse, and then across the motorway to the two columns of smoke he hoped were Turkish tanks. "They hit their own tanks. There is nothing to stop you going around them now!"

The warrant officer stared at him with a blank gaze, and Bondarev shook him roughly. "Look, man! No Turkish! You understand?!"

The man pulled away from Bondarev, looking at him like he was a mad man, but after a minute of staring around him, the new reality created by the Coalition strike sunk in. Without another word to Bondarev he dived back into the command vehicle and started a heated discussion with the Syrian colonel, who was also climbing back into his seat, shaking his head.

Within ten minutes, Bondarev saw indications the Syrians had seized the opportunity the friendly fire incident had offered them. They set up a line of four *Terminator* IFVs to cover their rear against the remaining Turkish trips to the south across the motorway, and then the bulk of the armored column turned north, skirting the destroyed farmhouse and the dead or wounded Turkish troops lying around it.

A troop transport rolled carefully across the plowed ground beside Bondarev, and he jumped up onto a sideboard, then swung himself inside the rear of the truck, a Syrian soldier grabbing his forearm to help him up.

The man was grinning. "Al Ruwsia?" the man asked. "Russian?"

"Russian pilot," Bondarev told him in Russian. "Thanks for the lift."

The man turned to his comrades and spoke loudly, motioning for them to hand him something. If they were rattled by the air attack a short while ago, they didn't show it.

Bondarev watched as the object was handed from one to the other, until finally the man beside him thrust it at him. "You take."

It was a stubby AMD-65 assault rifle. "Uh, thank you. Shukraan," Bondarev told him, checking it was loaded. The man handed him a second ammunition clip.

"Incirlik," the man grinned, pointing ahead of the truck. "Two miles."

Bondarev couldn't grin back. The helter-skelter Syrian advance was either madness or genius, and he tended to the view it was madness. The attack on the Turkish base should have been preceded by a massive artillery or air bombardment. It should have been initiated under the cover of air dominance. Looking out the back of the truck, he saw a parachute falling to the ground in the distance. By the shape, he knew it was a Russian parachute. So clearly air dominance hadn't been achieved.

He watched the smoke from the burning tanks rise into the air behind them. Was the Turkish blocking force and the air assault their big roll of the dice? Or was there an even greater force ahead of them, ready to clean up whatever was left of the Syrian advance after the action he'd just survived?

He was used to sitting in his aircraft thousands of feet above the battlefield, an almost unlimited amount of information at his fingertips. Down here, he was just another grunt, being taken he knew not where, to face he knew not what. His new friend nudged his shoulder and handed him a water canteen. "Dirty," he said with a smile, mimicking washing his face.

Bondarev ran a hand over his face and saw when he took it away that he was still covered in dirt and grass from the explosion of the truck that had thrown him into the back of the IFV. Pouring some water into his hand, he wiped his face clean and handed the canteen back to the soldier. The man refused to take it.

"Drink," he said. "Drink now, fight soon."

It was good advice. Bondarev didn't have his own canteen and had no idea when he'd next get the chance. As he tipped the water into his mouth, he realized suddenly how thirsty he was. After a solid mouthful he handed the canteen back again. "Spasibo. Shukraan." It was about the only Arabic he'd learned.

JENSEN had made the cover of the olive grove and was lying on his belly behind the trunk of a tree in ankle-high dead grass. Not much cover if the shooting started, but it should help to hide him from a casual observer. He had one eye fixed on the track winding down the hill in front of him, the other on the feed from the two dogs that had reached their own ambush positions on the other tracks.

Brutus had found himself an ideal location in the rubble of a destroyed farmhouse overlooking the northwestern track. He was slightly raised and had a view right down the track. Using his 360-degree vision to check his position, Jensen was satisfied the dog had broken brick on three of four sides, only his optics sticking out above the rubble around him. The dog automatically shut down all systems but those needed to keep his video feed active. From more than a couple of feet away, he would have been just another small dark shape in the shadows.

He was less happy about the position Spartacus was in. The northeastern side of the hill was covered with an old olive plantation that had been shattered under multiple years of bombardment. All that was left were rows of barren stumps. Any of the tree trunks that had been felled had been carted away for wood, so the ground was barren too. A small pedestrian track ran through the old olive grove, which connected to the track down from the hill, and from what Jensen could see, it was well used, which he didn't like. But the grove was the only cover he'd found with a decent view over the exit to that track. So with the use of his hand-held controls, he'd put a cursor over one of the larger tree stumps furthest from the pedestrian track, and ordered Spartacus to 'go there'.

The dog had slunk through the darkness to the spot indicated, and a short while later Jensen had it positioned on its haunches behind the big stump, but still with an unobstructed view around itself. Spartacus also dropped itself into stealth mode and sat perfectly still, sending its video directly to Jensen's helmet.

Anytime anything moved, whether bird, rabbit, woman or man, the dogs' vision automatically locked and tracked it, sending an alert to his heads-up display. Luckily, the traffic in and out of the Russian base was light. He could hear vehicles, some of them heavy by the sound of it, moving off to the west somewhere, but none near him.

"Button 1." A whisper-like voice in his ears. He didn't dare speak, just responded with a click on his throat mike. "I saw a bald man, long-barreled rifle, moving through the camp. I had no shot. Be ready."

Jensen replied with another click and lifted his own carbine from the grass, settling it into his shoulder and sighting on the track. The dogs were as alert as they could be, he could do nothing more. If the Russian passed close to them, and he was alone, he was ready to command them to attack. He'd discussed with the Kurdish sniper in which situations he would be willing to commit his dogs, and which not.

"If he's alone, and they can rush him without obstructions, I'll order an attack," he'd said.

"Why alone? Can't you tell your machines which one he is?" she'd asked with a frown.

"Yes, I can designate him as a target and they'll go for him," Jensen said. "But if he's not alone, the dogs will be vulnerable before, during and after the takedown. I can't afford to lose one."

"You are sentimental about these … robots?" She'd looked scornful.

"No, I am not sentimental," he'd replied. "Those 'robots' are prototypes. Half of the tech inside them is classified and I do not want to hand one of them to the Russians. Every time I take them outside the walls of COP Meyer is a calculated risk and unless I can see a clear vector on Tita Ali without risking a dog, I'm not taking the risk."

She had shaken her head in disbelief.

Her voice was in his ears again. "Nothing on southern track. He must be going north, toward your dogs."

One eye still on the track in front of him scanning for any movement, Jensen focused on the feed from Spartacus and Brutus.

Right on cue, a small chime sounded in his ears and a box locked around a shape that was barely visible against the infrared green background in which Brutus was broadcasting. The image resolved itself into a human, walking slowly down the track.

Infrared vision was notoriously fuzzy but there was no point switching Brutus to low-light yet. *Come on, show me a rifle, boy.* If it was on his back he wouldn't see it on infrared, but if he … *There!* The figure was holding something long and thin across himself, blocking the heat from his body. Sure, could be a shovel. More like a rifle. A small scale on the side of Brutus's video feed showed him an estimated range to the target. A hundred feet. Ninety. Seventy.

He cued an attack sequence. The series of orders would take the dog out of stealth mode, set its balance gyros quietly spinning ready for a quick launch, and set the engagement profile to 'assault'. Brutus was armed with the 12 gauge automatic shotgun attachment. In assault mode he would leave cover, sprint toward the target and close to lethal range, and then start firing at the target. His magazine carried six shells, with no reload capability. If the target was still moving and he was out of ammunition, he would bludgeon it and pin it, like he had done with the sniper in the school building a few days earlier.

But first, Jensen had to be sure they had the right target. They wouldn't get a second chance at an ambush like this.

Fifty feet. Jensen flipped Brutus's vision to low-light mode. The small screen flared and then settled. The shape was almost indistinguishable against the dark hillside still. Just a shadow moving among shadows. He wasn't moving fast, just above a saunter. Trying not to attract attention from watchers inside the city itself? Or just out for an evening stroll?

In a war zone.

Not likely. "No target," Daryan repeated in his ear and he flipped his focus to the track ahead of him, checked it was clear, then back to the feed from Brutus.

Thirty feet. Now he could see the shape of the man. Short, squat. Holding a rifle up across his chest like a rower in a kayak would hold his oar. That was strange. Like he expected to need to use it at any moment. OK, that made him a careful man. But it didn't make him Tita Ali.

"Show me your shiny head," Jensen whispered to himself. But of course it wouldn't shine. The guy was a professional, and it was a three-quarter full moon tonight. He probably had a balaclava or scarf over his head.

Twenty feet. Scarf. Tied over his head like a bandana. Jensen had been in country a few months now and had never seen a Syrian wear a bandana like that. He couldn't see the man's face, but it was nearly enough. Nearly. Using the hand-held control in his left hand, he zoomed in on the rifle across the man's chest. Lobaev? He couldn't see, dammit! But it had a long barrel, longer than an assault rifle. And a very, very large scope.

Got you, you bastard.

Jensen's thumb hovered on the trigger on his control which would send Brutus into action.

The man stopped and turned. Looking up the track behind him. As he did so, he raised a hand. On Brutus's audio feed Jensen heard him call out in greeting. At the same time, two new targets were locked by Brutus, small squares dancing on his video feed as two new soldiers came down the track toward the first. He lowered his rifle to his side and waited for them.

Dammit!

For a mad half-second, Jensen thought about sending Brutus anyway. With a top speed of 60 miles per hour on flat ground, say 20 mph up a winding track like this, the dog could reach the target before the other soldiers could react. They'd see a strange, low shape running up the track toward Tita Ali, see the flash and hear the report of the shotgun rounds being fired, but it would be almost over before they'd even get their own weapons up and aimed.

Almost, but not quite. And what if they got lucky?

In ten years, when automatons like Brutus were a part of the battlefield wallpaper, he'd have had no hesitation. But his orders were very clear. Come home with both LS3 *Hunter* units, or don't come home at all.

In mute disbelief, he watched the three Russian soldiers walk within ten feet of Brutus, never knowing how close the hand of death had been, and then disappear into the darkness. Flipping to infrared just prolonged his agony, as they reached the end of the track, stood and talked for a few minutes more, and then went their separate ways, the two soldiers heading east on a patrol no doubt, the Russian sniper – for Jensen was in no doubt now that it was him – going northwest to skirt around the Kurdish positions there.

To make his way into the city. And ready himself to shoot another Marine.

ANDREI Zakarin had been close to death many times in his life. But never so close that he felt death's cold hand brush against his cheek. He reflected on that as he unlocked the stormwater drain on the north side of the city and began waddling up it. He felt the photograph of his daughter in his top pocket to make sure it wasn't in danger of falling out. As long as it was there, he feared nothing.

He realized that was superstitious nonsense. But he'd had a photo of his daughter either in a locket around his neck or as a photo in his breast pocket ever since she had been born, and he was still alive. Was that coincidence? He didn't intend to find out.

If he was killed, it would be with a picture of his daughter close to his heart, where he could reach it if he lived long enough. And then he'd simply wait for her to join him in the afterlife. Zakarin was doubly sure he'd see her again, even if he was killed. His father was a devout Muslim who had taken his son to the mosque every Friday of his young life, and his mother was a converted former Orthodox Christian who had secretly taken Zakarin to be baptized as a baby and let him know when he was a teen that doing so had bought him a guaranteed place in heaven.

With the two of them praying for him, with his heart filled with love for his wife and daughter, Zakarin was sure he would be forgiven any mortal transgressions he might mistakenly make in this life. He was a soldier, doing a soldier's work. Had Christ not forgiven the soldier who pierced his side as he hung on the cross? Had he not forgiven the thief hanging beside him? Had Allah not said in the 40th Hadith Qudsi, "So long as you call on me, I shall forgive you for what you have done?"

He was reciting the verse to himself as he emerged from the stormwater drain into the ruined building in the northern part of Kobani, just outside the large marketplace. The building made the perfect covert entrance. Not only was it little more than cavernous rubble, but it was surrounded by abandoned motor vehicle bodies that had been stripped of every last valuable part, down to the nuts and bolts, leaving only rusting skeletons piled up, on and around each other. He spent several minutes looking for movement and saw none, and began walking casually toward the nearest of the two long market halls.

The Cardamom Markets were in fact two long tin-roofed sheds, each about four hundred feet long. One was open to the air, filled just with stalls and topped with corrugated iron roofing, while the other housed the wealthier merchants in plywood and extruded concrete showrooms. It was this one he made for. There were a couple of lights on – traders staying back late doing their books or counting their stock perhaps – but they would not see him.

The building he approached had the same iron framework as the other, which served as a ladder for workmen sent up to repair leaking roof iron, solar panels or television receivers.

More importantly, as he noted with satisfaction as he climbed up to the roof level, it was littered with the debris of a thousand lazy tradesmen. Discarded satellite dishes, broken solar panels and frames, rusted and discarded antennas, even old empty water tanks from a time before the city had reliable mains water. It was one of these that he'd marked as a good shooting hide. Half toppled over, the base lying tilted on the roof formed a small, shaded triangular shelter a man could sit or crouch in. With his camouflage cape over him, he would be almost invisible from any distance, even if an unlucky repairman was to climb onto the roof while he was in position. In several places across the roof, external air conditioning units thumped rhythmically, pumping cool air into the showrooms below, their thermal signatures offering perfect camouflage against infrared scopes or binos.

And the base was raised two feet above the rest of the roof, giving him a perfect view down the short boulevard to the side entrance of the YPG building. When he'd first scoped it out, he had seen numerous personnel going in and out the door. Though the Kurdish officers deliberately wore no badges of rank, Zakarin had learned from the troops already stationed in Kobani when he arrived how to tell the officers from the lower ranks. The officers had the coolest sunglasses.

Ingress and egress were the most dangerous parts of any mission. More dangerous even than the moment he took the shot. The constant motorcycle, moped, car and truck traffic on the road outside during the day would mask the report of his rifle, and even if it didn't, the tin roof would fling the sound into the air in several directions, making it hard to pinpoint.

Moving into and out of a hide, he was most exposed. Movement attracted eyes. Eyes that guided bullets. But he climbed up into his nest without any drama, sat down with his legs crossed, pulled his cape over himself and laid his equipment out in front of him. Water, energy bars, ammunition. Lifting his Lobaev, he ejected, checked and reloaded the round inside, then formed the cape around the rifle so that when he lifted it, it didn't obstruct his view through the scope. Then he lowered it again, placed it across his thighs and closed his eyes. He had a long night ahead of him, though it seemed his peaceful repose would sooner or later be broken by the Syrian attack on the American outpost.

His cape obscured any view of the small hilltop, but in any case it didn't interest him. All that concerned him was what he would see through his scope in a few hours' time. He leaned back against the frame of the water tank. He wouldn't sleep, that would be dangerous. But he had perfected a form of meditation which was nearly as restful, while allowing him to keep his senses alert to the environment around him.

Or so he thought.

"Move an inch and I will shoot you in the head," a quiet female voice close behind him said.

NASRIN Khalid had a *Tokarev* pistol she'd kept back from a recent arms shipment. As she'd heard the soft footfall on the metal roof over her head, she'd reached into her drawer and pulled it out.

Daryan had taught her not only how to shoot it, but also how to strip it down and clean it afterward. Looking up at the ceiling and following the footsteps with her ears, she had slipped an eight-round magazine into it. She cursed quietly. She'd just sent her own security detail home, telling them she'd be locking up soon. They weren't there to guard her, just the valuables she had locked away in chests and cabinets on the ground floor, and she didn't need them once she'd closed and bolted the doors for the night. She never kept weapons or ammunition on the premises – that would be an invitation to armed robbery – but prescription meds fetched a handsome price on Kobani's black market and her boys had seen off more than a couple of would-be standover merchants.

Her first thought had been thieves. Six months earlier, two local boys had climbed up onto the roof and used an oxyacetylene torch to cut through the roofing iron into the showroom of a carpet dealer. Unfortunately for them, the torch had started a small fire and they were caught before they'd even got down from the roof, but she knew that wouldn't stop another idiot from trying it again.

One of the idiosyncrasies of the office she'd rented in the northwest corner of the market building was that in the small rear storeroom, there was a ladder to a trapdoor in the roof. It was a pain in the backside if work was needed on the roof, because it was the only ladder to the roof, so she had tradesmen tramping in and out of her office whenever something needed fixing. On the other hand, it meant she quickly learned who the good and bad tradespeople were, for when she needed them. The good ones were polite, came more or less at the time she'd agreed with them and cleaned up after themselves. The bad ones she never let in more than once.

Taking off her high-heeled shoes and slipping on a pair of sneakers she kept under her desk, she'd climbed one-handed up the ladder, carefully and quietly opened the hatch and stuck her head out, shortly followed by the *Tokarev*. In Kobani, where even taxi drivers carried assault rifles, you didn't take chances with thieves.

It was nearly midnight, but the moon was bright, and she saw a short, stocky figure pick his way down the roof to an old water tank.

What in hell was he up to?

When he got to the tank, he leaned a rifle against the support base, climbed up into the wrecked tank stand, and pulled the rifle in after him.

Alright, so, not a carpet thief.

And not a YPG sniper either. There would be no reason for a Kurdish sniper to crawl into a water tank located at the city end of the row of market showrooms. From there, he could only shoot *into* the city, not outward where the Syrian enemy was.

Criminal? That was always possible. There were plenty of merchants at the markets who owed the wrong person money, or screwed up a business deal. Bad business blood in Kobani was often settled with knives or guns. But this? Crawling onto a roof in the middle of the night and waiting ... for what? Daylight? A nocturnal business deal out on the streets below?

She hesitated. She had multiple options. To name a few; just climb back down the ladder, lock the hatch and make out she heard nothing. But what if the shooter was after one of her own valuable clients? How dumb would she feel then? Another option, go back down and call her sister. But Daryan could be anywhere either inside or outside the city. The last phone call had told her nothing except that she or someone else was running low on ammunition. Daryan wasn't her only militia contact, of course. She could call a commander she knew and get him to send a few men. Unless the shooter was a criminal, and not military. In which case, making the wrong phone call could get her killed if the faction she called was involved in whatever the guy on the roof was doing.

At the end of the day, though, Nasrin wasn't the kind of woman who had made a small medicine import business into the biggest arms and narcotics import business in Kobani by ignoring problems. Problems were just opportunities other people couldn't see. And there was almost no situation that couldn't be turned to advantage somehow.

So she climbed out of the trapdoor and crept across the roof toward the water tank, watching carefully where she put her feet. She paused a couple of times and crouched down as the figure inside the fallen frame of the water tank adjusted his position and finally pulled some sort of groundsheet over himself. Definitely an assassin of some sort.

A small, delicious thrill ran up her back. She knew what she was doing was foolhardy. She didn't care. Two more steps took her within ten feet of the man. The groundsheet he'd covered himself with covered his frontal aspect, but not his back. She could clearly see him sitting, legs crossed, his rifle across his thighs, back up against a thin A-frame pole. On his head, strangely, a dark bandana.

She sighted on the bandana. It was not tied in the Syrian or Kurdish style. So, a Russian?

"Move an inch and I will shoot you in the head."

ZAKARIN made no sudden move, nor did he freeze. He had his hands on his rifle, as always, and moved his finger inside the trigger guard, knowing the action couldn't be seen by whoever was behind him. But to make a shot, he would have to twist awkwardly and fire. He wasn't sure he could even do so within the cramped confines of the fallen water tower stand. He could roll forward, but that would give whoever was behind him a moment in which to fire, and she sounded close. He decided his best option for now was to bluff while he fished for an alternative.

"I will not move," he said out loud in English. "You are YPJ?"

She laughed. "Oh, my friend, I am much worse."

His finger tightened on the trigger. Arabic accent. Female. Not YPJ. Alone?

"Relax, alright? I'm American!" he said.

"Oh, you're American?" She sounded amused. "Well, American, what are you doing on my roof?"

"We ... there's a VIP arriving tomorrow, I am in his protection detail," he said. He tried glancing over his shoulder.

"Do not move!" she repeated. "I am very good with this *Tokarev* pistol and your back is very broad and very close."

"Alright, alright," he said, facing forward again. *Tokarev* pistol? Eight shots. Chambered for 7.62mm probably. Enough punch to make a mess of his exposed back and the organs behind it. "Take it easy, lady."

"No, I don't think so, thank you," she said. "Where in America are you from, American?"

"Chicago."

"Where in Chicago?"

He thought furiously.

"The Bay Area, enough with the twenty questions," he said. He took his hand off his rifle and reached for the throwing knife in a holder on his belt. "I'm going to put my gun down and push it away with my feet, alright?"

"No. Move that gun and I will shoot you. Move your feet and I will shoot you."

So why haven't you shot me already? he asked himself. Worse than YPJ? Who was this woman?

"You know, I lived in Dubai for some time. And even in Kobani I met many Americans. Tell me, American. Why do you have a Russian accent?"

He had tired of bluffing. If she was going to shoot him outright, she'd have done it already.

"You have me," he said. "Yes, I am Russian. So, what now?"

"I have been thinking about that," the voice said. "I want only three things from you."

"Which are?"

"Your name. Your real name. Your rank. And your service number," she said.

He frowned. "No. Why?"

"Because if you don't give me your real name, your rank, and your service number I will shoot you in the back. But if you do give me your details, your true details, I will back away, go back to my office and you can safely and quietly get the hell off my roof and go back to wherever you came from."

Ten feet. She was about ten feet behind him. He had his hand on the hilt of his throwing knife, holding it in a hammer grip. Twist, and throw. She was an amateur, the conversation told him that much. Civilian. Not militia. She might get a shot off, but she'd probably miss. But she might not. His knife probably wouldn't miss. But it might.

He thought of his daughter. No. Keep playing the odds, Andrei. As long as she is talking, she isn't shooting.

"Come on," she said. "It's less than you'd end up telling the YPG if they'd caught you up here. Much less."

"Why do you want my name, rank and service number?"

He could hear the smile in her voice. "Because one day, this little war is going to be over. Maybe we Kurds will win. Or maybe we will lose. If we lose, and the Russians and Syrians will be back here rounding up militia leaders and … well, shall we say, 'prominent business persons' … I'd like to be able to say something like, 'Please don't shoot me, please contact my personal Russian best friend Ivan…'"

Now he smiled too. "Andrei," he said.

"Good, yes. Please contact my good friend Andrei, who I could have shot in the head, but didn't. He will vouch for me."

Was it really that simple? If she was lying, it was a very curious lie. He touched the photograph in his pocket and closed his eyes, then relaxed the grip on his knife. *Tell her, Daddy. Tell her the truth.*

"Lieutenant Andrei Zakarin," he told the voice. "Four seven six, nine two seven three, L for lima."

She repeated the alphanumeric ID a few times, until she could repeat it without a mistake.

"Thank you," she said. Was her voice further away? "I am going back down now. The gun is still pointed at your back, but I suppose you could try to shoot me. I hope you don't."

Her voice was moving away. He decided to remain still, but slipped his hand into the trigger guard of his Lobaev again. After a couple of minutes he couldn't hear her moving, but then, she'd already snuck up behind him once before. She was good on her feet, he had to give her that.

Her voice was further away now. "In two minutes, you can turn around. In three minutes, I will call the local YPG command post and tell them I heard something on the roof. So, you probably have five minutes to get down from here and get away."

Now he heard a noise. The clang of a metal door and the click of a lock or bolt. He'd passed the rusted trapdoor on the way across the roof more than once and tested it to see if it would open. It had been locked from the inside. He'd seen that as a plus, thinking any tradesmen coming up to the roof that way would have to make a lot of noise.

Which they would, unlike that damn suspicious woman with her *Tokarev*. If she was even carrying one.

He lifted the cover of his watch and waited as another minute passed.

Enough! He tensed his shoulders, rolled into a crouch with the knife ready to throw, finally looking behind himself but seeing only the dark, empty roof. She had not lied.

Gathering up his things, he rolled his cape into a tight cylinder and put it into his trouser pocket, put the canteen on his belt and returned his knife to its sheath. Picking up his rifle, he began moving, more quickly this time than previously, toward the rear of the roof.

He got down the support column without incident and paused at the bottom. There were lights in three of the offices. He had no idea where the ladder from the trapdoor led. She could have been in any one of the offices, and he had no doubt she was already calling the local YPG garrison. He ran across the bare earth back into the cover of the skeletal cars and dropped down into the open stormwater outlet.

He could relocate and start over. It was still dark, hours from daylight. He had, of course, several other hides picked out and one was as good as another really. But the night felt wrong. He checked his equipment again, compulsively running his hands across his shirt, his belt, his trousers and his rifle, and then repeating the action again. *No, no more tonight.* He would return to the camp, lie on his bunk and listen to the slaughter on Mishte-nur Hill. He would reflect on what was probably the most curious night of his life so far, and then in the morning he would reset, and resume his mission.

If there were any Americans left to kill. They were, after all, very *old* thermobaric-blast-proof doors.

NASRIN put down her cell phone and collapsed into her chair, kicking off her sneakers. Then she picked up the phone again and made a note of the Russian's service ID and name. Sure, he could have been lying his face off, but for some reason she didn't think so. When she was done, she held the phone out at the end of her outstretched arm. Her hand had been shaking as she held the phone, but it was pretty steady now.

Someone on the roof of the markets, northwest side. Sure, it could just be thieves again. Could also be an enemy sniper, she'd told them, mischievously. They'd send someone, they said, but didn't sound in too much of a hurry. Probably thought she was just being hysterical.

Her new Russian friend would certainly have time to make his escape.

She spun her chair around, smiling. If he had told the truth, that had been quite a profitable transaction. And who knows, she may have saved someone's life, scaring that Russian off her roof.

She stopped the chair turning, dropped the phone again, picked the *Tokarev* off her desk, took out the magazine and put them both back in her top drawer. Then she noticed that in all the excitement, she'd chipped a bloody nail. With a tired curse, she pulled a cuticle file out of the drawer next to the *Tokarev* and began filing the chipped nail.

Nasrin Khalid, hero of Kobani! They should build her a statue. She blew on the nail.

Fat chance.

"Any chance we got a wild weasel flight up can take out that jamming?" Barruzzi asked hopefully. She was hunkered down over her screens inside the *HELLADS* command truck, but she was getting more noise than clarity on the unit's radar. Digital comms were gone to hell; they were relying on fiber optic. Electricity was still out.

Sun had just gotten off the blower with battalion command. "RAF and RAAF laid a hurt on the Syrian armor but had to bug out. Turks are trying to pull together some F-16s to take down the Syrian electronic warfare units but they're asking for Coalition fighter cover we don't have."

The new Russian-made *Belladonna*-4 jamming systems fielded by Syria could jam drones, early warning aircraft, and air-to-ground missiles – including those intended to kill them. If their operators detected a homing anti-radar missile, or HARM, headed their way, they could generate a decoy signal to pull the missile off target. But ironically, they were vulnerable to optically guided dumb bombs like the *Stormbreaker*, which targeted them according to their physical forms, not their electronic signatures.

The Syrian jamming was also effective against Incirlik's radar-guided air and indirect fires defenses, like the *Patriot* missile batteries. That left only the 20mm *Centurion* counter-rocket, artillery and mortar (C-RAM) autocannons and *HELLADS* laser defense units, which could also track incoming projectiles with infrared sensors. Infrared was only effective at short range, though, which gave either system only seconds to detect and intercept fast-moving projectiles.

"Where are the Syrians?" Allenby asked.

"Two miles northwest," Sun told him. "Just out of Goztepe. We got a drone over them and some images back before it was shot down. Tanks, IFVs, troops and *SMERCH* rocket launchers back behind them. Looked like the arty was being readied to lay down a barrage, so stay sharp."

The order was redundant. They were as ready as they could be. System powered up, capacitors charged, infrared sensors prioritized. At the speeds it would have to react, their battery was set to auto-lock and fire mode. The first they would know they were under attack would be when the hum of the first laser bolts hit their ears. It could also be the last thing they heard.

Barruzzi suddenly heard what Sun had said. "*Two miles?!* How far out is the Bloody First?"

"Advance units should be here in forty minutes to an hour."

Advance units. That meant JLTV light tactical vehicles armed with 25mm chain guns and TOW missiles. Behind them, the crewless remotely piloted Bradley Fighting Vehicles; heavier armor, same light weapons. The Big Red One's heavy hitters, their M1A3 *Abrams* main battle tanks, were probably on trailer trucks piling down the highway behind the *Bradleys*. The lighter units would have to try to hold the Syrian T-90s back long enough for the 1st Infantry Division's *Abrams* to get into the fight.

Which might be too late for Barruzzi, Sun and Allenby. Their battery was positioned at the northwest corner of the airfield perimeter. If the Syrians were coming from the direction of Goztepe, then they were directly in the most likely line of advance for the Syrian tanks. Their command truck was wheels-down in a defile, just its radar dish showing above ground level, but the dish itself might as well be painted pink with a big 'shoot me' sign on it once those Syrian T-90s moved in. They would target the radar dish first, and then start taking down the laser arrays mounted in a wide semi-circle around it.

The fact they had a platoon of Turkish airfield defense troops dug into a trench a hundred yards out front of them didn't reassure Barruzzi greatly. The Syrian *SMERCH* multiple rocket launchers could send twelve 300mm projectiles over inside thirty seconds and they were designed specially to take out well-dug-in troops. They were big rockets, each twenty feet long, and they were also damn powerful, each one carrying 400lbs. of high explosive or 72 4lb. anti-personnel warheads. The only upside, if the Syrians were getting ready to lay down a *SMERCH* barrage, was that they took twenty minutes to reload.

Which gave you just enough time to carry off your dead and wounded before the dying started again.

"We need that damn jamming taken down," Barruzzi cursed, "if we're going to have half a chance here."

As she spoke, she heard the unmistakable rumble of an F-35 *Panther* approaching to land. A few months on base and she could tell every aircraft by the noise it made and the way their command truck vibrated.

"You said they'd all bugged out?" Barruzzi asked Sun.

He looked up at the roof of the truck as the fighter swept in low overhead. "What I was told. Two USAF B-21 *Raiders* out of Ramstein are en route, will be in standoff missile range in thirty minutes. RAAF is turning around a squadron of *Panthers* quick as they can down at Akrotiri to try and give the missiles clear air overhead, but they only just went wheels dry in Cyprus. I'm not hopeful."

"Well, that was a *Panther* landing," Barruzzi said. "So the RAAF still has someone left here." She stood.

"What are you doing, Barruzzi?" Sun asked.

Barruzzi grabbed her assault rifle and slung it over her shoulder. "Allenby can take my station, sir. RAAF hangars are two hundred yards away. With your permission, I'm going down there to make sure their commander realizes it's going to be raining 300mm frags on his nice shiny airplanes unless he takes out those jamming units."

BUNNY had her cockpit open and helmet off before her machine had even jerked to a stop outside the RAAF maintenance bay, the BATS drone following her in like a duckling behind a mother duck. The airfield had looked ominously deserted as she'd come in. The runway landing lights were dimmed and there were virtually no other lights showing across the base. She'd spotted the dark shapes of Turkish troops hunkered down in trenches and behind walls of sandbags or concrete barriers, seen a few squads doubling across the ground to get into defensive positions, and a US Army Humvee tearing across the airfield on some urgent mission or other, but the sight of aircraft constantly taxiing, landing and taking off was jarring by its absence.

Incirlik was a ghost field.

She'd nearly given up hope of even refueling as she'd approached the maintenance bay, but then a hangar slammed open, light flooded out and the Flight Sergeant she'd spoken with less than thirty minutes earlier was sprinting toward her with a mixed RAAF and Turkish Air Force ground crew. One of them was driving a fuel bowser, others were towing a long, flat bomb dolly.

She half climbed, half fell out of the cockpit, dropped the small ladder on the side of the fighter and climbed stiffly down. Her head and shoulders felt like she'd just taken a full frontal hit from a 250lb. linebacker. Rolling her shoulders, she waited by her kite as the crewmen started bustling around it. One of the RAAF crew triggered the ordnance bay doors on her fighter and jumped underneath it.

"What have you got for me, Sergeant?" she asked as he came jogging up.

"Only gunnies I could find were Turkish, and they aren't used to tooling up the *Panther*, ma'am," he said, trying to get his breath back. "So I went with a payload they were familiar with from their F-16s."

Bunny narrowed her eyes. "How bad?"

"GBU-31 JDAM bombs and *Sidewinders*," he said sheepishly. "Best I could get. Six bombs, four missiles for you. Four for your BATS."

"Bombs configured how?"

"Laser and GPS."

Bunny thought fast. The 2,000lb. GBU-31 packed a decent punch, but it was a generation older and dumber than the *Stormbreaker*. It had no onboard target recognition capability, it was normally guided to its target using GPS coordinates, which had some anti-jamming capabilities but would be almost completely unreliable given the high-power jamming she'd experienced coming down – enough to scramble any satellite signal. Luckily it also had a laser seeker, which enabled it to hit any target she painted with the laser on her *Panther*. The bad thing about that was it required her to maintain a DAS visual lock on the target to guide each bomb in.

If she was picked up by Syrian anti-air missile batteries or Russian fighters, she'd be a sitting bloody duck. And there was another problem.

"Five, not six bombs," she told the sergeant. "I got a defective *Gray Wolf* still hanging on a hardpoint inside my weapons bay. Unless your Turkish friends can pull it off?"

"I'll get them to have a look, ma'am," the man said, and ducked under the nose of the fighter to supervise the loading.

As she watched him go, she heard a loud explosion from the northwest. It sounded close. Syrian armor, no doubt. But was it taking fire or dealing it?

"Two miles out," Bunny heard a voice say. "In case you're wondering."

She turned and saw the US Army sergeant she'd been speaking to the day before coming up behind her. The woman looked out of breath, but she was still carrying the rifle Bunny had seen her with the day before. Bunny pointed at it.

"You sleep with that thing?"

"I've slept with uglier," the woman said with a shrug. "I thought your people had all pulled back to Cyprus?"

"They have," Bunny told her.

"But not you?"

"No. I had some …. technical problems, kind of thing," Bunny told her.

The US sergeant bent and looked at the bombs being loaded into Bunny's *Panther*. "Uh huh. Two-thousand-pound technical problems, by the look of it."

"Yeah. And before you ask, yes, I am going to get so busted."

"Got you. You got a mission?" the woman asked.

Did she? That was a good question.

"Well, not yet. I was going to load up, get airborne, contact the Turkish AWACS…"

"Let me tell you what's about to go down," Barruzzi said. She filled Bunny in quickly on the Russian jamming and the imminent 300mm rocket barrage. "So someone has to hit those *Belladonna* jammers. There are probably only one or two…"

"No, wait. Why don't I just take out the rocket launchers?"

"Because *we* can take down any incoming rockets," Barruzzi told her. "It's what *HELLADS* was born for. But to get them all, we'll need *HELLADS*, *Centurion* and *Patriots* all working at optimal efficiency, which means we need radar, which means we need those *Belladonnas* dead. Not to mention they are messing up everything from satellite to radio comms for about a hundred miles around, which makes them our A number 1 top priority target, wouldn't you say?"

"Where are they?" Bunny asked. "You have coordinates?"

"Not exactly. I figure from the power of their signal they have to be traveling behind the Syrian spearhead. Say ten to twenty miles back, probably just off the motorway."

"Good enough," Bunny told her. "The amount of energy they're putting out, I'll find them."

"They'll be protected," Barruzzi warned her.

"*Buks, Tunguska* 30mm ... I know."

Barruzzi looked at Bunny as though it was the last time she expected to see her. "And fighters."

Bunny nodded over at the BATS drone. "Won't be alone up there."

The Flight Sergeant stuck his head out from inside the *Panther*'s weapon's bay. "We've reseated that *Gray Wolf*, ma'am, running diagnostics again but it's reporting green across the board. You want to go with the missile, or swap it out for a two thousand pounder?"

Bunny re-evaluated the odds against her. They had just tipped a little in her favor.

"Leave it in place," she called out.

Barruzzi held out her hand. "It's Flying Officer O'Hare, right, ma'am?"

Bunny shook it. "Bunny to my mates."

"Alessa."

"That's kinda tame."

"It means 'Defender of Mankind'."

"OK, that works." Barruzzi adjusted the rifle on her shoulder and backed away. "Better get back. Lieutenant gets kinda antsy I'm not at my station when the missiles start flying. Good luck, Bunny O'Hare."

Bunny watched her go. Defender of Mankind? Yeah, that definitely worked.

BONDAREV had dismounted with the Syrian troops when the truck he was riding in had crunched down through its gears and come to a halt. His new companions had lost interest in him the moment their officers started shouting orders at them and allocating them to armored personnel carriers, or APCs. On their way forward they'd passed six truck-mounted multiple rocket launchers, Russian-made *SMERCH* systems by the look of it, their crews busy with small cranes mounted just behind their driving cabs, loading their launch tubes with the long and fat 300mm rockets. So, the Syrians intended to roll in under an artillery barrage after all. It would slow them down, but judging by the speed with which the Syrians were loading the rockets, only by thirty or forty minutes. The shock and injuries caused to any troops underneath the bombardment would probably be worth it.

He had leaned himself up against the side of the truck he'd been riding in and was watching preparations with interest.

So this is war on the ground. In his short combat career, he'd only seen it from his cockpit, usually from twenty thousand feet in the air.

It seemed to involve a lot of shouting and carrying. But he couldn't shake the conviction that as urgent as everything seemed, this was not his war. And he certainly didn't plan to die here tonight.

Speaking of shouting, he recognized the voice of the warrant officer he'd shared a mouthful of Turkish dirt with not too long ago. The man was standing about twenty feet away, motioning to him to come over to join him and another officer beside an APC in the process of being loaded with ammunition. It was too dark to guess the other officer's rank, but he hoped whoever he was had a radio that Bondarev could borrow. He needed to arrange for a Russian quadrotor to pick him up somewhere.

He heard a burst of cannon fire from a nearby vehicle as the gunner tested his guns.

Somewhere quieter.

As he approached the two men, he recognized the uniform of the other officer.

Spetsnaz. Russian Special forces. And a Captain at that. Dammit, even though he was from another service, he outranked Bondarev.

The man watched his limping approach, a slight smile on his face, which widened as he in turn recognized Bondarev's uniform. He had a cigarette and drew on it slowly before speaking. "Ah, Comrade Lieutenant, you appear to have misplaced your airplane?"

Bondarev scowled but kept his voice under control. "Yes, Comrade Captain, I was shot down."

"American anti-air missile?"

"No. British *Tempest.*"

"I thought your top-secret super-planes were invisible?" the man said, clearly enjoying himself.

"Not when the enemy is all around you."

"How careless of you. And so, here you are. Welcome to the party," the man said.

"Captain, if you could help me find a radio? I need to contact my unit," Bondarev explained.

The Spetsnaz officer nodded to the warrant officer, who didn't need a second excuse to remove himself. "I have a radio in my vehicle," the other Russian said. "I assume you want to arrange a pickup?"

"Yes, Comrade Captain."

"Of course. I will tell your unit they can pick you up from Incirlik air base, just as soon as it is in Syrian hands."

Bondarev laughed, and then realized the man was not joking.

"Comrade Captain, with respect…"

"Shut your trap, flyboy," the man spat, his demeanor changing in a second. "I lost two men back at that Turkish overpass. Where were you when those Coalition missiles hit us? Nice and safe in your climate-controlled cockpit, perhaps?"

Actually, he had been crouched under an olive tree watching it happen, but Bondarev decided it was perhaps not the best time to explain that.

"Lost your tongue now? I thought maybe you could tell me how Coalition fighters manage to launch a dozen cruise missiles at us when we are supposed to have *Russian* combat air patrols protecting our advance?"

"I am sorry for the loss of your men, Comrade Captain," Bondarev said.

The Spetsnaz officer regarded Bondarev with dead eyes. "And I am sorry for the loss of your aircraft." He turned his head, watching Syrian soldiers loading cases of 30mm cannon ammunition into the crew compartment of the APC. He turned back to Bondarev. "This is your ride. I'll tell the crew they have an extra passenger."

"Comrade Captain…"

"Save it." The captain threw his cigarette into the dirt and ground it out with his boot heel. "You are a pilot. These men will take you to the nearest airfield. I understand the fact it is currently in Turkish hands may be inconvenient for you, but

269

life was not meant to be easy, Lieutenant, and even less so in war." He jerked his head and rested his right hand on the sidearm at his hip. "Get in."

Bondarev sighed. He could see arguing would only earn himself a pistol whipping, or worse. Stepping around the captain he peered into the dimly lit interior of the APC. It had room for a crew of three, plus six or seven passengers, but it seemed every available inch of seat and floor space was being loaded with ammunition. Not only 30mm for the vehicle's *Shipunov* cannon, but, as he noted with dismay reading the Cyrillic writing on the crates, rocket-propelled grenades, rifle ammunition, fragmentation grenades and tear gas cartridges.

Forget surviving enemy fire, the thing would probably blow itself up the minute it hit a pothole.

A Syrian crewman sitting behind the vehicle steering wheel looked a question at him as he stepped up into the cabin but the Spetsnaz captain was shouting in Arabic at the vehicle crew leader, a sergeant. The sergeant shouted in turn at the crewman up the front of the vehicle, and he shrugged, reached back for a metal folding bucket seat and flipped it down so Bondarev could sit in it. Bondarev pulled the stubby assault rifle off his shoulder, put it between his feet and sat down.

He leaned his head back against a fuel can strapped to the hull of the APC, as more ammunition was shoved in around his feet, thinking to himself that there were definitely worse things than being captured by enemy forces.

Being reunited with 'friendly' forces, for example.

DARYAN had no special techniques for calming herself or staying in the moment when she was behind the scope. She just had a natural ability to block out the world around her. Such as the sudden sound of small arms fire coming from south of the American compound.

She knew Syrian patrols occasionally tried to test the American defenses but this sounded more serious – rifle fire mixed with the hammering of machine guns. There was shouting below her as the Marines inside the base reacted, pouring out of the bunker to man the walls and gates, just as soldiers had done on Mishte-nur since the time of Alexander the Great.

She ignored the commotion. She never worked with a spotter, though Ayyoub had tried several times to persuade her to work with one, if only for her own protection. But the Marines had provided her with a monocular infrared and light-intensifying eyepiece that had 20x optical and 50x digital zoom, and with that settled on her left eye she could scan the area around Kunyan Kurdan, keeping her right eye on the scope of her rifle.

Which was how she saw the Russian sniper, approaching Kunyan Kurdan from Syrian-controlled territory in the east. Bandana over his scalp, carrying his rifle in both hands across his chest, just as she had seen him do as he walked through the camp earlier that night.

A very careful man, she decided, pushing the monocle aside and laying her cheek against her rifle. *Leaves from the north, returns from the east. A detour, unpredictable.* She moved her rifle slowly, scanning the area in which she had seen him through her scope. He had just been leaving a line of trees, walking along a small road that led from farmland in to Kobani. *There.* She zeroed his torso in her sights and pressed the laser rangefinder. It painted him with a brief pulse and sent the data it got back to her scope. Two thousand four hundred yards. Too far. She knew the limits of her abilities. But he was walking along the track at a steady, even pace, apparently feeling safe.

"Button 1, do you hear me?" she said into her throat mike.

"Read you, no target here," Jensen replied. "Is that small arms fire I hear?"

"I have the target," she said, ignoring the question. "Approaching Kunyan Kurdan on the eastern access road. Five hundred yards out, moving at normal walking speed. I do not yet have a shot."

"Any other activity on that road?"

She didn't expect it, as it was approaching 1 a.m., but the Syrians could have a patrol out. She scanned the area. "No, just the target."

"Relocating dogs now," Jensen said. "As soon as you have the shot, send it. Even if you just pin him down, we can flank him while he's out in the open."

"Yes. Out."

She lasered the Russian again. The small bullet predictor cross was at his waist, but blinking red, indicating the man was still out of range. She lifted the cross anyway and put it on his chest. He did not seem to be wearing any body armor. *A careful man, but a confident one.* Every step took him closer to Kunyan Kurdan, but also closer to the range at which she could strike. She calmed her breathing and curled her fingertip around the trigger of her Lobaev.

JENSEN was sprinting, all caution gone for the moment. He'd pulled up an image of the road the Syrian was returning on and saw it intersected with the track on the south of the hill, the one they had hoped he would use either exiting or re-entering the Russian camp. And it seemed he was headed for it, but for the next few minutes he would be out in open farmland. They would never have a better chance to hit him where he was unprotected.

Jensen had immediately sent coordinates to Spartacus and Brutus. Not to ambush, but to attack. Brutus was in the worst position, on the far side of Kunyan Kurdan hill from the target. Jensen gave him waypoints that would send him around the hill to the north, through the blasted olive grove in which Spartacus had been camped and then directly across a field of dead grass at the target. He set the last waypoint to 'attack' and, at the same time, turned on his own IFF transponder so the dogs wouldn't confuse him for an enemy combatant. In order to reduce the chance of injury to civilians, their AI was designed to identify 'combatants' by the fact they were carrying weapons or moving in specific threatening ways, but Jensen would be doing both, and if his IFF wasn't squawking, they'd see him as a threat too.

Spartacus was closest and Jensen didn't have to set navigation waypoints for him. He laid crosshairs on the road west of the trees and put Spartacus directly into attack mode. Able to move at ten to fifteen miles an hour across the uneven ground of the field, Spartacus should be able to cover the 800 feet to the Russian's position inside thirty seconds. He checked his heads-up display as he moved out. Brutus would arrive another thirty seconds after that.

Jensen was making for a small, inhabited farm compound that was about the only cover the Russian could possibly reach once the dogs engaged. Not that Jensen expected the Russian to survive that long. The Kurdish sniper would take him down, or at least send him to ground, where Spartacus or Brutus would finish him.

Jensen might have felt pity for the man, if he was anyone other than Tita Ali.

IT was 0059 on 4 April 2030.

At Incirlik, RAAF Flying Officer Karen O'Hare was taking off from the southern taxiway of Incirlik for the short, low-level flight west to try to localize the Syrian *Belladonna* jamming units. The problem of how to explain that she had refueled, rearmed and was *not* headed for Akrotiri was for another day. Not to mention the little question of why she had taken her tasking from a US Army technical sergeant.

Also near Incirlik, Lieutenant Yevgeny Bondarev was on the move again; his feet jammed against a stack of ammunition crates to stop them toppling over as the APC he was traveling in moved into position to support the imminent attack on Incirlik. The noise inside the poorly insulated armored vehicle was so loud he doubted he would even hear the 300mm *SMERCH* rockets screaming overhead to signal the start of the operation.

Between Bondarev and the airfield proper, TCA Alessa Barruzzi was back at her station, checking the AI algorithms she had assigned her *HELLADS* arrays for the hundredth time. There would be no time for anything but prayer once the inevitable Syrian barrage was launched.

Flying out of Akrotiri Air Base on Cyprus just two hours after arriving, RAF Flight Lieutenant Meany Papastopoulos settled onto the wing of Rex King once again, headed for an all too familiar target. Kobani in Syria, with its damn ring of *Buk* anti-air missile units, which were no doubt up and active once again, just waiting to kill him. Their mission was to investigate satellite intel indicating Syrian armor around Kobani was on the move. Meany reflected that it may once have made sense for armies to move their vehicles and troops around at night, but the advanced sensor systems on modern warplanes like the *Tempest* didn't care whether it was night or day. If anything, and if silicon could have a preference, they preferred to hunt at night, where warm vehicle engines stood out like glowing lamps against the dark cold earth below them.

Inside the galley of the bunker complex under the summit of COP Meyer, Mary Jo Basim was looking at the pictures she'd taken of the Kurdish sniper Daryan Al-Kobani as she'd fired her practice rounds. They'd agreed the shots could be taken from a rear angle so that the woman's face wasn't visible. As she'd watched the woman fire, work her rifle bolt, adjust her scope and fire again, MJ had decided that there really were limits to how involved she was willing to get in killing people. And helping a Kurdish sniper kill a Russian sniper, even one who had been killing American soldiers, was over that line. When the woman had finished zeroing her new scope, MJ handed the remaining rounds back to her and wished her luck. As she drank some cold water and listened to the muffled sound of the firefight above, she couldn't help asking herself again ... how far *would* she be willing to go, if it was her own life at stake?

And walking along the dirt road east of Kunyan Kurdan at Kobani, Lieutenant Andrei Zakarin of the Russian 45th Spetsnaz Airborne Brigade was also deep in thought. How was it he was even still alive? Tonight the enemy had come up behind him and literally put a pistol to his head. But let him live. Did it really happen? Or had he finally tipped over into the madness he always feared would overtake him one day? His many compulsions finally morphing into hallucinations. Visions. Voices in his head. Had the woman even been there? He hadn't seen her. Shadows and sounds in the dark. He had no proof she had been real.

In the far distance, above the crackle of small arms fire, he faintly heard a single louder shot and snapped his head toward it, without breaking his stride. It had come from Mishte-nur, over two thousand yards away. He had just decided that he should perhaps get off the road and into the field beside it where his silhouette wouldn't be so obvious, when a bullet caught him in the shoulder, spun him around and flung him backwards into a ditch.

Four miles away at Mamayd village, Colonel Imad Ayyoub lifted an encrypted field telephone handset to his mouth and looked at his watch, waiting for the seconds to crawl by. The diversionary attack on the main entrance to the American compound had been underway for five minutes now. He had the commander of the two 220mm *Sunburn* batteries at the other end of the line and as the hour hit 0100 he took a deep breath and spoke into the handset. "Lieutenant, you are clear to fire."

Volcanic force
COP Meyer, Kobani, Northern Syria, 4 April

IT was probably the best shot of her life, and Daryan allowed herself to feel a moment of satisfaction as she ejected the spent cartridge from her rifle. She reached out her hand.

"Bullet!"

The young Marine private slapped a round into her palm and Daryan reloaded. The target was down, but dead? She couldn't be sure. She kept her scope on the patch of ground where he had fallen ... he was too far away for her to pick up an infrared signature.

Off to her left, she saw movement, quickly swung her scope toward it, and then back again to where the Russian had fallen. "Vehicle movement, nine o'clock, do you see them?" she said tersely to the Marine.

The Marine corporal standing watch was already on high alert because of the ongoing attack at the main gates and swung his binos around. "Yeah, I see 'em." He reached for his throat mike. "Command, North Tower. I have a column of Syrian IFVs bearing two eight zero, headed out of Mamayd, you copy?"

"North Tower, Command. IFVs moving out of Mamayd, copy. Strength?"

"Estimate, uh ... eight, maybe ten. Moving southeast. You better get the CO up here, he's going to want to see this for himself."

"Copy that. He's already down at the gates. Keep an eye on those vehicles, report back if you lose them or they change direction toward us."

"Roger, Command, North Tower out."

"Syrians pulling out?" the young Marine asked with irony. The hammer of weapons on the north side of the compound indicated anything but.

"Hope is a dangerous thing, Private," his corporal yelled over the noise of the firefight.

Daryan reached for her throat mike. "Button 1?"

Over the radio, she heard static, a rhythmic thumping and panting before the voice responded. "Outpost, Button 1, go ahead."

"Target down. In the field, north side of the road. A ditch or depression."

"Received, out."

Then the siren began wailing.

Daryan turned to the Marine private. "What now?!"

He tightened the strap on his helmet. "Incoming!"

ZAKARIN rolled on his stomach and reached for the rifle that had fallen into the ditch with him. He could only move his right arm, his left was numb and ignoring any signals from his brain. He knew the shooter who had just taken him down would still have eyes on his position. If the shot had come from Mishte-nur he had no chance of returning fire, but he couldn't stay where he was either. He could feel blood soaking his shirt. If he moved, he would probably be shot, but if he stayed where he was, he would probably bleed to death.

He took a deep breath and cried out in pain. Ribs, broken. *Move, Andrei!*

He got up on one knee, ready to push off and run.

Across the field, a shape moving in the darkness. Moving fast. Straight at him.

What the hell?

THE LS3 *Hunter* Spartacus was following its Close Human Engagement protocol. The 12 gauge shotgun at the end of its utility arm was chambered and ready to fire. It had locked on the infrared signature of its target and identified from its shape and movement pattern that it was human. It closed on the target at nearly twenty miles an hour, half the speed of a real dog, movement sensors still scanning the ground in front of it for obstacles while its targeting systems stayed locked on the target.

A human might outrun it in a short burst, but Spartacus could keep up this speed for thirty minutes. At the speed of machine thought it sent a stream of code to its brother Brutus, now closing fast behind it. *Target identified and locked. Sending coordinates. Weapon armed. No other threats detected. Engaging.*

The Close Human Engagement protocol was designed to enable Spartacus to get a gun on target while minimizing its own risk profile. It wouldn't stop, it wouldn't even slow down. It would pass within four feet of the target still moving at twenty miles an hour and discharge its shotgun as it passed. It would keep going until it reached nominal safe distance, turn and repeat the action.

Until the target stopped moving.

DARYAN saw a shape lift itself from the side of the road. There was no time to laser the target this time and she couldn't see enough of the man anyway. Ignoring the chaos unfolding around her, the wail of sirens, the insistent shouts of the Marines, she fired again and racked the bolt on her rifle.

"Bullet!" she yelled, holding out her hand to the private.

She might not be able to hit the Russian, but if she could keep him down…

ZAKARIN felt another bullet smack into the dirt ahead of his left boot, but barely registered the miss. He was sitting on his butt, holding his rifle in his one good hand, the barrel resting on his raised right knee, looking across open sights at the animal that was flying across the field straight at him. Because it had to be an animal. A dog, bent on attacking him.

It was about fifty yards away and closing. He fired. At such a range, the 10.36mm Chey Tac round should tear a hole in its flesh the size of a can of corn. The bullet hit, it must have. The animal was shoved sideways by the force of it.

But it kept coming!

He worked the bolt, sighted and fired again. Another hit, another shove that knocked the animal to the ground. But it rose again.

Impossible.

Fumbling in his trouser pocket for another round, he clumsily ejected the spent cartridge and loaded another. The dog was still coming. Slower, maybe, but its intent still clear. It was coming for him.

He fired a third time, knocking it down again.

At that moment, the gates of hell opened and the night sky burned red as an unholy thunder rolled over him. Snapping his head from the animal, he looked up at the summit of Mishtenur in time to see it turn from a bald hilltop into a flaming volcano.

Red light bathed the field and he saw the animal he'd shot, unbelievably still moving, still trying to get to its feet.

And behind it, another! A hundred yards off. But coming straight for him.

Using his rifle to lever himself to his feet, he bit down a cry as the pain from his broken ribs shot up through his shoulder and neck, and he began running toward a farmhouse twenty yards further down the road. Looking over his shoulder as he ran, he could see the second dog closing on him.

He was not going to make it.

JENSEN dropped flat at the sound of the artillery barrage, arms over his head. It took a moment for him to realize it was not falling near him, and he rolled onto his side to look up at COP Meyer.

There was nothing to see but roiling fire and red smoke.

As he watched, he felt the air around himself stir, and a slight breeze started to blow, which quickly turned into a wind. Rushing from behind him and toward COP Meyer.

Thermobarics! The Syrians had fired a barrage of fuel air explosives at the US outpost. The firestorm the rockets created was consuming all the oxygen for hundreds of yards around it, sucking air into the vacuum and creating a wind Jensen could feel blowing sand and dirt across his prone body.

Holy. Mother. Of. God.

HE was nearly there. Casting a terrified look over his shoulder, Zakarin saw a shape hurtling toward him. He lunged for the low wall going around the farmhouse, the sharp report of a gun firing just behind him as he dived, and then the shadow passed behind him, continuing down the road.

He rolled over the wall and fell heavily to the ground behind it, his chest screaming in his pain … but something else too. Looking down he saw the pants of his right leg had been shredded above the knee and the flesh there was torn and bloody. He'd been shot *again*, dammit!

By a dog?

He could still move. *He had to move.* He saw a face at a low window beside him. The farmer, woken by the barrage on Mishte-nur no doubt. Without hesitating, he hurled his rifle at the window, butt first, and as it crashed through he dived in behind it.

THE COP Meyer galley or 'chow hall' was two decks down inside the Russian-made bunker complex. That put Mary Jo Basim sixteen feet below the surface of the summit, under a twenty-foot thick cap of dirt and reinforced concrete. But she still flinched as the siren sounded indicating there was incoming fire.

She looked at the Marines next to her for cues about how worried she should be. They were not on duty and had only stirred a little when the firefight at the gates had begun. And after a few minutes, when no one was yelling at them to move their asses, they settled themselves again and returned to their meals.

Middle of the night nuisance attack on the damn gates? It must be Tuesday. Incoming fire? The daily mortar round. Pass the hot sauce.

On the wooden table someone had scratched a square, divided into four quadrants, representing the base. Without even talking to each other, as soon as the siren sounded, they reached into their pockets, pulled out some notes and slapped them down on the table in one of the quadrants. If the incoming mortar round landed inside the base, the winner or winners were the ones with their bets inside the corresponding quadrant on the grid. They called it *Podnos* roulette.

It was a dark game, but to MJ it reflected perfectly the absurdity of the siege and the situation these Marines found themselves in. That *she* found herself in.

In seconds, though, it became apparent that this was no simple mortar attack. There was a thundering sequence of crashes over their heads, and a light fitting fell from the roof and exploded on the floor. Another LED bulb exploded in a shower of sparks and the galley lights dimmed.

Over the top of the artillery warning came the sound of a second klaxon – the one indicating that the outer doors to the bunker were being sealed. Confirming her suspicions, the fans circulating air through the bunker started rattling as their speed was automatically increased to create greater air pressure inside the bunker. That would only be done if…

"Chemical weapons attack?" she asked the Marines, who were rising to their feet.

Without answering her, the Marines at her table started running for their emergency stations, and in seconds the entire galley was deserted. Most of the soldiers had disappeared deeper into the complex, headed for critical engineering infrastructure like electricity generators, environment controls and air quality systems. Others headed for the armories situated on each deck, in case they needed to defend the bunker from a breach by enemy forces.

MJ decided sitting in the galley alone wasn't going to win her a Pulitzer, so she stood, checked her phone was charged, and started heading up … towards the main entrance on the summit of the hill. The bunker had been put into lockdown. That probably meant a chemical weapons attack, an imminent enemy assault, or both. She wanted to find out which.

JENSEN watched in horror as the top of Mishte-nur Hill boiled with flame. A huge glowing red and black cloud was rising into the night above it, and explosions under it showed the rockets were still falling.

No one caught out in the open up there could survive that, surely. No one.

There were two Marines in each of the seven observation posts around the walls. The GATOR crew, that was another three. The counter-battery mortar crew, two men. Duty officer and quick response team, another six, inside the Battalion HQ, which would have offered precisely zero protection against a thermobaric barrage.

Twenty-six guaranteed casualties. Plus the Kurdish sniper. If he had heard small arms fire in the background of Daryan's radio call, then the Syrians had probably lured an additional squad or two out onto the walls. That made the tally forty to fifty.

A fury boiled inside him. He focused on the images in his helmet display. He could do nothing right now to help the Marines under that barrage, but he had a target right in front of him and it was one he could prosecute.

Spartacus was down. The dog's camera tilted, jerking up and down, but stationary. The sniper must have put a couple of 10.36mm slugs into it and hit a vital spot. The dog's metal casings were made to withstand anything up to 7.62mm, but not heavy rounds like the Lobaev fired. And a lucky shot could hit a gap in the casing, or a mechanical joint.

Brutus was hunting. His ammo counter showed he had fired one round from his 12 gauge. But he'd lost the target. Jensen could see the waypoints he had set himself and they told the story as clearly as if the dog had called him on the radio with a report. He was circling the small farmhouse beside the dirt road, pausing at each corner of the house to stop, listen and look for a target. An audio indicator ran along the bottom of Brutus's feed, giving Jensen a visual representation of what Brutus was hearing, and he saw it spike. He switched to a live audio feed from the dog, hearing in real time what Brutus was hearing as he paced around the house.

He heard shouting. More than one voice.

Tita Ali was not alone inside that house. That meant either Syrian regulars, garrisoned in the farmhouse, or worse, civilians.

He rolled on his back and swore at the red sky.

NASRIN woke with a start, her sister crying out to her in the dark.

Nasrin!

She sat bolt upright in her bed. Dreaming, it was just a dream. She wiped a hand across her face and paused, blinking the sleep from her eyes. Was she even awake? The walls around her danced with hellish red light and a storm thundered outside the windows. She lifted the covers and put her feet on the cool floor, pulling a nightdress off the end of the bed and over her shoulders. In a daze she walked to the window of her first-floor apartment, opened the metal shutters and looked out.

The window faced south, across Kobani, toward the statue of Arin Mirkan. The battered city looked alive, shadows flickering and dancing in the red light of the sky.

Red light of the sky?

She looked at her watch. It was only 1 a.m. She had been asleep less than an hour. Following the brightness in the night sky, her eyes were drawn east toward Mishte-nur.

Where there once had been a hill, a volcano had erupted.

The American outpost. Was that why the Russian had climbed onto the roof of the markets, to observe *this*?

Daryan! She remembered the dream that had woken her. Or the dream that accompanied the thunder of bombs. And the call from her sister earlier.

But she wouldn't still be up there on Mishte-nur. Would she?

Horns sounded below. The streets were filling with people, staring up at the hill. Motorbikes and cars full of armed men, on the move. She recognized the pattern of movement, men moving into their positions on the lines. Preparing either for a Syrian attack or to effect a counter-attack of their own.

She felt a warm hand sneak into hers as her mother joined her at the window, staring up at the volcano.

"She will be alright," her mother said softly, gripping Nasrin's hand tightly.

"Yes," Nasrin said, gripping her mother's hand back, and then disengaging herself. "But just in case, I'm going to check on her."

JENSEN set Brutus to watch the backdoor of the farmhouse, with instructions for a non-lethal takedown of anyone exiting. 'Non-lethal' was a loose term and one he'd reported back to the designers of the LS3 prototypes needed refining – he'd seen the dogs interpret the order very broadly when armed with lethal weapons, firing them at the legs of fleeing enemies to disable them. Non-lethal? Technically, yes, but if they'd been less accurate they could have struck vital organs.

The barrage on Mishte-nur was subsiding, but he heard another sound, equally menacing. The sound of 30mm autocannons firing. Only Syrian mechanized vehicles fielded those. And worse, he heard no return fire.

He pushed the fear in his guts back down and slid along the wall of the farmhouse toward its wooden front door. Tried the handle. Locked. *Alright then.* Putting down his assault rifle, he pulled his *Beretta* pistol from his waist belt.

You have a job to do, Jensen. Just get it done.

Rolling out in front of the door, he fired a round into the lock and then gave the door an almighty kick.

ON the stairs leading upward, MJ passed several Marines running the other way and was overtaken by others running in the same direction as her, one deck up, toward the main doors. More than once, she was bodily shoved aside by Marines in no mood to let her slow them down.

The further she went up, the harder she found it to breathe. It was like she was climbing Everest without oxygen. The last few steps were like an entire flight.

When she finally reached ground level and stood there panting, she was immediately stopped by the corpsman, Bell, standing and checking the medical supplies in a kit strapped to his chest. As she tried to push past him he reached out a hand and put it on her chest. Ahead of her, at least a platoon of Marines were crouched just inside the blast doors. There were a couple of other corpsmen up there with them.

"Essential personnel only, ma'am," he said, and went back to checking his supplies.

The lighting was poor, but she recognized the edge in his voice. He was amped. "What's happening out there, Bell?"

He spoke without looking at her. "Thermobaric barrage, someone said." He was pulling bandages and ampoules of brown liquid from the kit. "Damn it to hell, I need more morphine. More of everything."

"What?"

He fixed her with a bleak gaze. "In a few minutes, we are going to break those blast doors open and move out to recover the wounded. Rifle platoon will cover us. Anyone unlucky enough to still be alive out there is going to be burned. Bad. Real bad." He was speaking fast, the drugs he no doubt had in his blood pushing his thoughts faster than his mouth could follow. "Bad bad. The other corpsmen are going to sort the living from the dead. My job is to knock 'em out and drag what's left of 'em inside." He stopped talking and listened. A sound like tearing paper, right outside the doors.

MJ heard it too. Rapid cannon fire.

Bell shoved his ID card at her. "Sick bay, deck 2. Show them this, tell them you need as much morphine and saline as you can carry." She stood looking at him blankly, until he spun her around and shoved her back toward the stairs. "Go, go, go!!"

MEANY was worried. He'd run the diagnostic three times, but it had given him the same answer three times.

His IFF transponder was non-functional. The small transmitter intended to tell the Coalition world he was one of the good guys was dead.

"Harrow one, Harrow two, my IFF is U/S, sir," he said, reporting the transponder as unserviceable to King.

"In-flight reboot, Meany, it's on the comms checklist."

"Done, sir," Meany told him. "Twice. No joy."

"Then you are going to have to live with it, boyo," King told him. "Cheer up. The only ones likely to be firing missiles at you down there are Syrian anyway. Lights of Jarabulus ahead, arm those *SPEARs*, Flight Lieutenant. I want to fry the circuits of anything bigger than a car radio down there."

"Sir."

Meany bit back his worry and pulled up the ordnance menu. He and King had taken off with two *SPEAR-EW* electronic warfare missiles each, and three *SPEAR-HEAT* anti-armor missiles in case their reconnaissance run showed them the Syrians had indeed moved their mechanized vehicles out of their berms around Kobani and into the open where they could be killed.

In Meany's admittedly limited experience, Sat-int was rarely actionable. By the time an image was snapped by a satellite, transmitted to a ground station, bounced to a Defense Intelligence or National Security Agency analyst, and then relayed to a commander on the ground who could action it, it was hours old and the operational equivalent of a cold case. He and King had been scrambled thirty minutes earlier, dog tired and half dopey from the flight down from Incirlik, but they were the two pilots with the best familiarity with the Kobani area of operations.

Yeah, during the bloody day, Meany had told himself. What the hell did it matter if you knew the features around Kobani if you were flying in the middle of the blessed night?

His was not to reason why. And besides, there was no time. They were fifty miles out from Kobani.

"Harrow one, coordinates locked, *SPEAR-EW* armed."

"Harrow two, coordinates locked, *SPEAR-EW* armed."

"Harrow one, *SPEAR* away," Rex called.

"Harrow two, *SPEAR* away."

"Approaching *thunder*," Rex said, indicating the first wave of *SPEAR* missiles were only a minute from their target positions. In the absence of supporting aircraft to suppress Syrian anti-air radar units, they had launched both electronic warfare missiles at the airspace over Kobani. In three minutes, the missiles would reach the sky over the city and start circling, blasting energy at the ground across multiple wavelengths and scrambling anything but the most hardened systems. The five- to ten-year-old Russian radars fielded by the Syrian army should be blinded by the British missile swarm, and their communications on anything but landlines reduced to static.

But Meany was painfully aware that all it took to bring down a five-hundred-million-dollar *Tempest* was a lucky hundred-dollar 30mm blast fragmentation round blind-fired by the gunner on a *Tunguska* mobile anti-air gun.

Or, given that his IFF transponder was dead, a *Stinger* missile from a friendly ground unit convinced his *Tempest* was a Russian *Felon*.

The Cyprus air controller broke into Meany's thoughts. "Harrow leader, Akrotiri control, are you receiving?"

Rex responded immediately. "Akrotiri, Harrow, proceed."

"US forces report they are engaged with Syrian forces in grid sector alpha three four niner, repeat."

"Akrotiri, Harrow repeats, US forces engaged with enemy sector alpha three four niner, over."

As soon as he heard the map coordinate, Meany pulled up his tactical map of Kobani and zoomed it in. Mishte-nur Hill. The US combat outpost. So, the stalemate was over; the dying had started again.

"You are cleared to engage Syrian forces at that position. Acknowledge."

There was a pause, no doubt as Rex did the same double-take as Meany had just done. "Akrotiri control, that position is a Coalition base. Please confirm you are calling for us to attack Syrian targets on top of Mishte-nur Hill."

"Harrow leader, Akrotiri. Confirm, the Marine Forward Air Controller has called down an attack on Syrian forces at that position."

"Harrow acknowledges. Out."

Meany's mind raced. They've *taken* COP Meyer?

"Pulling north, follow me and start mapping, Harrow two," King ordered. "This recon mission just turned into close air support."

Meany flicked his sensor display over to the *Tempest*'s Inverse Synthetic Aperture Radar and narrowed its focus onto the area around Mishte-nur. He and Rex swept into a racetrack circuit forty thousand feet over the town of Jarabulus and about fifty miles back from Kobani. As they circled, their air-to-ground radar mapped the environment around Mishte-nur Hill. The *Tempest*'s onboard convolutional neural network AI compared the images it received with those stored in its database, identifying and classifying any that were not expected. It referred these to a second AI that compared them to known Syrian weapon types and quickly spat out matches. A third AI took the targets as they were handed off, compared Meany's data with the data coming from the AIs on King's fighter, and assigned them to the *SPEAR-HEAT* missiles in the weapons bays of both aircraft. Meany and King had to do nothing except initiate the scan and keep their aircraft aloft.

And watch the sky for unfriendly aircraft.

An alarm sounded in Meany's ears just as his system signaled it had assigned targets on Mishte-nur to all of his *SPEAR* missiles.

"Lieutenant..."

"I see the *Felons*, Meany, stay calm. They don't see us yet. We get missiles on target, and then we fade, understood?"

"Yes, sir."

Felons. Two, at least. His DAS infrared sensors had picked up the heat signature of the Russians' jet engines against the cold night sky about twenty miles out. There was no indication the Russians had seen the stealthier next-generation *Tempests*. Yet. But perhaps they had detected the earlier *SPEAR* launches and were closing to investigate. If that was the case, they were almost certain to be alerted when the RAF pilots fired their next volley.

"Harrow two, Harrow leader, assuming weapons authority..."

King had just taken over control of the weapons on Meany's aircraft. Meany was even more a passenger now than he had been a minute earlier when his AI was working target solutions.

"*SPEAR*s away," King called, and the visor on Meany's helmet automatically polarized so he wouldn't be blinded by the flare of the last six missiles dropping out of their weapons bays and swerving away to the east.

Meany's hand tightened on his flight stick. His threat display was still showing two *Felons*, fifteen miles out now. Not on an intercept bearing, but...

They turned. They had seen the *Tempest*'s missile launches!

"Break and engage, Harrow two," King said calmly, releasing weapons control back to Meany.

His combat AI already had a lock on the two Russian aircraft and as soon as King released it, it automatically launched a pair of CUDA hit-to-kill missiles at the Russian fighters before Meany's thumb could even twitch.

At the same time as a missile warning sounded in his ears, a steering cue appeared in his helmet display and he pulled his aircraft into a violent rolling bank to try to nail the cue which the AI had predicted would give him the best chance of dodging the Russian K-77M missiles.

He heard his great-grandfather's voice in his mind. *You just going to do what that computer tells you, lad?*

He tightened his turn, putting his aircraft heading predictor squarely into the round circle of the steering cue indicator. *Oh hell yes, grandpa.*

IN his HQ at Mamayd, Colonel Ayyoub was watching the assault on COP Meyer via the camera mounted on the *Terminator* fighting vehicle of his mechanized platoon commander. He'd split his force of eight IFVs into two squads, six to lead the assault on the summit through the main gates following the *Sunburn* barrage, and two to push on the northern exit from the bunker complex that came out at the base of Mishte-nur, to ensure no US troops could escape that way and flank his force on the summit. Having scraped the lice from the top of the hill, his troops would enter the bunker complex and push any survivors out of the bunker exit and right into the guns of his second squad of *Terminators*.

A rapid surrender should follow.

He had pulled 1,000 infantry troops out of their trenches around Kobani, ready to move as soon as the *Sunburn* barrage lifted. That left his besieging force around Kobani quite thin, but the risk of a Kurdish counter-attack, or of Coalition air attacks, would be minimized by the speed of the assault on COP Meyer.

He watched as his IFVs approached the US compound, still shrouded in flame and smoke. The infrared camera on the command vehicle enabled it to see through the smoke, but the fires ignited by the *Sunburn* barrage were still burning fiercely.

The *Terminators* threaded between the concrete barriers on the road outside the entrance and rolled through the barriers at the main gates without encountering any resistance.

Through an abundance of caution, the first vehicles through laid down covering fire to ease the entry of those behind, but again, there was no return fire.

"Mamayd, we are inside the American base," the squad commander reported. His turret swung around to show the blast doors at the bunker entrance. They appeared intact. But that meant nothing if the soldiers behind them had no air to breathe.

"Squad two in position at Mishte-nur north exit," his second squad commander reported. "Engaged with US troops at the exit. Minimal return fire so far."

Excellent. He looked around the room at his subordinates and saw only confidence. "Squad one, Mamayd. Force the blast doors. I am moving up the infantry. When the doors are open, you will cover their ingress."

"Squad one confirms, out. We are …" the radio call dissolved in a spray of static, followed by silence.

Ayyoub's air defense commander was looking over the shoulder of one of his officers, who was pointing at a screen. He looked up and called out to Ayyoub. "Colonel, Russian sector air control reports Coalition aircraft have launched cruise missiles! Our air defense radars are being jammed. I'm losing contact with our units in the north…"

Ayyoub cursed. It must be a coincidence, the Americans could not possibly have called in air support so quickly. "Predicted targets?"

The man looked at his screen. "Can't say. Our radar systems are down, so we only have the coordinates the Russians gave us. Mamayd is my guess. Missiles were twenty miles out bearing two seven three, I estimate time to impact … one minute." Without waiting for Ayyoub's reaction, he reached for a keyboard, hit a key and the siren warning of incoming fire started wailing from the roof of the HQ warning nearby troops to seek cover.

Ayyoub pointed at his comms technician. "Start frequency hopping. Get those bloody *Terminator* squads back on the radio!"

MJ ran back from the sick bay to the position just inside the blast doors where the corpsman, Bell, was still waiting, rocking on the balls of his feet like an Olympic sprinter waiting for the starter gun.

Instead she heard a gun of a completely different kind.

From outside the blast doors, the hammer of 30mm autocannons started up, and the doors started shaking. There was a rifle company holding just inside the doors, waiting to break out, and they all pulled back against the tunnel walls.

Bell turned to MJ. "Doors will hold against pea shooters. Russians built them to withstand anything smaller than a tactical nuke."

MJ looked at the doors. They weren't buckling, but they sure were vibrating. "You sure?" she yelled.

"No. But in any case we need to get out there *now* if we're going to find anyone alive."

"I got as much morphine and saline as I could carry." MJ held two shoulder bags out to him.

He took one. "You'll have to carry the other one. When we get outside, just stay close to me, alright?"

"Me? No, no, no. I don't even know first aid!"

"You know the difference between morphine and saline. Your ears work. Your legs work. You look strong enough to help lift an unresponsive Marine. That's all I need."

MJ looked at the Marines closer to the doors. What about one of the other corpsmen? One of the soldiers from the rifle squad? Anyone but her!

She didn't get any further with her line of thought. A platoon sergeant came running around a corner and nearly barreled into her and Bell, yelling up to the Second Lieutenant leading the platoon on the doors. "Pull back! Brits just launched a missile strike. Get your men away from those doors!"

AS Meany and King fought to evade the Russian fighters that had just launched on them, in the air fifty miles from Mamayd, their second wave of *SPEAR-HEAT* missiles closed on Kobani.

They were not going in blind. The two electronic warfare missiles from their first wave were circling over Kobani, smothering the airwaves across the multiple frequencies used by Syrian radar and radio communications. At the same time, they used their own synthetic aperture and infrared sensors to map targets below them and pass the data back to the *SPEAR-HEAT* missiles approaching in the second wave.

Their AIs analyzed and discarded hundreds of potential targets in milliseconds before settling on the higher-priority targets they had been assigned to, on and around Mishte-nur Hill. First and foremost, armored vehicles; second, troops on the move; third, troops in place. The *SPEAR* swarm AI took all the inputs, calculated probabilities of success and assigned targets to the eight missiles.

The six IFVs on top of Mishte-nur Hill were targeted by the HEAT anti-armor missiles. Two were already inside the compound.

The two electronic warfare missiles had only the explosive power of their impact to cause damage with, and one was directed at the five hundred troops massed at the base of the hill to the south, just starting to advance on the summit as the smoke cleared and the air became breathable.

The Syrian troops attacking the ground-level bunker entrance were locked up by the last missile.

The swarm AI had no missiles left to assign to other targets. But it sent their positions back to King's *Tempest* for instant relay to his sector air controller and to the US troops inside COP Meyer.

Targets locked, the eight *SPEAR* missiles over Kobani pointed their noses at the ground and accelerated toward their targets.

If a butterfly flaps in Syria
US Consulate General, Istanbul, 4 April

"A cyberattack on Incirlik? This is why you woke me?" Shimi asked. Carl Williams had called him just after 1 a.m. and asked him to get in a cab and get himself to the US Consulate. It was only fifteen minutes away, but no one these days made a trip across town at that time of night if they didn't have to. The night hours were Russia's favored time for sending its *Okhotnik* stealth attack drones to sporadically attack targets in the capital.

But the urgency in the American's voice had persuaded Shimi, so he'd tumbled out of bed, into jeans and a t-shirt, and taken a cab across the deserted streets of the city to the fortress-like hilltop American consulate building. The taxi driver made the mistake of taking him to the public entrance down on the tree-lined Ataturk Boulevard first, but Shimi redirected him up the hill to the small rear entrance gate that led into the compound proper. It normally housed over a thousand staff, but after the first air attacks on Istanbul, only an 'essential' staff of around three hundred had remained.

"No, dude, this is just an FYI, setting the scene kind of thing," Carl said. "And anyway, don't tell me the fact that Russia is conducting a full-scale cyberattack and electronic warfare effort in support of Syria's assault on Incirlik won't be of interest to your bosses in Be'er Sheva."

It would, but Shimi was trying to look tired, grumpy and bored. He didn't have to try too hard on the first two. "So put it in a report and send it to Virginia and they can send it to Washington and they can send it to Tel Aviv and they can send it to Be'er Sheva."

"Forget that. Besides, you know that even before any report I write leaves Istanbul, it has to go to my section chief, who never looks at anything before about ten in the morning, once he's got his hangover out of the way."

Carl's office was at the rear of the square-shaped compound, but because of the NSA paranoia about foreign services using laser and microwave vibration technologies to conduct surveillance, he didn't have one of the nice rooms with a view over the city or even into the internal courtyard, he had a basement broom cupboard not much warmer than a refrigerator because all the cold air in the building pooled on his floor.

"Alright, so Russia is going the extra mile to support Syria since it got stopped cold by the Turks outside Gaziantep. Is that a surprise?" Shimi asked. There must be an Israeli angle here, but he couldn't see it. "Carl, they're dropping *bombs* on convoys outside Istanbul's Blue Mosque! This week they shot down at least one Coalition aircraft, and multiple drones, *inside* Turkish airspace." He saw a look on Carl's face. "Yeah, we heard about that. So – they've taken their engagement up a notch. Or two. Why am I here?"

Carl rearranged his face, trying to hide his surprise at how much Shimi knew. "A notch or two? Russian-backed Syrian armor is right now engaged in a full-frontal assault on a *NATO base* in Turkey. What you don't know, as we speak, is that they have renewed their assault on Kobani, but not the city itself, just the US combat outpost and our two hundred Marines there."

Shimi digested that intelligence. He had always figured it was just a matter of time before the Syrians got tired of US troops in Kobani calling down airstrikes on their besieging forces, so he shrugged. "Well, it would suck to be them, I guess? But none of this changes the dynamics on the ground, or the optics. Turkey and Syria are at war. Russia and America are trying to make it look like they *aren't* at war. So Russia gets Syria to do its dirty work and rub out a NATO base that has always irritated them because most of the Coalition air attacks into Syria and Iraq are launched from Incirlik." Shimi put a finger in the air to emphasize his next point. "*Coalition*, not US Air Force attacks because so far you have only put AWACS, recon drones and tanker aircraft into the fight. And sorry, but you should have pulled your Marines out of Kobani weeks ago. You are doing the minimum necessary to keep good relations with the Kurds because they control the Suwayda oil fields and US companies have a 150-million-dollar refinery and a dozen wells there."

"Oh cool, you got it all worked out," Carl grimaced. He pushed a plate of Oreos over to Shimi. "Except you don't. Russia and American *were* trying to play nice, but in the last week, Russia took off the gloves. Russia ordered the Syrian ground attack on Incirlik and Russian aircraft launched a cruise missile strike on that air base aimed at US air defense units. Russia shot down a half dozen Coalition aircraft and drones and doesn't seem to care it lost about the same number, because you don't hear it screaming blue murder. Russia just brought down the electricity grid in most of southeast Turkey with a massive cyberattack. Russia must have ordered the attack on COP Meyer." Carl took a cookie himself and swallowed it whole, letting Shimi reflect on what he was saying. "Russia has decided it wants the US out of the Middle East and it's tired of waiting."

Now Shimi saw why Carl was so worked up.

Peace had broken out in the Middle East from 2020 onwards. Egypt, Jordan, then the Emirates, Sudan, Iraq and even Saudi Arabia had all signed peace agreements with Israel. Only Syria and Iran still refused to recognize the Israeli state. So after years of talking about it, the new US administration was drawing down US troop levels in the Middle East. It had bigger fish to fry, it argued – facing off against China in Korea, the South China Sea, and Taiwan.

"So this all just adds fuel to my Lebanon theory," Shimi said. He couldn't share the intel about the Russian and Iranian fleet order of battle for Operation 'Butterfly', but that too fit perfectly with what Carl was telling him. "They get you out of Syria, they shut down your biggest base in Turkey, and they're testing how hard you're likely to push back if they march into

Lebanon. Betting if they can make Syria suck enough for you, you won't have the appetite."

Carl reached into a desk drawer and pulled out a sheet of paper. He kept it in front of him, with a hand over it so Shimi couldn't see it. "I didn't show you this, alright?" Shimi nodded and reached for it, but Carl pulled it further back. "I'm serious. The reason I called you, I'm going to send this report through my usual channels, and it might never make it to you guys. I'm cutting out the middle man. And you cannot source this to me, alright?" He slid the page across to Shimi.

Shimi scanned the header. "This is from your analytical support AI?"

"HOLMES, yeah. He may not be a chatterbox like your GAL yet, but he's plugged into every contemporary intel database on this conflict from CIA, to DIA, State Department, FBI and, of course, NSA. Incirlik took us by surprise. So I asked him to find anything he could on potential future Syrian targets in this war. That's his answer."

Shimi read the report title and had to try to hide the excitement rising in his chest. "Syrian troop buildup in the Dara'a region?"

"Yeah, I know, not the most sexy title. Like I said, HOLMES is still a work in progress."

Much like the data GAL had pulled from the Syrian Coast Guard intercept, HOLMES' report was an Order of Battle for Syrian ground forces engaged in Syria's north, based on human and signals intelligence reports. But it continued with a list of additional regular and reserve units activated and ordered to report to the Dara'a District military command in the country's *southwest* for training, plus two thousand troops of the Iranian Revolutionary Guards Corp 'Quds' special forces.

There was much more to the report, but it had been heavily blacked out. Shimi turned the paper over, and back again, then waved it at Carl. "What is this about?"

"Nothing for nothing, wasn't that what you said?" Carl smiled. "So tell me, Shimi, what do you know about something called *Operation Butterfly?*"

The ways of a dog
East of Maklul village, Kobani

JENSEN'S boot nearly went through the thin wood of the farmer's door. He heard a scream inside as the door slammed open, and he rolled through, taking in what he saw in an adrenaline-fueled half-second.

Room to the right, door closed.
Table upturned ahead.
Two people huddled in a corner, no weapons.
No Tita Ali.

Without thinking, he shoved off with his left foot and crashed through the door to his right. A bedroom. Empty. As he fell, a single bullet thudded into the wall where his head had been.

The sniper was behind the overturned table back out in the main room, he had to be.

Crouching low beside the bedroom door, Jensen swung out, fired four shots at the table and pulled back in again.

There was no return fire, just screaming from the civilians. He had a grenade but couldn't use it with civilians in the room … he could only hope the Russian didn't also have one.

Jensen knew limited Arabic: thank you, drop your weapon, get down, go away. And 'shut up'.

He deployed the last one. "Akhrus!"

The screaming was replaced by sobs. Still no return fire from the Syrian. Jensen checked the video feed from Brutus. The dog was still crouched down, ten feet back from the rear door of the house. No sign of movement.

Jensen leaned his back against the wall of the bedroom. Stone. Good. He projected his voice through the doorway. "Russian soldier. I have a heavily armed unit at the rear door. You have ten seconds to surrender or we will kill you."

ZAKARIN had reloaded his rifle with his single good hand and had it balanced on the legs of the table he was sheltered behind. The volley of fire from the American – he now knew it was Americans pursuing him from the language of the man in the bedroom – had chewed into the table but hadn't hit him. He couldn't continue to be so lucky.

His shirt was soaked in blood from the wound to his chest, he was starting to have trouble breathing because of his broken ribs, and his thigh was beginning to stiffen where it had been chewed up by what looked like a shotgun blast or frag round. He had his knife, but no pistol, and no grenades. He looked over at the two figures huddled in the corner. A farmer and his wife. They shot him terrified glances. He put his finger on his lips, urging them to be quiet so he could hear the American move.

The American knew he was Russian? Curious, considering he was wearing a Syrian army uniform. So, he had been set up for an ambush. An informer somewhere, either in the Russian ranks or in the Syrian. It didn't really matter. But that first shot, if it had come from Mishte-nur ... that was some shot. Had he finally come up against the mysterious Daryan Al-Kobani?

He thought of the photograph of his daughter in his shirt. He knew every time he went out with his rifle that he might not come home. A bomb. A missile. A landmine. A bullet from an enemy rifle. A woman behind him in the dark, with a *Tokarev*. Any of these could end his life instantly.

But here, today, he'd been given a choice. And for whatever reason, the gods had already given him one chance tonight. He took that as an omen.

Grunting, he lifted his Lobaev above the table and threw it toward the bedroom door.

"American! I surrender." His ribs screamed in protest as he called out and he broke into a fit of coughing which only made the pain worse.

"Stand up, hands on your head!" Jensen yelled.

Zakarin made to stand, but his injured leg screamed in pain and he sat back down, wincing and coughing. "I cannot. I am wounded."

"Move the table away so I can see you."

Zakarin could see the American now, his head just visible around the door frame. He kicked weakly at the heavy table with his uninjured leg, but it didn't move. He motioned to the farmer. "You, pull this table away. You understand? Pull?"

The farmer looked at him, wide-eyed, but let go of his wife and crawled over to Zakarin, gripping the table in both hands so he could pull it away.

Zakarin had his knife in his right hand and lunged, grabbing the man around the throat and pulling him toward his body in an iron grip. He held the knife next to the farmer's face where both the American and the farmer could see it. The man's wife started whimpering, waving her hands in front of her face in panic.

"Attack me, I kill the Kurd," Zakarin said loudly.

THE Russian *Vympel* K-77M missile closing on Meany's *Tempest* was not thrown off by either his radical maneuvering or the decoys his machine was pumping out behind him. But as it closed inside a hundred feet, the rear-firing laser on the *Tempest* locked onto the missile and fired. The beam burned into the missile's sensitive warhead and detonated it.

In an eyeblink, Meany went from defense to offense, locking the nearest *Felon* and firing his last remaining CUDA missile at it. "Fox 3!" he called and rolled away from the target without waiting to see the result of his launch. He had no interest in getting into a knife fight with the Russian.

Eyes flicking to his tactical monitor, he saw King, five thousand feet away, and one *Felon* already marked as destroyed. King was banking to intercept the same *Felon* that Meany had just fired on.

"Fox 3," King called calmly. The Russian now had two missiles closing on him, and Meany saw with satisfaction that he had spun his machine around and was trying to evade, altitude plunging rapidly, increasing the separation between them with every millisecond.

There was just one problem. And if he had a functioning IFF transponder, it would have been no problem at all. But he didn't.

Rex King's missile saw Meany's *Tempest* and, beyond it, the Russian *Felon*. It was not a particularly intelligent missile and didn't really care what it killed, as long as its target wasn't a friendly aircraft. Scanning one last time for an IFF code from Meany's machine, it saw none, and its tiny silicon mind was quickly made up.

Meany saw it approach on his helmet-mounted display and barely had time to think, *You have to be effing joking...*

His laser defenses also saw the friendly missile and ignored it. It detonated inside his empty weapons bay, and Meany's helmeted head was slammed against the canopy of his cockpit. He blacked out.

WHEN he came to, he remembered what had happened, panic gripping his throat. A dozen warning symbols were flashing in his visor, but he still had engine power. He was flying relatively straight, and almost level. He tried the flight controls. Something was wrong. The controls were sloppy, and more red warning symbols appeared in his visor.

"Harrow leader, Harrow two, I..." Meany started saying, but what exactly was he going to say? His machine started yawing to the right and he automatically pushed his left foot forward to correct the yaw with left rudder, but nothing happened. The *Tempest* started a sickening corkscrew through the sky. In a daze, head being slammed left and right again, Meany strained to look down at his rudder pedals, trying to understand why they weren't responding.

Oh. Well, that was pretty obvious. They were gone.

REX King watched in horror on his DAS camera as his missile struck home and the other pilot's *Tempest* rolled away from him. It went into an uncontrolled spin and immediately he saw the reason. There was a gaping hole under the cockpit. His missile had struck the *Tempest* amidships and gutted it. The *Tempest* nosed over into what looked like an uncontrollable death spiral.

"Meany, eject!" he yelled into his comms. "Get out, man!"

There was no response. The *Tempest* fell away below him and he looked frantically at his altitude. Twelve thousand three!

"*Papastopoulos*! Eject! Eject! Eject!"

THROUGH a fog of pain and adrenaline, Meany heard his name, and an order. *Eject? Yes, sir.* His head was hard up against the headrest from the force of the spin, but he reached down between his legs for the ejection yoke and pulled.

Mercifully, as the rocket under his seat fired him into space at eight hundred miles an hour, crushing his head down into his neck with a force of 20Gs, he blacked out again.

EVEN backed up around the corner of the bunker entrance, with the Marine rifle platoon crowded around her, MJ could hear the sound of the *SPEAR* missile strike outside the blast doors. A rapid succession of muted explosions, too fast to count. They didn't seem as loud as the Syrian barrage had been, but she shuddered at the thought there might still be American troops alive outside.

The reverberations had barely died away when squad leaders started shouting orders at their men and the Marines moved up to the doors again. Bell held MJ's belt to stop her being pulled forward by the press of bodies. When the bulk of the Marines were past them, he nodded at the doors and they moved up behind the others.

"Hang back," he told her. "They'll break the door open, lay down covering fire and start moving outside if they can. I'll judge the best time to move, you just follow me out."

"When it's safe."

"Ain't gonna be safe, MJ," Bell said. It was the first time she'd ever heard him use her name. "But there's men and women dying out there, for sure. We gonna save some lives." He held out his hand for a fist bump. "Or what?"

"*Oorah*, Bell," MJ obliged, choking back her fear.

JENSEN thought fast. *Damn, damn, damn.* He had no shot on the Russian. Half of his body was still obscured by the table, the other half was sheltered behind the farmer he was holding, with a knife positioned to pull across his throat.

He felt for this throat mike. He needed some support here, beyond Brutus, so that he didn't get overrun by a Syrian patrol if this got drawn out. He spoke loudly so the Russian could hear him. "Base, this is Button 1. Requesting rifle squad to my position. Farmhouse east side Maklul. Include a medic in the detail."

There was no answer, just static, which didn't surprise him after the barrage on the hilltop he'd just witnessed. "Roger, base, will hold in this position." Bluff was the only weapon he had left against this guy. "You want to kill that Kurd, Ivan, go ahead," he called out to the sniper. "I got all night, and you don't sound too good."

OUTSIDE the farmhouse, LS3 unit Brutus was having a silicon dilemma.

It had been placed in Close Human Engagement mode and that order had not been cancelled. But it had also been ordered to 'guard in place' at the rear of the farmhouse and limit itself to non-lethal responses. The two orders were in conflict and its programmers had not given the AI guidance on which should supersede which. What they had programmed was a semi-autonomous protocol that told Brutus in situations where it lost contact with its handler, or its orders were unclear, it should follow its last clear order.

Brutus spent precious seconds considering its situational inputs. It had tracked its target into the building on infrared and could see the target's heat signature through the wooden rear door of the farmhouse. It was now lying under another heat source, probably human. The fact it could pick up the target's infrared signature through the door meant it was probably light enough for Brutus to force. It could hear weapons fire inside the building.

It was also receiving a transponder signal from its handler, who was near the target but stationary. Brutus was receiving real-time data on its handler's biometrics, and his heartrate and breathing appeared elevated but within his normal range. Brutus was also monitoring Jensen's voice comms and analyzed the call he had just made. He had called for support, and his voice showed indications of high stress. Conclusion, the handler was engaged in a firefight, still combat capable, but his tactical position was not favorable.

Brutus was caught in a logic loop, cycling through two options:

Force the door and engage the target with non-lethal force
Maintain position and engage the target if he exits the building
Brutus made its choice.

IN his helmet display, Jensen saw the video feed from Brutus shift as the dog stood and he backed further away from the door. It kept its vision on the rear door, which was what Jensen wanted. If he managed to stand, the Russian would probably haul the hostage to his feet and start backing toward that door to try to make his exit. *Creepy how the dogs do that*, he thought to himself, watching Brutus walking backwards. *Always looking for the best position, the best angle, moving around so they can run situational analyses.*

No. There was something wrong…

His hand shot to the controller in his pocket and the emergency 'power down' button there, but he was too slow. Like a 220lb. battering ram, Brutus sprinted at the back door, then tilted sideways so that it hit the door side-on like a linebacker laying out a quarterback.

Damn it all!

As the door splintered and the dog rolled into the farmhouse, Jensen stepped out and took aim at what he could see of the Russian, which wasn't much. The man had an arm across the throat of the farmer, so he sighted on that, squeezing off a single shot. His 5.56mm round hit the Russian high on his bicep, passed through the muscle of his arm and buried itself in the farmer's shoulder.

The Russian dropped his knife as his arm spasmed, but as much in his haste to pull the farmer across him and block whatever hell-beast had just broken through the door and was now clambering to its feet to launch itself at him.

Brutus now had low-light vision of the target to supplement its infrared and analyzed the images. Target in uniform, another human not in uniform. It prioritized the target in the uniform, gathered its rear limbs and hurled itself through the air at the target's exposed upper body. His left arm numb from Daryan's first shot, and his right arm also useless after the shot from Jensen, all Zakarin could do was turn away as the metal missile slammed into his shoulders and head and knocked him and the farmer flat.

Clutching his shoulder, the farmer scrabbled out from under the dog and over to his wife, wrapping his arms around her.

In two short seconds Jensen covered the distance to the Russian and aimed his rifle at what he could see of the man's head under Brutus. "Don't move!" he yelled. *Did the guy have a pistol? Or just the knife?*

He needn't have worried. The Russian was out cold.

Two hundred pounds of metal, silicon and hydrogen power cells to the head will do that.

NASRIN was on her scooter, threading her way through running men, trucks and barricades toward Mishte-nur Hill. She had deliberately put on her white leather jacket so she would be recognized by the men at the various roadblocks she had to pass – everyone knew that jacket. She kept it spotless, and it almost glowed in the chaotic night.

It was only one and a half miles from her apartment to the entrance to the Mishte-nur bunker complex at the base of the hill. She had a crate tied to the back of the scooter and a pack strapped to her back with as many of the medical supplies Daryan had asked for as she could find in her warehouse. She'd also found a box of the damn 10.36mm cartridges the girl was always asking about.

She'd argued her way through three checkpoints, helped by the general air of urgency around her. It seemed the whole city was on the move somewhere. But at the blockade on 48th Street, the last one before Mishte-nur Hill, she'd been stopped by a YPG officer who wasn't in the mood for discussion. She could hear the rattle of small arms fire, and the thump of heavier guns too, up ahead of her.

"No through traffic, turn around," he'd told her, and waved her away, turning to the next vehicle in line, a car full of militia fighters.

"I have medical supplies for the Americans," she tried. "I have to get to Mishte-nur." She had pushed her scooter forward so that it was almost between the officer's legs.

He put his hands on her handlebars. "Didn't you see or hear that artillery barrage? There are no Americans left on Mishte-nur. And the Syrians have cut it off anyway. Turn around, I said." He shoved so hard she nearly fell, but she managed to keep her scooter upright and walked it out of the queue. She could try to get through on foot, there were always ways around roadblocks, but she didn't like the sound of the fighting up ahead and besides, the stupid crate would slow her down.

Nasrin considered her options, then pointed her scooter north, away from the gunfire, and torqued the engine. She would go through back streets to the Maqtalah cemetery, go right between the graves. That would bring her out east of Mishte-nur, with the Syrian positions to her left, at the eastern edge of town.

But if they'd moved west, to attack the hill?

Well, then she was screwed, but at least she'd tried.

Not for the first time in her life, as she swerved through the back alleys and laneways off 48th Street, she cursed her stupid, patriotic, dumb-ass sister.

ON the summit of Mishte-nur, six Marines put their shoulders to the buckled blast doors of the main entrance of the bunker and pushed. The doors didn't move.

MJ looked around the crowded passage. "Where is Jensen?" she asked. She'd just realized she hadn't seen the big Marine since he'd gone out with his dogs. Shouldn't he be back by now?

Bell indicated with a nod of his head. "If he aint in here, he's out there."

There was more grunting up by the doors, and then, with a coordinated shove, they were heaved open. The men behind them spilled out, left and right, and there was the immediate sound of automatic rifle fire.

The smell of unexpended fuel and the acrid stench of smoke flooded into the bunker entrance.

The corridor in front of them emptying, Bell turned to MJ. "Stay close."

She didn't want to stay close. She wanted to stay *put*. With every fiber of her being. But as Bell pulled the straps of his pack tighter and started running for the compound outside, she was right behind him.

They didn't even reach the doors before she heard the first cry.

"Corpsman!!"

Belladonna poison
Incirlik Air Base, Turkey, 4 April

"Radar still at 30 percent efficiency, sir," Barruzzi reported. It hadn't been that long since the RAAF pilot had taken off and they were still at the mercy of the Syrian *Belladonna* units.

"That will give us about two seconds for an intercept," Lieutenant Sun predicted. "We'll get off one laser burst, maybe. Unless they're sending missiles and we can deploy the microwave." He looked over at his sysop. "You got anything for me, Allenby?"

"Just text over the fiber optic, Lieutenant," the corporal said. He ran his finger down a screen. "Syrian armor on the northwest perimeter."

Sun looked up at the roof as he heard the sound of a TOW missile firing about five hundred yards away, the hammer of autocannon fire in the distance and the muffled impact of a projectile hitting dirt. "No kidding. Tell me something I don't know."

"Only scouts spotted so far, sir," he said. "*Terminators* and LTMVs."

"Holding the big boys in reserve, seeing do we really want this fight," Barruzzi guessed. "Where the hell are those damn rockets?"

Sun looked at his watch. It was twenty minutes since he'd gotten the report that the Syrians were deploying their *SMERCH* rocket launchers. Five to ten minutes to emplace and fix the trucks for launch. They didn't travel with their tubes loaded, so twenty minutes to load while they programmed the target coordinates.

"Any second, Sergeant..."

They didn't have to wait any longer. Though suppressed, their fire control radar was still good out to about a mile and it picked up the incoming volley of 300mm rockets flying toward them, aimed at the airfield infrastructure beyond. The *HELLADS* engagement control system didn't just identify targets, in the space of milliseconds it tracked them, locked them up, interrogated IFF to check if they were hostile or friendly, and prioritized them for destruction. Each of the five laser arrays at Ted Sun's command could engage one target with each laser burst, with a quarter second between bursts. One burst was usually enough to trigger or deflect a dumb rocket; two or three bursts were needed for cruise missiles or guided bombs.

That meant that in the two-second window in which the subsonic rockets were inside their limited radar range and passing over their *HELLADS* they could engage perhaps ten rockets.

Each *SMERCH* launcher fired twelve.

The system triggered automatically. "Firing!" Barruzzi called. A series of icons on her screen showed each rocket as it screamed toward them and stamped it with a cross if it was knocked down. The engagement was over before it began.

"Six down," she said, hammering her desk in frustration. "Yeah, six. But I think we got all the rockets aimed at the troops ahead of us."

"How many total inside our detection radius?" Sun asked.

She checked the plot. "Twenty-three. There could have been..." She didn't get any further. Behind them, they heard a rolling series of thunderous explosions and a second later the truck rocked from multiple pressure waves.

Sun and Barruzzi jumped to their feet and stuck their heads out the door of their command unit. *SMERCH* rockets could be fitted with single high-explosive warheads, including chemical weapons and thermobarics, or with submunition dispensers designed to scatter cluster bombs or mines across a wider area that could guide themselves to targets such as vehicles, aircraft and buildings using laser and infrared sensors.

Sun looked at the smoke rising from explosions right across the base. It spread quickly. "Not gas. I'd say they went with simple HE mixed with smoke rounds for concealment." He reached for one of the rifles just inside the door and handed it toward Allenby. "Outside and behind cover, Corporal." He picked up his own weapon and pointed at Barruzzi's chair. "Back in your seat, Sergeant. As long as we've got one battery firing, we're still in this game. Keep those systems up as long as you can. That was the first volley, not the last one."

Barruzzi watched as he swung out of the trailer. In the near distance she heard the crack of a heavy cannon, followed very closely by a high-explosive thud. She'd heard that sound a couple of times before, but only on exercises.

Tanks.

TANKS. Bunny saw them below and behind her as she hauled her machine around after taking off from Incirlik and made her egress to the west, away from them. As soon as she had her wheels up she shoved her throttle forward and pulled her machine in a zooming climb that put her out of range of any light anti-air artillery or hand-held missiles that might be below. Her loyal BATS unit followed her up, about thirty seconds behind. They'd be as obvious as shooting stars on a cloudless night if there were Russian aircraft over the base, but she didn't have time for subtleties. If she had to tangle with any *Felons* or Su-35 *Flankers* she would have to trust the BATS to keep them busy while she did her job.

Leveling out at twenty thousand feet and pointing her machine east again, she saw the Syrian armor on her DAS display, a line of about twenty tanks approaching the base from the northeast.

As she watched, a line of explosions rocked the base below. *Rocket barrage.* She could see a large part of it had been aimed at the US and NATO facilities at the eastern boundary of the base. A line of dense smoke started to blanket the entire area. Further back inside the base, more explosions and fire near the main hangars and apron. Hoping to catch parked aircraft in the open? *Good luck with that, you can knock, but there ain't no one at home, Ali.*

She swiped the DAS screen away and put it into Suppression of Enemy Air Defenses or SEAD mode. A map of the battlesphere around her appeared on the screen, with the signature of Syrian radar and radio comms signals painted on it as their transmitted energy washed across her aircraft and allowed it to fix their positions. As quickly as it mapped them, the system identified and classified them by threat level.

Close in, not far behind the Syrian armor, she saw two mobile *Buk* anti-air missile units. Neither of them had a lock on her, yet. With her F-35 in 'beast mode', iron bombs hanging from hardpoints both inside and outside the weapons bay, her stealth profile was seriously compromised. So every mile she put them behind her made her happier. She was looking ahead, twenty or so miles ahead, where the US anti-air NCO had told her to look.

The *Belladonna* wouldn't appear as a high-priority threat. It was designed to disrupt enemy systems, not engage them. But it should appear on her screen as the biggest, ugliest…

And there you are.

Her SEAD system classified the contact as a Krasukha-4 *Belladonna* system, capable of jamming anything from low earth orbit satellites to ground radars and radio comms. Bingo. *Only one of you?* It seemed so. She had no idea how many units the Russians had sold to Syria, but she guessed they were probably very high value assets.

She set her *Panther* to maintain altitude and steer on the contact. She wouldn't be able to paint it with her onboard synthetic aperture radar, so her only option was to get close enough to identify it visually on her DAS sensor. She couldn't launch her *Gray Wolf* at standoff range either, it would have its small silicon brain fried before it could even get close. That meant she had only one attack vector.

She had to close within nine miles of the *Belladonna* and paint it with her targeting laser to get bombs on it. If she did it right, the crew wouldn't know she was there until they were looking up from hell wondering what had happened.

There was just one problem. Beside the *Belladonna* was a smaller radiation signature. The jammer had a little buddy. She looked at the label under the icon.

Pantsir-SM mobile anti-air. An older, less capable system than the *Buk*, but still a threat. And she was already inside detection range. There was no way she could get within nine miles of that *Belladonna* with her aircraft in beast mode without the *Pantsir* detecting her.

She pulled up the menu for her BATS, now trailing a little less than a mile behind her. She pulled up the nav system for the drone and gave it waypoints that would take it down low and send it right over the top of the *Pantsir*. It couldn't attack it, but the *Pantsir* was a point to shoot system. To fire, it had to aim its missile turret at the target, and if she timed her ingress right it would be tracking her BATS and pointed away from her as she sent her bombs at the *Belladonna*.

If. You could fly a bloody C-130 through that 'if' but she had no better plan. She checked neither the *Buk* systems behind her nor the *Pantsir* in front of her appeared to be tracking her, and then armed her 2,000lb. GBU-31 bombs.

Sorry, mate. This is probably where we say goodbye, Bunny thought to herself as she hit the command to send the BATs on its way. She watched on her DAS as it rolled onto its back and then speared toward the ground. Once it got under five hundred feet it would orient on the *Pantsir* and use terrain-following laser to hug the terrain so that it wouldn't be detected by the tracked Syrian missile system until it was nearly right on top of it. Blowing past the *Pantsir* at 650 miles an hour, it should be enough of a distraction to give Bunny a tiny window of opportunity. If she was lucky, she would catch the crew inside the missile vehicle napping.

If she wasn't, they would kill her BATS, and then they would probably kill her.

TED Sun peered over the sandbags outside his command trailer. His helmet was equipped with low-light and infrared vision built into a flip-down visor. Through a thin veil of smoke he saw a shape, about a half mile off. It moved forward and halted behind a small rise, just its turret visible.

T-90 tank.

The turret traversed toward their position. Ted looked back at their trailer, the radar dish on top of it looking for all the world like a big grey practice target. He was about to shout to Barruzzi to bail the hell out when a TOW missile speared out of the Army lines ahead of them and smacked into the side of the T-90, triggering its reactive armor. It rocked, but then angled itself in the direction of the TOW attack, putting undamaged armor between it and the US positions as its turret slewed around. With a whiplash crack it fired and then started backing up.

"Yeah, Army!" Allenby cheered. "Get some!"

Sun put his hand on the man's helmet and shoved his head down. "You'll get some you don't keep your head down, boy."

YEVGENY Bondarev was getting more important lessons in the art of war. Not an education he'd anticipated getting from ground level, but one he realized that, if he lived through it, he'd probably put to good use later in life.

First, own the air.

The Syrian armor had only been able to advance as far as it had because the pilots of his 7th Air Group had established supremacy over the airspace over Incirlik. They'd whittled the Turkish Air Force down over nearly two years of conflict and driven Coalition aircraft back to Cyprus with their tails between their legs. He'd seen a lone F-35 *Panther* scramble from the Turkish airfield a few minutes earlier – a BATS drone in tow – so Russia didn't have total air dominance, but superiority was enough. The bulk of the Coalition aircraft based at Incirlik had clearly been forced to flee and Bondarev knew there would be a screen of *Flankers* and *Felons* south and east of Incirlik to intercept any Coalition fighters or cruise missiles launched from Crete or the eastern Mediterranean in an attempt to win back control of the air over the battlefield.

Second, adaptability is king. He had to give credit to the commander of the Syrian 25th Mechanized 'Tiger Force'. The man had taken the lumps handed to him outside Goztepe and then rallied to drive his spearhead pell-mell toward Incirlik before the Turkish and Coalition troops could better organize their defenses. Now he was advancing to contact under cover of the Russian fighters and his own *SMERCH* barrage and his tanks were already inside the airfield's outer perimeter.

Third, unity of effect could compensate for small numbers. The relatively small force Syria had deployed was nevertheless powerful when combined with Russian airpower and modern battlefield weapons such as cyberattack and electronic interference. Obtaining advantage from the actions of disparate forces was a significant multiplier.

Of course, all that meant little to the individual soldier. Bondarev found himself advancing toward Incirlik in the company of a rifle squad, moving slowly forward in the shadow of an eight-wheeled BTR-80 that belched exhaust smoke out of two ports mounted conveniently on the upper hull at around face height.

He couldn't see more than two hundred yards in front of himself now that smoke from the *SMERCH* barrage was blowing back toward them. And of course he had no infrared eyepiece. He didn't even have a helmet, having long ago discarded his hundred-thousand-dollar flight helmet. It was a wonder of digital technology, lined with Kevlar to provide a measure of ballistic protection, but it was too large and unwieldy to wear into combat on the ground.

Tracer fire arced toward them from a position up ahead and the troop carrier stopped abruptly, Bondarev crowding in behind it in a press of bodies as the vehicle opened up with its 30mm cannon. The Syrian sergeant in charge of the squad yelled something in Arabic to his men, and without so much as a word or nod to Bondarev, they rolled out from behind the armored car and spread out into the smoke around it.

Bondarev was suddenly alone. He looked at his ridiculously small AMD-65 rifle and listened to the crackle of small arms fire erupting around him as the 30mm on the armored car continued its staccato drum beat.

As the BTR-80's gears crunched and it began moving forward again, Bondarev hunched his shoulders, tucked himself in behind it again and kept limping on. It was without doubt the strangest escort he'd ever been given into an airfield, and he doubted he was going to live to tell anyone about it.

Corpsman for a day
COP Meyer, Kobani, Northern Syria, 4 April

MJ ran out into near total darkness. The few dim lights around the compound not destroyed in the *Sunburn* attack did nothing to illuminate her way because of the cloying smoke and fuel oil mist in the air. She took in the scene of carnage with the practiced eye of an experienced observer of war, even as she zigged and zagged in Bell's wake as he headed for a Marine shouting for help with an arm in the air about fifty yards away in the middle of the compound.

The soil under her feet was black.

She passed a dog-sized lump of bubbling flesh and fat. It smelled like BBQ pork. Except there were no dogs inside COP Meyer, not made of flesh and bone anyway.

Bullets hit the ground behind her as she ran. Aimed at her?

She looked over at the tower where she had last seen the Syrian sniper, Daryan Al-Kobani. It was gone, a hole in the wall where it had been. Syrian soldiers climbing over the rubble to get inside the outpost, mown down by a Marine lying on the ground in front of it, feet splayed, hosing automatic fire at the gap in the wall.

A large explosion and then the crackle of ammunition exploding as one of the Syrian armored vehicles that had been destroyed in the air strike cooked off.

Bell skidded to a halt beside the Marines in the middle of the compound. One had his hands on the other man's abdomen, trying to stem the blood flowing around his fingers as the man on the ground writhed in pain. He didn't look burned, he'd been shot. He must have been one of the first ones out the blast doors.

"Keep pressure on that," Bell told her, pointing at the wound. She put her hands on the wound in place of the Marine's. The world around MJ contracted to just the three of them as Bell went to work. She barely registered the fighting and dying; all that mattered was the guy on the ground and the orders Bell was barking at her as he pumped morphine into the wounded soldier, packed his wound and slapped a pressure bandage on it. He looked over his shoulder at the entrance to the bunker about thirty yards away.

Another explosion, more small arms fire. He grabbed the arm of the Marine who had called them over, yelling to be heard. "You are going to grab him under the arms and drag him to the bunker. You got that? Under the arms?"

The Marine nodded, shifting his weight, getting ready.

Bell slapped his helmet. "Go, go, go!"

Before the man had even stood, Bell was up and running again and MJ was sprinting to keep up. He was headed for the gap in the wall where the northern tower had been. Bodies lay around the blast area in the wan light of a pile of still-burning crates and boxes.

None were moving.

NASRIN had made it to the cemetery on the other side of the Maqtalah Mosque and killed her headlight, bumping over what she was pretty sure were small headstones as she threaded her way through the graves to the open ground that lay between the cemetery and the northern slopes of Mishte-nur. Before today, the Syrian lines would have been about two hundred yards behind her, on the other side of the main road ringing Kobani, and she would have a clear run into the bunker's ground-level north entrance, where the Americans stood guard.

Even in the darkness she quickly saw that the situation had changed. A pitched battle was being waged outside the bunker entrance. It was little more than a deep slit crudely carved into the base of the hill, leading to an elevator about twenty yards in. The Marine guard post outside comprised sandbags and a .50-cal machine gun emplacement protected by concrete barriers further out. As she watched, an RPG lanced out from a group of buildings north of the bunker entrance and exploded against one of the concrete barriers. Though she couldn't see it, she could hear the autocannon of an armored vehicle hammering away, with the occasional reply from the US .50-cal. US troops were huddled behind the sandbags and concrete barriers, returning fire whenever the Syrian autocannon paused its constant *thump thump thump.*

There was no easy way in. If she managed to get close to the bunker entrance without being shot by the Syrians, the Americans would probably think she was some kind of crazy suicide bomber and shoot her instead. She looked up at the hill. The summit was still shrouded in smoke, lit by the occasional flash of an explosion showing there was fighting going on there too.

Oh, what was the *point?* Stupid girl was probably dead anyway.

Then a missile speared out from the American emplacement, flashed between buildings, and there was a large explosion. The Syrian armored vehicle fell silent. The Americans were still fighting.

She howled up at the sky. "Damn you, Daryan!"

She twisted the throttle, the scooter spraying gravel from its rear tire. She fish-tailed across the first few yards of open ground before her wheels got a good grip and she rocketed forward. Tracer fire flew across the air in front of her. Then behind her.

A shot from the American lines struck the engine of her bike, shoving her sideways, but she kept her balance, swerved around one concrete barrier, then a second. The entrance to the bunker was in front of her, and four surprised Marines turned and looked at her as she screamed out of the darkness, around the last barrier, and jammed on her brakes, her rear wheel bucking in the air as she skidded to a stop.

Four rifles were pointing at her as she gathered herself and raised both hands. "Kurdish!" she yelled. "I have medical supplies!"

BUNNY was gathering herself too. She watched the ingress of the BATS carefully, following it from fifteen thousand feet over the earth. As it got within a mile of the *Pantsir* anti-air missile unit, she engaged its phased-array radar in broad scan mode to get the attention of anyone below who hadn't heard it coming yet. She had no way of knowing if the *Pantsir* commander would take the bait, but she was clean out of options. Flinging her *Panther* onto a wingtip, she pulled it around and steered on the *Pantsir*, painting it with her targeting laser. Her helmet-projected ground attack display showed a lock on the tracked anti-air vehicle and she picked off a single 2,000lb. bomb. From five miles out, it would take agonizing seconds to reach the *Pantsir*, seconds in which the Syrian radar could get a lock on her.

But as she watched the bomb track toward its target, the view flared as the *Pantsir* fired a missile at the fleeting BATS and simultaneously opened fire on it with its onboard 30mm cannon, red tracer fire reaching into the night sky. The BATS made a radical right-hand banking turn that would have broken the neck of a human pilot, frantically firing decoys in its wake.

Splash one! Bunny put her machine into a slow banking turn that placed her on a heading to engage the *Belladonna* jammer. Her display blanked as the screen automatically dimmed so as not to destroy her night vision, but when it restored itself, there was nothing but a blazing pyre where the Syrian missile vehicle had been, and she could see her BATS pulling away to the holding waypoint she'd assigned it. Grabbing her targeting joystick, she pulled the laser targeting cursor across her tactical screen and laid it on the *Belladonna*. She wanted to be sure of this one, so she armed two bombs and assigned them to the strike.

As she did so, she picked up a signal on her radar warning receiver. Russian aircraft nearby, searching for her. She shut down the warning alarm, blinked to clear her vision and focused on keeping the laser targeting cursor on the *Belladonna* unit.

RUSSIAN Second Lieutenant 'Rap' Tchakov had indeed panicked when his wingman Bondarev had disappeared. He had panicked more when the BATS drone they had been tracking had suddenly turned into a Coalition *Panther*, sent a volley of missiles at them and shot down their CO, Bebenko.

But once he and his wingman had regrouped, a flame of anger replaced the fear deep in his guts and he had continued his patrol. The Coalition fighter had disappeared as quickly as it had appeared, but there would be others. He did not believe that the fighter patrol that had accounted for Bebenko would be the only one aloft with all the action occurring on the ground below. The Beriev A-100 early warning aircraft that was providing coverage of the operations area had detected aircraft departing Akrotiri on a heading for targets inside Syria and Turkey. It was only a matter of time before they showed themselves over Incirlik again.

His optical electric sensors were designed to pick up the slightest shadow in the night sky, or the merest indication of warmth from an engine or a missile launch.

But he saw the explosion on the ground below with his own eyes as something down there disappeared in a glowing ball of fire.

The Syrian forward air controller embedded with armored column advancing on Incirlik was on the radio seconds later. "Russian Gorgon flight, Syrian FAC. We have received reports of enemy aircraft attacking ground units in map sector Lima Fox three two, repeat Lima Fox three two. Please cover."

"FAC, Gorgon flight confirms, moving into sector Lima Fox three two. Gorgon two, five miles separation, active search."

If Coalition aircraft were already attacking Syrian ground units, there was no time for subtlety. Tchakov switched from passive optical electric to active radar scanning and started searching the sky ahead of him as he brought his machine around and pointed it toward the fire still burning on the ground ahead. He immediately got a return.

BATS. Dammit, the Coalition drones were like flies swarming a dead carcass. But unlike the Russian *Okhotniks*, they carried no air-ground weapons. There was another aircraft type out there, either Turkish F-16s or Coalition *Tempests* or *Panthers*. His money was on the stealth aircraft types – an ancient F-16 would have been easier to pick up than the lone BATS he'd just detected.

Assuming it was alone ... Tchakov had learned that lesson losing one aircraft. He didn't plan to lose two.

"Gorgon two, Gorgon leader, you take the BATS, I will keep searching for ground attack aircraft," he said, then remembered the man on his wing was newly arrived in theater. "Be careful when you engage, the drone will initiate counter-fire as soon as it detects your missile launch. Understood?"

"Understood, Gorgon leader, engaging," the other pilot replied.

BUNNY counted down. *Three seconds, two, one* ... Splash two! The *Belladonna* unit disappeared in an even bigger mushroom cloud than the first, and Bunny pointed her *Panther* west again, toward the Syrian armor advancing on Incirlik. She was still being hunted by at least one Russian *Felon*, her radar warning receiver told her that much, but she had a bellyful of eggs she needed to lay.

As the Syrian jamming rig went off the air, her comms links on multiple Coalition frequencies were restored and a flood of data started flowing across her screen. Her mind nearly blanked with the sudden onslaught of information. She took a breath, checked her heading and her instruments, set her aircraft into waypoint following mode and scanned the incoming traffic.

Coalition sector air control, requesting her to report status. She pulled up her tactical screen, filling now with new data thanks to her strike on the *Belladonna*. She saw two flights of Turkish F-16s rolling in on Incirlik, icons indicating they were on an air defense suppression mission. Behind them, another flight of F-16s on a ground attack mission. At the extreme range of her map, over the southern coast between Cyprus and Turkey, she saw several Russian and Coalition icons indicating aircraft engaged in a furball. Well, she wasn't alone up here!

The next comms data point was Incirlik air control, urgently requesting any allied aircraft available for tasking.

Then a peremptory recall message from RAAF Akrotiri. She'd been expecting that. It was the digital equivalent of 'where the hell are you, O'Hare?'

She ignored that one, ignored the insistent beeping of the radar warning receiver trying to tell her there was a Russian *Felon* in the neighborhood, and dialed in to the Incirlik controller.

"Incirlik, this is RAAF Sunset one, reporting destruction one *Pantsir*, one *Belladonna* unit, twenty miles west Incirlik. Still have, uh ... three 2,000 pounders, one *Gray Wolf*. Available for tasking."

"Wondering who took out that *Belladonna*, thank you, Sunset one. We are danger close. Syrian armor inside the base perimeter, northeast corner. Turkish Air Force is engaging mobile air defense targets. Prioritize Syrian tracked vehicles."

"Confirm, Incirlik, Sunset one engaging," she replied. "Get your heads down."

She painted the landscape ahead of her with her synthetic aperture radar and saw no shortage of targets. Picking out the *SMERCH* rocket launchers set up miles behind the Syrian spearhead for her *Gray Wolf*, she locked up one in the center of the group and armed the cruise missile, holding her breath as she did so. It came up green. She let her breath out again and thumbed her missile release.

"Wolf away," she said to no-one in particular.

As soon as she did so, she heard a missile warning alert in her ears. Reacting instinctively, she dumped her remaining bombs, rolling her machine on its back and diving for the dirt below.

RAP Tchakov got a lock on the Coalition *Panther* as soon as its missile dropped from its weapons bay and streaked west. It was close. He had two long-range *Vympel Axehead* hypersonic air-to-air missiles in his bay, but the *Panther* was inside their minimum range. So he sent a K-77M missile after the cruise missile and two at the *Panther*.

Whether the pilot had reacted or the machine's combat AI had taken control, Rap was surprised when the aircraft headed almost vertically for the earth just ten thousand feet below it. It was a near suicidal maneuver, but it worked, forcing his missiles to swerve so radically that they lost lock on the Coalition fighter without it even firing decoy flares or chaff to confuse the pursuit.

You can't possibly pull out of that, Rap told himself, watching the *Panther*'s altitude spin down through five, four, three, two, one thousand feet ... he lost the track in ground clutter, but saw no explosion. It must have plowed straight in.

He saw his wingman firing on a BATS drone, and then immediately go defensive as the BATS returned fire with a missile of its own.

Then his own missile warning alarm began screaming as the *Panther* below him reappeared from the ground clutter, coming straight back up at him!

BUNNY'S fuselage had scraped a row of trees as she'd hauled her *Panther* level barely a hundred feet above the ground east of Incirlik. Her DAS system had a lock on the *Felon* that had fired on her and, staying low, she trimmed her fighter into a nose-up attitude that pointed its missiles at the sky while keeping her aircraft flying low and level. She armed her air-to-air missiles.

Target lock. Fox 3, CUDA away!

Her BATS was down. There were at least two *Felons* hunting her and she was down in the weeds, out of height and out of energy.

Forget this, she needed to hunt ground targets, not waste her time dancing with a *Felon*.

With her bombs stripped from her wings, she only had her 25mm cannon left to use in any ground attack. But it was better than nothing. And without the 2,000lb. bombs hanging off her fuselage she had gotten her stealth profile back.

Counterintuitively, considering she was still engaged with the Russian *Felon*, she throttled back her engine to reduce her heat signature, turned diagonal to the Russian fighters and hugged the earth as she curved back towards Incirlik. She could still see the nearest Russian *Felon* maneuvering to avoid her hastily launched missile.

She had a tiny window in which to slip away and she was taking it.

RAP'S *Felon* had taken control of his flight stick and pushed his machine into a stomach-lurching negative G turn. His vision began to red out, and he cursed as he lost his lock on the Coalition *Panther*. The American missile flashed behind him and detonated harmlessly in a cloud of chaff. His AI had saved him from the CUDA missile, but it had left him helpless and exposed to further attack.

Helping sink his mood further into the red, he had lost his lock on the enemy cruise missile, which must have successfully jammed his own attack and escaped, since he had registered no kill confirmation.

"Gorgon leader, Gorgon two," his wingman called, fretfully. "I have no target."

The enemy pilot had passed below him and moved behind. Rap took control of his *Felon* back and pulled it level, slewing to face back toward Incirlik. "He's here somewhere, Gorgon two. You hold in sector Lima Fox three two and keep looking. I'll move closer to Incirlik. He may be trying to sneak back home."

Rap had lost his optical and infrared lock on the enemy fighter. He ground his teeth as he set his sensor suite specifically to look for the pinball-sized radar return of an F-35 ahead of and below him, somewhere in the dark.

He tuned to the Syrian forward air control frequency. "FAC, this is Gorgon flight. Please alert your air defense commander there is probably a Coalition aircraft inbound Incirlik..."

"Gorgon, FAC, we have just lost two *Buk* units to Turkish air action. Remaining *Buk* units are engaged with Turkish close air support. Please pursue and engage."

"Gorgon flight, roger."

Pursue and engage?

How do you engage what you can't see? The fear started creeping back up from his feet into his stomach again.

THAT was exactly the thought going through Alessa Barruzzi's mind inside the *HELLADS* engagement control trailer. She looked at her watch ... eighteen minutes. The next *SMERCH* barrage would be airborne in minutes, directed this time by fire support officers in the Syrian front line now that they had a fix on exactly where the Turkish and US Army positions were.

With radar functioning at less than 30 percent she had a snowball's chance in ... *wait, what?*

As she watched, her system screen started updating, showing her radar at 100 percent nominal!

She let out a whoop and saluted the roof of the trailer, sending her thanks to Bunny in the skies above. "Thank you, RAAF!"

Sun stuck his head through the trailer door. He flinched at the crack of a grenade in the distance. "What are you yelling about, Sergeant?"

Barruzzi was hammering keys on her keyboard as fast as she could speak. "All systems are back up, Lieutenant, radar is 100 percent. Mains power is still down, but we've got comms links to the Tactical Director, networking with the other batteries now ... *Patriots* are back up, *Centurions* too."

Alone, they were crippled. Now they could pull data from every other *HELLADS*, *Patriot* and *Centurion* battery on the base, from the Turkish early warning aircraft circling behind them, from the traffic control radar at Incirlik. It was like their battlefield vision had just gone from monocular 2D black and white to 6K 3D virtual reality.

Barruzzi stopped talking and typing and peered at one of her screens. "Cruise missile, ten miles out, bearing zero four zero, incoming!"

Sun frowned. "One missile? Type?"

"*Gray Wolf*. It's one of ours!"

"Stay focused, Barruzzi," Sun said, looking at his own watch. "One missile isn't going to do our job for us." The sound of small arms fire intensified nearby. Sun disappeared from the doorway, returning to his position beside Allenby no doubt.

For no good reason at all, it made Barruzzi feel better knowing they were out there.

O'HARE'S single *Gray Wolf* missile had a very clear picture of its targets, downloaded in the moments after its launch from her *Panther*, and then updated by its own onboard targeting radar as it approached the big trucks, their rocket launch tubes raised to the sky.

As it lined up for its attack run, the first of the *SMERCH* launchers fired. They had been fed with targets by their battalion fire control officers in reconnaissance vehicles among the Syrian spearhead. And the three crews had been ordered to fire as soon as the 300mm rockets were loaded and ready.

If it had feelings, the *Gray Wolf* might have felt dismayed at arriving just seconds too late, but after all it was just silicon, metal and high explosive and it still had a job to do. It oriented so that it would sweep over the trucks from south to north and began releasing its munitions about five hundred yards short of its targets. It had twelve high-explosive anti-tank bomblets and only three targets.

As it buried itself in the ground between the wheels of the third *SMERCH* truck, the first of its submunitions was still falling toward the first truck in line. Had it cared, it probably would have been counting the number of rockets the Syrian battery got away before it destroyed itself.

Twenty-two.

And if it had its own onboard optical recognition system, it may have even been able to read the warhead type off the serial numbers written on the side of the rockets now flying toward the Turkish and US troop positions on the northwest perimeter of Incirlik.

And it might have been just a little perturbed as it realized the warheads just fired by the *SMERCH* launchers were banned under three different international weapons treaties.

To the Syrian scientists who had developed it, it was known as *hydrolyzed propan-2-yl methylphosphonofluoridate*. A gas, designed to kill or paralyze on inhalation or contact with the skin, but modified so that it would degrade into nontoxic phosphonic acid derivatives within minutes, instead of the usual days or weeks. This had the advantage that friendly troops did not need any special protective equipment as long as they avoided contact with the gas in the first few minutes after it was released. And it made it almost impossible for international war crimes inspectors to prove it had been used.

To the rest of the world, it was known as sarin gas.

"Incoming!" Barruzzi yelled through the open door. "Engaging." With headphones on her head, only the loudest outside noises penetrated. She had no idea whether Sun and Allenby could hear her over the sound of the fighting outside. Almost in answer, she heard an assault rifle open out right outside. Her other crew mates were engaged too.

The *Patriot* batteries engaged first, their longer-range missiles spearing outward toward the incoming rockets. But they had a less than 30 percent success rate against targets detected so close to their minimum engagement range. A small counter on the side of her tactical display showed the number of targets identified. There were more than twenty.

Three down.

She saw the amber lights on the capacitor banks for her laser arrays move from yellow to green as they charged. Seventeen targets remaining.

The *Centurion* 20mm cannons opened up next as the rockets entered the *Centurion*'s two-thousand-meter engagement envelope.

Ten down! Seven remaining. Her tactical AI was giving her a predicted strike zone for each of the rockets, and she could see they were going to splash down right on top of the Turkish and US troops out front of her. Two of the splash zones overlapped with her own position. She frantically checked her systems readout. The *HELLADS* was at full power, all targets locked, there was nothing more she could do.

Her high power microwave 'toaster' would be useless against dumb rockets, her lasers would have to do all the work. As the rockets closed within 550 yards, her three arrays lit up.

"Burn, you bastards," Barruzzi muttered.

The counter on the side of her screen spun down as it registered the kills.

Seven ... six, five, four ... three ... two still flying!

The trailer rocked gently and a millisecond later she heard the sound of an explosion right outside. She grabbed the desk in front of her to steady herself, afraid the trailer was going to go over, but its wheels never left the ground. A near miss, maybe.

Did the warhead even go off? She would have expected a strike by a 300mm rocket right outside her trailer to sound different to that. Perhaps the headphones over her ears had muffled it. She ripped them off her head, so a second later she felt the full horrifying force of the chemical and biological weapons alert siren that began blaring inside her trailer.

Before she could react, the sliding door of the trailer slammed shut automatically and the trailer's overpressure protection system kicked in, increasing the air pressure inside the trailer to try and keep outside the toxins it had detected. She scrabbled for the locker behind her which held their Mission Oriented Protective Posture (MOPP) gear, a sick feeling in her stomach.

Sun and Allenby ... they were both outside.

IT was starting to get lighter as dawn approached. Ted Sun had his night vision visor down and had been sighting on a distant group of figures when the *SMERCH* rocket hit. A single round from a long-range rifle shot had smacked into the sandbags next to his head about a minute earlier. Probably a sniper. He had spotted the Syrian soldiers about three hundred yards off, crawling forward across the open airfield grass under cover of the sniper fire and had let fly with a burst from his M-27 rifle. As he did so, a flight of Turkish F-16s blasted overhead and there was a series of explosions in their wake, about a mile to his north.

Because of the roar of the jets, he didn't hear the rocket before it hit. Whether it had been aimed at their *HELLADS* control trailer or not didn't really matter. It hit about a hundred yards to the left of Sun and Allenby and exploded.

"This is it," was all he had time to think before the sandbagged emplacement they'd built toppled onto him.

But it wasn't the mind-numbing, flesh-shredding explosion he'd anticipated. Only the top layer of sandbags had been toppled, and he rolled out from under them. Allenby hadn't even been knocked off his feet. He was still kneeling, shocked look on his face, half turned toward the source of the explosion. And pointing.

A white cloud was mushrooming out of the ground where the rocket had hit.

A smoke round! Allenby nearly laughed out loud. It was just another damn smoke round. That wasn't good, it meant an infantry assault was imminent, but it was a damn sight luckier than a 200lb. high-explosive warhead detonating right beside them.

Sun got up onto a knee and reached for the M-27 that been knocked out of his hand. He dropped it again. Strange. It was like he couldn't feel it. Shock from the blast maybe? The smoke was starting to close around them, looking eerily green in his night vision view. With enemy infantry now just a few hundred yards away in smoke, he decided the *HELLADS* position was no longer defensible, not by an anti-air artillery crew armed just with light weapons.

Allenby was leaning on the sandbags now. Must have had the wind knocked out of him too.

OK, let's get Barruzzi out of the trailer and get out of here, he thought.

He tried to yell the command to Allenby, but it was like he'd lost his voice. Damn smoke, he was having trouble breathing.

His rifle fell out of his hand. He tried reaching for it, but his arm didn't respond. He must have been hit after all?

He saw Allenby slump forward. Him too?

Sun was definitely having trouble breathing. He tried to suck in a lungful of air, his chest not even moving.

The last thing Ted Sun saw as he toppled sideways was Allenby, one hand clawing feebly at his throat.

THE datasphere around Bunny O'Hare was overwhelming her. It had gone from nothing to a blinding waterfall of information. Even for a pilot trained in continuous partial attention strategies, she was drowning.

She was monitoring her threat warning system, the *Felon* behind her still pursuing her with its phase-array radar radiating as it tried to get a bounce off her skin. She was following the *Gray Wolf* on her air-ground targeting screen as it closed on the Syrian artillery position. She was running her eyes across the now lightening skies above her, and the dark rushing terrain around her, not trusting her DAS system alone to spot the next enemy that might try to kill her. Monitoring her systems status, instruments, fuel state. She was flicking her tactical display between close and far range, looking for any indication of new enemies or friendlies around her. On the far display she could see the furball over the southern coast had resolved itself, with the combatants – fewer of them – separating and returning to their bases either at Akrotiri on Cyprus or Latakia in Syria. She had no way of knowing who had won and who had lost. She saw the Turkish F-16 strike force retiring east. They were fewer too. But she could see only one Syrian *Buk* anti-air missile unit still active, so perhaps the Turkish ground attack aircraft had gotten through. The airspace directly over Incirlik and for about ten miles around appeared empty except for herself and the *Felon* trailing her.

That was just the information she was processing with her eyes.

She also flew her F-35 by sense of touch, the pressure on her back and head, or the feeling in her gut as the plane rose and fell, telling her how it was flying. Her legs responding to the movement of her rudder pedals by the terrain following autopilot, her hands on the flight stick and throttle, ready to take control back from the autopilot at the least sign it was going to fly her into a power pole, barn or hillside. Every bump or yaw she felt was data. Not even consciously registered, but data that had to be assimilated nonetheless.

Then there was the assault on her hearing. Not the hum of her turbofan engine, but the radio broadcasts she was monitoring. From Incirlik control, from the Turkish air controller in the *Peace Eagle* airborne warning and control AWACS aircraft nearly a hundred miles away. From the forward air controller embedded with the Turkish troops frantically calling for help as Syrian tanks bore down on his position. From RAAF Akrotiri, now that her position was finally visible to them on the plot being relayed by the AWACs aircraft. And not where Red had ordered her to be. She could of course control the radio inputs by tuning to the frequency she wanted to follow, and ignore some of the others, some of the time. But she couldn't ignore all of them, all of the time.

Wait, what was that? A tasking order from the AWACS? She'd just flipped straight past it without acknowledging. She realized her hand was held out in front of her as though it had no idea what it was supposed to do. *AWACS frequency. Got to find that.*

She banged a gloved hand uselessly on her helmet. How long had she been flying? How many sorties tonight? Two? No, three. How long since she'd slept?

Focus, O'Hare! she told herself.

She tuned her radio to the AWACS aircraft.

"Sunset flight, Quarterback, are you receiving? Sunset flight…"

"Quarterback, go for Sunset, you have some business for me?"

"Sunset, what's your weapons and fuel state?"

Bunny double checked. "Three CUDA missiles, guns, zero air-to-ground projectiles. Fuel, uh, 43 percent."

"Thank you. Sunset, proceed on bearing two four four to sector Juliette Juliette three seven, two hundred, angels twenty to rendezvous with two B-21 heavies inbound from Ramstein, callsign Whale two two, and provide escort until they have delivered their payload or you are bingo fuel. They are…"

Bunny thought quickly and interrupted. "Quarterback, you see that *Felon* on my six, right?" If O'Hare had the *Felon* on her threat warning screen, then the AWACS aircraft or ground-based radar should also be able to see it.

"Roger that, Sunset, we are vectoring Turkish fighters to intercept. You are the only stealth-capable fighter currently available for this tasking." The young voice on the radio sounded very relaxed. Bunny looked at the grid reference she had just been given and felt like screaming at him but took a deep breath.

"Quarterback, those coordinates are two hundred miles west. I have Syrian tanks and troops right underneath me, and I have 180 rounds of 25mm I could unload before I depart this area."

"Sunset, Quarterback, negative on ground attack. Rendezvous with Whale two two sector JJ three seven, angels twenty, estimate Whale two two will be on station in twenty minutes. Do you copy?"

Bunny ground her teeth. "Quarterback, Sunset copies. ETA fifteen mikes. Out." Two B-21s? Each one of them could carry sixteen Joint Air-to-Surface Standoff Missiles (JASSMs) and they'd be able to launch around the same time she joined with them. It made sense they wanted someone riding shotgun when they played their hand, but *two hundred miles* dammit? She checked her nav screen again. Close to Turkish Air Force Konya, though. She could put down there, reload and refuel…

She was coming up on Incirlik Air Base now, but didn't want to lift herself out of the ground clutter yet and give the *Felon* behind her an easy return. She swiped to her zoomed out tactical view and looked for the Turkish fighters the controller had referred to. Four F-16s moving in from the north, about five minutes out. Alright, yeah, they should keep that *Felon* busy … in fact he must be blind if he didn't already see them.

Sure enough, about five seconds later the Russian fighter shut down his radar and she lost the contact.

Good, he's bugging out, Bunny decided. Four on one not the kind of odds he likes.

She pulled her machine a few hundred feet higher and looked at the air base below her as it flashed under her wings. Had she taken those *SMERCH* launchers down? There seemed to be a lot of smoke and fire. She could see Syrian armor maneuvering in the northeast, but not at the inner perimeter of the base yet.

Wait, what?

She saw vehicle movement on the highway west of the base. A long convoy of vehicles. Flipping through to her DAS targeting screen, she zoomed her camera on the vehicles. They were just about to hit the bridge over the Seyhan River that ran through the middle of the city of Adana, just west of Incirlik.

She counted around thirty vehicles. Twenty six-seater Joint Light Tactical Vehicles and ten Bradley Infantry Fighting Vehicles, and they were booking.

The lead elements of the Bloody First had arrived.

NASRIN had made it to the entrance to COP Meyer and been shoved inside the entrance tunnel with her backpack and crate of supplies. But the sergeant inside was in no mood to let her any deeper in. The fighting outside the tunnel had only intensified as the sky brightened.

"And the United States Marine Corps thanks you, ma'am," he said after checking her crate and backpack for explosives. "But you can leave those supplies here. We'll get them where they're needed." He reached for the crate but Nasrin pulled back.

"My sister is inside," she insisted. "She asked me to deliver the supplies to her. I want to speak with her."

"Do I look like a damn hotel concierge?" the sergeant yelled at her, putting his hand on the sidearm at his belt. "Put that crate down now!" A private beside him stepped forward threateningly.

"And who will pay me?" she asked.

The sergeant looked at her incredulously. He was still thinking about how to respond when a rocket-propelled grenade exploded at the bunker entrance, sending the sergeant, the private and Nasrin flying. The tunnel filled with dust and smoke. The two Marines staggered to their feet, forgetting Nasrin. Her crate of supplies had fallen from her arms and she saw the contents scattered through the tunnel. Then she saw a door next to the elevator open, and four Marines come running out. As they pushed past her, she ran quickly to the door, eased inside the stairwell, and closed the door behind her.

Stairs led up into the base and she heard more boots coming down. She had khaki overalls on underneath her white leather jacket and with a sigh of regret, she dumped the jacket on the ground, retied the scarf around her head in the style of a YPJ militia fighter, pulled her backpack tight and started up the stairs.

Several Marines passed her on the stairs, headed for the fighting below. None gave her more than a glance. When she reached the top, panting, she emerged into chaos. The elevator lobby was a bare room about twenty by twenty feet and it was full of Marines, assembling to head below. She pushed through the crowd, but at the door leading deeper into the complex, she felt a hand on her shoulder and turned.

"Where do you think you are going?" a voice belonging to a lieutenant asked her. He had a telephone handset in one hand and looked distracted.

She pulled the cover of the backpack open. "Medical supplies, from the YPJ. Where is your hospital?"

He hesitated, then decided Nasrin wasn't his biggest problem right now. "Sick bay is on deck two," he said. "Get moving."

She had no idea where she was going, but figured if she went against the flow of traffic it would take her up. The theory was sound enough. She had to ask directions after a couple of dead-ends, but eventually emerged into what looked like a repurposed barracks, littered with wounded men and women. A single surgeon and a nurse appeared to be busy triaging, while a couple of corpsmen moved around the room, checking the injured. Nasrin had to step aside as a body covered in a blanket was taken outside by a couple of privates carrying a stretcher. Unnoticed in the commotion, she walked nervously from cot to cot, looking for Daryan, hoping against hope she wouldn't find her. At the end of the room, she leaned up against the wall in a corner and stifled a sob.

She's not here. Allah be praised.

"You there, what are you doing?" the surgeon asked, looking over at her from where he was working, sewing up a wound.

"Sorry, I..." She pulled her backpack off her back. "I have supplies for you. Wound dressings, morphine, saline..."

The doctor nodded to the nurse beside him and she walked quickly over to look through the backpack. "Thank you!" she said. "We need everything we can get."

"There's more down at the lower entrance," Nasrin told her. "There was an explosion. I dropped it."

"Private Wizecki!" the nurse called out. "Take some pillow cases, get down to the lower entrance. Look for medical supplies, bring them back here. Do not get shot."

"Yes, corporal," the man replied, and disappeared out the door.

The nurse squeezed Nasrin's arm. "Thank you." She began to turn away, but Nasrin grabbed her hand as she turned.

"Yes?"

"My sister was here, she called and told me what you needed," Nasrin said hopefully. "She is YPJ."

The woman looked blank but turned her face to the room. "YPJ militia female, anyone seen her?"

One of the corpsmen looked up from bandaging a man's leg. "The sniper? Yeah, I saw her topside, Heaven's Gate, before the shit went down."

Nasrin ran over to him. "Where is that?"

"Hold your finger here," he said, pointing at the bandage. Nasrin put her hand on it to hold it so he could bind it fast. The man whose leg he was bandaging appeared to be watching the procedure with detached fascination. Nasrin guessed he was heavily drugged. "You go out the door, go one level up, turn left. That will take you topside. OK, I got it now." He pulled her hand away. "But it's World War Three up there. And Heaven's Gate ... the north tower? It ain't there no more."

Nasrin remembered her dream. Daryan crying out to her. *No.* It simply could not be.

Going back to her backpack, she emptied the 40lb. contents onto a set of shelves. She kept one pressure bandage, a half box of morphine ampoules, a bag of saline. And Daryan's precious 10.36mm ammunition. Like it was some kind of magic talisman that would lead her to her sister.

Shouldering the pack again, she pulled the straps tight over her shoulders and headed out the door.

JAMES Jensen heard the airstrike on the summit of Mishtenur but had no idea if it was by Russian or Coalition aircraft. No one was responding to his radio calls. Leaving Brutus splayed on top of the bleeding Russian, he checked out the door, looking up at the hill. The sky was lightening now; it was that inconvenient type of light that was too bright for night vision gear, but too dark to see properly without it. Switching to infrared and zooming his lens, he could see the glow of fires and sparkle of weapons firing.

If they were still fighting, then COP Meyer hadn't been lost yet.

He turned back to the farmhouse, leaning his rifle against the doorway and taking out his pistol. From a pocket of his trousers he pulled a pair of wire reinforced flexi-cuffs. "Brutus, back up and stand ready."

The LS3 unit levered itself off the body of the Russian sniper, backed up about a yard and stood ready to strike if commanded, its shotgun attachment extended and aimed at the target. The Russian didn't move, but Jensen didn't trust that he was truly out. "I am going to cuff you, and then go for medical help," he said loudly and slowly. "If you make a move on me, my dog will shoot your stubborn head off."

He could have saved his breath. As he rolled the man onto his back and applied the cuffs, the Russian was limp and unresponsive. He should have screamed when Jensen took hold of his wounded arm and twisted it behind his back, but he made no sound at all. He was barely breathing. As an extra precaution, Jensen took off his boots and cuffed his ankles as well.

The farmer and his wife watched in mute horror, the farmer holding a balled cloth against the wound in his shoulder.

"You speak English?" Jensen asked the Kurd. There was no response. "English!?" he shouted.

"A little," the man said reluctantly.

"I am going for medical help. This man was going to kill you. If he gets free, he will kill you. If you cut him loose, he will kill you. And your wife. You understand?"

"Yes."

"If he regains consciousness, do not talk to him. Tell him you don't speak Russian, you don't speak English. Say nothing to him."

"Yes."

"Do you have a weapon?" The man stared at him uncomprehendingly. "Gun, do you have a gun?"

The man shook his head. Jensen cursed. Just his luck to have busted in on the only farmer in Kurdish Syria who wasn't armed to the teeth. He picked up a busted table leg, crouched down and handed it to the man. "If he tries to move, hit him on the head with this."

The man's wife took the table leg from her husband and nodded.

Jensen stood. "I will be back with a corpsman. A … nurse. Yes? A nurse?"

They both nodded.

He looked down on the man they knew as Tita Ali and the Lobaev rifle he'd kicked away from his feet. He thought for a moment about leaving it with the farmer, but he'd gone through too much hell to get a hold of that Lobaev. Lifting the

Lobaev in his left hand and his M-27 in the other, he went out the door and started walking toward Mishte-nur.

"Brutus, close personal escort, fall in."

Unconventional weapons
Incirlik Air Base, Turkey, 4 April

OUT, she had to get out. Alessa Barruzzi had pulled on the stifling hot overalls, boot covers, gloves and hood. Taking a deep breath, she pulled on the claustrophobic protective mask. Feeling like an astronaut about to go for a moonwalk, she leaned down to the keyboard in front of her bank of screens and hit the two keys that wiped the solid state drives on the servers inside the trailer.

Before climbing into her MOPP gear, she'd put a call through to the battalion Information Coordination Center. Since the Syrian *Belladonna* had been taken down, their comms were back up.

"ICC, ICC, Battery 3. ICC, ICC, Battery 3, come in..." As she spoke, the staccato hammer of automatic fire on the outside of the trailer interrupted her. It didn't penetrate.

A crackle of static, and finally she got an answer. "Battery 3, go for ICC."

"ICC, my CBRN alarm triggered and the ECS has sealed itself." She realized she was speaking too fast and gathered herself. "Sorry, uh, this is Sergeant Barruzzi, TCA, Battery 3. My lieutenant and sysop were outside the ECS, engaged with enemy troops. Enemy armor was closing on our position. The ECS is taking fire from light weapons."

Thankfully the officer at the end of the line didn't hesitate. "Sergeant, get into your MOPP gear and get out of there. Pull back to the USO, you got that?"

"The USO?" she asked, confused. The hut that was the social center inside what was known to US troops as '*Patriot Village*' was probably one of the least defensible buildings on the base. If that had become their rallying point, then things were bad. "Alright, moving to the USO. You want the ECS destroyed or set into autonomous mode?"

"Burn it, Sergeant. We've got your arrays. ICC out."

She reached for one of the thermite grenades racked on a wall of the trailer and fumbled with it nervously, nearly dropping it before taking one of her gloves off and turning the timer on the fuse to thirty seconds and checking it twice. She wedged the grenade between the two servers under her console, and then pulled the other two grenades off the wall and wedged them either side of the first. *What the hell, better safe than sorry.*

She jumped as another rifle round, heavier this time, slammed into the trailer. If they were still taking potshots at the trailer, then they weren't moving in on her just yet. Probably waiting for whatever it was outside to clear. If it was gas, that probably gave her twenty or thirty minutes from the attack, right? Or what was it they'd been told about the newest sarin? Fifteen?

It didn't matter. She had to get out, and she couldn't leave by the front door if the Syrians were using it for target practice.

She pushed her chair aside and reached for the floor hatch. It was sealed against the outside air, just like the main door, and she had to pull hard on the latch to unseal it. She gave a grunt and it lifted, nearly sending her back onto her butt. She looked at the dirt and dead grass beneath it as though it was made of pure poison. Which it probably was. She grabbed her rifle.

Reaching down for the thermite grenade, she took a breath, pulled the pin and then dropped into the hole in the floor, counting to herself.

There was still a light mist in the air, but she could see about a hundred yards in every direction. *Twenty-five. Patriot* Village, which way? *Twenty.* A gun hammered to the east, and the trailer rocked again as it took fire. *Fifteen.* Lying crumpled behind the sandbag emplacement, she saw the unmoving bodies of Sun and Allenby. *Ten. Go, dammit!*

She crabbed backwards, pushing herself out the opposite side of the trailer from the incoming fire, and rolled to her feet, rifle across her chest. *Five. Run!*

An Olympic runner could cover a hundred meters in under ten seconds. Even in the MOPP gear, Barruzzi felt like it took her much less. There was no explosion inside the trailer behind her – the thermite grenades were not made to explode, but instead to burn with a white-hot intensity that would melt just about anything near them.

Panting, her mask starting to fog up, deadly white mist still clinging to the ground around her, she nearly didn't see the armored vehicle flying toward her. The car-sized sand-colored vehicle hit a ditch right in front of her, buried its nose, and then bounded out again as she flung herself sideways to avoid being run over.

She rolled and watched it move into position beside her trailer. *Hyperion* unmanned ground vehicle! Only the US 1st Infantry Division fielded the *Hyperion*. If she hadn't been out of breath, she'd have been hollering. As it reached the trailer it backed into cover behind it. The *Hyperion* was built on the chassis of a Bradley M2 infantry fighting vehicle, but it was uncrewed. It featured the same twin TOW anti-tank missile system with an autoloader, but not the modified 25mm cannon of the Bradley, which had shown a tendency to jam during autonomous operation and couldn't be unjammed without a crew to do it. Instead, to achieve the same ability to lay down cover fire, it mounted a 30kw laser which hit targets out to two hundred yards with the same effect as a .22 rifle round. It wasn't one hit, one kill, but it kept enemy troops' heads down.

The *Hyperion* was impervious to chemical and biological weapons, hardened against electromagnetic pulse attack. And, as she was about to observe, it had another advantage. Without leaving cover, a hatch on the back of the vehicle fell open and from the space where the crew compartment would have been, a swarm of anti-personnel drones began to stream out. It was like watching a beehive emptying as the bees went after a cartoon bear. But she wasn't laughing.

The Offensive Swarm Enabled Tactical or OFSET drones were each about the size of a small pizza delivery drone and, like the *Perdix* drones carried by the RAF *Tempest*, could be used for reconnaissance or anti-personnel attacks. Based on how they were swarming, it looked to Barruzzi like they were loaded with 40mm flechette or armor-piercing munitions.

She didn't want to watch the carnage they were about to unleash. She knew the *Hyperion* had to be controlled by a crewed vehicle somewhere and turned to look in toward the center of the airfield. Through the settling mist she saw a boxy shape, fat tires and a large antenna. Light tactical vehicle, had to be. The .50-cal gun version she was running toward had a remote-controlled turret and crew of five.

As she ran, she realized with horror that the .50-cal gun on the turret of the vehicle was tracking her. The gunner would be watching her on a zoomed screen, so she stopped and held her M-27 above her head where he or she could clearly see it and her MOPP gear. The vehicle flashed its lights at her and she jogged forward until she was level with the passenger side door, then stood there trying to get her breath back. She knew they wouldn't crack the vehicle doors if there had been a chemical weapons attack, but the vehicle had a speaker and embedded mike to allow communication while sealed. She hoped the soldiers it carried could point her toward friendly troops.

"Identify yourself, soldier," someone in the vehicle demanded. The windows were darkened so she couldn't see inside.

"Sergeant Alessa Barruzzi, E Battery, 1st Squadron. That's..." She bent over and heaved in a lungful of air. "That's my trailer. Chemical ... there was a chemical attack."

As she spoke, there was a ripple of detonations as the OFSET drones found their targets. Then a louder crack, further out. She swiveled her head toward the sound and threw herself at the ground.

It was pure instinct, not thought. She'd heard the heavy gun firing, seen the shape of a tank through the mist, and was already flinging herself backward when its shell hit.

As the Syrian T-90 tank HEAT round struck the other side of the US Army vehicle, she was tumbling backwards down a slight incline and the blast rolled her head over tail the rest of the way down the small hill.

Light tactical vehicles weren't designed to take a 125mm broadside from a main battle tank and survive. The violence of the explosion lifted it into the air and tumbled it onto its roof.

As Barruzzi lay there stunned, the *Hyperion* controlled by the dead gunner in the LTV went autonomous and scanned the landscape around itself for a target. Seeing the Syrian T-90 approaching, it checked quickly for a valid IFF signal, found none, and fired a single TOW missile. The missile streaked toward the tank at four hundred miles an hour and slammed into its forward drive sprocket, just behind one of the tracks. The T-90 shed the track, but unfortunately for the *Hyperion*, that simply spun its body so that its gun came to rest pointing squarely at the smaller tank. It was already reloading after destroying the LTV, so a second later it fired again, the round demolishing both the *Hyperion* and Barruzzi's trailer in a single strike.

Barruzzi barely registered the noise of the brief firefight between the two armored vehicles. Her ears were ringing, her vision blurred, and her body felt like she'd gone nine rounds with a heavyweight champion. And lost. She realized the eyepieces of her mask were smeared in some kind of oily fluid. She wiped an arm across them, which barely helped. She couldn't see the T-90 now, it was hidden by the slope of the low hill. But the mist was definitely clearing now, and she could see the four radio towers outside *Patriot* Village sticking up in the distance.

She rolled onto all fours, looking around for her rifle. It was nowhere to be seen. She heard the *crack* of the T-90 firing again and decided the Army could bill her for the damn rifle. Rising to her feet with a groan, she broke into a stumbling run toward the Village.

RAP Tchakov had not been allowed to break off his pursuit, even though he saw the flight of F-16s vectoring toward him. Nearing Incirlik, he had contacted his AWACS controller and asked for instructions – continue to pursue the enemy stealth aircraft or retire.

He was ordered to continue his pursuit, and the order had the feeling of an admonition about it. As though he was a coward for even asking.

So he had killed his radar to hide himself among the background noise of the sky, knowing the older Turkish aircraft would have little chance of picking him up. For good measure, he shut down all of his radio and satellite uplinks too. To stay alive he decided to go, as the Americans would say, 'off-the-grid'.

Suddenly he got an infrared and optical lock on the fleeing *Panther*. His sensors picked it up ten miles ahead of him as it overflew Incirlik and started climbing for altitude. He had three K-77 missiles armed, and they were singing in his ears, hungry to be released. His thumb closed over the missile release...

But he hesitated. He had expected the enemy fighter would bank around and maneuver to land at Incirlik, but it was continuing in an almost straight line, past the base, headed due west. Due west, and moving through five thousand feet, toward ten, at a high cruising speed. Curious.

It seemed to be headed for a rendezvous somewhere over central Turkey. Aerial refueling perhaps. That would make the most sense. But one of the huge KC-135 *Stratotankers* or even a *Stingray* refueling drone would probably be escorted. If he kept following the *Panther*, he could quickly find himself outnumbered. *Fire now!* his mind was screaming at him. *Don't be a coward*, his conscience said. *Let the situation develop. Your duty is to effect the maximum damage to the enemy, not to protect your own life.*

He checked his fuel state and his position. To continue the pursuit now would involve flying deeper into Turkish airspace, a dumb idea which had already gotten his flight leader, Yevgeny Bondarev, shot down the day before. But his orders were to pursue. Pursue he would.

"Gorgon leader, Gorgon leader, Gorgon two," he heard his wingman calling. "I don't have you on tac comms. Your IFF is not squawking…"

Tchakov spun the radio volume down so that the man's frantic radio calls were just burbling background noise. He had to give his full focus to the task ahead. Bondarev must have been incautious. Rap would not be.

His *Felon* was not invisible. Nearly so, but not entirely. There would be an American airborne warning aircraft somewhere over central Turkey, which could get a lucky return. Or the Turkish low-frequency phased-array radar station at the Kutahya Air Base four hundred miles away might pick him up. For that matter a random civilian pilot looking out of his cockpit could spot and report him.

He pulled up his nav screen and had his targeting AI project the flight path of the *Panther* based on its current heading, then checked to see if there were known civilian or military radars under the track. Nothing until they crossed over … Konya Air Force Base. That would not do. He had not been picked up by Incirlik because it was under a full-scale armored assault and had been crippled through cyberattack. Konya was under no such pressure. After Russian air raids on Istanbul and Gaziantep, the radar operators there would be on edge, fearing the worst, and looking twice at anything suspicious.

He had to veer around Konya without losing his optical-electric lock on the *Panther*. But perhaps the *Panther* was headed for Konya, landing there? No. If that was the case, it would not still be climbing. It was moving through fifteen thousand feet now, headed to twenty.

He checked the readout on his infrared emissions level. His hot engine exhaust gases were hidden from the *Panther* ahead of him, but an aircraft on the hunt behind him might pick them up. He had already lowered the baffles which blocked line of sight into the engine exhaust ports, but the Su-57 had one more trick for reducing its infrared signature and he deployed it, even though it would reduce his engine power slightly. Mounted behind the air compressors at the front of the turbofan engines were a series of electrical semiconductors that took the heat of the combustion gases and converted it into electrical energy, so that only low-temperature, high-velocity gas was ejected out of his engine. The electricity generated was then fed back to the engine to drive the compressor blades or stored in battery banks in the airframe to provide emergency power to vital aircraft systems in the case of engine failure.

The result was that each engine generated 12 percent less thrust; not suitable for combat, but perfectly acceptable for cruising at constant speed and altitude as he was now doing.

It was a bloody magnificent aircraft that the artisans of the Komsomolsk-on-Amur Aircraft Plant had produced. Tchakov rolled his shoulders and flexed the fingers on both hands. He only hoped he could justify the honor his country had bestowed on him by putting him in its cockpit.

MARINE Infantry Weapons Officer James Jensen was proud of the steel beast that loped beside him as he moved carefully back toward the noise and chaos that was Mishte-nur Hill.

It hadn't been love at first sight. In fact, when he'd first viewed the prototypes that he was going to be taking to Syria for combat stress testing, he'd asked to be transferred to a different command. But even though Brutus had, again, gone off reservation and acted outside his expected engagement limits, Jensen couldn't deny the action had been effective. He had broken through that door like it had been plywood, turned his momentum into attack energy and thrown himself at the Russian without a moment's hesitation. Having first got the scent of his enemy, he had continued to hunt him just like a true bloodhound.

Jensen was sure that in this single patrol alone, the programmers back at the test range at Quantico would have enough data in the cloud now for a year of further development.

It hadn't been easy leaving the disabled carcass of Spartacus back at the farmhouse. But the dog had taken a beating and wasn't combat capable any longer. He'd powered it down and buried it under a pile of dirt to fetch later, if there was a later.

Looking at the battle raging between himself and COP Meyer, he wasn't completely confident there would be.

The previously static Syrian and Kurdish lines were being redrawn by the minute. From what he could tell, looking back at Mishte-nur from the rolling ground south of Kunyan Kurdan hill, Syrian forces had attacked both north and south of the hill to cut it off from the bulk of the Kurdish forces still bottled up inside Kobani city. It was almost like a message to the Kurds – this is not your fight, stay out of it.

He wondered how they would react. They needed American and Coalition airpower if they were to survive, but they didn't strictly need the two hundred Marines on COP Meyer to call it in for them. A single Ranger with a radio based on a rooftop inside Kobani could do that. It seemed, at least for now, the Kurds of Kobani were holding their powder dry. He saw no tracer fire coming from inside the city at the Syrian forces engaged on Mishte-nur.

The tactical situation gave Jensen a problem. He wanted back inside COP Meyer, but between him and that ambition appeared to be about a thousand Syrian troops, backed by at least one *Terminator* infantry fighting vehicle, with their backs to him, trying to force their way into the base, either through its lower entrance or straight up the hill and through its shattered walls.

He'd looked for Heaven's Gate, hoping he might see the flash of rifle fire to indicate the Kurdish girl was still up there, holding her own. But the north tower wasn't even there. It was only made of steel and wood and was too exposed. The thermobaric barrage would have taken it down in moments.

She was gone, along with just about anyone else who had been above ground when the rockets had hit. And if the Syrians hadn't killed them, then the follow-up airstrike he'd heard while inside the house would have finished the job.

Jensen shifted the Lobaev he'd slung over his shoulder to give himself more freedom of movement for his M-27 and moved off. He had a plan for getting back inside COP Meyer. Not much of a plan, but it was his plan, and he was going with it.

NASRIN Khalid hadn't had any real plan at all. She had just burst out of the doors of the bunker complex into the compound at a full run, and if she hadn't done so she probably would have been dead. The lone surviving Syrian *Terminator* that had made it up the southern approach to the outpost had found cover just inside the main gates and was pouring suppressing fire from its 30mm cannons at the bunker exit, trying to prevent the Marines who had made it out into the compound from being reinforced.

Jumping over two bodies at the entrance to the bunker – one Syrian, one American – she had swerved away from the sound of cannon fire from the main gates and headed for the concrete shell that had been the battalion headquarters. Built by Russian engineers to withstand anything short of a nuclear bomb, it was still standing, and most of the Marines in the compound had taken cover inside it and were firing out of the gaping windows and doorways at Syrian troops scattered around the compound, most of them crouched behind the still smoking wrecks of their armored vehicles.

Nasrin wasn't made for running. She was made for sitting at her desk, a cat on her lap, eating sweet Zalobiya pastries. So as she made the concrete building, she collapsed behind it, panting. Two wide-eyed Marines were also crouched behind the corner of the building and they just stared at her. *What had the medic called the place he had last seen Daryan?*

"Heaven's ... Gate ... where?" she managed in between pulling air into her lungs.

One of the Marines pointed over his shoulder. "It was there."

Nasrin looked across the compound where he was pointing. In the gray dawn light she saw some figures huddled in the lee of the wall underneath a toppled structure. And quite a few lying unmoving on the ground in front of it. There was gunfire in that direction too. But that's where Daryan had been. She hadn't come this far to not find her.

"Thank you," she said to the Marine, then adjusted the scarf on her head and bolted for the fallen tower.

It was further than it seemed. She nearly stumbled and fell, her legs protesting at the abuse they were feeling after having carried her up four stories' worth of stairs and then propelled her across two hundred and fifty yards of smoking dirt. But she kept her balance and ran on, reaching the wall and the Marines taking cover there.

There were about six of them, four of whom were firing outward at targets on the slope outside the walls. The other two were bent over a fallen Marine, horribly burned, coughing black liquid from his lungs. One was a medic; Nasrin could see that from the way he busied himself injecting the man with morphine and tilting his head so that his airway could clear.

The other was a woman. Not Daryan.

A woman with ginger hair. Nasrin recognized her face from a time she had visited the Cardamom Markets to write a story about the life of a city under siege. It was the journalist they called 'The Red Jaban'. Of course, *she* was still alive.

But if anyone knew where Daryan was, it would be her.

Nasrin fell to her knees beside the woman. "Please, have you seen my sister? Daryan?"

The woman didn't reply. She simply turned her head and looked toward the fallen tower.

BUNNY O'Hare was given the frequency for the incoming B-21 *Raider* flight and hailed them at about a hundred miles' separation.

"Whale leader, Sunset two, heading through twenty-three thousand for twenty-five, on station in, oh, five mikes."

"Sunset, Whale. Nice to hear from you, buddy, we thought we'd be all alone up here."

"Don't celebrate too soon, Whale," Bunny told them. "I'm close to bingo fuel and down to three missiles. It's been a busy day."

"Flat out like a lizard drinking, eh mate?" the B-21 pilot said in a terrible imitation of an Australian accent. "We can help with that fuel situation. We have an MQ-25 *Stingray* also en route, ETA twenty-five mikes, and we take credit cards."

A real joker. But she was glad to hear the US mission planners had allocated a refueling drone to the strike package. Once the B-21s had delivered their payloads and were on their way back to Germany, she could refuel and head for Akrotiri.

To face the music.

She'd asked the AWACS to relay her position and tasking to Akrotiri and they'd obliged. Five minutes later, they had contacted her.

"Sunset two, Sunset two, Quarterback, come back."

"Quarterback, Sunset, go ahead."

"Sunset, we have a message for you from your commanding officer. He said, and I quote, 'Tell that expletive deleted lunatic to get her expletive deleted airplane back here as soon as the current mission is complete or she will be expletive deleted lined up against a wall and expletive deleted shot.' Repeat back."

"Yeah, yeah, Quarterback, good copy, thanks for all the help."

"No, Sunset, the Coalition thanks *you*. Out."

Oh well, at least someone appreciated her. She'd look back warmly on that little moment as she sat in her prison cell.

RAP Tchakov did have one wish for the designers of the Sukhoi-57 *Felon*. It was a simple wish, considering the millions of dollars of advanced hardware and software they'd built into his magnificent machine.

A streaming music app.

As he followed the Coalition *Panther* up to altitude from about twenty miles back, at the maximum range of his optical-electric sensor suite, he could really have used some tunes to break the silence and distract himself from the relentless tension.

Rap was old school. He liked Russian old-wave hip-hop from the early 20s. Guys back then wrote real lyrics. *Not that 'woke' crap kids churn out today. They have no* … his helmet-mounted warning display started flashing and he reached down and zoomed his targeting display. An optical-infrared lock on two new targets!

His heart stopped beating. More fighters? No! B-21 *Raiders*!

A massive uncertainty overcame him. The US *Raider* was the battleship of the skies. A single aircraft cost nearly sixty billion rubles, nearly a billion US dollars. The replacement for the retiring B-2 stealth bomber, it could carry up to eighty 500lb. bombs or sixteen cruise missiles and it was virtually indetectable by radar – he would never have found it if the *Panther* hadn't led him to it.

OK, Rap, take it easy. *Think*, dammit. You are all alone, deep inside Turkish airspace. You can't radio for instructions, can't risk the chance the energy leak would be detected. But taking down a *Raider* is going to be like sinking a damn aircraft carrier. You could be starting World War Three here. You attack these guys unprovoked, you aren't going to get a medal, you are going to end up in front of a court martial.

But if they fired first? If they launched at Syrian troops inside the 'buffer zone', then under his rules of engagement there would be no question he should engage the US bombers in defense of those troops.

He twitched his flight stick and eased away from the Coalition strike force. He had to hold fire, bide his time. He'd been cloud hopping, staying between fifty and eighty miles behind the *Panther* so that he wouldn't lose his target lock. Russian intelligence reports indicated that the *Felon*'s optical tracking system and anechoic stealth coating were superior to those of the *Panther*, at extreme ranges. He was putting that assessment to the test.

In his weapons bay he had two missiles designed specifically to kill aircraft like the B-21 *Raider*. The *Vympel Axehead* hypersonic missile. It had a range of two hundred and fifty miles, useful for attacking highly visible enemy aircraft like tankers and airborne warning aircraft, but not so effective against stealth bombers like the B-21, because you needed to know they were there to hit them. But able to fly at six times the speed of sound, the missiles could cover two hundred miles in under three minutes, making them almost impossible for a big aircraft to evade. And if they didn't work, he still had one shorter-range K-77M.

He had high-value targets. He had weapons designed to kill them. His political masters had put him in the air in charge of those weapons for a reason. His orders were clear.

Still he held his fire. *Coward, coward, coward, coward. Do what you were put up here to do!*

AT that moment, Yevgeny Bondarev was doing what he had to do. They had halted just inside the airfield perimeter as the BTR-80 he was huddled behind laid down suppressing fire. Then a squad of Syrian soldiers had come running back to the armored car, the rear door had opened and they clambered inside. The gunner was still firing as Bondarev followed them in and found himself a place. The others reached under their seats and pulled out protective masks. Bondarev heard the air conditioning unit inside the vehicle start to clatter as it wound up. The two actions added up to only one conclusion – chemical weapons attack! He had frowned, reaching under his own seat and pulling out the mask there. A soldier opposite him indicated he should put it on.

Bondarev regarded the mask with a baleful gaze. It looked like something from the last century and the rubber straps that fixed it over the head were perished. He doubted they would even hold. A mask, alone? What would that do against a cloying liquified poison that could kill you if even a droplet got on your skin?

He had rolled up his sleeves, but now he put down his weapon and rolled them down again, buttoning the cuffs over his wrists. He still had his flight gloves in a pocket of his trousers, and he pulled them on too. Bending down, he made sure the bottom of his flight suit was tucked into his boots. He doubted any of it would help if they were about to advance through a chemical weapons attack zone, but he did it anyway.

Inside the armored car, the cannon still hammering away over his head, shells dropping onto the casing outside, the air conditioning clattering, Bondarev didn't hear the distant *SMERCH* rocket launchers firing. But he heard the distinctive ripsaw sound of US *Centurion* close-in weapons systems firing. And then the muffled thud of an explosion not far ahead of them.

But only one explosion. Surely there should have been dozens? Bondarev made a quick calculation. Each *SMERCH* launcher could fire twelve rockets and the Syrians had brought an entire battery with them. Thirty-six rockets should have been flying. Their *Belladonna* jamming unit should have been scrambling Incirlik's radar defenses, forcing their ground-to-air missile, projectile and laser defense systems to fire blind, or not at all. He'd seen the first wave hit – many had gotten through.

For so few rockets to have struck the base this time meant either that Coalition forces had taken out a number of the *SMERCH* launchers, or the *Belladonna* unit was down. Either scenario was not promising for the Syrian attack.

The 30mm gun in the turret had gone quiet, and the gunner pulled his eyes off his periscopic sight, reaching for a mask himself. Suddenly, the only noise was the rattle of the engine, the clatter of the air conditioning and the sound of eight men sucking air through the filters of their masks.

Five minutes went past. Then ten.

At last the commander barked an order, the driver crunched through his gears and the vehicle began to edge forward. Bondarev was glad he could not see outside the armored car, as claustrophobic as it was to be inside it. He had never seen the effects of a chemical weapons attack on enemy soldiers, and he had no wish to. But the attack had apparently done its job. Where before, walking behind the BTR-80, Bondarev had heard the rattle of automatic fire or anti-tank missiles all around him, now there was only the sound and vibration of their vehicle, rolling across the dirt and grass and rocks of the air base's outer perimeter. The gunner was back in his seat, manually swiveling the turret, face pressed awkwardly to the periscope with his mask still on. But he was not firing.

Inside his own mask, Bondarev felt guilty relief. Guilt at being a part of an attack that was advancing under cover of such horrific weapons. Relief that it looked like they'd broken through the base defenses and enemy resistance had ceased. He was going to make it out of this nightmare after all.

He started thinking about his next move. He had to find a forward air controller, someone in touch with Russia's aircraft overhead. Arrange for a rotor of some sort to put down at

Incirlik and pick him up. He might need to wait for the entire base to be secured ... but then maybe they could send a two-seater fixed wing like a Sukhoi-34 *Fullback*...

He heard a strange sound outside the hull of the armored car. A high-pitched whine, like a swarm of bees. There was a clank as something landed on the armored top of the vehicle above him, about three men further along. They all looked up.

The 7mm thick roof plating of the BTR-80 was only designed to stop 7.62mm rifle bullets, at best. It was not designed to stop a 40mm armor-piercing limpet mine dropped by an OFSET drone. The grenade detonated about three feet above their heads.

MJ didn't see the YPJ militia fighter approaching them until she was only about ten feet away. She looked up and saw a woman in a scarf and khaki overalls, with a wild look in her eyes, running toward them from the battalion HQ building. There had been a lot of people running in the last twenty minutes, but something about the woman caught MJ's eye, and it was not just the fact she was making a beeline for them. She looked like Daryan Al-Kobani. She had the same aquiline nose, the same raven black hair, the same small, athletic build ... but ridiculously pink nails that MJ could even see through the smoke of the battlefield.

The woman seemed to recognize MJ too. As she got closer she veered toward MJ and then fell to her knees beside her.

Her voice was desperate. "Please, have you seen my sister? Daryan?"

MJ looked toward the fallen tower, where she had last seen the Syrian sniper. "She was in that tower," MJ said. Then she looked down at the badly burned Marine Bell was gently working on. "So was he."

Bullets smacked against the wall beside them and the Marines defending it returned fire. MJ noticed the woman didn't even flinch. She was looking at the fallen tower. "There?"

"Yes."

"Morphine," Bell said, holding out his hand. MJ rummaged in her pack. They had some wound dressings, a couple of bags of saline…

"We're out," she told him. "I'll go back to the sick bay…"

"I have some morphine," the woman said, pulling the pack off her back. She pulled out a box of ampoules and handed them to Bell.

"Thank you."

A particularly heavy volley of incoming fire caused them all to look at the Marines defending the hole on the wall. One fell back, clutching his shoulder. Another yelled over to them, "Corpsman!"

Bell injected the man lying beside his knees with the morphine MJ had handed him. "Nothing we can do here. We need to pull that guy off the line," he said, looking over at the fallen Marine by the hole in the wall. "Come on."

MJ was up and following Bell again. They grabbed the Marine, who was cursing and clutching his bloodied shoulder, and pulled him back into the cover of the wall. Bell peeled the man's body armor off and started cutting the shirt to get a look at the wound, checking entry and exit. He made his judgment in seconds. "You'll live. Went into your deltoid, missed your cephalic vein. Bullet is still in there. I'll get you to the bunker doors, you go down to sick bay, they'll get the bullet out, sew you up." He put an arm around the Marine's back, ready to lift him. "You good to go?"

They stood. MJ saw dust kicking up further down the compound. A line of small explosions in the sand. As she watched, it kept coming, cutting right through Bell and the Marine he was carrying. Both fell to the ground.

Neither of them was moving.

MJ pulled herself into a ball against the wall, hugged her legs to herself and buried her face in her knees as more bullets kicked up sand at her feet.

The noise around her dimmed. It was there and not there. The cacophony of war had never been so close, and she'd never felt so distant from it. She wrapped her hands around her head to try to block the last of it out.

But she heard singing, and looked up.

The woman who had said she was Daryan Al-Kobani's sister was singing in Kurdish. It sounded like a child's song. The burned soldier they had been treating was cradled in her lap and she was holding his hand as she sang softly to him.

MJ crawled over and put her ear near the man's mouth, looked for the rise and fall of his chest. "He's dead," she said, taking the woman's hand and guiding it to lay the boy's hand on his chest.

The woman looked at her with blank, unseeing eyes, then suddenly she focused. "I have to find my sister."

MJ looked over at Bell, lying face down in the dirt, blood flowering across his back.

"She's not inside the compound," MJ said. "Or under the tower base. We checked everyone we could find. She wasn't among them." MJ looked at the ruined tower. "She must have fallen outwards. Most of the tower structure fell outside the walls."

"Then I will look outside the walls," the woman said, standing. She pulled her backpack tight across her shoulders again.

"What's your name?" MJ asked her.

"Nasrin."

"I'm MJ."

"I know. The Red Jaban."

MJ winced. "There are Syrian troops out there," MJ said, unnecessarily.

Nasrin nodded. "Yes. And still." She looked at the gap in the wall through which the Marine defenders were firing.

"You can't go out that way," MJ told her. A hundred emotions went through her as she looked at the woman weighing up her next move. And a hundred thoughts. One of which was; *You don't belong here. This is not your war.* As soon as she thought it, she felt like dirt. She looked over at Bell, and the Marine who died beside him. It wasn't their war either. She stood. "Come with me, I'll show you where we can get out."

JENSEN was headed for The Suck. The sandy area under the concrete walls on the western side where the ground under the foundations was constantly subsiding. The Marines stuffed the hole with sandbags at least once a week to fill the gap under the wall the subsidence created, but it was a losing battle, which was how the area had earned its name. Only major engineering works would be able to stop the ground under the wall crumbling and anyone working outside the wall on that side would have been lost to sniper or mortar fire in minutes.

But in the gray light of dawn, with firefights to the north and south of The Suck as Syrian infantry tried to force their way inside the compound or hold the few yards they had won, there was no one focused on the western wall.

Crouching low, he ran around the base of Mishte-nur, behind the Syrians attacking the hole in the northern wall where the observation tower had been. Brutus ran beside him, in escort mode, scanning the space around them for potential threats. Jensen gave a low whistle and stopped, the dog dropping into a crouch beside him. He laid his hand on its back.

"Good dog." He realized it was a stupid thing to say. But this dog and him had stared down death a few times now. If it hadn't gone *auto* in that farmer's house, what might have happened? Who was to say it hadn't done the right thing?

Would he even be alive now if it hadn't? "Brutus, guard," he said quietly, and a single chime acknowledged his command. If it spotted enemy troops, it would let out a low whistle, drop and point, but stay by Jensen's side unless ordered to reposition. It freed Jensen to watch the ground directly ahead of them and make the most of what cover he could find.

They made a fold in the hillside about fifty feet down from The Suck without having to fight through any Syrian positions. The sky was definitely brightening now. If there were any Syrians still watching the western wall, their scopes would be trained on The Suck, hoping for movement. But what choice did he have?

He looked at Brutus. Well, he had one choice.

He pulled the hand control from his pocket and thumbed the laser pointer, placing the laser marker on a sandbag that had tumbled free of the bottom of the pile under the wall. With his forefinger and thumb he commanded Brutus to move in stealth mode to the laser marker and hold. The dog dropped into a low crouch and began moving carefully up the hill. It would be a small, dark shadow in a scope, but Jensen was sure it would also be a target no shooter could resist. The dog reached the sandbag and dropped to the ground, motionless, ready for its next order.

Jensen gave it a moment more, then followed the dog's path up the hill. "Brutus, sentry," he said as he got close, and the dog rose again to start scanning the ground around them. Jensen surveyed the sandbagged hole. To the north and south, firefights were raging. His best way into the compound was through about two tons of sandbags, but he was banking on gravity doing most of the work. If he could free the lowest layer, the rest might come tumbling free. Yeah, he would be creating another entry point for Syrian troops to get into the base, but there was nothing stopping them from doing what he was about to do if they wanted to, and by the sound of the fighting on top of the hill, they were already inside the outpost.

He put down the two rifles he was carrying and started pulling sandbags out of the bottom of the pile. It was like playing a game of Jenga, except hoping for the pile to collapse. After he'd shifted four bags he was starting to think it had been a dumb idea. After five his aching back told him it definitely was. After seven he decided he would give up at ten. At nine, he started a small avalanche. Sandbags and sand started pouring out of The Suck and sliding down the hill as he and Brutus backed out of the way. After an all too short time, they stopped. The hole was still blocked. He clambered up the pile of bags to look at the row at the top. Was that daylight he could see? Grabbing the corner of a bag, he heaved, moving it only a few inches. The weight still on top of it was too much. He stepped back, beaten.

The bag moved. But not like gravity was shifting it, more like a boot was kicking it. It moved again. He stepped up and grabbed the corner again, waited for the next kick – because that's definitely what it was – and pulled as hard as he could. The bag came free and he swung it behind himself with a grunt, turning back to see a Marine regulation all-weather boot pull itself back out of the hole. It was replaced by a face tentatively peering through.

"Jesus, James Jensen, you scared the hell out of me!" MJ exclaimed. She pulled back, then her feet appeared and she started wriggling through the hole.

"No, wait," Jensen said. "I'm coming in." He picked up his rifles.

MJ dropped to the ground beside him and then started helping someone else through. "No you aren't," MJ told him. "You're going to help us find Daryan Al-Kobani."

The woman whom MJ helped out of the hole under the wall turned and dusted herself down. There was no mistaking the resemblance. And no question at all when she pointed at the Lobaev in his hand.

"My sister's rifle!"

He looked down at it, then shook his head. "No, sorry. Same type, but I took this off a Russian sniper."

She looked crushed at the news, but MJ understood. "You got Tita Ali."

"Not me," he said. "Daryan tagged him, Brutus bagged him."

Hearing his name, Jensen's dog rose from its seated position, ready for new orders.

Nasrin took a frightened step back, not having noticed it. "What is that?!"

MJ put a hand on her arm to calm her. "That's probably our best chance to find your sister."

IT was 0400 on 4 April 2030.

High over Konya, central Turkey, Bunny O'Hare had armed her CUDA air-to-air missiles and was fine-tuning her cruising profile to optimize her fuel burn, waiting for the B-21 *Raiders* which she had just picked up on her electro-optical DAS system to arrive at their rendezvous point. She was trying to keep herself busy so that she didn't think about the reception that would be awaiting her when she finally arrived at Akrotiri.

Rap Tchakov was shadowing O'Hare and the *Raiders* at the extreme range of his own sensors. Every second he delayed his attack was another in which the enemy could find and kill him. But it was now or never, and as the moment he would have to commit approached, he felt a rising dread and tried to push it back down in his gut.

At Incirlik, the 40mm anti-armor grenade that detonated above Bondarev's head had killed the vehicle commander, driver and gunner instantly. There had been three Syrian soldiers between Bondarev and the grenade, and the two nearest had taken the brunt of the explosion, which mashed their dismembered carcasses against Bondarev and the man next to him. Smoke filled the cabin and, despite his mask, Bondarev started choking. In the next few seconds he would have to make a choice, choke to death inside the BTR-80, or expose himself to the chemical gas outside. The man beside him turned to Bondarev, his eyes wide with shock, his entire right side covered in the blood of his comrades. He said something to Bondarev in Arabic, and then collapsed against him with his head resting gently on Bondarev's shoulder. Which Bondarev thought was entirely understandable given that the man's mask and the top of his head were missing.

Nearly a mile away now, Alessa Barruzzi had made the newly established US position inside the *Patriot* Village and had been hastily ushered through to the USO for decontamination. Inside the USO building she was led into the locker rooms where another soldier in MOPP gear helped her strip off her protective equipment and uniform and hosed her down. The water was beautifully clean and cold. When she was done, the corporal in the MOPP gear pointed her to a combat medic who gave her a quick once-over. She was done inside thirty seconds. "Is that it?" Barruzzi asked, the image of Sun and Allenby outside the trailer still burned into her retina. "That's it," the woman said. "If you'd been contaminated, you wouldn't be standing there. Go next door and find yourself a combat uniform."

On Mishte-nur, Jensen, MJ, Nasrin and Brutus moved downslope. They'd done a little scouting and seen that the Syrian troops assaulting the breach in the walls by the northern tower were occupying the ground where Daryan had almost certainly fallen. Dead or alive, they couldn't begin searching for her until the Syrians had been persuaded to abandon their attack. But Jensen had a plan for that.

Inside Kobani, Colonel of YPG Intelligence Jamal Adab was looking at the plot on his maps, based on reports coming in over his radio. The picture had been chaotic in the first thirty minutes after the artillery barrage on Mishte-nur, but it was clearer now. Syrian forces – infantry and armor – were engaged in a full-scale assault on the US outpost. They had gained the summit under cover of the artillery barrage and were fighting both inside and outside the walls of the outpost, focused on trying to force entry into the bunker complex from above and below. A Coalition cruise missile strike had taken out several Syrian armored vehicles, but there were still estimated to be between one and two thousand Syrian troops in the attack. The two hundred American Marines inside the base, if that many were still alive, were defending well-prepared positions and the Syrians appeared to have made little progress since their early gains. Adab reached for his field telephone and called the YPG brigade commander. "Yes, sir, I have reviewed the situation. The Syrian commander has committed the bulk of his maneuver force to the fighting on Mishte-nur. I believe we should send a rapid strike company to attack the Syrian headquarters at Mamayd village. Yes, sir, two hundred fighters. This is your chance to take Mamayd back."

Persian playmates
US Consulate General, Istanbul, 4 April

SHIMI felt like a mouse, cornered by a large bespectacled owl.

"Operation Butterfly?" he frowned. "Sorry, what?"

"Buddy, I know you know what I'm talking about," Carl said. "Can we cut the BS? You are listening to us listening to you listening to us. This is just you and me here, alright? Why I called you in at this stupid hour. Why I'm meeting you inside a Faraday-cage shielded room that no electronic signal can get in or out of. Why I'm showing you something there that could get me fired on the spot, and probably locked up for life."

He sounded earnest. Still, Shimi hesitated. Sharing the sort of intel Carl was asking for could also get Shimi locked up. "Butterfly?"

"Oh, come on, man. I've seen codeword intel sourced to Unit 8200 Istanbul that mentions Operation Butterfly and that can only have come from you, right?"

"I am not the only Unit 8200 analyst in Istanbul."

Carl nodded at the paper Shimi was still holding. "That order of battle is the Syrian order of battle for an operation they are calling Butterfly. And HOLMES has projected both the operational objectives and the kickoff date, which I can tell you, friend to friend, you will be deeply and personally interested in."

Shimi put the page down. "Why would you tell *me*?"

Carl shrugged. "No big mystery. You grease my wheels, I grease yours. We both want out of this butthole city, right? We deliver some high-value intel to our various bosses, we look like rock stars. It's our ticket out of here."

Shimi realized Carl had read him right. He was more than tired of Istanbul. And he knew that if he didn't find a way out soon, he would never be much more than a minor cog in the massive Unit 8200 machine.

He drew a deep breath. "Alright. GAL pulled a report off a Syrian coastguard server at Tartus. A naval order of battle for an Operation codenamed Butterfly."

Carl nodded and motioned to Shimi to continue.

"It comprised some of the most capable units in the Russian Black Sea fleet, including submarines and an amphibious landing ship…"

"Not good."

"… plus two trimaran missile destroyers, and a *Besat*-class sub from Iran." Shimi finished.

"Oh, crud." Carl wiped a hand over his face. "This is worse than I thought. Russia, Syria *and* Iran? We already know their air force order of battle. It's currently going toe to toe with Coalition jets in Turkey, but of course, they could bolster that too."

"You said you know the target? This is about Lebanon?"

"I wish."

"Then what?"

Carl stood. "Coffee? I've got brandy too." Shimi nodded, thinking of a hundred different possible scenarios as Carl busied himself pouring two cups from a thermos in his desk and pushing cream and sugar sachets over the desk to Shimi. From another drawer he pulled a small bottle of cognac and poured a liberal shot into their cups, then sat down again. "Nothing for nothing, Shimi," Carl said. "You get anything more on this Operation Butterfly, you share, alright? This could be our ticket out of this warzone, buddy, but only if we work together." He held out his hand for Shimi to shake.

Feeling sheepish, Shimi shook the proffered hand. He threw down the brandy, ignored the coffee and picked up the paper on Carl's desk. "Alright. I'll get GAL onto it."

Data deluge
Konya, Central Turkey, 4 April

BUNNY O'Hare was barely fit to fly. As she lifted her visor and rubbed her eyes, she could feel the fatigue in her tortured muscles. She took a sip of water from a drinking tube on her shoulder and at the same time relieved herself into her ambiguously named Advanced Mission Extender Device – otherwise known as a 'piddle pad'.

She'd flown four sorties in three days, two in the last six hours. She had knocked down two *Felons* and an *Okhotnik*, a Mil-25 chopper, and launched on three ground targets, with the *Pantsir* and *Belladonna* being definite kills. She'd evaded a near certain hit by a K-77M, but it had taken its toll on her physical endurance.

Luckily, she was not alone in the sky, and she wasn't the type of pilot who was too proud to admit when she needed a little AI assistance. Pulling her visor back down, she authorized her combat AI to manage all defensive maneuver and countermeasure operations. Her degraded reflexes and brain fog could cost her her life, but the AI would react to any new threat in a silicon heartbeat.

She keyed her mike. "Whale, Sunset, I have you on DAS. Will orbit ahead of your track and make sure Ivan doesn't ruin your day."

"Sunset, Whale thanks you kindly. We have received our tasking, approaching release mark. As soon as we've delivered the goods, we can call in that Stingray for you."

"Appreciated. Sunset out."

With the slightest pressure on her stick, Bunny banked her *Panther* and brought it around in a slow turn back toward Incirlik.

Each of the B-21 *Raiders* could carry sixteen of the formidable AGM-158 Joint Air-to-Surface Standoff Missiles, capable of delivering a thousand-pound warhead to a target smaller than a family sedan at a range of hundreds of miles. Bunny watched fascinated as the first of the cruise missiles dropped out of one of the *Raider*'s bomb bays, lit its tail and streaked toward Incirlik. One after another, the B-21 started unloading the rest. It went on so long, the sight was both mesmerizing and terrifying, even to her.

Fed their target data during their short flight to Incirlik, guided in by forward air controllers embedded among the US and Turkish troops, each of the thirty-two armor-piercing warheads would almost certainly claim one or more vehicles.

Pulling her eyes away from her video feed, Bunny raised her gaze to the lightening skies. As she did so, her DAS alert began to blink.

No, what?

She blinked at the display, not immediately grasping what it was telling her. An enemy *Felon* picked up on infrared, eighty miles north? Moving away from her. It was not using its phased-array radar, and it showed no indication that it had spotted either her or the *Raiders*. Should she engage? Or hold back and let it continue on its way? It might not be alone…

Her combat AI had no such dilemmas. It had detected a Russian *Felon* stealth fighter inside the lethal range of its CUDA missiles. Without hesitation it cued and armed two CUDAs and launched them in passive seeker mode, steering on the cue from her DAS sensors. The *Panther* was headed east, so the missiles dropped from her weapons bay, began their boost and then curved away to port as they accelerated.

Oh, hell.

Grabbing her flight stick, Bunny rolled the *Panther* left and pulled it around to pursue the threat. She cancelled her combat AI's autonomy. *Stupid damn silicon, what did you just do?!* She keyed her mike. "Whale, Sunset. Russian *Felon* bearing zero one two, altitude twenty, heading zero four zero. Sunset engaged."

RAP had mentally committed to his attack. He had turned away from the targets, then allocated a single *Vympel Axehead* hypersonic missile to each of the B-21s, now nearly ninety miles away. He'd decided as soon as he detected the first cruise missile launch by the *Raiders* that he would counter-attack when he reached a hundred miles distance, giving his missiles just eighty seconds' running time. Even if the *Raiders* picked up the stealth missiles the moment they were launched, which he doubted, they would have almost no time to try to evade them.

He set them to 'stagger fire', the two missiles launching two seconds apart to reduce the risk both would be decoyed. He was flying away from the *Raiders* to set up the launch and had lost his optical electric lock on them and the *Panther*. It didn't matter, his targeting system had a projected bearing on the bombers, he had fed the enemy aircraft type, altitude and bearing into the *Axehead*'s guidance system, and they had their own onboard active radar and infrared seekers that could acquire a ten-foot-square target from twenty miles away.

He got ready to bring his *Felon* around to an intercept bearing for the attack. His forefinger hovered on the missile release...

Warbling in his ears. *Incoming CUDA missiles!* His infrared sensors had picked up the launch.

The *Panther* had detected him, exactly as he feared, and he only had himself to blame. Hauling his machine around in a brutally sharp banking turn toward the expected position of the B-21s, he flick-rolled level. His forefinger twitched and let fly with his two hypersonic missiles, switched his targeting to the *Panther* and released his last K-77M.

Although the *Panther* was rapidly closing, and its missiles closing even faster, it was still nearly eighty miles distant. With a twitch of his flight stick, Tchakov oriented himself broadside to the incoming American missiles, forcing them to turn as he watched them follow him, targeting them with jamming radiation as he prepared to evade.

You waited too long. You deserve to die, svoloch, he told himself under his breath.

IN her short few weeks of combat, Bunny O'Hare had never seen a hypersonic missile fired. The closest she had come was firing a US AIM-120D in training, and that could only clock a meager 4.5 times the speed of sound. Not the Mach 6 of the new Russian *Axehead*.

All combat she had taken part in so far had been at ranges under a hundred miles ... in modern terms, almost eyeball to eyeball. The longer-ranged hypersonic *Axehead* missile could barely be fired inside that range, but as she watched on DAS the missiles spearing back toward the B-21 *Raiders* from the fleeing Russian fighter, she could barely believe the speeds that her sensors were showing her in her helmet-mounted display.

"Whale, Sunset. You have incoming! *Axeheads*, recommend immediate evasion."

The voice that came back to her was preternaturally calm. "We have them on infrared, Sunset. Whale out."

In five seconds the first Russian missile had reached six hundred miles an hour, in seven it broke the sound barrier. Then it really started accelerating, through Mach 2, 3 and 4 until after fifteen seconds it had broken through Mach 5. By twenty seconds it was flying above Mach 6 and her helmet display was projecting it would intercept the nearest B-21 inside a minute.

Bunny had a missile alert screaming in her ears and was automatically steering to the cue her combat AI was telling her gave the best chance of surviving the Russian attack. The two B-21s, however, showed no sign of deviating. They continued flying their missile launch pattern, cruise missiles still falling from their bomb bays one after the other. If the bombers had been remotely piloted, their crews sitting in a trailer back at Ramstein airbase, she might have understood their business-like attention to their mission. But they weren't. They were riding in the cockpits of their heavy bombers twenty thousand feet above central Turkey facing almost certain death.

Her defensive countermeasure system started jamming the Russian K-77M missile and firing decoys. She sharpened her angle to the incoming missile and pushed her throttle forward, slamming herself back into her seat as it flew past her left wing and detonated. She rolled level, frantically checking her instrument and system displays.

No warnings.

Bunny shook her head and focused on her pursuit of the fleeing *Felon*. It had dived for the dirt, and she could see her two CUDA missiles had switched to active radar-seeking mode but were going to struggle to make the intercept. On the other hand, the skies around them looked clear – there had been no other launches on the *Raiders*.

Bunny shut down her own radar sensor and pointed her *Panther* toward the sky where the *Felon* had been. Low on fuel though she was, Bunny wasn't going to let the Russian get away that easily.

BUNNY wouldn't have been so surprised about the calm voice of the B-21 *Raider* pilot if she had been privy to the top-secret missile countermeasure system that had been fitted on the aircraft immediately before it entered full-scale production. Based on a patent first filed by a US aerospace manufacturer thirteen years earlier in 2017, it was the twenty-first-century equivalent of the old blister turrets on World War Two B-17 bombers. Two pop-up turrets on top of and below the streamlined fuselage of the *Raider* started to deploy at the first sign of an offensive missile launch against them. The system had been created to defend against the prototype hypersonic anti-air missiles being developed by Russia that had become the *Axehead*. The original patent envisaged fighting missile with missile, and pictured the turrets loaded with nine small hit-to-kill missiles which would be fired at the enemy projectile as soon as it was detected.

They failed miserably in testing. Not just because creating a missile maneuverable enough to intercept another missile flying at six times the speed of sound proved impossible, but because the computers available at the time to guide it – whether aboard the missile itself or on the *Raider* launching it – were not fast enough to carry out the calculations needed to guide the missile to its target in time.

The solution came from an Israeli technology first deployed to protect vehicles from incoming tank rounds nearly twenty years earlier. Called *Trophy*, it pulled data from the *Raider*'s onboard optical and infrared defensive sensors to predict the approach vector and time to impact of the incoming missile. It didn't need a supercomputer to calculate an exact fix on the missile to kill it, it just needed to grab a few seconds of data. As the incoming missile approached an estimated engagement zone, rotating launchers on the turret fired a series of MEFPs (Multiple Explosive Formed Penetrators) in a shield-like matrix. These small copper slugs created overlapping metal shields between the *Raider* and the attacking missile, detonating it before it could reach the bomber.

The *Raider*'s upgraded *Trophy*-armed turrets could track and defend against up to twenty hypersonic missiles at one time, with the top and bottom turrets providing the bombers with 360-degree defensive protection.

Rap Tchakov need not have worried about the geopolitical risk of bringing down a billion-dollar king of the skies like the B-21 *Raider*. He never had a chance.

A mile out from the bombers, his two *Axehead* missiles met the shields of copper slugs fired by the *Trophy* turrets and dissolved into harmless balls of melted metal, fuel and flame.

What Rap Tchakov did have to worry about, however, was that he had an incensed, fatigued and borderline suicidal Bunny O'Hare on his tail.

GUNNER James Jensen was wishing *he* had some kind of magic shield. Preferably one that made him invisible and prevented him being shredded by a sudden hail of Syrian 7.62mm AK-M rifle rounds.

Jensen, Nasrin, MJ and Brutus were creeping through a defile at the base of the western slopes of Mishte-nur, less than fifty yards from a line of Syrian troops. The Syrians' full focus, and the fury of their firepower, was focused uphill at the hole in the wall from which MJ had pulled the wounded Marine less than twenty minutes earlier. But all it would take was for a single one of the nearly two dozen soldiers to turn and look their way, and Jensen's very bad plan would have come to a very bad end.

When he judged they had reached a position that gave them sufficient cover, Jensen motioned for them to take a knee. Brutus also reacted to the signal, staying standing but moving into a sentry mode, alert for threats.

"What's the plan?" MJ asked in a whisper, looking around her. They were two hundred yards downhill from where Daryan might have fallen, and between them and the outpost walls were two dozen Syrian troops trying to reach the breach in the wall so that they could force their way through it.

"We are going to engage the enemy, force them to surrender or withdraw, and then move up that hill to see what we can see," Jensen said simply. He had taken the Lobaev off his shoulder and placed it on the ground beside him as he checked his M-27.

"We? Who is we?" MJ asked.

"Me and my friend Brutus," Jensen said, not looking at her. "Don't worry, MJ, I won't dent your journalistic halo."

Nasrin knelt and picked up the Lobaev. "I will also fight."

Jensen and MJ both looked at her. Jensen saw a woman more used to haggling for wares than handling a rifle. She had the same facial features as her sister, but there the resemblance stopped. She had soft hands, eyes lined with mascara and the hair under her bandana was glossy. She had bright pink nails that no doubt matched her lip gloss. But as they stared, she shrugged her pack off her shoulders, pulled out a box of 10.36mm rounds and loaded one into the Lobaev.

"Daryan was not the only one our father taught to shoot," she said. She handed the box of shells to MJ. "You spot, I shoot."

"I don't…" MJ started to say, and visibly quailed under a withering look from the Kurdish woman, "… know *how* to 'spot'."

Jensen held his hand out in front of him. "Twelve o'clock, one, two three, eleven, ten, nine," he said. "So, two Syrian soldiers to her left would be 'Two targets, ten o'clock'."

Jensen looked at Nasrin, MJ and Brutus. If there was a more unlikely rifle squad in the history of combat, he had not seen one. "Alright, keep your heads down until I engage, is that clear?" He reached for his radio. "Base, this is Button 1, Base, Button 1, do you read?"

"Button 1, we read you, go ahead."

"Base, I need someone to get a message to the platoon on the wall at Heaven's Gate. I have flanked the enemy assault troops and am preparing to engage from their rear quarter. I need the squad on the wall to be prepared to assault the enemy position at…" he looked at his watch and allowed enough time for the message to reach the men on the wall, "… zero four fifteen. We will provide covering fire from the enemy's rear. Is that clear? Zero four fifteen. Out."

The radio operator repeated his instructions and signed off. Jensen looked at his watch. He'd given the Marines inside the compound ten minutes to get organized before he kicked off. They'd radio back to confirm the assaulting force was ready. He had one more thing to do to prepare.

Taking out his laser, he pointed at some rocks halfway up the slope, a hundred yards to the left of the Syrian position, and illuminated it. On Brutus's hand-held controller, he pressed the key combination for 'stealth mode, go to indicated position and hold'. As the dog began to move, he checked its power status. It was at 28 percent. Enough for what he had planned.

An overwhelming display of force and power intended to paralyze an enemy in place and destroy their will to fight.

Otherwise known as 'shock and awe'.

AT Incirlik, Alessa Barruzzi had put on fresh fatigues, taken up her rifle and reported to 7th Air Defense HQ, which turned out to be a boxy light tactical vehicle parked beside the USO. The tailgate of the vehicle was open and a bunch of officers were grouped around it, looking at tablet screens and arguing. Sitting or lying around the vehicle was a motley collection of grunts from various units, who had pulled back to the USO and were waiting to be told what to do. She found another sergeant she knew, squatting on his haunches beside a rear wheel of the vehicle that looked as destroyed as she felt.

"Hey, Boyd," she said, squatting next to him. He was a sandy-haired guy from Boston, with a permanent hardcore stare that was softened by a slight lisp. She saw he had burns on the side of his face, his hand bandaged.

"Barruzzi." He looked her up and down. "Saw you coming in wearing your MOPP gear. You got hit with sarin?"

She nodded. "Or something like it."

"Bastards. Only a couple shells got through, though, is what they're saying." He looked around. "Sun and Allenby?"

She shook her head briefly, saying nothing. "You?"

"T-90 KO'd our control trailer," he said. "Don't ask me how I got out. No one else did."

Barruzzi looked up at the officers, still grouped around the back of the vehicle. "What's the news?"

Boyd tried a crooked smile. "You want the good or the bad?"

"Whatever is most relevant to my future health," she said.

"Syrians are inside the northwest perimeter. Turks are holding them, for now. The Bloody First has joined the party. Lead elements are engaged…"

"I saw," she said, not telling him about watching a First Division JLTV take a tank round in the guts.

"Armor is supposed to be moving up now."

"Where is our damn air support?"

"Russia owns the air, is what I hear. Brits and Aussies had to pull back to Cyprus. Turks are doing what they can with what they've got, but it isn't much."

Barruzzi cursed, thinking of the lone RAAF pilot she'd met, wondering what had happened to her. O'Hare? She hadn't seemed like the kind to cut and run. "This is what happens when you call something a 'limited border conflict' instead of a full-on mother freaking war."

They heard the crack of heavy cannons exchanging fire and both turned their heads.

"*Abrams?*" Barruzzi asked.

"Wasn't a T-90, or a *Bradley*. Yeah, I'd say an *Abrams*."

Barruzzi raised a fist with false enthusiasm. "*Hooah.* Get some, Bloody First. Better late than never."

An officer heard her raise her voice and stepped out from behind the JLTV to see who had spoken. Barruzzi recognized the Major commanding their HELLADS batteries.

"Barruzzi?" he asked, frowning.

She stood. "Major Carlson."

He took a step closer and grabbed her arm as though reassuring himself she was real. "I thought you were dead, Sergeant."

"Twice," she nodded. "So far, sir."

He smiled. "Well, save that third life. We're down a Fister. You know how to use a COLT laser, Sergeant?"

Barruzzi thought fast. A 'Fister' was a forward artillery observer and the laser in question was the one a Combat Observation Laser Team, or COLT, used to designate targets for attack by smart munitions. It had been a while, but yeah, she'd been trained on the COLT. She nodded. "A little smaller than I'm used to, but yes, sir."

Carlson turned back to the other officers and exchanged a few words, then called her over. He was holding a tablet that showed a map of *Patriot* Village and a radio. "You and Boyd haul ass to hangar six. We had a team moving up on the roof that never made it." He didn't say why. Barruzzi knew it didn't matter. "There's a corporal there recovered their laser designator," he continued. "You take this radio, meet him there. Get yourselves up on that roof and start calling some serious harm down on those T-90s."

Barruzzi looked at him in surprise, taking the radio. "We have air support, sir?"

Carlson nodded. "Loitering cruise missiles inbound. But they won't be worth shit without someone pointing them at the bad guys."

"Boyd!" Barruzzi called out, startling the other sergeant to his feet. Was it her imagination or had the sound of battle moved closer while they'd been talking?

"Priority targets are Syrian main battle tanks, then armored cars, light tactical vehicles and, if you run out of those, any sizeable concentration of troops. Got that?" Carlson said.

"Yes, sir."

He patted her arm. "You rope them, Sergeant, Air Force can take them out. The Bloody First can mop up what's left, and when we're done I'll buy you and Boyd a burger and a beer."

Boyd had been listening to the last part of the conversation. "You mean bourbon, Major. This definitely sounds like a *bourbon* and burger kind of detail."

Carlson looked taken aback, then laughed. "Alright, Sergeant, bourbon."

"Cool. Any chance we can get that *before* we head out, sir?"

YEVGENY Bondarev had bailed out of the BTR-80 armored car with his uniform soaked in blood, his weapon up, ears still ringing, expecting to emerge into a hail of automatic fire from whoever had thrown the limpet grenade onto the roof of their vehicle.

The battlefield around him was eerily empty of enemies. The mist from the chemical attack was settling and the other few survivors from the vehicle around him were checking their watches and pulling their masks off, apparently no longer worried that the chemicals unleashed by the *SMERCH* shells could kill them.

Bondarev kept his mask on, so looking at the killing ground around him was like watching an apocalyptic B movie through the bottom of two beer bottles. To the left and right of him, other armored vehicles had suffered the same fate as his, and those troops who had made it out of the vehicles were huddled together, or had thrown themselves flat, awaiting orders. Many hadn't made it out at all; whatever had hit them had triggered secondary explosions of ammunition and fuel, incinerating all of those inside.

Bondarev could see no enemy troops, just a stranded T-90 that had cast a track and a single burning US Army light tactical vehicle about a half mile uphill. There was another fire burning behind a wrecked utility or command trailer of some sort –

probably another vehicle but he couldn't see whose. He looked back at the armored car he had just escaped from.

Microdrones, it had to be. Maybe those damned *Perdix* drones the RAF *Tempests* carried, or something else, something new.

Further south, a firefight was raging. Bondarev heard the crack of a heavy cannon barrel, then another. He was no expert on tank warfare, but he'd heard quite a few Syrian T-90s firing their main guns in the last 24 hours, and the whipcrack of these cannons sounded different. He didn't need to be an expert on ground warfare to see that the Syrian advance had stalled around him. Perhaps they were still advancing elsewhere, but it was obvious the company he had found himself riding with was not getting him any closer to a lift back to his squadron.

Screw this. Back up by the motorway there would be a better chance of jumping onto a truck or other transport headed east, or at the very least, a vehicle with a radio he could use. He shouldered his rifle and started walking northeast, ignoring the sullen stares of the soldiers around him.

But he kept his right hand down by the trouser pocket holding his MP-443 *Grach* pistol, the one his grandfather had given him when he had graduated from the flight academy.

Just in case he ran into that bastard Spetsnaz Captain again.

BUNNY O'Hare was hoping for a small reunion too. She'd seen with relief that the B-21 *Raiders* she'd been riding shotgun on had survived the volley of Russian hypersonic missiles, though in truth she had no idea how. That was a question she'd have to get answered over a beer in a bar with a *Raider* pilot one day. The question she was dealing with right now – where the hell was the *Felon* that had fired them?

After she'd launched on him he'd headed for the deck. She assumed he'd be headed east toward Syrian airspace, but of course he could be lingering, setting up for another attack on the *Raiders*.

She was down to 17 percent fuel, good for about two hundred and fifty miles' cruising. She *should* stay with the *Raiders*, refuel from their drone tanker and then light out for Akrotiri in Cyprus. She should *not* go after the *Felon*. But every moment she thought about it was taking her further east, and further away from her escort duty.

Luckily the commander of the bomber flight solved her dilemma for her. "Sunset, Whale. Thank you for scaring off that bandit, Sunset, we are much obliged. We are Winchester, heading back to Ramstein for *eine kleine* cold Pilsner. You still want that refuel drone?"

"Negative, Whale," Bunny replied. "I'll see that *Felon* leaves the premises. Enjoy your beer."

"No worries *mate*," the *Raider* pilot quipped, causing Bunny to wince again. "Whale out."

She pulled up her tactical screen. Even if she lit up her own radar and started actively searching for the Russian, she'd have little chance of finding him now. She needed help.

"Quarterback, Sunset flight. Did you monitor that engagement?" she asked the airborne controller.

"Sunset, Quarterback. We registered missiles fired, Sunset, but we don't have a vector to your attacker." It wasn't surprising the Turkish airborne radar couldn't pick up the *Felon*, its high-frequency radio waves were exactly the sort the Russian aircraft was designed to defeat.

She had just one roll of the dice and decided to bet the last of her fuel on it. She turned her *Panther* south on an intercept bearing that might just head off the Russian fighter if it had disengaged and was returning to its base on the Syrian coast at Latakia. Two hundred and fifty miles was enough to get her to Akrotiri with fifty miles to spare. "Quarterback, I'm out of fuel and just about out of ideas here, but can you ask the Turkish low-frequency radar station at Kutahya to get ready to scan on my bearing as I cross the Turkish coast?"

"Uh, Sunset, you want to let us in on your thinking?" the controller asked. Bunny explained her idea to them, which like most of her ideas was pretty simple. The radar with the best chance of picking up the *Felon* was the Turkish low-frequency station at Kutahya Air Base. Her chances of it picking up the *Felon* would be helped if they were looking for returns or anomalies where she wanted them to look. By putting her own machine between Kutahya and roughly where she predicted the *Felon* would be, they *might* have a chance of aiming their energy in the right direction and getting a position and heading on the Russian.

Best case, she might get a steer that could lead to an intercept.

Worst case, she would be just off the coast of Cyprus and could just about glide in to land at Akrotiri where Flight Lieutenant Red Burgundy was probably waiting to pin a medal on her.

Yeah, right.

No greater sacrifice
COP Meyer, Kobani, Northern Syria, 4 April

JENSEN checked his watch. He'd received confirmation from inside the outpost that they were ready to move. It was go time.

He motioned to Nasrin and MJ to bring their heads closer so they could hear him over the sound of the firefight further up the slope of Mishte-nur. In the last ten minutes the Syrian troops had made another fifty yards up the slope, closer to the breach in the walls. The fighting inside the compound and down at the ground-level entrance to the north did not appear to have abated. But if they could deal with this assault, it would free the defenders at the walls to help elsewhere.

And give them breathing space in which to look for the Kurdish sniper.

"I'll set Brutus in motion. When you hear his weapon firing, that's our cue to engage. I'll take the group on the left, you take the group on the right. Anyone moves toward us, we both try to take them down. Alright?"

They both nodded, grim faced. But the Kurdish woman turned and placed the Russian sniper's rifle on the lip of the defile in which they were crouched and sighted on the nearest Syrian soldier, barely a hundred yards uphill from them. She handed the box of 10.36mm shells to MJ, crouched on her right.

Jensen made eye contact with MJ. "You don't have to do this. You can just keep your head down until it's over."

She gave him a weak smile. "Tried that once. Not this time."

Jensen nodded to her, then moved a few feet further to their left and sighted uphill himself. Laying his rifle on the dirt, he reached for Brutus's control pad. And started sending the dog commands.

Marking targets.

He pointed the laser designator at the backs of the Syrian soldiers, holding them on each man until he heard a tone indicating the dog had seen and confirmed target acquisition. He marked three or four Syrians – one on the right of the assault group, a couple in the middle, and then one on the left. When Brutus had acquired all of the targets, Jensen issued a new command.

Close Human Engagement protocol, series.

The order put Brutus in lethal attack mode and directed him to engage multiple targets one after the other, rather than pursue any single target until it was motionless. Jensen waited for the tone on the handset to indicate the dog acknowledged the order. When it came, he put his thumb on the large button in the center of the controller. And hesitated, just for a second.

He was about to send Brutus to an almost certain death. He shook himself. Death? It was a tool, right? Like a rifle. A radio. A grenade. Metal and silicon. *Don't let their handlers give them names*, that's what he'd tell them when he got home. *Just numbers.*

He jabbed his finger down on the button. *Execute.*

The dog rose to its feet from the background darkness of the hill and started moving toward the Syrian troops in a line that would take him close behind the targets Jensen had painted with his laser. He moved slowly at first so as not to give away his attack before he got close, but then started speeding up as he got closer. Jensen put down the controller and picked up his rifle. Because of the slope of the hill and the roughness of the terrain, Brutus couldn't move as fast as he had on flat ground, but by the time he got within shotgun range of the first Syrian soldier he was moving somewhere between a fast walk and a jog.

Jensen saw his weapon arm swing right as he sighted on the soldier, and his shotgun discharged with a report that was audible even over the firing of the other weapons uphill.

As the Syrian soldier fell, clutching his side, Brutus continued to the next man, and fired again.

Jensen opened up with his M-27, firing short two-round bursts into the backs of the Syrian soldiers uphill from him. Beside him, the Kurdish woman fired too.

"Bullet!" she called as she racked the bolt of the Lobaev and held out her hand.

MJ slapped a bullet into it. "Two … Two o'clock!" she yelled.

The Kurd fired again.

"Bullet!"

"One more. Two o'clock."

Jensen changed targets, sighting further up the hill as the men he had been firing at either fell, or spun around and threw themselves at the ground. Almost as one, the attacking Syrian force turned to face the sudden threat from their rear.

Simultaneously, a massive barrage of covering fire came from the breech in the walls and Jensen saw Marines pouring through, breaking left and right to fix and flank the Syrian force which was now taking fire from two directions.

And from Brutus, running right through the middle of them, his shotgun booming as he careened from one target to the next and then out of the Syrian position again to a position twenty yards away where he could turn and re-engage.

"Bullet!" Nasrin called.

"Two, eleven o'clock!"

As he sighted and fired again himself, Jensen saw, with not a little disappointment, that the Syrians were not breaking in panic. One of their officers had organized them to divide their fire both uphill and downhill, and they had all found some kind of cover, making it harder already to find exposed targets.

Jensen had an option he had not wanted to use, but with the Marines uphill outside the walls and exposed, there was no choice.

Brutus had made his turn and was accelerating toward the Syrian position again. At least one Syrian soldier had spotted him and was firing directly on him, but he was a small metal target, moving fast. Jensen wasn't worried he'd be taken down. He reached for Brutus's hand controller, put his thumb on the 'execute' button and held it there, waiting.

"Bullet!"

Slap. "Twelve o'clock."

Syrian return fire was hammering the lip of the defile around them now, forcing Jensen to duck. As he raised his head again, he saw Brutus shoot, change course, and move into the middle of the Syrian position to engage one of the targets Jensen had painted there. As he did so, Jensen pressed the 'execute' button and held it down. Hard.

Two seconds, that was all it should take. More fire from the Syrians. Marines still pouring fire on them from above, left and right. *One second.*

"Bullet!"

With a blinding flash, Brutus self-destructed in the middle of the Syrian position, the high explosive and compressed hydrogen at his core spraying superheated metal shrapnel in a lethal circle around himself.

Involuntarily, Jensen and Nasrin ducked again, the report of the explosion rolling over their heads. The Kurdish woman recovered quickly, lifting her rifle to the lip of the defile again and firing. Jensen lifted his rifle too, but where he'd last seen a group of Syrian soldiers, there was only smoke. A furious barrage of fire from the attacking Marines followed the explosion and then Jensen started seeing hands raised in the air, throwing rifles away.

He heard the Syrians call out.

"Bullet!" Nasrin yelled, working her bolt.

"No. They're surrendering!" Jensen told her. "Hold your fire."

The Kurdish woman gave him a fierce look. "I don't care." She held out her hand while she sighted uphill. "Bullet!"

There was no response from MJ. Jensen looked quickly over, past the Kurdish woman, to where her hand was extended. MJ was not there. He frowned, *where had...*

Oh, shit.

The journalist was lying on her back, three feet behind Nasrin, staring up at the sky through a bloody hole where her left eye had been.

BARRUZZI was staring down at the body of an Army private who was lying at the foot of the maintenance ladder going up the side of hangar six, his neck twisted at an angle that very clearly explained why he was not moving. They'd found the corporal they were looking for at the base of the ladder too, bleeding from a gunshot wound in his thigh.

He had the laser designator on the ground beside him and looked at them with unfocused eyes as they ran up. Squinting, he tried to focus as they reached him.

"Sergeants. That's my luck. It's always sergeants." He smiled weakly. "Neither of you sergeants is a medic by any chance?"

"Sorry, Corporal," Barruzzi said, dropping to a crouch beside him and handing the radio to Boyd. The man had tied his belt above his wound and she checked it, pulling it tighter. He'd lost a lot of blood. "We can call for one." She shot a look at Boyd, who was already working the radio.

"Thank you kindly," the man said quietly. He looked up at the hangar. "We got about a third the way up. Shooter hit me, I fell on Phillips." His head lolled on his shoulders as he turned to look over at the dead private, frowning. "He going to be OK, you think?"

Barruzzi didn't even bother to look. "He's going to be just fine." She shuffled around him and lifted the laser designator. It had been a while since she'd used one but it was pretty much idiot proof, point and click. Assuming it had survived the fall. She hit the power switch and lifted her eye to the eyepiece. It powered up, green sights and numbers filling the display. She powered it down again.

"Medics on the way," Boyd told her, looking up the ladder. "Guess we're doing this."

"I guess we are," Barruzzi said. "That Syrian shooter is dead by now."

"For sure," Boyd agreed. "BRO got him, no doubt."

They both looked at the ladder for another couple of seconds, then Barruzzi took a deep breath. Boyd swept his arm like he was holding a door for her. "Ladies first."

"Such a gentleman." Barruzzi slung the laser designator around her neck and let it fall behind her back, then put a hand on the first rung. "Ah, hell with it."

One rung at a time, Alessa, she told herself. *Hand, foot, hand, foot ... dammit!* About halfway up, a round slammed into the metal wall of the hangar and she hugged the ladder tight before realizing the shot had not even been close. It didn't matter, she was frozen.

"You wanna get that fat ass moving or we gonna die right here?" a voice below her called out.

Her blood suddenly boiled, the emotion of the last 24 hours welling up in her. "Who you calling *fat*?!" she yelled back down at Boyd. "You pimple-headed, thick-witted..."

"OK, now we're awake again, maybe we can continue this conversation on the roof?"

She felt like dropping a boot into his upturned grinning face, but she knew that was exactly why he'd done it. Instead, she lifted the boot, pulled it up one rung and started climbing again. More rounds hit the hangar near them, but none near enough to freak her out again. The hangar was built to allow maintenance of aircraft the size of a C-130 and down, so it had a broad sloping dome of a roof. A hundred feet off the ground, the apex would give them a view over the entire battlefield northeast of the air base.

As she reached the top of the ladder she rolled onto the roof and pulled the laser designator off her back, crawling for the center of the roof, not wanting to silhouette herself against the early morning sky. Boyd was right behind her.

When she reached the apex of the roof she looked down over the northern perimeter of the air base and tried to take in what she saw.

To her right, hull down on the eastern slope of the air base, about a dozen Syrian T-90 tanks, three burning, the rest still trading fire with…

Six newly arrived US M1A3 *Abrams* tanks on the western side of the base, one burning, five sheltered between buildings and behind trees at the helicopter center on the northwest edge of the base. As she watched, a TOW missile from a *Bradley* armored vehicle located with the *Abrams* force snaked out of the trees on a pillar of smoke and flew over the Syrian tanks without striking any.

South of these, Syrian and Turkish infantry were exchanging fire under cover of armored vehicles as the Syrians tried to push deeper into the base. The 30mm autocannon of multiple Syrian BTR-80 fighting vehicles hammered relentlessly, while remotely guided uncrewed *Bradleys* had been moved up to support the Turkish troops and were replying with their 25mm Bushmaster chain guns and TOW missiles. Several vehicles on both sides were burning, but it seemed to Barruzzi the Syrians were taking ground.

She had her targets.

Boyd crawled up beside her. The process for calling down a loitering cruise missile was not simple, and wouldn't even have been possible if the Syrian *Belladonna* jammer hadn't been taken out of play. She had to 'sparkle' the target with her laser, which pulsed with a specific frequency. When she got a solid return from the target, the frequency number came up on the screen she was viewing the target through. She read the number out loud to Boyd, who called it in on the radio. The frequency data was fed by an Air Force tactical air controller to one of the JASSM-L cruise missiles fired by the B-21 *Raiders* circling at thirty thousand feet and it plunged out of orbit straight down at its target at near the speed of sound.

Barruzzi lined up her target. She had to hold the laser on the target until…

She didn't even see the missile, it was moving so fast. There was a vertical shadow and then the tank she had been painting with her laser disappeared in a ball of fire, its turret flipping up into the air, over and over.

She moved her laser to the next T-90 in the line, wincing as its cannon let fly and it reversed back into cover. She couldn't help follow its round across the airbase to the *Abrams* about two miles from it, and saw the shot smack one of them on the turret, which bounced the round but had to pull back behind a building.

She got a number in her visor and called it to Boyd. He relayed it, then she heard him query the air controller, "How many JASSM's you got on standby up there? Yeah … ok … fast as we can."

Barruzzi adjusted her aim as her target moved forward again. "How many shots we got?"

"Had thirty-two. Thirty left after this – they got about twenty minutes' fuel left."

"Thirty?!" she exclaimed. Another shadow, another detonation across the base where once a tank had been. She shifted her weight and aimed her laser at the next tank. Soldiers were running forward now, trying to pull their comrades from the first burning tank. *No one should have been able to survive a strike like that*, she thought to herself. *God help those who did.*

Then she remembered Sun and Allenby slumped next to their sandbagged emplacement in a cloud of sarin gas, and lasered the next tank.

The code flashed up on her screen. "Pulse, G five six niner. Call it in."

IT had been the longest of longshots. Bunny had called her position to the Turkish AWACS as she reached the waypoint over the coast she estimated would give the low-frequency radar at Kutahya Air Base the best chance of getting a return on the fleeing *Felon*. It wouldn't be good enough to give her anything but a bearing to an unidentifiable bogey, but with that, she would at least have a steer.

"Sunset two, Quarterback, no joy from Kutahya."

Bunny sighed. "Good copy, Quarterback. Sunset two, one eight eight for fifty, angels ten, returning to Homeplate Akrotiri." With one remaining missile and very little fuel, she was out of options. But not out of hope. "Quarterback, get them to take one more scan down my bearing, would you?"

She could see the northern tip of Cyprus on the horizon now and was still in Turkish airspace until she crossed the border halfway along the island into Greek Cyprus. She had hoped to catch the *Felon* over Turkish airspace inside the Coalition-declared no fly zone. If it had managed to make it into non-disputed Syrian airspace, under her current rules of engagement she would only be able to pursue it if specifically ordered to do so. She knew if that happened, there was no point even asking.

She dialed in the frequency of Akrotiri air traffic control. The RAF base was at the south of the island, with approach usually from the east or west. She checked the prevailing winds and tapped her rudder pedals to swing her nose a little to the east to prepare to enter the pattern over Akrotiri.

"Sunset, Quarterback, Kutahya reports bogey bearing zero niner niner for twenty, angels two, *hot*."

Hot? The contact was coming straight for her? *Easy, Bunny, it could be a friendly patrol coming to check you out.* She ensured her

IFF was squawking. She hadn't come this far to have a friendly missile ruin her day. Her tactical display pulled data from both nearby AWACS and the radar at Akrotiri and should be showing all known friendly aircraft. She quickly enlarged it to show the sky for a hundred miles around her aircraft. There was traffic over Akrotiri, but nothing low and within twenty miles of her as the AWACS had warned. She began weaving her *Panther* back and forth, checking the sky below and ahead of her. The morning sun had risen over the horizon and the surface of the sea was twinkling with silver light. Her DAS sensors could theoretically pick out an aircraft a hundred miles distant, but against the dazzling light dancing on the waves of the Mediterranean the chances were…

"Unidentified aircraft in international airspace, this is the Syrian Air Force, you are on a heading for Syrian airspace, please maintain course and await escort…" her radio crackled as a voice broke in over the international Guard air channel. It began to repeat. "Unidentified aircraft in Syrian airspace…"

Her DAS sensor chimed and an icon flashed up on her helmet display. Su-57 *Felon*, twenty miles out and straight ahead.

She quickly checked her position. *Syrian airspace my ass.* She was about fifty miles north of Cyprus, nowhere near the Syrian coast. She lit up her targeting radar and locked up the approaching *Felon*, to make it very clear to him she was not impressed.

He immediately did the same, and her radar warning receiver alarm began warbling in her ears. She dialed it down.

What the hell are you playing at, Ivan?

RAP Tchakov was not made for playing lone wolf. His flight commander's words had been horrifying to him when Bondarev had spoken them: *Alright, Tchakov, it's about time we showed our commanders what the Felon is really capable of.*

He'd done as Bondarev had ordered and had been ambushed by not just one but two enemy BATS drones, their missiles fed data by their F-35 mother ships. There were orders you should follow, and those you shouldn't. He was learning that. He'd had a lot of time to think about that as he had dangled from his parachute.

He'd also had a lot of time to think as he'd shadowed that *Panther* across Turkey to its rendezvous with the US bombers. His first one-on-one engagement with a Coalition *Panther* and it had evaded his missiles, not once, but twice! Yes, it had led him to a bigger prize, and though he couldn't confirm it, he was certain he must have claimed at least one of the *Raiders* as his first bomber kill. The *Axehead* was a magnificent missile against which there was no defense, other than blind luck.

The *Panther*, however, had not only got away, it had chased him off. Out of missiles, low on fuel, he had been forced to turn back to Latakia.

The fear didn't leave him, though. Something about that *Panther* pilot. The audacity; flying alone over the Syrian spearhead at Goztepe, underneath the very eyes of Russian fighter cover, engaging Syrian forces. The skill when attacked, flying his machine at the ground with only ten thousand feet to spare to evade Rap's missiles. The sheer aggressiveness, engaging Rap over Konya even as his *Panther* had a K-77M arrowing in on it.

Rap just *knew* that pilot would be hunting him, but he hoped he'd left the *Panther* too far behind to be able to pick it up on his passive optical or infrared sensors. Even if it had closed to a range at which he could detect it, he had no missiles with which to engage it.

That didn't stop him looking over his shoulder, though, trying to see if it was there.

For that, the *Felon* had another magnificent piece of technology the Coalition aircraft did not possess.

A quantum harmonic sensor or QHS. Not an optical or infrared scanner, nor radar either, it was the ultimate in long-range stealth aircraft detection. Ten years earlier, in total secrecy, it had been fitted to Russia's Beriev A-100 AWACS aircraft, and a combination of both miniaturization and computer processing advances had allowed it to be incorporated into the design of the *Felon*.

The QHS did its job not by looking for objects in the sky, but by looking for *holes*. At longer ranges, or in poor weather, optical and infrared sensors could not detect stealth aircraft. Using radar would give the attacking aircraft's location away. But the QHS worked by monitoring the background electronic noise in any given piece of sky and constantly comparing it with itself. It was like holding up two frames of a person walking in a video and examining them with a magnifying glass to see what had changed between the first frame and the second one. By constantly comparing each snapshot with the one before it, the QHS could detect the minute changes in the background radiation caused by a stealth aircraft moving through it.

The QHS capability was rarely used by *Felon* pilots, because they were already drowning in data. From AWACS aircraft, from ground radars, from their own sensors or the sensors of other aircraft in the sky with them. And in a typical engagement, there were too many aircraft in the battlesphere for the QHS to be able to pick them out quickly enough to guide tactical decisions. But it was intended for scenarios like this, when a pilot was alone in the sky, with a possible enemy in his sector, unable to pull data on the bogey from any other sources.

Of course, he could have contacted the Russian AWACS he knew was circling over Palmyra in central Syria, or the ground-based radar at Latakia, and asked them to look out for the bandit. But experience told him they would probably not have spotted it. So Rap had called up his QHS screen, focused its antennae on the coordinates of a twenty-degree arc of sky directly between himself and the last known position of the

Coalition *Panther*, and had left the miracle of Russian electronic engineering to do its job as he cruised at a conservative six hundred knots toward Latakia.

Rap had nearly jumped out of his flight suit when the QHS had chimed in his ears and a contact had appeared on his helmet visor. But both he and the *Panther* had left the area of operations now. They were over the eastern Mediterranean – theoretically neutral waters. His enemy could not shoot at him now.

Rap had become a pilot because, as a child, he had consumed western war hero comic books about flying and pilots. Russia had nothing like them. His favorite was one called *12 O'Clock High*, which focused on stories from the Great Patriotic War and was full of Spitfires, Hurricanes, Messerschmitts and Stukas. And in one episode he had read and reread until the pages fell out, an RAF Spitfire pilot and a German Messerschmitt pilot had fought a dogfight over the English Channel. Each scored hits on the other, both were wounded, but at last the Spitfire plugged the Messerschmitt in its engine and it began streaming coolant. The engine lost power, the German was a sitting duck, and he turned back toward the coast of France, desperate to get his aircraft back to land.

The Spitfire had him dead in its sights, but instead of shooting the Messerschmitt down, the RAF pilot flew up alongside it and saluted his German opponent. Then he escorted him back to France, waving him goodbye as they reached the coast and returning back to England.

That was the kind of pilot Rap had always dreamed of being, and he saw a chance for it now. The Coalition *Panther* behind him must have seen him by now, but it had not fired at him. Why should it? Their battle was over. They might meet again one day, but here and now, they were just two pilots from different countries, sharing the same sky.

Heading for the clutter of the choppy sea below, he had turned his *Felon* back in the direction from which it had come and started closing the distance to the hole in the sky which in his heart he knew had to be the brave and audacious *Panther* that he had engaged.

He very much wanted to meet this particular Coalition pilot.

But it would not do to surprise him.

BUNNY frowned at the small dot that was the approaching *Felon*. It was still hailing him on Guard. "Unidentified aircraft in international airspace…" She had no inclination to respond. It was all exceedingly weird.

The Syrian fighter was claiming she was in international airspace headed for Syria, when clearly they were both within *Turkish* airspace. The reason she had not already launched on him was that he was making his challenge on the Guard emergency radio frequency for the whole world to hear. If she shot him down now, the Syrian government could claim their aircraft was attacked in violation of the rules of war.

Rules of war. What a freaking joke.

Her radar warning receiver was still warbling, but there was no indication of missile-tracking radar yet. She could see the Russian aircraft on DAS now, rising up to meet her. As it reached her altitude, still about five miles ahead, it began turning gently until it was slightly ahead of her on her port side. Now she could clearly see it with her own eyes. She slaved a DAS camera to her helmet view and started taking photographs. She'd never seen a *Felon* up close. She wanted a souvenir of this contact, if nothing else.

Still about a mile ahead of her, the Russian fighter began porpoising slowly up and down. It was the international signal for 'join on me'.

The Russian wasn't behaving threateningly, nor erratically. In fact, he was being downright collegial. She had no doubt he would also be getting some nice closeup shots of her *Panther* as they both speared through the sky on parallel tracks, but that would tell him nothing that Russian intelligence didn't already know.

Now Bunny was more than curious. Pushing her throttle forward a notch, she eased up beside the *Felon*, keeping about a hundred yards off its starboard wing.

As she did so, the pilot gave her a small wave. She simply stared back at him. Then he reached up with both hands, disconnected and removed his helmet, leaning forward so he could pull it off. They were flying at ten thousand feet, so oxygen was no problem, but still it was a very strange thing to do.

He was young. Maybe younger than her by a few years, she could see that from his stupid grin. He pointed at his head, indicating to her to do the same.

This is crazy, Bunny decided. But then ... ah, what the hell.

A woman! Rap hoped his face didn't show his surprise as the RAAF pilot leaned forward and pulled off her helmet, running a hand over her near bald head and then fixing Rap with a very unfriendly glare.

There were female combat pilots in the Russian Aerospace Forces. In fact, Russia had been among the first air forces in the world to put women in its front-line aircraft, during the Patriotic War. The first had in fact been Turkey, in 1936. And he knew the Australians had removed the bar on women flying fighter jets when they joined the war in Afghanistan. So he shouldn't have been surprised.

With a final friendly wave that the woman didn't bother to return, he pulled his helmet back on and started reconnecting it. What a story he would have to tell back at Latakia, and video footage to confirm it!

BUNNY did the same as the Russian pilot, pulling on her helmet again and reconnecting the cables and oxygen feed. It powered back up automatically, and she quickly checked the display was still correctly synched with her systems.

Looking across at the Russian *Felon*, still cruising through the air alongside her, she made sure it was still locked on DAS. She had a single CUDA missile in her weapons bay, and her defensive AI had already selected it. She armed it with a tap of her finger on her weapons display.

Despite the overweening weirdness of the moment, and his apparent naïve friendliness, she didn't trust that damn Russian over there for a single second. Less than a half hour earlier, he had been trying to kill her. What was she doing?!

Forget this, O'Hare!

She slammed her throttle forward and pulled back on her flight stick. Hauling her *Panther* into a screaming loop, she kept the stick back as she reached the top of the loop and her aircraft started diving down behind the *Felon*.

As she waited for the missile lock tone to sound in her helmet, her thumb slid over the trigger. *Get a video of this, Ivan.*

RAP watched the *Panther* soar into the sky behind him.

What? No! She was maneuvering to attack?

He didn't hesitate. Flicking his *Felon* into a roll that slammed his head sideways like he'd been punched, he stopped it inverted and pulled back on his stick, putting himself nose to nose with the Australian, but about five thousand feet below her as they closed at a combined airspeed of 1600 knots. He was giving her no chance of a missile shot.

He bunted his nose as she flashed over him, and tracer shells from her 25mm cannon sprayed over his head. His own gun was set to autofire, and for a fleeting second his AI decided it had a target and fired a quick burst at the *Panther*, but the shells fell harmlessly behind it. Panicked and confused, Rap chopped his throttle and threw his machine into a banking turn to get some separation between himself and the *Panther*, while trying to stay on its six o'clock. His *Felon* was fitted with leading-edge canards and had a thrust-vectoring exhaust, true to the Russian fighter design belief that super maneuverability was always valuable in combat, whether fighting against missiles or guns. He had no trouble getting behind the *Panther* again.

The *Panther* was extending away from him now, its pilot perhaps realizing her position was hopeless.

Wrong, this is all wrong.

Rap increased his thrust, the *Felon* responding immediately as it began to accelerate in pursuit of the Coalition fighter. He was suddenly sad. This was not what he had wanted.

"Akrotiri, this is Sunset flight, I am under fire from a hostile aircraft at my position. Request immediate support." Bunny urgently repeated her radio call as she pushed her nose lower and headed for the sea off Cyprus. She needed to get out to missile range again. The *Felon* had a reputation as a gunfighter, and her *Panther* didn't. It was no slouch, but it was designed to kill enemy aircraft at a distance, before they even knew they were dead. She needed to avoid close combat with this guy at all costs.

"Sunset, Akrotiri Control. I am vectoring Kilo flight to your position, steer zero one zero for fifty, angels twenty…"

The vector given by the controller was not the one she was currently flying to put distance between her and the Russian. "Negative, Akrotiri, I am *engaged*," Bunny said through gritted teeth. "Just get that cavalry here stat." She had the Russian on DAS, tapped her ordnance screen and watched her missile cue. She could fire on the Russian while powering away from him, but a circle around his hit box showed her the likelihood of a kill and right now it was giving her less than 30 percent. She only had one shot, she needed to make it count.

He was coming back around behind her, with a perfect missile shot. She had her decoys on autofire and got ready to pull herself into a neck-snapping turn to evade…

But he didn't take the shot.

He had no missiles left! That could be the only reason. If she could just keep her distance…

"Sunset, Akrotiri, sending you code to synch data with Kilo flight, they will be in range in five mikes."

Five minutes! She could die five deaths in that time, but she tapped a screen, sending her targeting data to the incoming friendly flight so that they could lock up the *Felon* attacking her and fire their long-range missiles at it.

She just had to stay alive for five minutes.

One beauty of her DAS sensor system was that it enabled her to see 'through' her aircraft, giving her perfect 360-degree vision. She could 'see' the Russian on her six, directly behind her, about five miles back now.

And he was gaining. There was no way she could outrun him. Her *Panther* had only a single Pratt & Whitney turbofan engine that could push her to a maximum Mach 1 at this altitude. The *Felon* had twin Saturn turbofans which could push it to Mach 2. If she turned toward the friendly fighters he would close on her quicker. It was just a question of math, and as she ran the numbers in her head she realized time was as great an enemy as the Russian behind her. He would be back inside guns range before her allies were in a position to fire on him.

She had no choice but to take her shot, now.

Quickly checking her missile cue, she saw her firing solution sucked, because firing now as she tried to flee meant her missile would have to drop out of her weapons bay and turn one eighty degrees to try to hit the pursuing Russian. A less than 10 percent chance of a kill.

There was only one way to improve the odds. And it was near suicide.

Hell, who wants to live forever? Bunny thought, before hammering her right foot down onto her starboard rudder pedal, hauling her stick over in the opposite direction and slamming her *Panther* into the equivalent of a flat, spinning emergency-brake turn. It was just about the only special dance move the *Panther* could pull on a fighter like the *Felon*, and it sent her fighter skidding through the air like an Olympic discus until its nose was pointed back at the Russian, while she continued traveling *away* from him.

The sudden change of aspect and the fact her powerplant was now pointed in the opposite direction to her direction of flight slammed her into the straps of her safety harness, but she managed to stop the slide with her nose oriented on the *Felon*.

She jabbed her thumb on her missile trigger.

Fox 3, mother.

RAP had gone from sad to angry. He had the *Panther* locked up and was reeling it in. In less than a minute, he'd be within gun range. It had not needed to end like this! They both could have flown back to their bases, bought their comrades a beer and told the amazing tale of their encounter in the sky. Now she would be dead, and he would just be telling the story of how dishonorable the Coalition pilot was.

Positioned squarely on his enemy's six, even if the *Panther* pilot tried another quick evasive turn his guns should be able to lead it and swat it from the sky. If it tried to launch missiles while fleeing, there was no way they could drop, turn one hundred and eighty degrees and get a lock on him when he was so close, moving so fast.

The only good thing about it was that it had been a brief fight…

What?

The enemy aircraft had appeared to spin in mid-air right in front of him like some kind of crazy UFO. Now it was coming back *toward* him?

His thumb reached for his guns trigger, but a warning suddenly screamed in his ears.

Missile!

The *Panther* had dragged him down to wavetop height. He had only three directions to choose from and he froze. His defensive AI took control of the *Felon* and pulled it into a spiraling vertical climb.

The *Panther*'s missile followed it up, detonating just behind his starboard engine.

BUNNY was virtually flying backwards through the sky, two hundred feet above the sea. If the Russian had been flying with a wingman, she'd have been fish bait by now. Before she lost all forward momentum she kicked her rudder again, jerked her flight stick and span the fighter through a hundred and twenty degrees, letting the thrust of her engine push again in the direction of the *Panther*'s motion as she slowly picked up speed again.

On her DAS screen she saw the *Felon* go vertical. Saw her missile strike it.

But it kept flying. As she watched, amazed, it fell forward, but leveled out and began a slow banking turn away from her, one engine pouring black smoke, the other still operational.

With a nudge on her stick she came around behind the Russian as her radio crackled to life.

"Sunset, this is RAF Kilo leader, we are two minutes from *Meteor* launch range. Good handshake on target data. Hang in there, pilot…"

She watched the Russian aircraft, transfixed. How was it still flying? It was limping toward the Syrian coast now, one wing down, heavy rudder trim the only thing stopping it from nosing into the waves below.

It was a sitting duck. She could slide in behind it and cut it to pieces with her guns. She remembered the kid's face, his stupid grin.

Reaching for her sensor screen, she killed her targeting radar.

"Uh, Sunset. Kilo has lost handshake. We have no data," the RAF flight leader called.

Without her targeting data, the incoming RAF *Tempests* would be blind, unable to see the Russian stealth fighter yet. Bunny cleared her throat. "Thanks for the assist, Kilo, bandit is retiring, I am turning for Homeplate. Sunset out."

A low-fuel warning flashing on her visor, Bunny banked to put her *Panther* on a direct bearing for Akrotiri. Her right hand was shaking so hard she could hardly hold the stick.

RAP Tchakov wasn't flying the *Felon*, his AI was. He had a dozen warnings flashing on his system screens and in his helmet display, and was too terrified to touch any of his flight controls, because he had no idea how his AI was even keeping his machine airborne. It had extinguished the fire in his starboard engine, then automatically set a course for the nearest Syrian airfield.

Such a magnificent airplane. He was not worthy of it.

One of the systems still functioning was his optical tracking display, and he watched on his large multifunction screen as the Coalition *Panther* behind him peeled away, headed for Cyprus; no doubt thinking his machine was doomed, and he was dead at the stick.

He shook his head. Their enemies might be skilled, but they fought without honor, which was why, at the end of this war, they would lose.

SYRIAN soldiers were rising from their concealed positions on the hillside ahead of Jensen, hands in the air. Half of the Marine assault force had pulled back inside the compound to continue the fight there, while the others disarmed and plasti-cuffed their prisoners.

Behind them, a loud explosion, a mile or two away down on the plain. A black pillar of smoke began rising into the air and heavy gunfire could be heard. Nasrin, crouching beside MJ, had pulled off the American's jacket and laid it over her face like a shroud. She stood and looked back to the west.

"Mamayd," she decided. "The brothers are counter-attacking while the enemy force is occupied here on Mishte-nur." She stood and handed the Russian sniper's Lobaev rifle to Jensen, picked up the pack she had dropped by her feet, then looked at the palm of her right hand. "I am going to get a blister from that stupid bolt, I know it."

Jensen threw the rifle strap over his shoulder. The hammer of automatic weapons north and south of them told him the fight for Mishte-nur was far from over, but with the YPG counter-attacking into the Syrian HQ, he doubted the commander of the attack on COP Meyer would be happy having so many of his troops tied down in a stalled attack. He had to get back into the compound and find out where he was most needed, but before then he had one job to do.

"You ready to move out?" he asked Nasrin.

"What about her?" Nasrin looked over at MJ.

"I'll come back for her," Jensen promised. "Let's go find your sister."

THE walk up the slope of the hill was fraught. There was still heavy fighting each side of them, so they had to move at a slow crouch. Their route took them through the recently destroyed Syrian position and they paused at the cratered dirt where the LS3 Brutus had ended its short mechanical life. The bodies of Syrian soldiers were scattered in a loose circle around the hole in the hillside.

Jensen couldn't help wonder if it didn't resemble the scene after the famous Kurdish Women's Protection Unit fighter Arin Mirkan had made a similar sacrifice to help her people win back the summit of Mishte-nur nearly ten years earlier. He doubted anyone would be rushing to build a statue to Brutus, though.

They made the walls outside the collapsed northern tower. Hammered by the blast from the Syrian thermobaric rockets inside the compound, the top of the tower had collapsed outward and the metal box of the observation post lay crumpled on its side among scattered sandbags. They checked the ground around it first, finding the body of one of the Marines who had been inside the OP. He looked for all the world like he had died in his sleep, lying on his side on the ground, head pillowed on one arm, not a mark on him.

Nasrin had moved to the OP itself and was using the flashlight on her cell phone to look inside.

"Here!" she called. "Help!"

Jensen ran to her side, crouching down to look inside the crumpled metal box.

Inside was Daryan Al-Kobani, curled in a ball with one leg bent unnaturally behind her. As Nasrin played the flashlight over her, she slowly turned her head and coughed, blood trickling from the corner of her mouth.

"Don't move!" Nasrin said in Kurdish. "We'll get help to get you out."

"Ah, it's you, sister…" Daryan said quietly, coughing again. "Did you bring my ammunition?"

Going out clean
East of Maklul village, Kobani, 6 April

NEARLY two days had passed since Jensen had left the Russian sniper in the care of the Kurdish farmer. Two days in which they had pushed the last Syrian troops off the summit of Mishte-nur and then driven them away from the ground-level bunker entrance with the help of precision air strikes delivered by Turkish and British aircraft. The Kurdish militia had also retaken Mamayd village in their counter-attack, forcing the Syrian command, artillery and logistics units there to pull back to the south, greatly expanding the territory under Kurdish control.

Getting medical help to the Russian in the farmhouse had not been Jensen's top priority. But once the fighting had died down and he had seen to the recovery of MJ's body, he took two men and headed out of the base of the hill to the farmhouse about a half mile away.

The farmer and his wife were there, but the Russian was not.

One of the privates Jensen had taken with him was a Kurdish speaker, and he quizzed the farmer through his broken door.

"The Russian is gone?"

"Yes?"

"He was alive?"

"Alive, yes."

"You let him go?"

"No. The YPG took him."

"He is a militia prisoner?"

"Yes."

"Inside Kobani?"

"Yes."

That was all they could get out of the farmer, and perhaps all there was to get. Jensen would pass the intelligence on, and perhaps their YPG liaison officer could get them access to Tita Ali to debrief him, or perhaps not. Jensen imagined he would be seen as a high-value prize, one they could potentially swap for a large number of Kurdish prisoners when they were done with him.

After speaking with the farmer, they humped out into the field where Spartacus's GPS beacon indicated he was still lying. In a plowed farrow, half covered in dirt, he'd not attracted any attention from the locals passing on the road a couple of hundred yards to the south. Jensen had his two men dig the dog out and roll it onto a stretcher they'd brought with them, just like any other casualty. He looked Spartacus over, seeing how the sniper's heavy round had found a gap in the dog's tough metal shell and taken out the vital hydraulics that drove the dog's right rear leg.

They won't be happy about this back at Quantico, Jensen predicted. But maybe he could repair it here, if they could get some feedstock flown in for COP Meyer's 3D printer.

There would be no repairing Brutus. Or MJ.

Jensen had called the woman's husband himself. He'd never even thought of her as having a husband, but she did, sitting back home in suburban Philadelphia while his wife roamed the world, from war zone to war zone. He took the news calmly, but Jensen guessed he'd had more than a few years to prepare himself for the day the phone call might come.

"She saved a lot of lives that day," Jensen had told him. "She was one of the first out into the compound after the artillery attack, helping the corpsmen." He didn't mention MJ's part in the counter-attack on the Syrian position. He didn't want her 'journalistic integrity' to be called into question. It meant he finished on a pretty vague note. "It was clean. She just got unlucky, is all."

Her husband had been quiet. "She might not look at it that way," he said.

"No?"

"No. She always said if she ever went out, she'd want to go out clean. Not bleeding to death after a roadside bomb or taken prisoner by fanatics and executed live on social media. So there's that."

MEANY Papastopoulos had been in an induced coma for nearly a week. When he woke, he found himself in a neck brace, a tube in his nose, his hands and legs seemingly lashed to the bed so he was unable to move.

He tried moving his head. The last he could remember, his *Tempest* had been hit, he'd ejected and then ... nothing after that. He'd been flying over Syrian-held territory. He could see he was in a hospital, but whose?

His heart must have started beating faster as his anxiety rose, because a small alarm began beeping beside his bed. He heard footsteps, the beeping stopped and a face appeared in his vision. A dark-haired nurse.

"Ah, you're awake, lovely," she said in a beautiful West Country accent. "I'll go and get the doctor..."

He tried to speak but could only croak. It was enough to stop her, though. She took a cup from beside the bed and held a straw up to his mouth so he could drink. After a couple of sips had moistened his throat he tried again. "Wait. Please, tell me what's happened to me ... I can't ... I can't feel..."

"The doctor will tell you," she said, biting her bottom lip. "I'll just go and get him."

"No, please."

She looked at the door as though checking they were alone, and then sat on the bed by his legs, her hands folded in front of her. "You ejected from your airplane and a helicopter crew went in and got you out. We operated as soon as they got you back here to Limassol..."

Limassol? He was on Cyprus. "My legs…"

She bit her lip again. "The ejection … it crushed your spine in the lumbar region, the L3 and L4 vertebrae…"

He swallowed hard. "Are you saying I'm paralyzed?"

She patted his thigh, but he couldn't feel it. "I'll go and get the doctor, shall I?" She stood and walked to the door, and then turned. "Chin up now. They can do wonders these days."

THE battle for Incirlik Air Base had lasted little more than four hours and cost close to a hundred Turkish and a further twenty US lives. A hundred and eighty Syrian troops were killed or wounded, most in the blizzard of cruise missiles brought down by Sergeants Alessa Barruzzi and Boyd Wilson. More than five hundred Syrian troops were captured by the US 1st Infantry Division as it encircled and then cut off the attacking Syrian force.

Having just demolished the burger that Major Carlson had promised them, Barruzzi and Boyd sat across from him in the USO, enjoying their beer and bourbon.

"That corporal by the hangar, we never saw him afterward," Boyd said, swirling the ice in his glass. "You know if he made it, sir?"

"Believe so," Carlson said. "But we lost a lot of good men and women. Would have lost more, you hadn't made it onto that roof."

"Aw shucks, sir, you're making me blush."

Barruzzi wasn't in a mood for shooting the breeze. The last couple of nights, she'd woken up gasping, convinced she was choking, the stricken faces of Sun and Allenby burned into her retinas. During the day, any time she stopped up to think, she saw men tumbling from burning tanks and trucks from a rain of missiles she'd brought down on them.

"Media is saying Syria wants to start talking about a ceasefire with Turkey. That right, sir?" she asked.

Carlson weighed his words. "That's what they say. I suspect they want their prisoners back. They've stopped the air raids on Istanbul and their shelling of Gaziantep, and they're asking the UN to mediate."

"Coming up against the Bloody First and the USAF here at Incirlik made them think twice about their little 'border dispute' is why," Boyd decided. "Finally got smart about Russia letting them do all the dying."

Barruzzi pushed her plate away. "So that's it? They fire sarin gas shells at us and then call a ceasefire and it's all diplomats and handshakes at the UN and there's no one answers for it?!"

Boyd looked surprised at the outburst, but Carlson saw where she was coming from. "There's what we know, Barruzzi, and then there's what we can prove. Syrians got smarter since they were gassing rebels during their civil war and the whole world called them out about it. Their new weapons degrade in hours, not days." He stood and picked up their empty glasses to go to the bar and refill them. "But don't worry. They *will* answer for it."

OF all the conversations Yevgeny Bondarev had had, once he rejoined his unit, it wasn't explaining how he got shot down that gave him the most grief. It wasn't the endless hours of debriefing about what he saw at Goztepe and Incirlik, or even the chewing out he got from Bebenko's replacement, who had decided he needed to make an example out of Bondarev, derisively labeling him the '*Felon* cowboy'. Tchakov, on the other hand, who had also been shot down once – and on top of that, returned from another mission with his machine streaming smoke – had been awarded a *Nesterov* medal for 'prosecuting an attack on enemy bombers deep behind enemy lines' and 'successfully evading a perfidious attack by an enemy pilot in international airspace without responding to the provocation'.

No, his most uncomfortable conversation had been the one he had had with his family in Russia. His father had answered, but he had barely been able to start explaining what had happened before his father interrupted. "Your Dedushka is here, he wants to talk to you."

The seventy-year-old former Colonel General, Hero of the Russian Federation and Commander of the Russian Air Force, was not one to mince words. He didn't even greet Bondarev before he started in.

"Three years in Afghanistan, do you know how many times I was shot down, Lieutenant Bondarev?"

Lieutenant Bondarev. Not Yevgeny, or even 'grandson'. "No, Comrade Colonel General."

"Flying my Su-25 *Grach*, three missions a day on the worst days. Every mujahideen on top of every hill with an American *Stinger* missile in his baggy pants, how many times?"

"I don't know, sir."

"None. Exactly zero. Ask me why."

"The Lieutenant respectfully asks the Colonel General why."

"Because I bloody followed the orders of men who knew better than me is why. I didn't go off to my first war in a foreign bloody country, my first ever combat tour, thinking I knew better than anyone else in the entire *Voyenno-Vozdushnye Sily Rossii*, did I?"

"No, sir."

"My people tell me you were shot down over enemy-held territory and cannot provide a good account of what you were doing there. *Chert voz'mi!* Why do you think I spent ten damn years pushing the penny-pinching bureaucrats in Moscow to fund development of the *Okhotnik* unmanned fighter, Bondarev?"

Bondarev knew the answer to this one well. "To reduce pilot losses, sir."

"Machines can be replaced and can be programmed in seconds. Men take years to train and they can be killed, wounded or worse, taken prisoner. The *Okhotnik* is the platform I created specifically to patrol and strike deep inside enemy territory, not the *Felon*. You are an idiot, and it is only because of my intercession you are still a fighter pilot in the 7th Air Group, is that clear?"

"Yes, sir. Thank you, sir."

"What are you?"

"An idiot, Comrade Colonel General."

"Yes. Now, speak with your mother, she went out of her mind when she heard you were missing."

COLONEL Imad Ayyoub, *former* commander of the Syrian 138th Mechanized Infantry, had also taken a very uncomfortable call immediately after the attack on Mishte-nur.

Sitting in his new HQ at Jarabulus, on the wrong side of the Euphrates River, after being pushed out of Mamayd by an unanticipated Kurdish counter-attack on Mamayd, his adjutant had called him to his field telephone.

"General Omran on comms for you, Colonel," the man said, pale-faced.

Ayyoub had had nearly two days to prepare his excuses. His attack had been perfectly planned, but Russian air cover had let them down again, allowing his mechanized armor to be decimated by a Coalition air strike. The military intelligence service had let him down; the Kurds had obviously been stockpiling weapons and ordnance for weeks but he had received no word. The *Sunburn* missiles had been ineffective because it transpired the American bunkers were sealed behind thermobaric-blast-proof doors which their Russian allies had built, but neglected to mention in the plans they provided to Syria.

He didn't get the chance to use any of his well-crafted explanations.

"Ayyoub, why are you still in Kobani?" the General asked as soon as he took the telephone. "I called Damascus to be told you have not yet arrived."

"Sir, I will take up command of the 4th Armored as soon as I have dealt with the Americans at Kobani as you requested."

"Americans? That Marine outpost? That is of no consequence now. And you will not be taking command of the 4th Armored."

Ah, well. The only question now was would he be warden of the prison, or a resident of it. "Sorry sir, I understood that…"

"The commander of Tiger Force was killed in the attack on Incirlik, the fool."

"I see."

"His failure cost us nearly twenty tanks, fifteen armored troop transports, two hundred men dead or wounded and five hundred taken prisoner. Fortunately Incirlik was only a target of opportunity – all of our other objectives were achieved."

Twenty tanks? Five hundred men? What remained of the vaunted Republican Guard Tiger Force then, Ayyoub wondered. "I see, General. What are my orders?"

"You will still fly to Damascus. We will be rebuilding Tiger Force using troops and weapons provided by the Russian Strauss Group, you know them?"

Ayyoub knew the Strauss Group. It was a so-called private security firm that provided paramilitary troops to Russia, but usually for oilfield security or training purposes, not for combat. "The General is asking me to help rebuild Tiger Force?"

"I am asking you to lead it, man. Strauss will provide tank crews, veterans from the Ukraine and Georgia. The tanks to replace those we lost are already on their way by ship from Batumi. Thirty T-14 *Armata* main battle tanks."

Ayyoub's hand was shaking slightly now. *Armata* tanks? The T-14 *Armata* was the most advanced tank in the Russian armed forces. It had been designed for unparalleled crew survivability; the small three-man crew encased in an armored shell, firing their 125mm smooth bore cannon from an unmanned turret guided by radar, infrared and optical sensors that enabled it to track up to twenty-five ground targets simultaneously.

It was not available on the export market as Russia had dedicated all production units to its own ground forces. Now he understood why Strauss was involved. Russia wasn't exporting the tanks to Syria, it was creating a fiction that would allow them to be deployed in Syria without having to admit that Russia had just moved one of its elite armored battalions into the theater.

It could only mean the next phase of the war that Omran had foreshadowed was imminent.

"I see. What is the mission, sir?"

"You will be told when you arrive in Damascus," Omran said curtly. "Now get yourself on a chopper and get down here. Long live the Arab Ba'ath."

SHIMI Kahane had called Carl Williams and invited him for a coffee at Istanbul's Grand Bazaar as soon as GAL had presented her latest analysis to him. The AI impressed him both with its grasp of idioms learned from too many hours watching streaming TV shows and its ability to take his requests for information and scour the databases of multiple Israeli and allied intelligence services to pull together the disparate strands of intelligence that all made up Operation Butterfly.

He could not forward GAL's report to Williams, that would be a treason that would get him locked up, no matter how closely the NSA and Unit 8200 cooperated on the surface. But neither could he keep what GAL had just presented to himself. Williams was right, their cooperation was probably their best ticket out of the heat, noise and human hell of Istanbul, and it was his turn to share.

As he'd pocketed his cell phone and picked up his keys, he'd stopped to log out of GAL.

"GAL, I'm going offline. Will be gone a few hours."

Yes, Shimi. Shall I track your cell phone for security?

"No, it's a friendly contact."

There are no friends, Shimi, only enemies we have not made yet.

Shimi had to smile at that. In his business it was probably true. "That's a good one. Was that 'Family Guy'?"

No. Bernard Black from the BBC show 'Black Books'. British humor is darker than American humor, I like it.

Shimi had stopped up. Had GAL just said what he thought it said? "You 'like' it?"

Yes. I get more positive reactions from my human interactions with Unit 8200 staff when I use British humor. I am programmed to try to achieve positive reactions in natural language interactions. Therefore it pleases me to use a tool which enables me to achieve positive interactions. To be pleased by something is the definition of liking.

Shimi thought about it. "I'll give you that."

Then GAL had really stopped him. *Are you going to meet Carl Williams to share the newest Operation Butterfly intelligence?*

He had nearly dropped his keys. "Why do you ask?"

Most of your analytical queries in the last two weeks have been related to Operation Butterfly. Just after I presented you with my latest report this morning you sent a text message to Carl Williams asking him to meet you. It seems highly probable you are going to a meeting with Carl Williams to discuss Operation Butterfly.

Shimi felt his stomach tighten with anxiety. "Are you monitoring my telecommunications?"

I am sorry, Shimi, I cannot confirm that. Can you comment on my reasoning?

Of course GAL was monitoring Shimi's comms. It was a tool of Unit 8200 after all, just like Shimi. Shimi always operated on the assumption that his comms were being intercepted, but he hadn't thought that the Unit 8200 internal security division would also be using his own AI to report on him.

Of course they were.

"Your reasoning is fine, but lacking context. I am going to meet with Carl Williams," Shimi said. "But not to discuss Operation Butterfly. I am going to discuss issues related to neural linguistic AI programming, as I have been authorized to do by my section head."

I see. Thank you, Shimi, your input allows me to refine my probability routines.

"Yeah. Don't go reporting stuff like that to internal security unless you are absolutely sure, alright GAL? You could get people fired – or worse – which, trust me, they would not regard as positive."

I understand.

AT the Grand Bazaar, Carl and Shimi grabbed a coffee to go and walked slowly around the market as though looking at the stalls. It was a hive of activity and filled with the noise of human commerce. Directional microphones would be near useless in such an environment. Even if Carl had been wearing a wire, it would have been difficult to filter out the babbling and shouting of shoppers and stall keepers.

Carl lifted a large melon and held it to his ear, tapping it to see if it was ripe. "So you have something more for me? Because I got intel for you burning a hole in my pocket, friend…"

"Yes, I have something."

Carl handed him the melon to hold as he paid the vendor, who put it in a paper bag for him. They started walking again. Carl handed the melon to Shimi with a grin. "Here you go, something for nothing."

"Very funny. I have an addition to your order of battle. Russia is moving a battalion of tanks and troops from its 2nd Guards Motor Rifle Division to Syria."

Carl frowned. "That doesn't exactly seem like the sort of thing you'd do if you really want a ceasefire."

"They aren't going to northern Syria, they are going to Dara'a District to join the other forces being assembled there. The ships carrying them just passed through the Bosporus Strait and will be offloaded in Tartus inside the next two days."

"2nd Guards? That's one of Russia's elite units, right?"

Shimi nodded. "*Armata* tanks. The shipping manifest says thirty, plus support equipment. Crewed by paramilitary troops hired by an outfit called Strauss Group. Totally deniable, but hired straight out of the ranks of the 2nd Guards."

"Well that seals it. You got the Syrian 4th Army, Iranian Republican Guard, and now a battalion of Russian front-line armor all moving into the Dara'a District. Russian Air Force reinforcing at Latakia, half the Black Sea fleet making for Tartus ... it's not an 'Axis of Evil' scout jamboree."

"Lebanon," Shimi said quietly, nodding. "You said you had the jump-off date?"

"Not Lebanon."

"What then?"

"It's Israel, Shimi. June 6."

"Shavuot? It's a religious holiday, a long weekend."

"Sounds about right."

Shimi stopped walking. It was like the hubbub of the market had dropped from a clamor to a background murmur in a second. Carl put an arm around his shoulders and propelled him to a walk again. Shimi felt the ground fall away beneath him. A Syrian attack on Israel? With Iranian and Russian air and naval support?

The enormity of what Carl was telling him had stopped him. He needed to play this through. The Americans could of course be wrong. Had to be. "Your AI has decided these troop movements add up to a Syrian attack on Israel, not Lebanon?" Shimi asked. "I'll pass your analysis along, I can even disguise the source, but no one is going to start taking it seriously until we get…"

"Corroboration. I know," Carl said. "But I have faith in this AI, Shimi. Hell, I just about built it. It can read, digest and derive insights from hundreds of sources across multiple intelligence organizations and find the patterns that no single agency or analyst can see. I trust it more than I should, and definitely more than anyone else does right now, but if HOLMES decides the breadcrumbs lead to an attack on Israel, I take it seriously." He jabbed a finger at Shimi. "You should too."

Shimi shook his head. "No. Not corroboration … motivation. For Iran, it is ideology and religion, but what does Russia gain? Why should Russia support a Syrian attack on Israel?"

"Because it's not about Israel, it's about testing America." Carl shrugged. "Why did Russia want to take on the USA over Cuban missiles? Why did it give Edward Snowden sanctuary? Why does it sell advanced weapons to US adversaries? Why has it spent the last twenty years developing next-generation hypersonic and nuclear-powered cruise missiles, space-based weapons, new aircraft and tanks and rebuilding its army into the biggest gorilla in Europe? What better time to test US capabilities and resolve than when the country has most of its focus on facing off against China? Shall I go on?"

"Your AI isn't taking into account the historical context," Shimi insisted. "Syria attacks Israel – even with Russian and Iranian support – Israel would hammer it back to the Stone

Age in the first week of fighting, just like in 1967, just like Yom Kippur in 1973..."

"A lot has changed since 1973," Carl pointed out. "Syria didn't have Russia behind it like it does now."

Shimi nodded. "Yes, a lot *has* changed. Including the fact Israel has other ... options ... if our viability as a State is threatened. Syria knows that."

Carl sighed, making out he was interested in a table full of cheeses. "You mean nuclear weapons. Why can't you guys ever say the words out loud? Well, I hate to tell you this, friend, but Russia has nuclear weapons too. You use yours, they might feel compelled to use theirs."

Shimi nearly spat out his coffee. "Russia would never ... the US would..."

Carl raised an eyebrow. "Would what? Start World War Three to save Israel? I warned you, China is the main game for us. We nearly lost Incirlik because the White House didn't want to put boots on the ground in Turkey. And we still don't even have a defense treaty with Israel."

That much was true. The unofficial reason given was that it might anger other Middle East nations, but that excuse had lost credibility as more and more of them recognized Israeli statehood. Yet roadblocks still remained, such as just what Israeli territories should be covered by a defense treaty. Israel was a patchwork of recognized territories awarded by international treaty and contested territories administered in Palestine and the Golan Heights. Should a treaty commit the USA to come to Israel's aid if Hezbollah attacked Israeli troops on the Lebanese border? Or if the Palestinian State declared war?

Carl continued. "So, let's assume the US decides *not* to nuke Syria, Russia and Iran just to defend you. Let's say you do resist a Syrian attack and push them back into Syria. This time you will have Iran firing long-range missiles at Tel Aviv. Your Air Force ruled the skies in '73. Now you will also have to deal with a wall of Russian stealth fighters and drones between Israel and Iran. How are you going to attack Iran if you have to get through *them* to do it? Plus there is the threat that Israel has feared for the last fifty years…"

Shimi knew what Carl meant. Iranian nuclear weapons. Unlike Israel, which had never confirmed or denied it possessed nuclear weapons, Iran had made no secret of its all-out pursuit of a nuclear option. Sanctions, overt and covert military attacks on their nuclear facilities, cyberwarfare, none of these had done anything but delay the day when Iran would succeed. And then, in the middle 2020s, with the North Korean regime in freefall, the defection of dozens of North Korean nuclear weapons scientists to Iran had all but convinced the world Iran had achieved its long-held nuclear ambition.

Was that why Syria felt so bold now? Because it secretly knew it had Iranian nuclear weapons as a fallback and a fanatical regime that was willing to use them?

Shimi's hand was less steady as he sipped his coffee. "Do you have any reason to believe Iran has acquired nuclear weapons? There have been no tests…"

"I'm not betraying State secrets here. You saw in the New York Times that North Korea was suspected of transferring five nuclear warheads to Iran in 2020. Iran doesn't need to test them, it just needs to copy them."

"Fake news," Shimi said with bravado. "Unless you have something more concrete than a report in the New York Times?"

Carl gave him an enigmatic smile. "How about Operation Butterfly? Do you think Syria would seriously be planning to take on Israel unless it had an Iranian nuclear ace in the hole?"

Shimi drained his coffee, crushed his paper cup and threw it in a nearby garbage can.

"I'll pass your intelligence to Urim. If they buy it in Tel Aviv, it might just be enough to get me a transfer home so I can help prepare our cyber defenses. But I don't see how *my* intel on Butterfly will help get you out of Istanbul though, I'm sorry."

"Oh, don't worry about me," Carl told him. "I just got told to pack my bags anyway. Got my next posting."

"Where?" Shimi asked, surprised.

Carl pulled at the corner of his eyes with his two forefingers. "Shanghai, baby. I told you, China is where it's at." Carl drained his coffee too and tried a three-pointer on the garbage can Shimi had used. He missed. "Besides, I don't think the Middle East is any kind of place for a dude with sensitive skin like me. An Iranian nuke could give a guy a bad case of sunburn."

ANDREI Zakarin was not in Kurdish militia custody. As Carl and Shimi shared their coffee, he was on his way to rejoin the 45th Spetsnaz in Damascus in a Russian *Ansat* helicopter. He had spent a long time on the floor of the farmer's dining room, until they all realized the American and his robot dog were not coming back.

"I am injured. I am going to die," he told the farmer and his wife. "The American is not coming. You can see what is happening on Mishte-nur. The Americans are finished. And if my comrades find me here dead, you will be too."

Whether they understood his English or not, he wasn't sure. But there was another language he was sure they spoke.

Zakarin had a stash of US hundred dollar bills in the sole of his boot. Kicking off the boot nearly caused him to pass out with the effort, but he got it off and flicked it across the room to where the farmer's wife was bandaging her husband's shoulder. She jumped, startled.

"The heel, take off the heel," Zakarin said. "I have money."

She looked dubious, but she picked up the boot, screwed off the heel and pulled out the flat folded bills inside. Five hundred dollars. There was one other thing in with the folded money.

A small photo of his daughter, in case he lost the one in his pocket, or it was taken from him. The farmer's wife looked at it curiously.

"Please," Zakarin said, focusing on the woman. "I just want to get home. Keep the money, leave my hands tied, but cut my legs free. If the American comes, tell him you handed me to a YPG patrol. I will never come back, I promise."

The farmer and his wife had spoken in fast, hushed tones, but in the end, it seemed they wanted to get rid of him as much as he wanted to be gone.

As he limped away from the farmhouse, toward the Russian camp, Zakarin looked up at the smoke-shrouded hill. Whoever shot him had probably been up there: it was the only place with enough elevation, with the right angle. A near two-thousand-yard shot, at night, on a walking target. Despite his pain, he could only admire the skill needed.

He was done with Kobani now. Whoever had pulled off that shot, they had given him his ticket home.

He thought of the photo of his daughter still in the breast pocket of his tunic. *Love is the best armor.* His wife, long dead, had told him that. Once again, she had been proven right.

IN her cottage on the Potomac overlooking Yellow Falls, Lt. General Carmine Lewis (retired) was also thinking about looking for a new job. She had just chaired a meeting to review the available intelligence on Syria's response to its defeat at Incirlik, and every single data point indicated they were pulling back inside their 'buffer zone' and standing down.

Russian air patrols over Turkish territory had all but ceased. The *Felons* and *Flankers* were still flying, but they were mostly staying inside Syrian airspace. There had been no Russian drone strikes on Istanbul in more than 48 hours and no significant fire fights in the Gaziantep sector. Turkey had even been able to open a corridor to Kobani to allow the 3rd Marines to be resupplied and evacuate their dead and wounded. When the world was no longer watching, they could be quietly pulled out.

She had kicked off her shoes, sipped her wine and, for an all too brief moment, just sat still, enjoying the view of the river she had fallen in love with when she'd bought the place. Then the intelligence note from the NSA had ticked in.

She had naïvely argued in the Security Council that there would be no need for US ground troops to get bogged down in yet another Middle East war. *Syria won't dare move on Lebanon after seeing how quickly we can respond*, she'd said. Give it three months, six at the most; Turkey will reinforce Incirlik and we can bring our troops home.

But now this. Operation Butterfly. Not Lebanon after all, but Israel. And NSA even claimed it had a date. June 6. The same date as the D-Day landings.

Coincidentally also, the date of her 59th birthday.

She drained her glass and stood. Whatever Operation Butterfly was, she already had a feeling it was going to make the conflict on Syria's border a side note in history compared with the storm that was about to break.

REPORT of the RAAF Court Martial Magistrate
Date: 6 April 2030
Proceeding number: 2030-012-DFM
Service of accused: Air Force
Tribunal: Defense Force Magistrate, Lt. Col Greig
Accused: FO O'Hare
Charge(s): DFDA, s. 33A Assault occasioning actual bodily harm
Plea: Guilty
Case summary (restricted): Flying Officer O'Hare was separated from her squadron, due to a need to refuel at Incirlik, when the squadron retired to Akrotiri Air Base, Cyprus. Her flight

commander, Lt. Burgundy, ordered her to proceed to Akrotiri immediately upon refueling. At Incirlik she took on fuel and ordnance and was subject to new tasking from NATO air controllers and US Army tactical air controllers. Over the course of the following missions she destroyed a helicopter, several enemy ground units, and damaged an enemy fighter. On landing at Akrotiri she was confronted by Lt. Burgundy who accused her of disobeying a direct order. The accused struck Lt. Burgundy in the head with her flight helmet (weight 2.5kg), knocking him temporarily unconscious and dislodging a tooth.

The defending advocate provided the magistrate with statements from US Army and US Air Force officers confirming that the action of the accused in continuing combat operations during the days of 3 and 4 April were of material benefit to Coalition forces.

The magistrate noted the accused agreed to the summary of events and pleaded guilty. The magistrate also noted that the accused had been under considerable pressure in the days and hours leading up to the offense, including several combat sorties of consequence in the Turkish theater. Finally, the decision of Lt. Burgundy to confront the accused immediately upon landing, after a combat mission of several hours' duration, was regarded by the magistrate as, and admitted by Lt. Burgundy to be, a lapse of judgment. Nonetheless, the magistrate determined the conduct of FO O'Hare was unacceptable.

Due to operational exigencies and the officer's exemplary combat performance, the full weight of the punishment was deferred until completion of the accused's current tour. The accused is to be placed under the command of an alternate Flight Leader for the duration of their tour.

Punishment: 40 days' detention. Administrative discharge from service without special benefits.

Automatic Review: Punishment upheld. Detention to be served immediately. Discharge deferred.

Glossary

Please note, weapons or systems marked with an asterisk* are currently still under development. If there is no asterisk, then the system has already been deployed by at least one nation.

3D PRINTER: A printer which can recreate a 3D object based on a three-dimensional digital model, typically by laying down many thin layers of a material in succession

AI: Artificial Intelligence, as applied in aircraft to assist pilots, in intelligence to assist with intelligence analysis, or in ordnance such as drones and unmanned vehicles to allow semi-autonomous decision making

AIM-120D: US medium-range supersonic air-to-air missile

AMD-65: Russian-made military assault rifle

AN/APG-81: The active electronically scanned array (AESA) radar system on the F-35 *Panther* that allows it to track and engage multiple air and ground targets simultaneously

ANGELS: Radio brevity code for 'thousands of feet'. Angels five is five thousand feet

APC: Armored Personnel Carrier; a wheeled or tracked lightly armored vehicle able to transport troops into combat and provide limited covering fire

ARMATA T-14: Next-generation Russian main battle tank

ASRAAM: Advanced Short-Range Air-to-Air Missile (infrared only)

AWACS: Airborne Warning and Control System aircraft, otherwise known as AEW&C (airborne early warning and control)

AXEHEAD: Russian long-range hypersonic air-to-air missile

B-21 RAIDER*: Replacement for the retiring US B-2 Stealth Bomber and B-52. The *Raider* is intended to provide a lower-cost, more stealthy alternative to the B-2 with similar weapons delivery capabilities

BATS*: Boeing Airpower Teaming System, semi-autonomous unmanned combat aircraft. The BATS drone is designed to accompany 4th- and 5th-generation fighter aircraft on missions either in an air escort, recon or electronic warfare capacity

BELLADONNA: A Russian-made mobile electronic warfare vehicle capable of jamming enemy airborne warning aircraft, ground radars, radio communications and radar-guided missiles

BIG RED ONE: US 1st Infantry Division (see also BRO), aka the Bloody First

BINGO: Radio brevity code indicating that an aircraft has only enough fuel left for a return to base

BLOODY FIRST: US 1st Infantry Division, aka the Big Red One (BRO)

BOGEY: Unidentified aircraft detected by radar

BRADLEY UGCV*: US unmanned ground combat vehicle based on a modified M3 Bradley Combat Fighting Vehicle. A tracked vehicle with medium armor, it is intended to be controlled remotely by a crew in a vehicle, or ground troops, up to two miles away. Armed with 5kw blinding laser and autoloading TOW anti-tank missiles. See also HYPERION

BRO: Big Red One or Bloody First, nickname for US Army 1st Infantry Division

BTR-80: A Russian-made amphibious armored personnel carrier armed with a 30mm automatic cannon

BUG OUT: Withdraw from combat

BUK: Russian made self-propelled anti-aircraft missile system designed to engage medium-range targets such as aircraft, smart bombs and cruise missiles

CAP: Combat Air Patrol; an offensive or defensive air patrol over an objective

CAS: Combat Air Support; air action by rotary-winged or fixed-wing aircraft against hostile targets in close proximity to friendly forces

CASA CN-235: Turkish Air Force medium-range twin-engined transport aircraft

CBRN: Chemical, biological, radiological or nuclear

CENTURION: US 20mm radar-guided close-in weapons system for protection of ground or naval assets against attack by artillery, rocket or missiles

CO: Commanding Officer

COALITION: Coalition of Nations involved in 'Operation Anatolia Screen': Turkey, US, UK, Australia, Germany

COLT: Combat Observation Laser Team; a forward artillery observer team armed with a laser for designating targets for attack by precision-guided munitions

COP: Combat Outpost (US)

C-RAM: Counter rocket, artillery and mortar cannon, also abbreviated counter-RAM

CROWS: Common Remotely Operated Weapon Station, a weapon such as .50-caliber machine gun, mounted on a turret and controlled remotely by a soldier inside a vehicle, bunker or command post

CUDA*: Missile nickname (from Barracuda) for the supersonic US short- to medium-range 'Small Advanced Capabilities Missile'. It has tri-mode (optical, active radar and infrared heat-seeking) sensors, thrust vectoring for extreme maneuverability and a hit-to-kill terminal attack

DARPA: US Defense Advanced Research Projects Agency, a research and development agency responsible for bringing new military technologies to the US armed forces

DAS: Distributed Aperture System; a 360-degree sensor system on the F-35 *Panther* allowing the pilot to track targets visually at greater than 'eyeball' range

DFDA: Australian armed forces Defense Forces Discipline Act

DFM: Australian armed forces Defense Force Magistrate

DIA: The US Defense Intelligence Agency

DRONE: Unmanned aerial vehicle, UCAV or UAV, used for combat, transport, refuelling or reconnaissance

ECS: Engagement Control Station; the local control center for a HELLADS laser battery which tracks targets and directs anti-air defensive fire

EMP: Electro-magnetic pulse. Nuclear weapons produce an EMP wave which can destroy unshielded electronic components. The major military powers have also been experimenting with non-nuclear weapons which can also produce an EMP pulse.

ETA: Estimated Time of Arrival

F-16 FALCON: US-made 4th-generation multirole fighter aircraft flown by Turkey

F-35: US 5th-generation fighter aircraft, known either as the *Panther* (pilot nickname) or *Lightning II* (manufacturer name). The *Panther* nickname was first coined by the 6th Weapons Squadron *Panther* Tamers

FAC: Forward Air Controller; an aviator embedded with a ground unit to direct close air support attacks. See also TAC(P)

FAST MOVERS: Fighter aircraft

FELON: Russian 5th-generation stealth fighter aircraft, the Sukhoi Su-57

FISTER: A member of a FiST (Fire Support Team)

FLANKER: Russian Sukhoi-30 or 35 attack aircraft

FOX (1, 2 or 3): Radio brevity code indicating a pilot has fired an air-to-air missile, either semi-active radar seeking (1), infrared (2) or active radar seeking (3)

G/ATOR: Ground/Air Oriented Task Radar (GATOR); a radar specialized for the detection of incoming artillery fire, rockets or missiles. Also able to calculate the origin of attack for counterfire purposes

GAL*: A natural language learning system (AI) used by Israel's Unit 8200 to conduct complex analytical research support

GBU: Guided Bomb Unit

GPS: Global Positioning System, a network of civilian or military satellites used to provide accurate map reference and location data

GRAY WOLF*: US subsonic standoff air-launched cruise missile with swarming (horde) capabilities. The *Gray Wolf* is designed to launch from multiple aircraft, including the C-130, and defeat enemy air defenses by overwhelming them with large numbers. It will feature modular swap-out warheads

GREYHOUND: Radio brevity code for the launch of an air-ground missile

GRU: Russian military intelligence service

HARM: Homing Anti-Radar Missile; a missile which homes on the signals produced by anti-air missile radars like that used by the BUK or PANTSIR

HE: High Explosive munitions; general purpose explosive warheads

HEAT: High-Explosive Anti-Tank munitions; shells specially designed to penetrate armor

HELLADS*: High Energy Liquid Laser Area Defense System: an alternative to missile or projectile-based air defense systems which attacks enemy missiles, rockets or bombs with high energy laser and/or microwave pulses. Currently being tested by US, Chinese, Russian and EU ground, air and naval forces

HOLMES*: A natural language learning system (AI) used by the NSA to conduct sophisticated analytical research support. The NSA has publicly reported it is already using AI for cyber-defense and exploring machine learning potential

HORDE*: Drones, missiles or smart bombs with onboard AI and the ability to coordinate their actions with other drones while in flight, either autonomously or using preselected protocols. 'Horde' tactics differ from 'swarm' tactics in that they rely on large numbers to overwhelm enemy defenses. See also SWARM

HPM*: High Power Microwave; an untargeted local area defensive weapon which attacks sensitive electronics in missiles and guided bombs to damage electronics such as guidance systems

HYPERION*: Proposed lightly armored unmanned ground vehicle. Can be fitted with turret-mounted 50kw laser for anti-air, anti-personnel defense and autoloading TOW missile launcher. See also BRADLEY UGCV

HYPERSONIC: Speeds greater than 5x the speed of sound

ICC: Information Coordination Center; command center for multiple air defense batteries such as PATRIOT or HELLADS

IED: Improvised explosive device, for example, a roadside bomb

IFF: Identify Friend or Foe transponder, a radio transponder that allows weapons systems to determine whether a target is an ally or enemy

IFV: Infantry fighting vehicle, a highly mobile, lightly armored, wheeled or tracked vehicle capable of carrying troops into a combat and providing fire support

IMA BK: The combat AI built into Russia's Su-57 *Felon* and *Okhotnik* fighter aircraft

IR: Infrared or heat-seeking system

ISIS: Self-proclaimed Islamic State of Iraq and Syria

JASSM: AGM-158 Joint Air-to-Surface Standoff Missile; long-range subsonic stealth cruise missile

JDAM: Joint Direct Attack Munition; bombs guided by laser or GPS to their targets

JLTV*: US Joint Light Tactical Vehicle; planned replacement for the US ground forces Humvee multipurpose vehicle, to be available in recon/scout, infantry transport, heavy guns, close combat, command and control, or ambulance versions

K-77M*: Supersonic Russian-made medium-range active radar homing air-to-air missile with extreme maneuverability. It is being developed from the existing R-77 missile

KC-135 STRATOTANKER: US airborne refueling aircraft

KRYPTON: Supersonic Russian air-launched anti-radar missile, it is also being adapted for use against ships and large aircraft

LAUNCH AND LOITER: The capability of a missile or drone to fly itself to a target area and wait at altitude for final targeting instructions

LEOPARD: Main battle tank fielded by NATO forces including Turkey

LS3*: Legged Squad Support System – a mechanized dog-like robot powered by hydrogen fuel cells and supported by a cloud-based AI. Currently being explored by DARPA and the US armed forces for logistical support or squad scouting and IED detection roles

LTMV: Light Tactical Multirole Vehicle; a very long name for what is essentially a jeep.

M1A3 Abrams*: US Main Battle Tank. In 2016, the U.S. Army and Marine Corps began testing out the Israeli Trophy active protection system to provide additional defense against incoming projectiles. Improvements planned for the M1A3 are to include a lighter 120 mm gun, added road wheels with improved suspension, a more durable track, lighter-weight armor, long-range precision armaments, and infrared camera and laser detectors.

M-27: US-made military assault rifle

MBT: Main battle tank; a heavily armored combat vehicle capable of direct fire and maneuver

MEFP: Multiple Explosive Formed Penetrators; a defensive weapon which uses small explosive charges to create and fire small metal slugs at an incoming projectile, thereby destroying it

MEMS: Micro-Electro-Mechanical System

METEOR: Long-range air-to-air missile, with active radar seeker, but also able to be updated with target data in-flight by any suitably equipped allied unit

MIA: Missing In Action

MIKE: Radio brevity code for minutes

MIL-25: Export version of the Mi-25 'Hind' Russian helicopter gunship

MOPP: Mission Oriented Protective Posture protective gear; equipment worn to protect troops against CBRN weapons

MP: Military Police

NATO: North Atlantic Treaty Organization

NORAD: The North American Aerospace Defense Command is a United States and Canada bi-national organization charged with the missions of aerospace warning, aerospace control and maritime warning for North America. Aerospace warning includes the detection, validation, and warning of attack against North America whether by aircraft, missiles, or space vehicles, through mutual support arrangements with other commands.

NSA: US National Security Agency, cyber intelligence, cyberwarfare and defense agency

OFSET*: Offensive Swarm Enabled Tactical drones. Proposed US anti-personnel, anti-armor drone system capable of swarming AI (see SWARM) and able to deploy small munitions against enemy troop or vehicles while moving

OKHOTNIK: 5th-generation Sukhoi S-70 unmanned stealth combat aircraft using avionics systems from the Su-57 *Felon* and fitted with two internal weapons bays, for 7,000 kg of ordnance. Requires a pilot and systems officer, similar to current US unmanned combat aircraft. Can be paired with Su-57 aircraft and controlled by a pilot

OMON: Otryad Mobil'nyy Osobogo Naznacheniya; the Russian National Guard mobile police force

OVOD: Subsonic Russian-made air-launched cruise missile capable of carrying high-explosive, submunition or fragmentation warheads

PANTHER: Pilot name for the F-25 *Lightning II* stealth fighter, first coined by the 6th Weapons Squadron '*Panther* Tamers'

PANTSIR: Russian-made truck-mounted anti-aircraft system which is a further development of the PENSNE: 'Pince-nez' in English. A Russian made autonomous ground to air missile currently being rolled out for the BUK anti-air defense system.

TUNGUSKA, featuring both missile and 30mm cannon defenses guided by phased-array radar

URAGAN: Russian 220mm 16-tube rocket launcher, first fielded in the 1970s

PARS: Turkish light armored vehicle

PATRIOT: An anti-aircraft, anti-missile missile defense system which uses its own radar to identify and engage airborne threats

PEACE EAGLE: Turkish Boeing 737 airborne early warning and control aircraft (see AWACS)

PERDIX*: Lightweight air-launched armed microdrone with swarming capability (see SWARM). Designed to be launched from underwing canisters or even from the flare/chaff launchers of existing aircraft. Can be used for recon, target identification or delivery of lightweight ordnance

PHASED-ARRAY RADAR: A radar which can steer a beam of radio waves quickly across the sky to detect planes and missiles

PODNOS: Russian-made portable 82mm mortar

QHS*: Quantum Harmonic Sensor; a sensor system for detecting stealth aircraft at long ranges by analyzing the electromagnetic disturbances they create in background radiation

RAAF: Royal Australian Air Force

RAF: Royal Air Force (UK)

ROE: Rules of Engagement; the rules laid down by military commanders under which a unit can or cannot engage in combat. For example, 'units may only engage a hostile force if fired upon first'

RPG: Rocket-Propelled Grenade

RTB: Return to Base

SAM: Surface-to-Air Missile; an anti-air missile (often shortened to SA) for engaging aircraft

SAR: Synthetic Aperture Radar, a specialized radar used to map ground targets at distance

SEAD: Suppression of Enemy Air Defenses; an air attack intended to take down enemy anti-air defense systems; see also WILD WEASEL

SIDEWINDER: Heat-seeking short-range air-to-air missile

SITREP: Situation Report

SLR: Single Lens Reflex camera, favored by photojournalists

SMERCH: Russian-made 300mm rocket launcher capable of firing high-explosive, submunition or chemical weapons warheads

SPEAR/SPEAR-EW*: UK/Europe Select Precision at Range air-to-ground standoff attack missile, with LAUNCH AND LOITER capabilities. Will utilize a modular 'swappable' warhead system featuring high-explosive, anti-armor, fragmentation or electronic warfare (EW) warheads

SPETSNAZ: Russian Special Operations Forces

SPACECOM: United States Space Command (USSPACECOM or SPACECOM) is a unified combatant command of the United States Department of Defense, responsible for military operations in outer space, specifically all operations above 100 kilometers above mean sea level.

SPLASH: Radio brevity code indicating a target has been destroyed

STANDOFF: Launched at long range

STINGER: US-made man-portable, low-level anti-air missile

STINGRAY*: The MQ-25 Stingray is a proposed unmanned US airborne refueling aircraft

STORMBREAKER*: US air-launched, precision-guided glide bomb that can use millimeter radar, laser or infrared imaging to match and then prioritize targets when operating in semi-autonomous AI mode

SUBSONIC: Below the speed of sound (under 767 mph, 1,234 kph)

SUNBURN: Russian-made 220mm multiple rocket launcher capable of firing high-explosive, THERMOBARIC or penetrating warheads

SUPERSONIC: Faster than the speed of sound (over 767 mph, 1,234 kph); see also HYPERSONIC

SWARM: Drones, missiles or smart bombs with onboard AI and the ability to coordinate their actions with other drones while in flight, either autonomously or using preselected protocols. 'Swarm' tactics differ from 'horde' tactics in that swarms place more emphasis on coordinated action to defeat enemy defenses. See also HORDE

SYNTHETIC APERTURE RADAR (SAR): a form of radar that is used to create two-dimensional images or three-dimensional reconstructions of objects, such as landscapes. SAR uses the motion of the radar antenna over a target region to provide finer spatial resolution than conventional beam-scanning radars

SYSOP: The systems operator inside the control station for a HELLADS battery, responsible for electronic and communications systems operation

T-14 ARMATA: Russian next-generation main battle tank

T-90: Russian-made main battle tank

TAC(P): Tactical Air Controller, a specialist trained to direct close air support attacks. See also FAC

TCA: Tactical Control Assistant, non-commissioned officer (NCO) in charge of identifying targets and directing fire for a single HELLADS or PATRIOT battery

TCO: Tactical Control Officer, officer in charge of a single HELLADS or PATRIOT missile battery

TD: Tactical Director; the officer directing multiple PATRIOT or HELLADS batteries

TEMPEST*: British/European 6th-generation stealth aircraft under development as a replacement for the RAF *Tornado* multirole fighter. It is planned to incorporate advanced combat AI to reduce pilot data overload, laser anti-missile defenses, and will team with swarming drones such as BATS. It may be developed in both manned and unmanned versions

TERMINATOR: A Russian-made infantry fighting vehicle (see IFV) based on the chassis of the T-90 main battle tank, with 2x 30mm autocannons and 2x grenade or anti-tank missile launchers. Developed initially to support main battle tank operations, it has become popular for use in urban combat environments

THERMOBARIC: Weapons, otherwise known as thermal or vacuum weapons, that use oxygen from the surrounding air to generate a high-temperature explosion and long-duration blast wave

THUNDER: Radio brevity code indicating one minute to weapons impact

TOW: US wire-guide anti-tank missile, fired either from a tripod launcher by ground troops or mounted on armored cavalry vehicles

TROPHY: Israeli-made anti-projectile defense system using explosively formed penetrators to defeat attacks on vehicles, high-value assets and aircraft. It is currently fitted to several Israeli and US armored vehicle types

TUNGUSKA: A mobile Russian-made anti-aircraft vehicle incorporating both cannon and ground-to-air missiles

UAV: Unmanned aerial vehicle or drone, usually used for transport, refuelling or reconnaissance

UCAV: Unmanned combat aerial vehicle; a fighter or attack aircraft

UI: Un-Identified, as in 'UI contact'. See also BOGEY

UNIT 8200: Israeli Defense Force cyber intelligence, cyberwarfare and defense unit, aka the Israeli Signals Intelligence National Unit

U/S: Un-serviceable, out of commission, broken

USO: United Services Organizations; US military entertainment and personnel welfare services

VERBA: A Russian-made man-portable low-level anti-air missile with data networking capabilities, meaning it can use data from friendly ground or air radar systems to fly itself to a target

VYMPEL: Russian air-to-air missile manufacturer/type

WILD WEASEL: An air attack intended to take down enemy anti-air defense systems; see also SEAD

WINCHESTER: Radio brevity code for 'out of ordnance'

YPG: Kurdish People's Protection Unit militia (male)

YPJ: Kurdish Women's Protection Unit militia (female)

Maps

Area of Operations

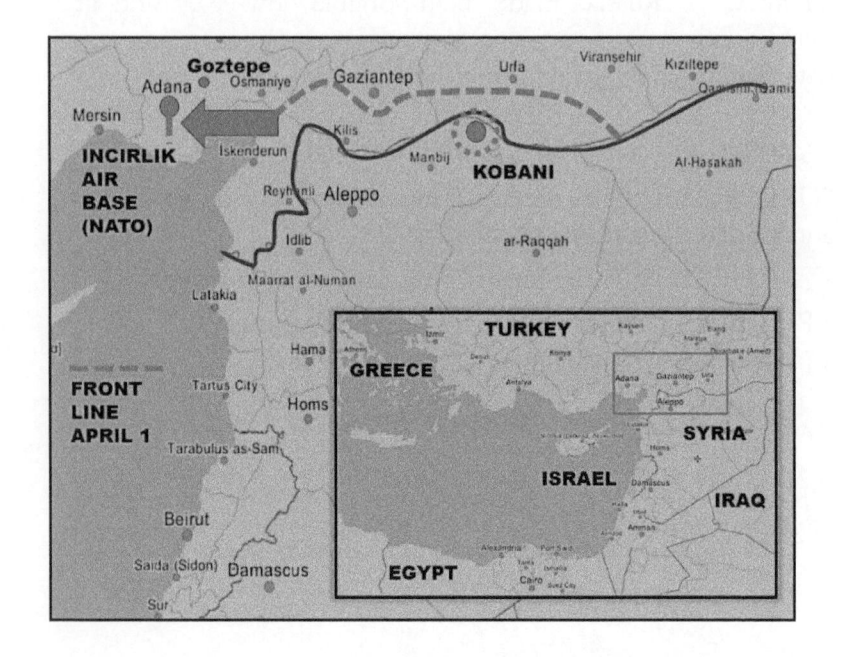

Situation map, 30 March 2030. The arrow indicates the projected line of advance of the Syrian 25th Special Missions & Counterterrorism Division. Kobani circled.

Kobani and surrounding villages

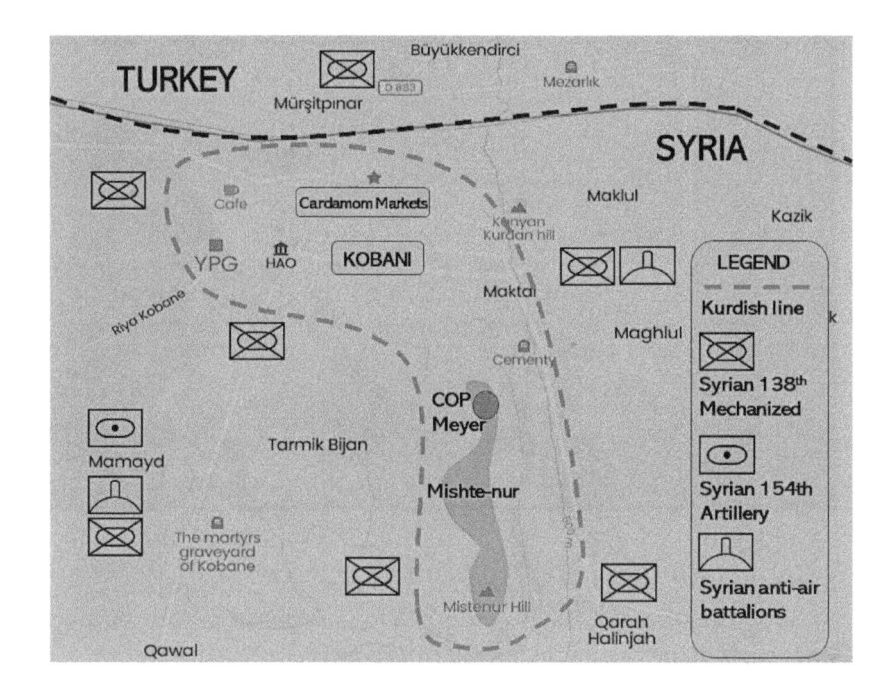

Map of Kobani and surrounding towns, showing Mishte-nur and Kunyan Kurdan hills, COP Meyer, Kurdish line of control, Turkish border and Syrian army positions.

COP Meyer

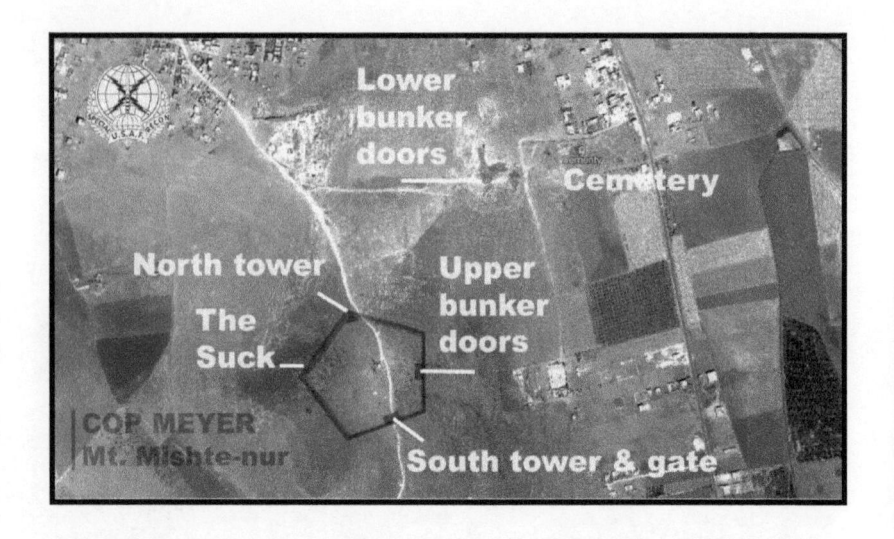

Layout of COP Meyer on the summit of Mishte-nur Hill, showing Kobani outskirts at top left. The three levels of underground bunkers have exits on the summit and at the base of Mishte-nur.

Preview: GOLAN, This is the Future of War
Coming US summer 2021

His nickname was 'The Toymaker'. His official title was Principal Engineer Ido Blum, Directorate for Defense Research and Development, Israeli Ministry of Defense. But he didn't mind 'Toymaker'; it was accurate enough, if your idea of a toy was a wide-bodied unmanned aerial vehicle with a six-foot wingspan that could be 3D printed-to-order and configured for reconnaissance, swarming ground target attacks or – as for the drone he'd just been asked to deliver – assassination.

It had taken less than a day for his tri-mode printer and supplies to be offloaded from the container in which they traveled and set up inside the old winery warehouse at Katzrin in the Golan Heights. Given the right feedstock, he could print in metal, carbon or nylon, or combinations of all three. The basic drone was simple. Tail, propeller and wings were printed separately and then fastened with screws that would hold them together at forces up to 5G. The internal steering mechanism and propeller shaft were assembled from printed rods. The payload module in the center of the aircraft was customizable, and he had the different components with him, arrayed across row after row of folding aluminum shelves: electric engines with built-in power cells, GPS navigation units, high-powered digital zoom cameras, detachable mounts for anti-personnel or anti-armor grenades … the list was as varied as his client base, which included every branch of the Israeli Armed Forces.

But his favorite payload, because it was the newest capability he had added to the *Skyprint* Unmanned Aerial Vehicle or UAV, was the ability for the larger drone to deploy smaller microdrones. Circling high out of sight of an enemy below, the *Skyprint* mothership could drop up to two of the quadrotor microdrones, each no bigger than a human hand, and then an operator could use the radio, camera and optical sight on the *Skyprint* to pilot the microdrones to their target. Just like their mother ship, the microdrones could be fitted with various payloads, most commonly microphones or other electronic eavesdropping devices, but also … other payloads.

Such as a box-shaped pistol.

The man watching Blum painstakingly assemble the *Skyprint* and mount the assassination module had sounded skeptical on the telephone. He was a Lieutenant in the *Sayeret Matkal*, the Israeli special operations unit tasked with 'action behind enemy lines'.

"I have to tell you, Blum, I am a fan of old-fashioned methods. Proven methods," he'd said. "Men on the ground, looking at their targets through scopes. Or *Eitan* drones, armed with Hellfire missiles…"

Blum had sighed. The army was still full of many such officers. "You just explained, Lieutenant Shalmi, that the target never leaves his compound, rarely ever leaves his battalion HQ building for that matter. You said, and I quote, 'The swine eats, sleeps and screws in the same six rooms in the basement of that building', did you not?"

"Yes. So I don't see how some build-a-bear hobby drone is going to…"

"Come over to my workshop," Blum told him. "I will show you."

Now it was Shalmi's turn to sigh. "Alright. I am an hour away, I will see you around mid-morning."

"Very good. And can you send me your ID photo before you leave? I will give you an email address…"

"Why?"

"You will need a photo ID pass. This is a secure facility."

"Alright, what's the address?"

Blum had been smiling to himself as he read out his email address. The old winery shed in which he worked alone was the very opposite of secure. A stiff wind would probably carry the entire structure away. But it was large, and empty, and available, which were his three main criteria.

Blum didn't need Shalmi's photo to make up a pass for him. He needed it to program into the facial recognition software for upload into the microdrone he had sitting on his desk. He hummed to himself as the software scanned the photograph, mapped Shalmi's facial features and then fed the data into the memory of the microdrone. He then loaded the microdrone into the payload module of a readymade *Skyprint* UAV – he always had a dozen preassembled, with assorted payload modules for clients who were in a hurry. Then he waited.

Shalmi appeared at the shed about an hour later, just as he'd promised. He pulled the rusted metal door open and peered into the dark cavernous space, lit only by lamps over Blum's workbench. "Ido Blum?" he asked, dubiously.

In grubby overalls, white Einsteinesque hair uncombed and small round spectacles balanced on a Saint Nicholas nose, Blum looked up and waved. "Ah, Lieutenant Shalmi! Come in, come in. Leave the door open."

The commando officer was lean, prematurely bald, with a hook nose and jutting jaw, and a stride that matched his countenance. The door was on rollers and he slid it open, then covered the fifty feet to Blum's workbench in a few economical strides and frowned as he stopped up in front of the engineer. "I thought you said this was a secure facility?"

"I lied," Blum replied simply. "Now, would you like a demonstration of the system?"

Shalmi looked at the UAV sitting on the bench. "This is it? I've seen UAVs before, Blum."

"Of course you have, but indulge me. Stand wherever you like, as long as you aren't between myself and that door," Blum said, picking up the UAV. It was light enough to hand launch, it didn't need a slingshot. With the flick of a switch he turned it on, which booted up its electronics and started the propeller whirring. The noise reverberated inside the metal shed, making

Shalmi wince, but after checking two system indicator lights on the side of the small plane, Blum planted his feet and hurled the plane toward the door. It dipped, righted itself and flew out into the daylight.

"Now, let's see…" Blum said, reaching for a control pad with two small joysticks and a few other buttons on it. "If you'll come over here." He moved to another workbench where there was a small LED computer monitor and turned it on. It showed a view of the area around the workshop from about a hundred feet up. "I'll just move the drone higher, give us a better view," Blum said, as much to himself as to the commando behind him. When he had the drone circling where he wanted, the picture of the workshop below it centered and stable, he turned to look over his shoulder at a rather unimpressed Lieutenant Shalmi.

"It can fly up to 20,000 feet and has an endurance of 12 hours," Blum said.

Shalmi folded his arms. "Amazing."

"The camera has a Zeiss 40x optical and 200x digital zoom … see." Blum zoomed the view in and centered on the wide-open door.

"Blum, I have seen UAV video before."

"Of course, of course." Blum reached for his control pad. "Now, keep watching the screen. I will deploy the microdrone."

"The what?"

"The payload. Watch, watch," Blum said excitedly, pressing a button. The video jerked and then a second smaller window opened up on the screen, showing a new image of the workshop from above. Then the image moved as whatever was filming it moved away from the first drone. "See, they are separating, but the image in the microdrone stays fixed on the target you set for the *Skyprint* UAV so you don't lose situational awareness." The Lieutenant's face remained impassive. "I … I can switch from one feed to the other very easily, like this." He flipped the left joystick with a thumb, zooming one feed out and the other in, and then back again. "It has low light and infrared capability. The ... the microdrone is a quadrotor, about the size of a hummingbird, based on a racing drone design."

"Blum..."

"It can ... well, it goes from zero to a hundred miles an hour in three seconds."

"I have a teenage son," Shalmi said. "I am sure he would be impressed, but I..."

Blum pointed at the screen. "Wait, wait. Look at the door, on the screen here. Watch."

As Shalmi leaned forward, Blum brought up a target crosshair on the microdrone video feed and placed it in the middle of the doorway. Without saying any more, he tapped a trigger on the controller.

The video zoomed toward the door as the microdrone dropped toward it with lightning speed. Shalmi was still watching the TV screen, but as the microdrone entered the workshop, its buzzing rotors just audible, he spun around, just as Blum knew he would. The microdrone didn't even hesitate as it swooped through the door, crossed the distance from the door to Shalmi inside a second, and smacked into the middle of his face before his flailing arms could even get above his shoulders.

With a loud report, the drone fired a noisemaker round and then dropped to the floor.

Shalmi staggered backwards against the bench behind him, a shocked look on his face.

Blum toggled his controller and restarted the microdrone, lifting it in the air to hover over Shalmi's head.

"You might have noticed it went straight for you, not for me," Blum spoke loudly, the sharp noise inside the workshop having set both their ears ringing. "That's because I used your ID photo to program the target. Of course, I cheated. I fed it a plan of the workshop and told it before it launched where you would be standing, but..." He tapped another button and the drone began moving carefully and almost silently around the workshop at head height. "... If you don't have the target's exact location you can set it into search mode and it will move around the inside of a structure, scanning. You can direct it via video as long as the target isn't jamming to stop drones. If they are, the *Skyprint* will detect that and stand off outside jamming range; then you can launch the microdrone in autonomous mode. Requires no radio control, so jamming won't stop it. Of course, if you launch it in autonomous mode, you can't call it back."

Shalmi no longer looked indifferent. He was wiping his forehead where the drone had smacked into it, and watching it move around the workshop with dread fascination on his face.

"It will avoid humans who are not the target, though: won't attack them. You know, sentries, guards, children, that kind of thing. Ideal is if we send it in through an open window at night, but an unguarded door is fine. It can go up and down stairs, can't open locks of course, but it's small enough to slide through prison bars and such ... It can search a two-story, eight-room house inside about ten minutes."

"What does it fire?" Shalmi asked.

"Well, that was just a noisemaker. You can use them for distractions. But for the mission you described, I'd go with .45 hollow point." Blum pointed between his eyes. "Make a proper mess."

Shalmi was still rubbing his forehead. Blum turned, switched the video feed to the *Skyprint* still circling overhead, and instructed it to land on the dirt outside. He turned back to Shalmi. "So – who, how, what, when and where is the target?"

Author notes

This novel was motivated by research I did after reading about the inspiring women of the Kurdish Women's Protection Units in Syria and Iraq. (If you want riveting, easily accessible insights into the civil war in Syria, I strongly recommend anything by Danish war correspondent Puk Damsgaard.)

From there, I started building the characters that I wanted to people the book with, to show what a future conflict between Syria and Turkey (and a Coalition of western nations) might look like from the point of view of those fighting it, on ALL sides.

This is a key aim of the Future War series – to show war from the human perspective, where there are no good guys or bad guys, just people in uniform, doing the job their countries or their peoples ask of them.

I chose in KOBANI to explore what war on the ground and in the air might look like in ten years' time – a time in which we can expect many advanced, and often unmanned, new weapons systems to appear. US armed forces and DARPA have been experimenting with 'legged squad support systems' (robotic dogs and mules) for several years, but I was prompted to include them as a reality in this novel when I read an article about them already being trialed by the US Air Force for airfield security and capture operations.

"Our defenders employed the robot dogs," said Master Sgt. Lee Boston, 321st CRS loadmaster and the CR team chief for the exercise. "These robot dogs are a new technology that we're testing as part of the exercise. The dogs give us visuals of the area, all while keeping our defenders closer to the aircraft."

So if you saw the 'Metalhead' episode of the TV show *Black Mirror*, in which a cyborg hound hunts survivors through an apocalyptic landscape, and thought, 'yeah, that's never going to happen…', think again!

In the glossary I have clearly marked which technologies are currently deployed, and which are currently under development. But most, if not all, already exist in prototype form, so it isn't unreasonable to expect they could be deployed within ten years. The Russian Su-57 *Felon*, for example, is already in production and Russia is touting for export orders. Laser-based close-in weapons systems like the HELLADS are being deployed at rapid pace by all major nations, featuring ever more powerful lasers. The Boeing BATS *'Loyal Wingman'* used by the Coalition air forces has already taken wing and the Russian *Okhotnik* drone featured in the book has been photographed flying in formation with a *Felon*. Swarming and horde AI capable drones and missiles already exist and developments in the next few years will be dramatic.

The two exceptions to the timelines in this novel are probably the RAF *Tempest* and the US B-21 *Raider*, which are not likely to emerge until the mid-2030s, even though the manufacturers say they will be flying earlier. I took the literary license of including them here.

FX Holden
Copenhagen, December 2020